PENGUIN CLASSICS

THE BIRD'S NEST

SHIRLEY JACKSON was born in San Francisco in 1916. She first received wide critical acclaim for her short story "The Lottery," which was first published in *The New Yorker* in 1948. Her novels—which include *The Sundial, The Bird's Nest, Hangsaman, The Road Through the Wall, We Have Always Lived in the Castle,* and *The Haunting of Hill House*—are characterized by her use of realistic settings for tales that often involve elements of horror and the occult. *Raising Demons* and *Life Among the Savages* are her two works of nonfiction. She died in 1965.

KEVIN WILSON is the bestselling author of *The Family Fang* and the recipient of a Shirley Jackson Award for his story collection *Tunneling to the Center of the Earth.* His writing has appeared in *Tin House, Ploughshares, One Story,* and elsewhere. He lives in Sewanee, Tennessee, and is an assistant professor at The University of the South.

T0033344

SHIRLEY JACKSON

The Bird's Nest

Foreword by
KEVIN WILSON

PENGUIN BOOKS

PENGUIN BOOKS

Published by the Penguin Group
Penguin Group (USA) LLC
375 Hudson Street
New York, New York 10014

USA | Canada | UK | Ireland | Australia | New Zealand | India | South Africa | China
penguin.com
A Penguin Random House Company

First published in the United States of America by Farrar, Straus and Young 1954
This edition with a foreword by Kevin Wilson published in Penguin Books 2014

Copyright 1954 by Shirley Jackson
Foreword copyright © 2014 by Kevin Wilson
Penguin supports copyright. Copyright fuels creativity, encourages diverse voices,
promotes free speech, and creates a vibrant culture. Thank you for buying an authorized
edition of this book and for complying with copyright laws by not reproducing, scanning,
or distributing any part of it in any form without permission. You are supporting writers
and allowing Penguin to continue to publish books for every reader.

LIBRARY OF CONGRESS CATALOGING-IN-PUBLICATION DATA
Jackson, Shirley, 1916–1965.
The bird's nest / Shirley Jackson ; foreword by Kevin Wilson.
pages ; cm.—(Penguin classics)
ISBN 978-0-14-310703-3
1. Psychological fiction. I. Title.
PS3519.A392B5 2014
813'.54—dc23   2013033710

Printed in the United States of America

For
Stanley Edgar Hyman

Contents

Foreword

Shirley Jackson was, and continues to be, one of my greatest influences, a writer who suggested a way to engage with the strangeness of the larger world and yet stay true to whatever complicated ideas I wanted to express. I first read "The Lottery" when I was a preteen, still one of the most transformative reading experiences of my life, which led me to *Hangsaman* and *The Haunting of Hill House*, then her earlier works, as I searched for every written word that Jackson created, and ended when I finally read, long overdue, *We Have Always Lived in the Castle*. Jackson has remained the writer I look to when I want to understand the darkness of the world and how human beings internalize that darkness or, perhaps even more terrifying, create it themselves. The larger world has always been difficult for me to process, a constant source of anxiety, and Jackson's work gave me a blueprint for how I might navigate that world without succumbing to paranoia; her stories were cautionary tales in which I somehow lived comfortably. *The Bird's Nest*, though written early in her career, showcases what I find so engaging about Jackson's work: her ability to create situations of quiet chaos that, no matter how much the reader seeks to find a tangible explanation, defy our attempts to categorize or fully understand it. The world, I understood through Jackson's novels, could never be fully explained, and it was in those mysterious places that resisted definition that offered the most interesting stories.

The Bird's Nest opens on a building in need of repair, a museum that features an "odd, and disturbingly apparent, list to the west." When I reread this novel, the image immediately reminded me of Jackson's exceptional later novels, *We Have Always Lived in the Castle* and *The Haunting of Hill House*, where the reader encounters ominous structures, domiciles that house strange and fascinating characters. A few pages into the story, we meet our main character, Elizabeth Richmond, a quiet, lonely young woman mourning the recent death of her mother, and we learn the possibility that "Elizabeth's personal equilibrium was set off balance by the slant of the office floor" of the museum, where she works in the clerical department. Elizabeth's office is on the highest floor of the museum and now, thanks to the renovation project, offers an open hole in the wall next to her desk that exposes "the innermost skeleton of the building" and induces the temptation to "hurl herself downward into the primeval sands upon which the museum presumably stood."

For those of us who love Jackson's work, this is familiar territory, and we are prepared for the listing structure to slowly drive Miss Richmond mad. Darkness enters the narrative when we learn that she is receiving threatening letters that exacerbate her recurring headaches and back pain. All of the elements are now in place and then, a testament to Jackson's genius and a reason why *The Bird's Nest* remains one of my favorite novels, Jackson shifts the narrative into a new and altogether more interesting direction. Elizabeth Richmond possesses multiple personalities, one of which leads her to sneak out of the house she shares with her aunt and into all manner of unsavory activities. The threatening letters have no source other than Elizabeth's own hand. She admits to being unaware of these terrible events, but she can't be sure. We now see that the structure housing strange and fascinating characters is not the museum but, rather, Elizabeth's own body. And thus we discover the true focus of Jackson's genius: the mysterious contents within all of us, the self-destructive tendencies that threaten to ruin the structure that keeps them hidden from the rest of the world.

As we leave the museum behind and enter into the unique workings of Elizabeth's mind, the story becomes an examination of

mental illness, the darkness inside us that we struggle to understand and keep at bay. Like Constance in *We Have Always Lived
in the Castle*, Eleanor of *The Haunting of Hill House*, and Nata-
lie of *Hangsaman*, Elizabeth is a fragile, isolated young woman,
but Jackson experiments with voice by revealing each distinctive
personality, each one broken in some unique way. While sections
of the novel are given over to Elizabeth's sometimes unwilling
psychiatrist, Dr. Wright, and her aunt Morgen, who possesses her
own secrets, my favorite passages focus on the difficult inner
workings of the mind of Elizabeth, or whichever personality cur-
rently inhabits her form. Jackson has always written with such
precision about the delicate nature of our psyches, and as someone who has struggled with mental illness for my entire adult life,
I think that there are few writers who know the ways in which
our minds betray us as well as she does. When Betsy, Elizabeth's
most problematic and difficult personality, sneaks away from the
care of Dr. Wright and Aunt Morgen to run off to New York in
search of the mother she believes is still alive, the novel becomes
electric and disturbing; it is hard to tell exactly what is happening, as Betsy's thought processes are jumbled, but the world becomes a dangerous place, every human interaction fraught with
the possibility of violence, every landmark simply another space
that remains unknown to Betsy. It is some of the most thrilling
and terrifying writing found in any of Jackson's work.

While the good doctor's work with Elizabeth, especially his
use of hypnosis to treat multiple personalities, might provide
the occasional breakthrough, I don't believe Jackson intends
to suggest that he truly holds sway over the bottomless depths
of Elizabeth's own mysterious desires and behaviors. The doctor in fact has an edge of something ominous in his own manner, played nicely against his self-deprecating humor. His
interior complications explain his horror when he is confronted with the true nature of Elizabeth's darkness. The doctor is merely a lion tamer attempting to subdue the human
psyche, and one can't help inferring Jackson's opinion on the
lasting success of domesticating such a wild animal.

While the book ends with the suggestion of happiness, or at
least temporary calm, there is no happy ending. The threat of

the world around us and the even more potent threats inside us cannot offer much in the way of happiness. Elizabeth, whatever her fate, is a sympathetic character, entirely human in her desires and actions, however strange they might be. This explains why, much like *The Bird's Nest* itself and, in fact, all of Jackson's work, it is so unsettling to see the darkness and chaos beneath the surface. We encounter a world where, thanks to Jackson's talent, we recoil from the danger and then move closer to see it more clearly.

KEVIN WILSON

The Bird's Nest

ELIZABETH

Although the museum was well known to be a seat of enormous learning, its foundations had begun to sag. This produced in the building an odd, and disturbingly apparent, list to the west, and in the daughters of the town, whose energetic borrowings had raised the funds to sustain the museum, infinite shame and a tendency to blame one another. It was at the same time a cause of much amusement among the museum personnel, whose several vocations were most immediately affected by the decided slant given to the floors of their building. The proprietor of the dinosaur was, as a matter of fact, very humorous about the almost foetal tilt of his august bones, and the numismatist, whose specimens tended to slide together and jar one another, was heard to remark—almost to tedium— upon the classical juxtapositions thus achieved. The stuffed bird man and the astronomer, whose lives were spent in any case almost out of earthly equilibrium, professed themselves unaffected by the drop of one side of the building, unless driven toward a kind of banking curve to offset the natural results of walking on tipped floors; walking was, in any case, an unfamiliar movement to either of them, one tending toward flight and the other toward the complacent whirling of the spheres. The very learned professor of archeology, going inattentively along the slanted corridors, had been seen hopefully contemplating the buckled foundations. The contractor and the architect, along with the ill-tempered daughters of the town, endeavored to blame first the inefficient materials supplied for the building and second the extraordinary weight of some of the antiquities contained therein; the local paper printed an editorial criticizing the museum authorities for allowing a meteor and a mineral collection and an entire arsenal from the Civil War, dug up just outside of town and including two cannon, to be lodged all on the west side of the building; the editorial pointed out soberly that, had the exhibit of famous signatures, and of local costume through the ages, been settled on the west side, the building might not have sagged, or might at least not have done so during the lifetimes of its sponsors. Since the local paper—current and impermanent—was not permitted below the third, or clerical, floor of the museum, the exhibits were allowed to retain their impractical arrangements unmoved by the editorials, although the clerical employees on the third floor read the comics daily and studied the front pages hoping to discover the manners of their deaths. They were given, on the third floor, to meditation, and they believed almost everything they read. In this, of course, they differed in almost no way from the educated inhabitants of the first and second floors who dwelt among unperishing remnants of the past, and made little wry jokes about disintegration.

Elizabeth Richmond had a corner of an office on the third floor; it was the section of the museum closest, as it were, to the surface, that section where correspondence with the large world outside was carried on freely, where least shelter was offered to cringing scholarly souls. At Elizabeth's desk on the highest floor of the building, in the most western corner of the office, she sat daily answering letters offering the museum collections of pressed flowers, or old sea-chests brought back from Cathay. It is not proven that Elizabeth's personal equilibrium was set off balance by the slant of the office floor, nor could it be proven that it was Elizabeth who pushed the building off its foundations, but it is undeniable that they began to slip at about the same time.

The instinctive thought of every person connected with the museum, up to and including the paleontologist, had been to repair, to patch together, to reconstruct, rather than to build anew in a new site, and in order to repair the building at all the carpenters had found it necessary to drive a hole the height of the building, from the roof to the cellar, and had chosen Elizabeth's corner of the third floor to effect an entrance to their shaft. On the second floor the hole in the wall was discovered through a sarcophagus, and on the first floor, not unreasonably, behind a little door marked "Do not enter"; Elizabeth's office allowed of no concealment, and so she came to work of a Monday morning to find that directly to the left of her desk, and within reaching distance of her left elbow as she typed, the wall had been taken away and the innermost skeleton of the building exposed. She was the first person in the room that morning; she hung her coat and hat neatly on the coat hanger just inside the door, and then went across the room and looked down with a swift sense of dizziness and an almost irresistible temptation to hurl herself downward into the primeval sands upon which the museum presumably stood; far below her she could hear the faintly echoing voices of the guides on the first floor; today was an Open Day and the guides were apparently cleaning their fingernails. The complaining voice which, slightly louder, seemed to come from the second floor may have been that of the archeologist, outside the tomb, finding fault with the air. Elizabeth, looking down, sighed because she had a headache, and because she had a headache nearly all the time, and turned to her desk to contemplate a letter offering the museum a model skyscraper made of matchsticks. The faint sense of holiday, inspired by not having a fourth wall to her office, had faded almost entirely by the time she opened the third letter on her desk. When she had read the letter once, she got up and looked down again into the cavity of the building, and then returned to her desk and sat down, thinking, I have a headache.

"dear lizzie," the letter read, "your fools paradise is gone now for good watch out for me lizzie watch out for me and dont do anything bad because i am going to catch you and you will be sorry and dont think i wont know lizzie because i do—dirty thoughts lizzie dirty lizzie"

Elizabeth Richmond was twenty-three years old. She had no friends, no parents, no associates, and no plans beyond that of enduring the necessary interval before her departure with as little pain as possible. Since the death of her mother four years before, Elizabeth had spoken intimately to no person, and the aunt with whom she lived required little of her beyond a portion of her weekly pay and her prompt presence at the dinner table. Although she had arrived daily at the museum for two years, since her employment the museum had been in no way different; the letters signed "per er" and the endless listings of exhibits vouched for by E. Richmond were the outstanding traces of her presence. There were half a dozen people who spent their time in the same office, and half a dozen others who occupied other offices on the third floor, and all of these knew Elizabeth, and said "Good morning" to her, and even "How are you today?"—this on particularly bright spring mornings—but those of them who, in philanthropy or mortal kindness, had endeavored to become more friendly with her had found her blank and unrecognizing. She was not even interesting enough to distinguish with a nickname; where the living, engrossed daily with the fragments and soiled trivia of the disagreeable past, or the vacancies of space, kept a precarious hold on individuality and identity, Elizabeth remained nameless; she was called Elizabeth or Miss Richmond because that was the name she had given when she came, and perhaps if she had fallen down the hole in the building she might have been missed because the museum tag reading Miss Elizabeth Richmond, anonymous gift, value undetermined, was left without a corresponding object.

She had not chosen employment at the museum because of a passionate fondness for learning, or in the hope of someday managing a public institution of her own, but because in her usual undirected way she had followed the information given by a friend of her aunt's, and found a job at the museum open, and because her aunt had added, most pressingly, that Elizabeth might very well try it, since it was necessary for Elizabeth to work at something now that she was old enough to be self-supporting. Her aunt forbore to comment upon her own uneasy sense that it might be easier to identify Elizabeth in some firmer manner if Elizabeth were located in a concrete spot (my niece Elizabeth, who works at the museum) rather than being merely herself and so very obviously unable to account for it. She went to work, then, with no further direction than this crossing of two lines to determine a point, and was taken on at the museum because the clerical work on the third floor required no very sparkling personality, and because her abilities, whatever her disadvantages, included a clear written hand and a moderate speed at the typewriter, and because whatever was given Elizabeth to do, if she understood it, was done. If she took any pride in anything, it was in the fact that everything about her was neat, and distinct, and right in a spot where she could see it. Her desk and her letters were squarely arranged; she came to the museum each morning at the hour she had been told to come, taking always the same bus to work and hanging up her coat and hat where they belonged; she wore always the dark dresses and small white collars which her aunt assumed were proper for an office worker, and when it came time to go home Elizabeth went home.

No one at the museum had stopped to think that driving an enormous hole through one side of Elizabeth's office might be unhealthy for Elizabeth; no one at the museum had mused, slide rule in hand, "Now, let's see, this shaft down the building ought to pass somewhere close to Miss Richmond's left elbow; will it, I wonder, trouble Miss Richmond to find one wall gone?"

On Monday, just before noon, Elizabeth took her letter out of the drawer of her desk and put it into her pocketbook; she meant to read it again at lunch. It had nagged her during the morning, with an odd urgency; it was somehow most pleasantly personal, and not at all the sort of thing she was used to. Over her sandwich in the drugstore she read it again, investigating the handwriting, and the paper, and the wording; the most exciting thing about it was probably its lingering familiarity. It did not distress her because she could not conceive of someone imagining it, and taking a pen and a sheet of paper and writing it, and putting it into an envelope addressed to Elizabeth at the museum; it was an act of intimacy from a stranger impossible to picture. Sitting in the drugstore Elizabeth touched the badly written words with her finger and smiled; she had very definite plans for this letter: she meant to take it home and put it into a box on the top shelf of her closet with another letter.

Although the museum people spent the greater part of their own time in hammering and measuring and patching, it was generally felt that the presence of carpenters and bricklayers repairing the building was out of place during museum hours, and so as Elizabeth left the building as usual at four o'clock, she met the carpenters coming in. It was of no importance to anyone at the museum, and of little significance to the carpenters, but as Elizabeth passed them in the hallway she smiled and said to them, "Hello, there." She went into the street, blinking in the sunlight because she still had her headache, stepped onto the usual bus, sat looking out of the window until she reached her own stop, stepped down from the bus, and walked the half block to her aunt's house. She unlocked the door with her key, glanced at the hall table to see if her aunt had left any message, and into the living room to see if her aunt had got home, then went upstairs to her own room, where she hung her hat and coat carefully in the closet, took off her good shoes and put on sensible slippers, got a chair to stand on to reach the closet shelf, and took down the red cardboard valentine box which had held chocolates on her twelfth birthday. She carefully set the box down on her bed, put the chair back where it belonged, and sat down on the bed with the box. Before she opened it she took the new letter out of her pocketbook and read it again, then folded it and slipped it back into its envelope, addressed so untidily to miss elizabeth richmond, owenstown museum. Then she opened the box and took out the other letter inside; this one was substantially older. It had been written seven years before by Elizabeth's mother and it read, "Robin, don't write again, caught my Betsy at the letters yesterday, she's a devil and you know how smart! Will write when I can and see you Sat. if possible. Hastily, L."

Elizabeth had found this letter, presumably never addressed and mailed, in her mother's desk shortly after her mother's death. Until now it had been hidden alone on the closet shelf, but today, after reading both letters again carefully, she put both into the valentine box and, taking the chair, put the box back again onto the closet shelf, set back the chair, and went into the bathroom and washed her hands with soap as her aunt came to the foot of the stairs and called "Elizabeth? You home yet?"

"I'm here," Elizabeth said.

"You want cocoa for dinner? It's turned cold out."

"All right. I'll be right down."

She came slowly down the stairs, kissed her aunt on the cheek because she usually kissed her aunt when she came home and she had not seen her aunt until now, and went into the kitchen.

"Well," said Aunt Morgen definitely. She sat down heavily at the kitchen table, and folded her hands before her on the table, steadfastly disregarding the chops and the bread and butter. "Now," she said. Elizabeth sat down hastily, and folded her own hands, and looked without expectancy at her aunt. "Lord, bless this food, our lives to Thy service," said Aunt Morgen, speaking the moment Elizabeth folded her hands and seeming with an "Amen" in one pure gesture to unclasp her own hands and reach for the chops, "have you had a pleasant day?"

"Same as usual," Elizabeth said. Food of any kind, under any circumstances, was a matter of substantial importance to Aunt Morgen, and her greed was only very slightly frosted over with conversation; there were, at best, only one or two topics in the world which could lift Aunt Morgen's eyes away from her plate, and Elizabeth had never succeeded in saying anything which could surprise Aunt Morgen into putting down her fork before the food was gone. Dinner was calculated exquisitely to Aunt Morgen's appetite, but she was fair; there were precisely as many chops and baked potatoes and slices of bread and pickles set out in Elizabeth's name as were calculated for Aunt Morgen; their conversation was divided as perfectly.

"Have *you* had a pleasant day?" Elizabeth asked Aunt Morgen.

"Not very," Aunt Morgen said. "Rained," she pointed out.

Although Aunt Morgen was the type of woman freely de-scribed as "masculine," if she had been a man she would have cut a very poor figure indeed. If she had been a man she would have been middle-sized, weak-jawed, shifty-eyed, and clumsy; fortunately, having been born not a man, she had turned out a woman, and had of necessity adopted from adolescence (with what grief, perhaps, and frantic railings against the iniquities of fate, which made her sister lovely) the personality of the gruff, loud-voiced woman so invariably described as "mascu-line." Her manner was free, her voice loud, she loved eating and drinking and said she loved men; she took toward her sober niece an attitude of avuncular heartiness, and among her few friends she was regarded as fairly dashing because of her fondness for blunt truths and her comprehensive state-ments about baseball. She had reached an age where sustain-ing this character was no longer quite such a strain as it might have been when she was, say, twenty, and had reached a posi-tion of comparative complacence, discovering how the pretty girls of her youth had by now become colorless and dismal, and sometimes blushed when she spoke. She had never once regretted taking her niece in charge after her sister's death, since in addition to being plain, Elizabeth was quiet and unob-trusive, and showed no inclination to interrupt her aunt's con-versation, which took place exclusively between the times of dinner's conclusion and their hour of retirement. In the morn-ings, before Elizabeth left for the museum, Aunt Morgen fre-quently inquired after her health, and occasionally advised her to wear overshoes; before dinner, in a peaceful hour which Aunt Morgen spent making dinner and drinking sherry by herself in the kitchen and Elizabeth spent, as today, in her room, conversation was impossible; while dinner was being served and while it was being eaten, Aunt Morgen was too much occupied to speak. After dinner, however, Aunt Morgen habitually took a small glass or two, or even several, of brandy, and it was then, lounging back in her kitchen armchair, with coffee, brandy, and a cigarette on the table before her, and

Elizabeth hesitating over her cooling cocoa, that Aunt Morgen held forth for the day.

"If you'd learn to drink coffee," she began tonight, as she frequently did, "I'd let you have some of my brandy."

"I don't care for any, thank you," Elizabeth said. "It makes me sick."

"That's because you drink it with cocoa," Aunt Morgen said. She shuddered. "Cocoa," she said. "Cocoa. Damn miserable puny stuff, fit for kittens and unwashed boys. Did *Shakespeare* drink cocoa?"

"I don't know," Elizabeth said.

"You ought to know things like that, *you* work in a museum. Me, I sit home all day on my fanny, living on my income." She smiled and bowed formally to Elizabeth. "Your mother's income, I should have said. Mine only by the merest faint chance, mine only because of deserving patience and superior intelligence. Mine," said Aunt Morgen with relish, "only because I outlived her. If I had killed her, mind you," she went on, pointing her cigarette at Elizabeth, "they would have caught me. I wouldn't have gotten her money, because they would have caught me if I *had* killed her, and don't think I didn't think of it often enough, but they would have caught me. I don't after all suppose that I'm *that* smart, kiddo."

Aunt Morgen very often called Elizabeth "kiddo" after dinner, and she talked so much of Elizabeth's mother when they were alone that Elizabeth, who had listened sometimes at first, found that she was now able to slip into a placid unlistening after-dinner state, almost as though she had taken a great deal of Aunt Morgen's brandy. As Aunt Morgen's voice went on, Elizabeth watched without awareness the changing lights on the silverware and the mirror over the sideboard, and the quick shadowy motion as Aunt Morgen lifted her brandy glass, and the endless pattern of rose-edged doorways on the wallpaper.

"—saw me first," Aunt Morgen was saying, "but of course then your mother, once he met my sister Elizabeth, then it was her of course, and of course there was nothing I could do. But

I flatter myself, Elizabeth junior, I flatter myself, that my intelligence and strength showed him finally what a mistake *he* made, choosing vacuity and prettiness. Vacuity," Aunt Morgen said, enjoying the word, although she used it almost nightly. "Toward the end, *I* noticed, he came to me more and more, asking *my* advice about the money, and telling *me* his problems. I knew about the other men, but of course he had made his choice, although I must say she wasn't so much by then, was she, up to her neck in mud. Well." Aunt Morgen breathed deeply, leaning back, her eyes half-closed and regarding the brandy bottle. "Stack the dishes, kiddo? Early bed for Auntie."

"I'll wash them. Mrs. Martin comes to clean tomorrow and she gets mad if she finds dirty dishes."

"Old fool," said Aunt Morgen obscurely. "You're a good girl, Elizabeth. No fancy notions."

Elizabeth took the dishes to the sink and turned on the water; because she had begun to recognize, from her headache all day and the first beginnings now of an intolerable stiffness in her back—as though stretching, or rubbing against a doorway like a cat, would relieve her—that she was in danger of another attack of what Aunt Morgen called migraine and what Elizabeth thought of as a "bad" time, she moved deliberately and slowly, taking as long as possible over small motions; activity of any kind helped when she felt "bad." These spells she remembered as from childhood, although Aunt Morgen believed that until the time of her mother's death Elizabeth had only had temper tantrums, and remarked wisely that Elizabeth's migraine was a "reaction of some kind." In any case, the "bad" times had come with increasing frequency of late, and Elizabeth, recalling that she had been away from her work for four days not two weeks ago, thought dully, against the pain, "They'll let me go if I keep staying home sick."

By the time she had finished slowly washing and drying the dishes, and putting them carefully away on the shelves, and scrubbing the frying pan and scouring the sink and washing the table, the pain in her back was considerable; no longer a warning, it was now substantial enough for her to come to the door of the living room, where Aunt Morgen sat doing the crossword puzzle in the evening paper, and ask for an aspirin.

"Migraine again?" said Aunt Morgen, looking up. "You ought to run in and see Harold Ryan, kiddo."

"I've always had it," Elizabeth said. "Doctor Ryan couldn't do anything."

"I'll get you a hot water bottle for that back," Aunt Morgen said good-naturedly, setting down her pencil, "and one of those little blue pills. *That*'ll put you right to sleep."

"I can sleep all right," Elizabeth said. She was already dizzy, and reached out for the door frame.

"Poor baby," said Aunt Morgen. "All you need is sleep."

"Me?"

"Night after night I hear you tossing and muttering," Aunt Morgen said. She put an arm around Elizabeth. "Come along, old lady."

She helped Elizabeth undress, because the backache, which came with suddenness and severity, and disappeared again without warning, was by now severe enough to make it difficult for Elizabeth to move.

"Poor baby," Aunt Morgen said over and over, taking off Elizabeth's clothes, "many's the time I undressed your mother before you were born. *She*," said Aunt Morgen, chuckling, "was so clumsy then that when you got her on one side she couldn't roll over without help. *There* you are, now the nightgown. Those last couple months were the only time she ever let anyone help her, anyone *female*, that is, and even then only me. Always private, she was. I must say, you didn't get her body; more like your father, you are. Other arm, kiddo. She was a lovely girl, my sister Elizabeth, but mud clear up to the neck. Now for the hot water bottle and that nice little sleeping pill."

"I'm almost asleep now, Aunt Morgen."

"Not going to have you tossing all night tonight."

When Aunt Morgen, walking very softly but stumbling over the night table, had finally turned off the light and gone away, Elizabeth lay in the darkness alone and tried to close her eyes. There was a line of light where Aunt Morgen had left the door a little open—it had not occurred to her that Elizabeth might need her in the night, but she was unable to remember to close a door completely—and Elizabeth could hear, from downstairs, Aunt Morgen's easy movements, from the living room to the kitchen, and the subsequent slam of the refrigerator door, and Aunt Morgen's voice humming to herself, in a kind of pride that *she* was well, and had outlived so many people.

Bad old woman, Elizabeth thought, and then was surprised at herself; Aunt Morgen had been very kind to her. "Bad old woman," and she realized that she had spoken it aloud. Suppose she hears me, Elizabeth thought, and giggled. "Bad old woman," she said, very loudly indeed.

"Did you call me, kiddo?"

"No, thank you, Aunt Morgen."

Lying softly in her bed, the pain in her back lessening and the headache fading in the darkness, Elizabeth sang, wordlessly and almost without sound, to herself. The tune she used was of nursery rhymes, of faded popular songs, of whispers and fragments of tune she had heard long ago, and, singing, she fell asleep. She did not hear Aunt Morgen pass down the hall, nor perceive Aunt Morgen's belated conscientious glance in through her doorway; she did not hear Aunt Morgen whisper, "You all right, kiddo?"

Aunt Morgen slept soundly of a night and awoke, ordinarily, ill-humored; it did not, therefore, surprise Elizabeth to awaken to Aunt Morgen's displeasure. Elizabeth had lain quietly in bed for perhaps ten minutes, knowing from experience that, once awake, she would not fall asleep again, and, testing delicately, had decided that although she still had her backache, it was so much improved by a good night's rest that she might certainly get up and go to work. The headache still pulsed somewhere at the back of her head, and she repeated what was—although she was not aware of it—an habitual gesture, that of rubbing her hand violently against the back of her neck, as though she might possibly rub the nerves there into submission, and anesthetize them against the pain; this habit was one of several persistent nervous gestures she used, and it did her headache no good whatsoever. When she came downstairs, dressed as neatly as usual, she came into the kitchen where Aunt Morgen, still in her bathrobe, sat sullenly at the kitchen table drinking her coffee. Elizabeth said "Good morning," and went to the refrigerator for milk. When she sat down at the table opposite Aunt Morgen she said "Good morning, Aunt," and still received no answer; when she looked up she realized that Aunt Morgen was regarding her angrily and without the ordinarily misty look of early morning. "My headache is better," Elizabeth said timidly.

"So I see," said Aunt Morgen. She tapped ominously on the edge of her coffee cup and prepared her face, by turning down the corners of her mouth and narrowing her eyes, for heavy irony. "I am happy," she said deeply, "to know that your health was so much improved that you were able to leave your bed."

"I thought I would go to work; I—"

"I was not referring," said Aunt Morgen, "to your present state. The improvement in your health to which I refer took place, I should say, at approximately one o'clock this morning." She stopped to light a cigarette, her hand shaking noticeably with fury. "When you decided to go out," she finished.

"But I didn't go out anywhere, Aunt Morgen. I slept all night."

"Do you really suppose," Aunt Morgen said, "that *I* am unaware of what goes on in my own house? Do you really suppose, you overgrown baby, that *I* am going to be taken in by your pretense of being sick and be sympathetic and bring you hot water bottles and give you pills and come to see how you are and put you to bed and be as nice as I can, and then for all my pains get laughed at? Do you really *suppose*," Aunt Morgen went on, her voice rising intolerably, "that I don't *know* what you're *doing?*"

Elizabeth stared, speechless; childish defenses came back to her, and she dropped her eyes and looked at her glass of milk, and twisted her fingers together, and trembled her lip, and stayed quiet.

"Well?" Aunt Morgen leaned back. "Well?"

"I don't know," Elizabeth said.

"You don't know *what?*" Aunt Morgen's voice, softer for a moment, rose again. "*What* don't you know, fool?"

"I don't know what you mean."

"I mean what's going on in my house, I mean what you're doing, I mean whatever dirty horrible nasty business you do in the middle of the night that even your own aunt can't know about and you have to sneak out like a dirty thief, going down the stairs with your shoes in your hand—"

"I *didn't.*"

"You did. And I will *not* be lied to. Now," said Aunt Morgen, rising and leaning terribly across the table, "I mean to hear, before you leave this house today, exactly what you think you're getting away with. And the sooner," said Aunt Morgen, "the better."

"I didn't."

"It won't do you any good. Where did you go?"

"I didn't go anywhere."

"Did you walk? Or was someone waiting for you?"

"I didn't."

"*Who?* Who was waiting to meet you?"

"No one. I didn't do anything."

"Who was he?" Aunt Morgen slammed her hand down onto the table so that Elizabeth's glass of milk rocked and spilled; the milk ran to the edge of the table and dripped onto the floor, and Elizabeth was afraid to move to find a cloth to wipe it up; she was afraid to do anything more than sit, avoiding Aunt Morgen's eyes and twisting her hands under the table. "Who?" Aunt Morgen demanded.

"No one."

Aunt Morgen opened her mouth, gasped, and took hold of the edge of the table with both hands. She closed her eyes tightly, shut her mouth, and stood, visibly calming herself.

After a minute she opened her eyes and sat down, and spoke quietly. "Elizabeth," she said, "I didn't want to frighten you. I'm sorry I lost my temper. I realize that by yelling at you I'm doing more harm than good; suppose I try to explain."

"All right," Elizabeth said. She looked quickly at the milk, and it was still running off onto the floor.

"Look," Aunt Morgen said persuasively, "you know that as your only guardian I feel a great deal of responsibility. After all," she said with a friendly grin, "I was your age once, much as I hate to admit it, and I can remember how hard it is to feel that people are keeping an eye on you. You feel independent, and free, and sort of as though you don't *have* to account to anybody for what you do. But please try to realize, kiddo, that as far as I'm concerned, you can go ahead and do whatever you please. I'm not a dragon, or one of your fidgety old maids who faints when she sees a man. I'm your same crazy aunt, and I may be an old maid but I bet there's not much left can make me faint." Aunt Morgen hesitated and then, obviously resisting a train of thought which threatened to carry her away, went on firmly, "What I'm trying to say *is*, you don't need to sneak in and out, and be afraid of my finding out something you're ashamed of. If there's some fellow you want to see, and you think for some reason I might mind your seeing him, don't you think you'd be smarter to have me mad at you for seeing him—which I certainly couldn't do anything about—than to have me mad at you for sneaking around and hiding things behind my back—which I certainly *can* do something about, and you just *watch* me—and all things considered, doesn't it seem as though you'd be better off out in the open?" Aunt Morgen ran out of breath, and stopped.

"I guess so," Elizabeth said.

"Then, look, kiddo," Aunt Morgen said gently, "suppose you just tell auntie what it's all about. Believe me, nothing is going to happen to you. You've got a *right* to do what you please, and remember, I'm not going to scold you, because *I* always did what I pleased, and I can remember perfectly well how you feel."

"But I didn't," Elizabeth said. "I mean, I didn't do anything."

"Suppose you didn't *do* anything," Aunt Morgen said reasonably, "that's still no reason for not telling me, is it?" She laughed. "It's if you *did* do something you ought to be scared," she said.

"But I mean I didn't do *anything*."

"Then what *did* you do?" Aunt Morgen asked. "What on earth can you find to do at that hour of the night if you didn't *do* anything?" She laughed again, and shook her head, bewildered. "What a *hell* of a way to talk," she said. "Don't you know any honest words?"

"No." Elizabeth thought. "I mean," she said, "I didn't *do* anything."

"Good lord," Aunt Morgen said. "Good holy lord God almighty, I can't *say* it again. Are there any words," she asked delicately, "which might communicate with your dainty brain? I am trying to ask you precisely what occurred, and with whom, at one o'clock last night."

"Nothing," said Elizabeth, twisting her hands.

"I am by now completely convinced that it was nothing," said Aunt Morgen fervently. "I am only astonished that he could have expected anything else. There must be people," she said as though to herself, "like that in the world, but how does she find them? Who, then," she continued to Elizabeth, "was this optimistic young man?"

"No one," said Elizabeth.

"Blood from a stone," said Aunt Morgen, "gold from sea water, fire from snow. You're your mother's own daughter, mud up to the neck." She laughed, unexpectedly good-humored. "I don't know *why*," she said, still laughing, "I should believe that *you* would go out on a cold night to meet a young man. My own private guess, being you're your mother's daughter, is that you'd make a big mystery of going out to mail a letter, and hope someone would think the worst of it. Or to find a nickel you lost last week. And if it *is* some fellow," she added, pointing jeeringly at Elizabeth, "I'll bet your poor dear father's fortune *he* isn't fooled. You're like your mother, kiddo, a cheat and a liar, and neither of you could ever get around me."

"But I didn't," Elizabeth said helplessly.

"Of course you didn't," Aunt Morgen said. "Poor baby." She rose and left the kitchen, and Elizabeth was finally able to get the dishcloth and wipe up the spilled milk.

There was still a gaping hole in her room at the museum, and it stayed just beyond her left elbow all day. In the morning mail, which included a letter asking the museum for a complete listing of the exhibits in the Insect Room, and a letter asking for a final decision upon an unparalleled collection of Navajo hammered silver, there was another letter for Elizabeth. "ha ha ha," it read, "i know all about you dirty dirty lizzie and you cant get away from me and i wont ever leave you or tell you who i am ha ha ha."

Coming home that afternoon with the letter in her pocketbook Elizabeth stopped suddenly on the street between the bus stop and her aunt's house. Someone, she thought distinctly, is writing letters to *me*.

She put this letter also into the red valentine box which had held chocolates on her twelfth birthday, and opened and reread the other two. "i will catch you . . ." "She's all I have . . ." "you cant get away from me . . ."

"Well?" Aunt Morgen said after dinner. "You decided to give in?"

"I didn't do anything."

"You didn't do anything," Aunt Morgen said. "All right." She looked coldly at Elizabeth. "You got another one of your phony backaches?"

"Yes. I mean, I have my backache again. And my head aches."

"For all the sympathy you'll get from *me* tonight," Aunt Morgen said heavily. "How often you think you can get away with it?"

"And how is our poor head *this* morning?" Aunt Morgen inquired at breakfast.

"A little better, thank you," said Elizabeth, and then she saw Aunt Morgen's face. "I'm sorry," she said involuntarily.

"Have a pleasant time?" Aunt Morgen asked. "Poor devil still hoping?"

"I don't know—"

"You don't *know?*" Aunt Morgen's irony was heavy. "Surely, Elizabeth, even your mother—"

"I didn't."

"So you didn't." Aunt Morgen turned back to her coffee. "How do you feel?" she asked finally, grudgingly.

"About the same, Aunt Morgen. My back hurts, and my head."

"You ought to see a doctor," Aunt Morgen said, and then, standing abruptly, and slamming her hand on the table, "honest to *God*, kiddo, you *ought* to see a *doctor!*"

". . . and i can do whatever i want and you cant do anything about it and i hate you dirty lizzie and youll be sorry you ever heard of me because now we both know youre a dirty dirty dirty . . ."

Elizabeth sat on her bed, counting her letters. Someone had written her lots of letters, she thought fondly, lots of letters; here were five. She kept them all in the red valentine box and every afternoon now, when she came home from work, she put the new one in and counted them over. The very feel of them was important, as though at last someone had found her out, someone close and dear, someone who wanted to watch her all the time; someone who writes letters to me, Elizabeth thought, touching the papers gently. The clock on the stair landing struck five, and reluctantly she began to gather the letters together, folding them neatly and putting them back into their envelopes. She would not like to have Aunt Morgen see her letters. They were all safely back in the box and she had put away the chair she stood on to put the box onto the shelf of her closet, when the door crashed open and Aunt Morgen came in. "Elizabeth," she said, "kiddo, what's *wrong?*"

"Nothing," said Elizabeth.

Aunt Morgen's face was white, and she held tight to the doorknob. "I've been calling you," she said. "I've been knocking on your door and calling you and outdoors looking for you and calling you and you didn't answer." She stopped for a minute, holding tight to the doorknob. "I've been calling you," she said at last.

"I've been right here. I was just getting ready for dinner."

"I thought you were—" Aunt Morgen stopped. Elizabeth looked at her anxiously, and saw that she was staring at the table by the bed. Turning, Elizabeth saw one of Aunt Morgen's brandy bottles on the table. "Why did you put that in my room?" Elizabeth asked.

Aunt Morgen let go of the doorknob and came toward Elizabeth. "God almighty," she said, "you *stink* of the stuff."

"I don't." Elizabeth backed away; Aunt Morgen, unreasonably, frightened her. "Aunt Morgen, please let's go have dinner."

"Mud." Aunt Morgen took up the brandy bottle and held it to the light. "Dinner," she said, and laughed shortly.

"Please, Aunt Morgen, come downstairs."

"I," said Aunt Morgen, "am going to my room." Eyeing Elizabeth, she backed toward the door, the brandy bottle in her hand. "*I* think," she said, her hand again on the doorknob, "that *you* are drunk." And she slammed the door behind her.

Perplexed, Elizabeth went over to sit on the bed. Poor Aunt Morgen, she thought, I had her brandy. Absently, she noticed that the bedside clock said a quarter past twelve.

". . . i know all about it i know all about it i know all about it dirty dirty lizzie dirty dirty lizzie i know all about it . . ."

Because the next day there was proof to correct on the museum catalogue, Elizabeth, with her new letter safely in her pocketbook, did not leave the building until quarter past four, when the workmen were already engaged on the hidden structure of the building. As a result, she missed her usual bus home. When she finally came into the kitchen where Aunt Morgen sat drinking her brandy, Elizabeth saw first that Aunt Morgen had not eaten any dinner, and then she looked up into her aunt's hard stare. Wordless, Elizabeth could only hold out

placatingly the box of chocolates she suddenly discovered she
was carrying.

Mr. and Mrs. Arrow fancied themselves as homey folk in a
circle where all their acquaintance collected Indian masks, or
read plays together of an evening, or accompanied one another
on the sackbut; Mr. and Mrs. Arrow served sherry, and played
bridge, and attended lectures together, and even listened to the
radio. Mrs. Arrow was accustomed to deplore as extreme
Aunt Morgen's habit of going to the movies alone, and both
Mr. and Mrs. Arrow felt that Elizabeth was allowed too much
freedom; Mrs. Arrow had said as much, indeed, to Aunt Morgen when Elizabeth first went to work at the museum. "You
allow that girl too much leeway, Morgen," Mrs. Arrow had
said, making no bones about the way she felt, "a girl like Elizabeth takes more watching than one of your . . . one of
those . . . that is to say, Elizabeth, you know as well as I do,
takes watching. Not that Elizabeth's not *normal*." Mrs. Arrow
had stopped and lifted her eyes to heaven and spread her hands
innocently, so that no one would ever believe that Mrs. Arrow
meant to imply for a minute that Elizabeth was anything apart
from normal, "I don't mean that at all," Mrs. Arrow explained
earnestly. "What I mean is, Elizabeth is an unusually sensitive
girl, and if she is going to go off by herself every day for long
periods of time, it would be most judicious, Morgen, most
wise of you, to check *care*fully that she is always among people of the most genteel sort. Of course," Mrs. Arrow went on,
nodding reassuringly, "over at the museum they're mostly *vol-
unteer* workers. I always think," she finished, "that it's so *kind*
of them."

Mr. Arrow had at one decisive point of growth taken a set
of singing lessons to improve his poise, and he was still very
apt to sing when even very slightly invited to; Mr. Arrow cus-
tomarily entertained guests with songs like "Give a Man a
Horse He Can Ride," and "The Road to Mandalay," and Mrs.
Arrow accompanied him on the piano, pedalling furiously and
occasionally humming the easy parts; "For God's sake," Aunt

Morgen said to Elizabeth, pressing her finger insistently upon the doorbell, "don't ask Vergil to sing."

"All right," Elizabeth said.

"Ruth," Aunt Morgen said, as the door opened, "how good to see you again."

"How are you, how are you," said Mrs. Arrow, and Mr. Arrow, behind her in the hall and smiling largely, said "How are you? And here is Elizabeth, too; how are *you*, my dear?"

Because the Arrows neither collected Indian masks nor patronized a decorator, they were forced to use ordinary pictures on their walls, and whenever Elizabeth thought of the Arrows' home she remembered the bright reproductions of country gardens and placid smooth hills and sunsets; the Arrows also had an umbrella stand in their hallway, although both of them laughed about it and Mr. Arrow, in his faint deprecating way, said that after all it *was* the very best place to put wet umbrellas. When Elizabeth, coat neatly hung in the Arrows' hall closet, sat in a great chair in the Arrows' living room, with her hands folded correctly in her lap and Aunt Morgen spreading herself comfortably in just such another chair, and Mr. and Mrs. Arrow nervously together on the sofa, Elizabeth felt safe.

The whole room partook somehow of the smooth hills and sunsets; the chair in which Elizabeth sat was soft and deep and upholstered in a kind of cloudy orange, her feet lay on a carpet in which a scarlet key design ran in and out and around a geometric floral affair in green and brown, and the wallpaper, pervading and emphasizing the room, and somehow the Arrows, presented the inadvertent viewer with alternate squares of blue and green, relieved almost haphazardly by touches of black. There was nothing of harmony, nothing of humor, in the Arrows' way of life; there was everything of compromise and yet, comfortably, a kind of deep security in the unmistakable realization that all of this belonged without dispute to the Arrows, was unmovable and after a while almost tolerable, and was, beyond everything else, solid. Not even Aunt Morgen could deny the Arrows the reality of their living room, and when one met them at a lecture on reincarnation, or walking placidly together toward the park on a Sunday afternoon, or dining at the home of one of those odd people who always seemed to invite them, Mr. and Mrs. Arrow brought with them, and spread infectiously, an air of unfading wallpaper and practical carpeting, of ironclad and frequently unendurable mediocrity.

From where she sat Elizabeth could see her own reflection in the polish of the grand piano, and sparks from her own face glancing off the cut glass bowl of wax fruit, and glitters when she moved her hand, flashing and glinting, from the gilt mirror over the marble mantel and the glass beads on the lampshade and Mr. Arrow's cuff links and the painted jar on the table, kept always full of sugared almonds. Mr. Arrow was going to get them some sherry, Mrs. Arrow hoped they would take a chocolate, Mr. Arrow was willing to break the ice with a song, if anyone liked; Mrs. Arrow wondered if Elizabeth was not getting thin, and the lights danced on the glass of the picture where the roses and peonies were massed in the country garden. Elizabeth identified a disturbance; she was getting one of her headaches. She rubbed the back of her neck against the chair, and moved uneasily. The headache began, somehow, at the back of her head and progressed, creeping and fearful, down her back; Elizabeth thought of it as a live thing moving down her backbone, escaping from her head by the narrow avenue which was her neck, slipping onto and conquering her back, taking over her shoulders and finally settling, nestled in safety, in the small of her back, from which it could not be dislodged by any stretching or rubbing or rolling; to a large extent her rubbing the back of her neck was an attempt to cut off the path of this live pain; firm enough rubbing might make it turn back, discouraged, and keep only to her head; "—museum?" Mrs. Arrow asked her.

"I beg your pardon?" Elizabeth said to Mrs. Arrow.

"Are you well, Elizabeth?" Mrs. Arrow asked, peering. "Do you feel all right?"

"I have a headache," Elizabeth said.

"*Again?*" Aunt Morgen asked.

"It will go away," Elizabeth said, sitting still. Mr. Arrow

would bring her an aspirin, and thought he might better not sing until her poor head was better; Mr. Arrow remarked smilingly to Aunt Morgen that frequently the headtones of the human voice were most irritating to the sensitive membranes of the brain, although, of course, many people found it sooth-ing to be sung to when their heads ached. Mrs. Arrow had a kind of headache pill which she had always found more effi-cacious than aspirin, and would be delighted to bring one to Elizabeth; Mrs. Arrow herself always took two of these pills, but felt that Elizabeth had better not at first venture more than one. Aunt Morgen thought that Elizabeth should have her eyes examined, because these headaches came so often, and Mr. Arrow told about the headaches he had had before he got *his* glasses. Mrs. Arrow said that she would be very happy to go and get Elizabeth one of her headache pills if Elizabeth thought it would help and Elizabeth said untruthfully that she felt better now, thank you. Because everyone was look-ing at her she picked up the glass of sherry which Mr. Arrow had poured for her, and sipped at it daintily, loathing the underneath bitter taste of it, and feeling her head swim sick-eningly.

"—to breed Edmund," Mrs. Arrow was saying to Aunt Morgen. "It seems like a long way to go, of course, but we felt, Vergil and I, that it was worth it."

"Got to take a lot of care with that kind of thing," Mr. Arrow said.

"I remember," Aunt Morgen began, "when I was about sixteen—"

"Elizabeth," Mrs. Arrow said, "are you *sure* you feel all right?"

Everyone turned again and looked at her, and Elizabeth, sipping at her sherry, said, "I feel fine now, really."

"I don't like the way that girl looks," Mrs. Arrow said to Aunt Morgen, and shook her head worriedly, "she doesn't look well, Morgen."

"Peaked," Mr. Arrow amplified.

"She used to be strong as a horse," Aunt Morgen said, turn-ing to look intently at Elizabeth. "Lately she's been getting these headaches and backaches and she hasn't been sleeping at all well."

"Growing pains," Mrs. Arrow said tentatively, as though there was still a chance that it might turn out to be something worse. "She could be working too hard, too."

"Young girls," Mr. Arrow said profoundly.

"How old *is* Elizabeth?" Mrs. Arrow asked. "Sometimes when a girl spends too much of her time alone. . . ." She gestured delicately, and dropped her eyes.

"I'm all right," Elizabeth said uneasily.

"Fanciful," Mr. Arrow said, with a gesture reminiscent of Mrs. Arrow's. "Wrong ideas," he added.

"I've been wondering if she ought to see Doctor Ryan," Aunt Morgen said. "This business of not sleeping. . . ."

"Always just as well to go with the *first* symptoms," Mrs. Arrow said firmly. "You never know what might turn up *later*."

"General check-up," said Mr. Arrow roundly.

"I think so," Aunt Morgen said. She sighed and then smiled at Mr. and Mrs. Arrow. "It's a great responsibility," she said, "my own sister's child, and yet it's not as though I've been much of a *mother*."

"*No* one could have been more conscientious," Mrs. Arrow declared, immediately and positively. "Morgen, you must *not,* you simply must *not,* blame yourself; you've done a *splendid* job. Vergil?"

"Fine job," said Mr. Arrow hastily. "Often thought about it."

"I've always tried to think of her as though she was my own," Aunt Morgen said, and the sudden quick smile she sent across the room to Elizabeth made the words almost pathetic, because they were true. Elizabeth smiled back, and rubbed her neck against the chair.

"—Edmund," Mrs. Arrow was saying.

"But I don't understand," Aunt Morgen said. "Was the mother brown?"

"Apricot," Mrs. Arrow said reprovingly.

"That was why we had to go so far out of town," Mr. Arrow explained. "We wanted to get just the *right* color combination.

But of course," he went on mournfully, "as it turned out, we could have saved ourselves a trip."

"It *is* a shame," Aunt Morgen said.

"So of *course* we *had* to take the black one," Mrs. Arrow said, and shrugged, to show how helpless they had been.

Mr. Arrow touched his wife on the shoulder. "All water under the bridge," he said. "How about a little music? Elizabeth's head all right?"

"Fine," said Elizabeth.

"Well, then," said Mr. Arrow, moving with speed toward the piano. "Ruth? Care to play along?" As his wife rose and came toward the piano, Mr. Arrow turned to Aunt Morgen. "Which shall it be? Mandalay?"

"Lovely," said Aunt Morgen, settling herself into her chair and reaching without formality for the sherry decanter. "Mandalay would be perfectly grand."

Elizabeth opened her eyes then because instead of the sound of the piano playing the introduction to "The Road to Mandalay," there was a silence, and then Mr. Arrow said, "Well, really." He closed the music on the piano and said to Elizabeth, "I'm sorry. I *asked* if your head was all right. Really," he said to Mrs. Arrow.

"He did, you know, Elizabeth," Mrs. Arrow said. "I'm sure no one wants to *make* you listen."

"I beg your pardon?" Elizabeth said, perplexed. "I *want* to hear Mr. Arrow sing."

"Well, if it was a joke," Aunt Morgen said, "it was in extremely poor taste, Elizabeth."

"I don't understand," Elizabeth said.

"It's all forgotten now, anyway," Mr. Arrow said peaceably. "We'll go ahead, then."

Elizabeth, waiting again, again heard only silence and opened her eyes to find them all looking at her. *"Elizabeth,"* Aunt Morgen was saying, chokingly and half-rising from her chair, *"Elizabeth."*

"Never mind, Morgen, really," Mrs. Arrow said. She got up from the piano bench, her hands shaking and her mouth tight. "I'm certainly *surprised*," Mrs. Arrow said.

Mr. Arrow, not looking at Elizabeth, folded the music slowly and put it with some care onto the other music on the back of the piano. After a minute he looked around the room, smiling his faint smile. "Let's not have our nice evening spoiled, ladies," he said. "Sherry, Morgen?"

"I have never *been* so humiliated," Aunt Morgen said. "I can't understand it at *all*. I do apologize, Vergil, I honestly do. All I can say is—"

"Please don't mind it," Mrs. Arrow said. She put her hand gently on Aunt Morgen's arm. "Let's forget all about it."

"Elizabeth?" Aunt Morgen said.

"What?" said Elizabeth.

"—feel all right?"

"What?" said Elizabeth.

"She ought to lie down or something," Mr. Arrow said.

"I had no idea—" Mrs. Arrow said.

"She's taken eight glasses of sherry, by *my* count," Aunt Morgen said grimly. "Where she ought to be is home in bed; I never saw her drink *any*thing before."

"But just sweet sherry—"

"—see a doctor," said Mrs. Arrow wisely. "Can't be too careful."

"Elizabeth," Aunt Morgen said sharply, "put down your cards and get up and put on your coat. We're going home."

"Must you?" Mrs. Arrow asked. "I don't really think she needs to go *home*."

Aunt Morgen laughed. "Three rubbers of bridge is about *my* limit," she said. "And Elizabeth has to get up in the morning."

"Well, it's been lovely to have you," Mrs. Arrow said.

"Come again soon," Mr. Arrow said.

"We've enjoyed it *so* much," Aunt Morgen said.

"Thank you for a very nice time," Elizabeth said.

"It was nice to see you, Elizabeth. And, Morgen, do make a point of getting to that science lecture. Maybe we can all go together—"

"Thanks again," Aunt Morgen said.

When the door had closed behind them and they were going down the walk in the cool night air Aunt Morgen took Elizabeth's arm and said, "Look, kiddo, you frightened me. Are you sick?"

"I have a headache."

"No wonder, after all that sherry." Aunt Morgen stopped under the street light and took Elizabeth's chin and turned her face to look at her. "You're *not* tight on sherry," Aunt Morgen said, wondering. "You look all right and you talk all right and you walk all right—there *is* something wrong. Elizabeth," she said urgently, "*what* is it, kiddo?"

"Headache," Elizabeth said.

"I wish you'd talk to me," Aunt Morgen said. She put her arm through Elizabeth's and they began to walk on. "I get so goddamned *worried*," Aunt Morgen said. "All during the bridge game I—"

"What bridge game?" Elizabeth said.

"Well, now, Morgen," Doctor Ryan said. He leaned back in his chair and the chair creaked under his huge weight, as it had been doing, Elizabeth thought, all her lifetime; she had never thought of it so clearly before, but all she remembered of Doctor Ryan after leaving his office was the way his chair creaked. "Well, now, Morgen," Doctor Ryan said. He put his fingers together in front of him and raised his eyebrows and looked quizzically at Aunt Morgen. "Always *were* one to get het up about trifles," he said.

"Hah," said Aunt Morgen. "*I* can remember a time, Harold Ryan—"

They both laughed, similarly, greatly, looking at one another with wrinkles of laughter around their eyes. "Damn disrespectful woman," Doctor Ryan said, and they laughed.

Elizabeth looked at Doctor Ryan's office; she had been here before, with her mother, with Aunt Morgen; Doctor Ryan had been here in this office ever since Elizabeth could remember, and so far as Elizabeth knew he had no other home. He had been in Aunt Morgen's house when her mother died, his arm around Aunt Morgen's shoulders, his great voice saying small things; he had come once in the night, looming jovially at the foot of Elizabeth's bed, speaking coolly through the feverish, inflamed phantoms crowding the pillow; "You're making quite a fuss, my girl," he had said then, "over nothing but a couple of measles." The rest of the time, the rest of Elizabeth's life, Doctor Ryan had been here in this office, leaning back in his chair and making it creak. Elizabeth did not know the names on the backs of any of the books in the glass-doored case behind Doctor Ryan's back, but she knew peculiarly well the tear on the leather spine of the one third from the end on the second shelf, and wondered, now, if Doctor Ryan ever turned around and took down one of the books to look at. While Doctor Ryan and Aunt Morgen laughed, Elizabeth looked at the grey curtains over the window, and the books, and the glass inkwell on Doctor Ryan's desk, and the little ship model which Doctor Ryan had made himself, long ago, when his fingers were nimbler.

"But honestly, Harold," Aunt Morgen said, "she *did* frighten me. There was poor old Vergil, just opening his mouth, and Elizabeth shouts out this *obscenity*—I mean, honestly—" Aunt Morgen's lips moved, and she made a visible effort to keep from smiling. "I mean," she said helplessly, "I've thought of it *myself*, when Vergil—" She put her hands over her face and began to rock back and forth. "If you could have seen . . ." she said. "Mandalay . . ."

Doctor Ryan covered his eyes with his hand. "Mandalay," he said in confirmation. "I've heard Vergil do Mandalay," he added.

"I didn't," Elizabeth said. "I mean, I didn't say anything."

Aunt Morgen and Doctor Ryan both turned their heads to look at her, both soberly interested.

"That's it," Aunt Morgen said. "I really don't think she *remembers*."

Doctor Ryan nodded. "Physically, of course," he said, shrugging, "all you can do is check the things you *know* about. I can tell you she's overtired, or nervous, or some such nonsense, but then you can come right back at me with something you and I both know is impossible, and we're right back where we started. Tell you what *I* think we ought to do," Doctor Ryan said, suddenly determined, and reaching across his desk for a prescription pad, "there's an old friend of mine, fellow named Wright, Victor Wright. *You* know, Morgen, and *I* know, that I'd be the last person in the world to send Elizabeth to one of these psychoanalysts, knowing her the way I do; no telling *what* they might say. But I *do* want you to run over and see Wright, Elizabeth, and have him take a look at you. He's an odd duck," Doctor Ryan said to Aunt Morgen, "always been kind of interested in this kind of problem. No . . ." Doctor Ryan gestured, reassuringly. "No *couch* or anything, Morgen, you understand."

"You're a dirty old man, Harold," Aunt Morgen said agreeably.

Doctor Ryan looked up and grinned. "Aren't I?" he asked, pleased.

"Do you think if there's anything wrong this fellow will find it?" Aunt Morgen asked.

"There's nothing *wrong* with Elizabeth," Doctor Ryan said. "I think she's worried about something. Boys, maybe. You ever ask her about boy friends?"

Aunt Morgen shook her head. "I can't get her to talk to me at all."

"Well," Doctor Ryan said, rising, "if anyone can get it out of her, it's Wright."

Aunt Morgen got up and turned to Elizabeth, and then yelped. "Harold Ryan," she said, "I've been telling you to cut that out for twenty-five years."

"Still the best pinching surface in town," Doctor Ryan said, and winked at Elizabeth.

2

DOCTOR WRIGHT

I believe I am an honest man. Not one of your namby-pamby modern doctors, with all kinds of names for nothing, and all kinds of cures for ailments that don't exist, and none of them able to look a patient in the eye for shame—no, I believe I am an honest man, and there are not many of us left. The young flashy fellows just starting out, who do everything except put their names in neon lights and run bingo games in the waiting room, are my particular detestation, and that is largely why I am putting my notes on the case of Miss R. into some coherent form; perhaps some one of your young fellows may read them and be instructed, perhaps not. I can remember joking with my late wife about a patient a doctor could get his teeth into—although that, too, I suppose, will be liable to misconstruction by your head doctors with their dreams and their Freuds; boys I brought into the world, too, some of them. It is gratifying to know that the extraordinary case of Miss R. was taken and solved and lies transcribed here for all the world to read, by an honest man; gratifying, at any rate, to myself. I make no excuses or apologies for my medical views, although perhaps my literary style will leave something to be desired, and I preface this account by saying, as I have said for forty years or more, that an honest doctor is an honest man, and considers his patient's welfare before the bills are sent in. My own practice has dwindled because most of my patients are dead—(that is another of my little jokes, and we'll have to get used to them, reader, before you and I can go on together; I am a whimsical man and must have my smile)—naturally, because they grew old along with me, and I survived 'em, being a medical man.

Thackeray says somewhere (and I had my finger on it not two days ago, somewhere in *Esmond,* anyway) that a man's vanity is stronger than any other passion in him; I've read that twenty times and more in as many years, and I daresay a good writer is much the same as a good doctor; honest, decent, self-respecting men, with no use for fads or foibles, going on trying to make our sensible best of the material we get, and all of it no better and no worse than human nature, and who can quarrel with that for durable cloth? And yet, along with Thackeray, I have my prides and my little passions, and perhaps fancying myself Author is not the least of them.

With all of this, there wasn't much joking in me the first time I met Miss R., poor girl. Ryan had made the appointment for her, and, to tell the truth, I wasn't much inclined to her at first, thought her a sullen type, perhaps. Young women who fancy "character-reading" or "fortune-telling" might have thought her shy. Colorless was a word came to my mind when I looked at her. She had brown hair, taken smoothly to the back of her head, and fastened there with strong combs or a bit of ribbon, maybe; brown eyes, hands long and graceful and quiet when she sat down, not fussing with her gloves or her pocketbook like these nervous women; altogether, if I may be permitted a term which has got sadly out of use, I thought Miss R. a gentlewoman. Her gown was suitable for her age and position; dark, neatly made and not at all stylish, perhaps even—although I liked it, I recall—a bit prim. Her voice was low and level, and I thought her cultured. I cannot recall that she ever laughed genuinely, although when she came to know me she frequently smiled.

Miss R.'s symptoms—dizzy spells, occasional *aboulia,** periods of forgetfulness, panic, fears and weaknesses which were causing her to function poorly at her employment, listlessness, insomnia—all indications of a highly nervous condition, perhaps of an hysteric, had been faithfully reported to me by that amiable blackguard Ryan, to whom her family had taken her

aboulia; a state which I can describe for the layman who reads and runs as an inhibition of will, preventing a desired action; Miss R. showed this largely in speech, almost as though she were *prevented* from uttering a syllable.

when her state became too apparent to be ignored; like most
families, the members of this one—in this particular case, I believe, only a middle-aged aunt—chose to overlook the obvious
symptoms of nervousness in the patient, and excuse them vari-
ously and charitably until the case' was too far advanced to be
dismissed; I know of one family where it was not until a lad had
made off with some thousands of dollars from his father's safe
that his doting family confessed that he had been a sleepwalker
since childhood! At any rate, Ryan, finding himself at a loss
with regard to Miss R. when she did not respond to his usual
treatments (nerve tonic, sedatives, rest in the afternoon), and
knowing of my own interest in the deep problems of the mind
(although, as I cannot say often enough, I am not one of your
psychoanalysts, but merely an honest general practitioner who
believes that the illnesses of the mind are as reasonable as the
illnesses of the body, and that your analytical nastiness has no
place in the thoughts of a decent and modest girl like Miss R.)
he arranged with me to give her an appointment.

Miss Hartley, my nurse, had taken down the name of the
patient, her address, age, and such vital information, and the
card bearing these facts was set upon my desk when Miss R.
entered.[†]

She smiled at me almost timidly as she sat down; my office
is so constructed as to display the maximum reassurance to
timid patients—something your chromium and enamel physi-
cians seem to regard as superfluous—and its dark rows of
books (from my school days, madam; I admit it before you
charge me) against the walls, its heavily curtained windows
(enriched, my dear miss, with cigar smoke and ashes and a terror to moths therefrom) and its deep chairs and pillowed sofa
(to which, sir, I would gladly at any convenient time admit
your ample bottom, for an hour or so of comfortable sitting,
and a glass of good wine and one of the cigars which Miss dis-
likes so much)—all this seemed to bring a measure of quiet to
Miss R., who looked about her almost stupidly, but showed, at

---

[†]Naturally, for reasons of discretion, I cannot call this young woman by her
full name. V.W.

least, no immediate signs of hysterical terror, a reaction, I might point out, not unheard of in patients forwarded to me by good old Ryan. Miss R. set her long hands upon her lap, as one who has been well brought up and taught that a lady seats herself quietly, and looked steadily to one side of me, and wet her lips nervously, and smiled without meaning at the corner of my desk, and opened her mouth, and closed it again. "Well," I said heartily, to show that I knew she was there and that our interview had, so to speak, commenced itself, and my valuable time for which her aunt was paying had been placed at her entire disposal, "well, Miss R.," I said, "what seems to be the trouble?"

I half-expected her to tell me. Sometimes—it is astonishing—a quiet girl who regards the corner of your desk will, without more than the faintest encouragement, bring herself readily to recount the most amazing fantasies, but she only dropped her eyes to examine the foot of the ashstand and said "Nothing."

"Probably," I agreed. "Probably nothing at all. But Doctor Ryan seemed to feel that you and I should have a little talk, and perhaps—"

"It's just wasting your time," she said.

"I suppose so." I dislike being interrupted, but Miss R. seemed so sure that she was well that I was curious; I confess I almost thought at that moment never to see her again. "Doctor Ryan says," I told her, consulting Ryan's note, "that you have difficulty sleeping."

"I don't," she said. "I sleep all right. My aunt told him I didn't sleep but I do."

"I see." I made a meaningless note, and said cautiously, "And the headaches?"

"Well," she said, moving her hands together slightly. I waited, thinking that she was going to continue, and then looked up expectantly. She was gazing raptly at my desk calendar, as though she had never seen such a thing before.

"And the headaches?" I repeated, a little sharp.

She looked at me squarely for the first time, dull, uninterested, stupid, turning her hands one within the other. "And the headaches?" I said. As though I had reminded her, she put one hand to the back of her neck, and closed her eyes; "And the headaches?" I said, and she looked at me, her eyes wide and aware of me, and said loudly, "I'm frightened."

"Frightened, Miss R.?"

"I haven't any headache," she said. "I feel fine."

"But frightened," I said. I noticed that I had begun to fidget with my letter opener, and put it down firmly on the desk and set my hands evenly one beside the other.

Miss R. folded her own hands neatly in her lap and smiled dully at the corner of the curtain.

"Well, now, Miss R.," I said, wondering at myself for an intense desire to turn and look at the curtain with her, "suppose we . . ."

"Thank you very much, Doctor Wright," she said, rising. "I am sure you have done me a great deal of good. Am I to come again?"

"Please do," I said, scrambling out from behind the desk as she started for the door. "Perhaps Miss Hartley can give you an appointment for the day after tomorrow."

"Goodbye," she said. I sat down again as the door closed behind her, and had my look at the curtain, and reflected that if Miss R. could be brought to tell me anything at all of her ailments, it would not be willingly or even—I perceived even then—consciously.

That, then, was my first introduction to Miss R. (and before my reader gasps, and stops, and turns jeering to point at a grammatical error in the good doctor's notes, let me interject with dignity that I use the tautology "first introduction" deliberately, almost in the nature of a joke; I had, as my reader, abashed, will soon see, more than one introduction to this remarkable girl). My own opinion then, I will say honestly, was of a personality disturbed and beset with problems it was incapable of solving alone; I am not a maker of quick judgments and could not, even then, damn Miss R. with a pat name for her illness.

My own special hobbyhorse has long been hypnosis; the great and enduring good brought about by hypnotic treatments, its value in a case such as Miss R.'s, its soothing and

consoling effect on the patient, have persuaded me after much
practice and definite estimate of results that the skillful and
sympathetic use of hypnosis is of inestimable value to the medical man whose patients justly fear placing themselves in the
hands of your modern name-callers; I had determined already
that hypnosis was the best—indeed, as I saw it, the only—
method to induce Miss R. to reveal enough of her difficulties
to aid us toward alleviating them, and hypnosis I determined
to try.

On her second visit to my office, we again scrutinized the
curtains, the ashstand, the calendar, and I spared a moment to
wonder what poor old Ryan had made of her; I hesitated to return directly to her statement that she was frightened, and so
began by covering the same ground as before; again she insisted that she slept perfectly well, that she had no headaches,
and, going by her words alone, it would seem that a visit to a
doctor was, to her way of thinking, an absurd and unreasonable imposition; when she looked at me directly, however,
there was in her eyes the mute appeal of an animal (and I am
an animal lover; I do not degrade Miss R. by the comparison;
indeed, I have seen many dogs more intelligent and aware than
Miss R. seemed then, on our second meeting) hurt beyond its
understanding and longing for help.

"Are you afraid of me?" I asked her gently, at last.

She shook her head no.

"Are you afraid of Doctor Ryan?"

Again no.

"Of speaking to me of your illness?"

And she nodded her head yes. She regarded still the edge of
the carpet, but I was persuaded that her answers related to my
questions, and continued, heartened, "Do you have difficulty
speaking?"

Yes again.

"Then will you permit me to hypnotize you?"

Staring at me then, eyes wide, she first shook her head violently no, and afterward, as one less frightened of the cure
than its practitioner, nodded her head yes.

That, then, was Miss R.'s second priceless interview with

Doctor Wright. I felt, however, that I had made progress; I could hardly boast that I had won my patient's confidence, but I had, at least—and I defy Ryan to say the same—had from her an answer to a question.

When she left I remarked casually that we would, then, attempt an hypnotic trance upon her next visit and so I was—from bitter and long-suffering experience—not more than mildly surprised when she entered my office upon the occasion of her next appointment with a step slower than usual and a look so furtive that she dared not face the curtain squarely, but regarded instead the toe of her shoe. She spoke at once, from the doorway, before I had even time to tell her good afternoon; "Doctor Wright," she said, "I have to go. I can't stay."

"And why not, Miss R.?"

"Because," she said.

"Because, Miss R.?"

"I have an appointment," she said.

"With me, surely."

"No, with someone else. I have to go back to work," she added, inspired.

Our appointments, for alternate days, were always at four-thirty, since Miss R. left her employment at four; it was remotely possible that Miss R. might today be required to return to her office, but I said in a leisurely fashion, "Well, Miss R., and is this all true?"

She was unused to falsehood, and had the grace to blush. "No," she said. She shifted her pocketbook to her other hand and said, "The truth is that my aunt is opposed to hypnotism."

"Indeed?" I said. "I am astonished that it was not mentioned. Surely Doctor Ryan—"

"I agree with my aunt," said Miss R. "I oppose hypnotism."

I might perhaps have accepted this as a moderately reasonable attitude (considering, heaven help us, the fakeries and lies practiced upon the general public in the name of hypnosis, I am only surprised, sometimes, that the uninformed people of this world continue to respect medical men at all), even considering Miss R.'s extremely limited area of experience, and the unlikelihood of her having formed any very decided opinions about anything whatsoever, had I not observed, glancing at her at that moment, that her eyes were imploring me, almost as though, speaking, she wanted one thing and looking, another.

"Nevertheless," I said firmly, "I intend to continue with the treatment as we agreed at your last visit."

"How?" she asked, surprised. "If I don't want you to?"

The look of entreaty which accompanied these words caused me to continue, as firmly, "It would be foolish to suppose that I could or would treat you against your will, nor would I wish to do so, but surely you cannot find any objection to continuing our conversation of your last visit? I found it most enjoyable."

Warily, as though afraid that I might perhaps leap at her and force upon her my horrendous treatments, she moved toward her usual chair, and I found myself experiencing a strong relief when she was at last induced to sit quietly, and fix her gaze, as always, upon some unoffending object.

How to begin was not a problem; Miss R. having once been brought to consent to treatment, needed no further persuasion, I knew; what Miss R. needed was some method, palatably presented, whereby what she actually wanted (and of this I was positive by now, that she *did* want treatment, and by the means I suggested) could be offered her in disguise, as it were, so that her objections, however unreasonable, might be circumvented with her own unconscious aid. At any rate, with Miss R., whose mental resources were, to say the least, untapped, nothing so patently on the surface as her rejection of treatment needed to be dealt with by any more than the most perfunctory deviousness; I smiled amiably down at my desk and remarked that *at least* I might have the pleasure of conversing with her; she looked at me swiftly and away, perceiving the heavy emphasis I used and seeing what I meant her to see, that I was both vexed and disappointed.

"I'm sorry," she said, and such a voluntary statement from Miss R. was worth almost any effort to me, in the step ahead it represented. "I wish I could let you hypnotize me."

I bowed politely, as befits a gentleman whose generous of-

fers have been civilly rejected (Victor Wright, Marquis of
Steyne!) and I repressed my smile as I said smoothly, "Perhaps
at another time; when we know one another better you will
trust me."

"I trust you," Miss R. said uncertainly to the floor.

I endeavored to turn the conversation onto Miss R.'s family
and her work, since discussion of her physical condition had
found her so reticent, but discovered, as I had more than half
expected, that Miss R. was ready with no more comprehensive
descriptions of her family life or the museum where she was
employed; indeed, at one point, despairing, I was almost persuaded that the girl was largely unaware of place and time,
and might, if asked suddenly, have difficulty remembering her
own name! I learned—through a cross-examination of which
the Spanish Inquisitors might have been proud—that she was
at this time doing a kind of menial clerical work at the museum, typing (the kind of a formal learned activity, requiring
no imagination or inventive qualities in discovering the correct
letters, which Miss R. might be expected to do splendidly) and
dealing with routine correspondence (again, I ascertained,
requiring no initiative) and matter-of-fact listings which required only the ability to copy down names and numbers.

It was this work which had suffered so extremely from her
ill health, since she depended upon its income for her liveli-
hood (although I strongly doubted whether her unknown aunt,
no matter how heartless, would have let poor Miss R. starve
for lack of an income, since various of Miss R.'s answers to my
questions indicated that her aunt was in possession of what
must have amounted, even today, to a fairly handsome fortune) and she would, without her occupation, have lost even
that shred of independence left to her, and as a result—*mutatis
mutandis*—suffered the worse. Her aunt had found her the
job, persuaded her to take it, and encouraged her to continue
at it, and I did Aunt the discourtesy of supposing that she, too,
might have found Miss R.'s daily, regular absence a source of
some refreshment. In answer to searching questions Miss R.
admitted to having her headache still, and was further persuaded to agree that she did, after all, suffer from headaches

almost constantly, and backaches almost as often. That Miss R. was entirely inert I soon had reason to doubt, for, seeing me glance once at the clock, she rose immediately, although I had supposed her regarding, as usual, the corner of the desk, and, remarking that her aunt expected her home, made as to take her leave. I assured her that I noted the clock because of an appointment of my own which was still almost two hours away, but could not prevail upon her to stay, although I felt most strongly that we were making a kind of progress.

"Doctor Wright," she said unexpectedly, pausing on her way to the door but not turning to look at me, "I think this is wasting your time. I have nothing wrong with me."

I smiled reassuringly, although unnecessarily, at her back. "If you were able to diagnose your own case, Miss R.," I said, "you would hardly have to come to a doctor. Moreover," I went on, before she could point out that she had not come to a doctor at all, but had been sent, "one or two hypnotic sessions will surely show if there is nothing wrong."

"Goodbye," Miss R. said, and took her departure.

I need not further detail for the impatient reader (you are patient, sir? Then you and I are left behind, inhabitants of a slower and more leisurely time, when we were not restless with an author for his painstaking efforts to entertain us, and demanded paragraphs of rich and rewarding meditation, and loved our books for the leather and the weight; we are forgotten, sir, you and I, and must take our quiet contemplation in secret, as some take opium and some count their gold)—I need not further trouble the reader, then, with a meticulous account of the progress which I made in persuading Miss R. to permit hypnosis; she was finally brought to agree to a brief experiment, although I am assured that she thought herself yielding to a kind of sinfulness rather than an honest attempt at therapeutic assistance, since she insisted upon the provision that she should not be required to answer any "embarrassing" questions, and was not to remain under hypnosis for more than a minute or so—too little time, I could not help noting cynically (although privately, sir; I am not a monster!) for any overt nefarious act on my part. To all of these stipulations I acceded willingly, knowing that even a brief experiment would certainly ease Miss R.'s fears, and might even prove of some assistance in quieting her nervous illness. As I had long suspected, she was, once she had brought herself to the point, a willing and cooperative subject, and in a very short space of time I had subdued her into a light hypnotic slumber.

When she was breathing easily and quietly, her hands and face relaxed, and her feet resting comfortably upon a small footstool, I was agreeably surprised at her appearance of pleasant, intelligent comeliness and reflected at the time that very possibly Miss R.'s nervous constraints stretched even farther than headaches and sleeplessness, and threw over her whole personality an air of timidity and stupidity; I recall that I even wondered briefly if Miss R. might not be a gay and merry companion under her mask of illness. Marveling at the relaxation in her face, which for the first time seemed to me pretty, I asked her quietly, "What is your name."

"Elizabeth R."—without hesitation.

"Where do you live?"

She named her street and city address.

"Who am I?"

"You are Doctor Wright."

"And are you afraid of me, Miss R.?"

"Of course not."—smiling slightly.

It was most gratifying to see that, just as the anxious lines upon Miss R.'s face smoothed out under hypnosis, just as the tightness of her mouth relaxed and her voice lost its reluctance, so her funds of information were ready-tapped, as it were, and she answered my questions readily and without hesitation, although I had before heard from her only the briefest of replies and those spoken falteringly and with much hesitation; I foresaw, what I had believed all along, that with the priceless assistance of Miss R.'s own mind, freed of its pressure of constraint, we might easily and without terror soon have her as free from nervous ailments as the best of us.

At this first attempt, I was most unwilling to rouse Miss R. from her happy sleep, but, mindful of my promise to keep her in trance for only a minute or two, I emphasized in her mind (in the form of what is called *post-hypnotic suggestion,* a most compelling influence) the conviction that she would sleep soundly and dreamlessly that night, and awaken the next morning refreshed (concluding that, once we had Miss R.'s insomnia under control, we might be strengthened to attack the headache and backaches, which I half believed to be little more than the result of fatigue) and awakened her. Immediately she became the Miss R. of my previous acquaintance, sullen, silent, looking anywhere but at me as she asked immediately, "What did I say?"

Silently I passed her my notes across the desk, and she glanced at them hastily and then said in great astonishment, "Is this all?"

"Every word," I told her truthfully, although, needless to add, I had prudently kept back my own words which were to instill in her the suggestion of a night's dreamless sleep.

"Why did you ask me if I was afraid of you?"

"Because naturally a doctor's first duty is to establish trust between himself and his patient," I said glibly, and, no doubt still marveling at my tremendous restraint when she was—as I have no doubt she thought of it vividly—in my power, she arose shortly afterward and took her leave.

My treatment, as generally planned at that time, was simple enough for the most untutored layman to understand. Shorn of technicalities, my intentions were thus: through the use of hypnosis, under which I suspected Miss R. might speak and act far more freely than in a waking state, to discover and eliminate whatever strain was causing her deliberately to confine herself in an iron cage of uncommunicativeness and fear. I was positive that at some time lost to conscious memory, Miss R. had forsaken herself as she was meant to be, and imposed upon herself the artificial state of stupidity in which she had been living for so many years; I may liken this state and its cure to (if my reader will forgive such an ignoble comparison) a stoppage in a water main; Miss R. had somehow contrived to stop up the main sewer of her mind (gracious heaven, how I have caught myself in my own analogy!) with some incident or traumatic occurrence which was, to her mind, indigestible, and could not be assimilated or passed through the pipe. This stoppage had prevented all but the merest trickle of Miss R.'s actual personality from getting through, and given us the stagnant creature we had known. My problem was, specifically, to get back through the pipe to where the obstruction was, and clear it away. Although the figure of speech is highly distasteful to one as timid of tight places as myself, the only way in which I might accomplish this removal is by going myself (through hypnosis, you will perceive) down the pipe until, the stoppage found, I could attack it with every tool of common sense and clear-sighted recognition. There; I am thankful to be out of my metaphor at last, although I confess I think Thackeray might be proud of me for exploring it so persistently, and it does, I fear, portray most vividly my own diagnosis of Miss R.'s difficulty and my own problem in relieving it. Let us assume, then, that the good Doctor Wright is steeling himself to creep manfully down a sewer pipe (and I wonder mirthfully, whether by calling poor Miss R.'s mind a sewer I might not be approaching wickedly close to your psychoanalytic fellows, those plumbers to whom all minds are cesspools and all hearts black!). Oh, Miss Elizabeth R., to what a pass have you brought your doctor!

One other matter remains (and now I speak more seriously) which, in the interests of future clarity, ought now to be clearly understood. It has long been my habit—and I believe the practice of many who use hypnosis professionally as a therapeutic method—to distinguish between the personality awake and the personality in hypnotic trance by the use of numerical symbols; thus, Miss R., awake and as I originally saw her, was automatically R1, although use of the prime number did not necessarily mean that I regarded R1 as Miss R. well, or healthy, or fundamental; R1 was Miss R. the first, in my mind and in my notes. Miss R., then, in the light hypnotic trance in which I had already seen her, was R2, and in my notes I was of course easily able to distinguish between Miss R.'s comments and answers awake or asleep by noting whether my questions had been answered by R1 or R2, with already in my own mind a distinct preference for the answers, and, indeed, the whole personality, of R2.

Indeed, when Miss R. came again to my office two days later, I thought I detected already traces of R2 in her manner; her step was lighter, perhaps, and although she did not look directly at me she contrived to speak, beyond the sulky "Good afternoon" with which she always responded to my greeting; "I feel better already," she remarked, and I thought I saw a brief lightening in her face.

I was heartened, as any doctor must have been. "Splendid," I said. "Have you slept well?"

"Very well," said Miss R.

"However," I said, "we must not therefore assume—"

"So I won't be hypnotized again," said Miss R.

I was sorely tempted to speak to her tartly, to point out to her that her purely temporary feeling of well-being might without my assistance suddenly forsake her and lower her once more into the deep despondency from which I had a little way lifted her, and yet I only said gently, "Any treatment, even any clear diagnosis, of your case, dear Miss R., is impossible without adequate knowledge. I do not believe that voluntarily you can or will give me the information I need; in a state of hypnosis you will answer me freely and truly." Had I at this moment remembered her stricture upon "embarrassing" questions, I might not have been so blunt; at any rate, she subsided sullenly into her chair and did not answer. Regretting immediately my sharp words, I fell silent for a moment, so that my self-annoyance might not find utterance in remarks which might seem to be taking out on Miss R. my own irritation. So silent we sat both, and then at last, fetching a deep sigh, I smiled at myself and said frankly, "I do not ordinarily become angry with my patients; perhaps, my dear Miss R., you will do *me* good."

I had, without realizing it, found a way of procedure; Miss R. looked at me, and almost laughed. "I won't make you angry again," she promised.

"Indeed I believe you will, and it may be good for a stern fellow who tends to think of his patients as problems rather than as people. By all means, whenever you find me regarding you as a problem in arithmetic—" (or in sewage, I might have said; O unfortunate analogy!) "—do at once bring me sharply up by an appeal to my temper. You shall never find me wanting in anger, my dear."

We gazed amiably upon one another, quite as though Miss R. were already the person she might someday become, and I verily believe that in the brief moment of anger, and my graceless apology, we came closer together than we had been before. In any case, the unkind question of treatment, brought up of necessity once more, found Miss R. less inclined to flat refusal, and it must suffice to say that she was once again brought to submit herself to hypnosis. "But no embarrassing questions, please?" she asked, blushing as though ashamed of this insistence and yet constrained to make it, as a patient will ask a dentist over and over again not to let the extraction hurt. Since I had at this time no slightest notion of what might seem to Miss R.'s tender sensibilities an embarrassing question, I could only agree helplessly, like the dentist, and promise myself privately to fulfill the obligation as nearly as possible; I had at the same time a notion that Miss R.'s reading of embarrassing questions might be wholly different from my own; I had a conviction that my own assumption, in a like case, of what might constitute an "embarrassment" would be a line of questioning tending toward the point of stoppage in the pipe, but I strongly suspected that what Miss R. meant by "embarrassing" was precisely what any untutored young girl might mean by the word: i.e., anything she would be ashamed to discuss before me, any secrets the poor girl might possess, although these need not be—indeed, very probably were not—the secret I was in search of; I thought tolerantly of love letters and such, and resolved roundly that Miss R.'s maiden sentiments should remain her own still, untampered with by me.

As Miss R. slipped softly into the trance state, I was anxious to meet again the pleasant girl I had spoken with before, and welcomed the amiable face with the delight of one greeting a charming acquaintance; I had decided that it would be most proper and practical to initiate the little series of questions I had first asked as a formal beginning for all hypnotic questioning, establishing, as it were, a little ritual of introduction, and I hoped that after a short time it might have the double effect of reassuring Miss R. in the first moments of trance, and in addition, perhaps, serve as a complementary trance-inducement; that is, when Miss R., falling asleep, heard my familiar pattern, she would be confirmed in the hypnotic state. So, I began again, "What is your name?"

"Elizabeth R."

She again told me where she lived, and assured me that she had no fear of me. When I asked her if she remembered what she had told me upon her previous visit, R2 smiled and said she did, that she had told me she was not afraid of me, and she was not. I felt that this emphasis upon complete trust in myself was very necessary, and endeavored to stress constantly, in my questions and my manner, my utter and entire sympathy with her. I thought of myself, frequently, as fatherly, and often found myself addressing her as a fond parent speaks to a precious child.

Since I had not been restricted, upon this second attempt, to "only a minute or so," I was able to question Miss R. at greater length about her illness, which she admitted frankly in this trance state, and about her daily life; I learned, for instance, much more clearly, about her work at the museum, and her routine homelife with her aunt. I also learned, without really intending to press the matter, that the substantial fortune which kept Miss R. and her aunt so easily was in actuality the future property of Miss R. herself, left in trust by her father; and for years to come, through a skillful and (I must confess I thought it) foresighted maneuver among lawyers and bankers, would be administered entirely by Aunt, with due deference to Miss R.'s comfort and convenience; I do not pretend to understand financial matters, and Miss R. obviously knew less of them, even, than I, but I could not help applauding the wisdom which would preserve Miss R. secure and safe from the many pitfalls which must beset a very young girl possessed of a large fortune and as passive and acquiescent as Miss R. had shown herself to be. Aside from the casual remark which elicited this information, my questions were largely trivial, aimed as much at establishing communication as at securing information, and we got along swimmingly, until I asked, "And why did you refuse to be hypnotized at first, then?"

She wrung her hands, and turned helplessly in her chair, which was so much unlike her relaxed R2 trance state that I felt suddenly and strongly that we were getting, at last, to a closer view of Miss R.; after a minute, still wringing her hands, she brought out, "I won't answer that question." She spoke harshly, and as though reluctantly, and it was the first sign she had shown as R2 of lack of cooperation. I smiled privately at the fancy that I might have asked an "embarrassing" question, and so meekly abandoned the subject and went on, "And so you slept well?"

"Very well," she said, relaxing and smiling. "And thank you for telling me to sleep soundly, because I know that it was your idea."

"Why are you turning your hands in that fashion?" she had commenced twisting her fingers together again and bringing her hands insistently to her eyes.

"I want to open my eyes, but they won't open."

"I should prefer that you keep your eyes closed, if you please."

"But I *want* to open them."—petulantly.

"Closed, please."

"If I could open my eyes," she said wheedlingly, "then I could look at you, dear Doctor Wright."

"There is no need for your looking at me, dear Miss R., so long as you can hear me."

"But if I can't see you, then I don't choose to hear you."

And no question of mine, after that, could provoke a response. She set her lips stubbornly, folded her arms, and scowled, eyes shut. Seeing at last that further questioning was worse than useless, I gave her finally the same suggestions about sleeping well, and added that her appetite should be better, and, in no very good humor with my patient, awakened her. Again she asked me what she had said, but this time, instead of passing her my notes as before, I told her that she had become cross with me and refused to answer me at all. In genuine dismay she said impulsively, "I can't believe it of myself; what will you think of me?" And then, slyly, "Are you going to give up my case?"

I told her, believing her sincerely contrite, that such stubbornness was not unusual, and added humorously that I really believed her to be more stubborn asleep than awake, which made her laugh. We parted amiably, and good friends, and she came to my office the next day but one substantially more cheerful and gay, and much easier with me, as though my human vexation at her last visit had somehow proven us equally fallible, and close. There was color in her cheeks at this next visit, and she reported, almost chattering, that not only had she slept well and without waking during the past two nights but that (as I had suggested to her in hypnosis) her appetite had improved and her headache, which had troubled her intermittently for the past several years and almost constantly for the last few months, had vanished for the whole of the previous day and had only returned briefly this morning, disappearing by breakfast-time; this did much to confirm, of course, one of my beliefs about the headache and the backache and the appetite being all outgrowths, as it were, of the insomnia, and I had great hopes of all of these symptoms clearing away readily as Miss R. rid herself of the extreme fatigue from which she suffered. This must not be taken to mean that I felt Miss R.'s difficulties to be merely physical, and that all I had to do was persuade her through posthypnotic suggestion that she should sleep well, and so cure her entirely; Ryan, even, could have accomplished *that* with a pill or two; my belief was sincerely that the trifling physical symptoms were precisely that—symptoms; the cure we were seeking must be applied for deeper and more insistently. I confess, too, that I perceived that the easier Miss R.'s physical state, the stronger her trust in me, and the easier, consequently, my endeavors toward understanding her.

She accepted the hypnotic trance readily by now, and fell without difficulty into her usual light slumber. Again I began formally by asking her who she was, and where she lived, and again she answered me without hesitation, smiling a little, and doing my heart good with her smiling, friendly face.

"Do you choose to hear me today?"

"Of course."—surprised.

"The other day you did not, you know."

"I? I could not have done such a thing."

I turned to my previous notes and read her her own remarks upon refusing to hear me if she could not open her eyes. As I read she brought up her hands and began again twisting them and rubbing at her face.

"Then," she asked, "may I open my eyes now?"

"I insist that you keep your eyes closed." I paused. "Do you choose to hear me with your eyes closed?"

"I suppose I must."—pettishly. "You won't leave me alone unless I do."

I frowned a little, at a momentary loss how to proceed, and it was at that moment, I think, that I received the most shocking blow of my life. I sat, as always, upon a stool next to Miss R.'s chair, with a low table next me upon which I could write my notes; Miss R. lay back in the large chair, with her feet on a footstool and a pillow behind her head. I remember that I looked at her for a minute, in the half-light the room was in with the curtain closed, and saw her almost clearly, her face pale against the dark chair, the merest line of late-afternoon sunlight touching her from the crack in the curtain. Her face was turned a little toward me, her lips still parted in a little smile, and her eyes, of course, closed. Her hands were at her breast, still twined together; she is like a sleeping beauty, I thought childishly; I wonder, though, how I ever thought her handsome. Because she was not, I saw, at all handsome, and as I watched her in horror, the smile upon her soft lips coarsened, and became sensual and gross, her eyelids fluttered in an attempt to open, her hands twisted together violently, and she laughed, evilly and roughly, throwing her head back and shouting, and I, seeing a devil's mask where a moment before I had seen Miss R.'s soft face, thought only, it cannot be Miss R.; this is not she.

A moment, and it was gone; the laughter ended, and she turned timidly toward me. "Please," she asked, "may I open my eyes?"

I awakened her at once; I was myself too shaken by the grotesque sight of her to be able to do more than bid her good afternoon; I believe she felt that I was displeased with her, and she would not have been far wrong; I was, as I say, shaken, and I am shaken now, writing of it. What I saw that afternoon was the dreadful grinning face of a fiend, and heaven help me, I have seen it a thousand times since.

I was not well in time for Miss R.'s next visit, nor the next, so it was nearly a week before she came again to my office. When she entered, and I greeted her, I felt rather than perceived what a good deal of our progress had been lost; from her reluctant step and sullen voice I realized that she was very nearly again the Miss R. who had come to me first. I felt this, I say, rather than perceived it, because when I glanced at her I saw only in her face the shadow of the grinning fiend who had laughed at me, and so I took my turn, in this visit, at looking at the table leg and the rug and a thousand other sane objects, that I might not look into Miss R.'s face. She for her part seemed restless, and in discomfort; she confessed to a return of her headache, and I had great difficulty in subduing her into the trance state; this may perhaps have been because of my own horror of hearing again that jeering laughter. Our visit was brief; I merely imposed the usual post-hypnotic suggestions, and awakened her; I was myself not entirely well, and unequal to great exertion.

On her next visit we seemed again to have gained ground; I felt that I had thrown off the clinging nervousness which resulted from my own illness, and was better able to cope—as one who has raised demons, and must deal with them—with any manifestation Miss R. might choose to exhibit while under hypnosis. We had very little difficulty, however; Miss R. fell almost immediately asleep, and we conversed, R2 and I, upon the several subjects we had before started, of her aunt, her home, her work. Once or twice she begged most pitifully to be allowed to open her eyes, but I was firm in my refusal, and she desisted for the time. When I awakened her, although there was still some constraint between us—the cause entirely unsuspected, I fear, on her side, poor girl—she bade me good-bye with a trace of her former friendliness. In my notes for that day I find the phrase "R2 unusually charming." She wore a dress I had not seen before, I recall, of a somewhat lighter blue than was usual for Miss R.

It seemed, however, that we were never to step forward without going an equal step back; for every time I found cause to congratulate myself on some appearance of progress, I was given equal cause to despair. For, the next visit after the one when R2 had been so unusually charming, R1, or Miss R., arrived at my office in a state where I could not persuade her to answer me, or, indeed, to speak at all. Hypnosis was out of the question under these circumstances, and I could hardly dismiss my patient in tears; I had no recourse but to administer a soothing draught, and to wait. I busied myself at my desk, and let Miss R. compose herself in her chair; after a time, when it seemed that her agitation had subsided, I half-turned toward her, affectionately, and asked, "What has disturbed you so, dear Miss R.?"

Handkerchief again to her eyes, she held out to me a letter which, as helplessly, I took. "Do you want me to read this?" I asked, and she nodded.

I took it to my desk, where I had set my glasses, and held it under the lamp, and read, half-aloud: "Dear Mr. Althrop, The Museum of Natural Arts and Sciences of the City of Owens-town, although it would be pleased to display your interesting collection of matchbook folders, is nevertheless a non-profit, endowed organization, and as such is not in a position to pay for donated exhibits. Therefore, with great regret, I must inform you that you are a silly silly foolish girl and you are going to be sorry when i catch you—"

"Indeed," I said. "Singular." The letter was typewritten carefully, up to the line which began "you are a silly silly," etcetera.

These last few words were handwritten in heavy black pencil, in a straggling, ill-formed hand. "Singular indeed," I said again.

"I typed it this morning," Miss R. said, tormented into speech. "It was on my desk to finish this afternoon and when I came back from lunch it was like that and I—"

"Quietly," I said, "Miss R., quietly, please."

"But I don't want *him* to get the letter. Mr. Althrop."

"Surely not. Now, you say you discovered this when you came back from lunch?"

"It was right on my desk where I left it."

"Pardon me, dear Miss R., but is there anyone in your office who might wish to do you an injury? Discredit your work, perhaps?"

"I don't think so. I don't know of anyone, Mostly," said the poor girl, "they don't care whether I work or not."

"I see." I longed to speak to R2, to ascertain the truth of R1's opinions of her office mates, but the time was certainly not ripe for summoning my friendly R2, and I had to make what unwilling use I could of R1. I questioned her closely about her office, its availability to others, the time she had taken for lunch, even the Mr. Althrop to whom the letter was addressed, of whom she knew nothing. His letter had simply been given her to answer in the form used for such refusals, and that was all she knew—that, and the fact that the letter would now have to be done over, which, even considering Miss R.'s feelings about her personal neatness, seemed a disproportionate cause for her grief; she told me over and over that Mr. Althrop *must not* have the letter; she wanted, with more passion than I had seen R1 bring to anything, to take the letter off with her and hide it, and, even though I smiled at the childish notion that an error hidden is an error forgotten, I agreed with her that the letter must surely be done over, and offered, indeed, to aid her in an apology to her superiors for the delay, if such was required.

When Miss R. had calmed herself sufficiently, I sent her home. Our usual treatment was impossible after the upsetting experience in her office; I sent her home tranquil, and resolved to question R2 at the earliest opportunity, to see if she in turn could throw any light upon this bewildering experience. My hoped-for opportunity came at Miss R.'s next visit, when, seeing her in what was almost her old sullen state, I ventured to suggest our usual hypnotic treatment, and got a sulky permission, although I knew by that time—I believe Miss R. did not—that her permission was hardly necessary; I could by then subdue her into the trance state at will; without some strong motive for resisting, she could no longer revolt against my treatment. Thus is was possible for me to summon my friend R2 with ease, and I was splendidly glad to see her that day. My usual formalities regarding her name and address were spoken, I believe, in a tone of real jubilation, and I know she greeted me with equal enthusiasm. I never met R2 without a strong impulsive regret for the person Miss R. might well have been for all this time, so securely shut away, so well forgotten, and I believe that a large part of my determination upon Miss R.'s cure was exerted upon R2's behalf; perhaps I saw myself—even I!—as setting free a captive princess.

At any rate, it was with deep disappointment that I heard that R2, usually so helpful, was now completely in the dark about the ugly lines scrawled upon the bottom of Miss R.'s letter, and unable to help me at all. She could only suggest that Miss R. had, through her very inoffensiveness, made an enemy in her office who had chosen this cowardly means of avenging herself. "Not everyone," said R2 in her gentle way, "is as lucky as I am; everyone I meet is kind to me," and she smiled at me.

This explanation, however, seemed to me manifestly impossible, if only because it was as difficult to imagine Miss R.'s making an enemy as it was to imagine her making a friend. Beyond this R2 had no suggestions to offer, and I determined at last upon trying a method which I had so far not found necessary—i.e., a deeper hypnotic trance, in which I hoped should stand revealed those facts and incidents about which R2 was as ignorant as myself.

It was certainly true that the answers to many of our questions lay deeply hidden in Miss R. herself, and I believed implicitly that only the most penetrating investigation would disclose them. I therefore threw R2, my pretty one, into a deeper hypnotic sleep, and watched aghast as her soft features coarsened again into those of the fiendish face I so well remembered and which I already feared sincerely and instinctively. She first began those twistings of her hands which I remembered so well, and then her face contorted and—I at the same time wanting badly to awaken her, and drive out the possessing demon—her mouth turned crookedly down into the evil smile I had seen before, and she brought her hands to her eyes in what seemed a desperate attempt to open them.

Hence, Asmodeous, I thought, and said quietly, "I prefer your eyes closed, please."

"What," she said, or rather shouted, in the roughest voice I have ever heard, "you giving me orders again, wicked man? I warn you that one of these days I am going to eat you!" She began to laugh again, and, dismayed, I thought of adverting to my opening formula, hoping to quiet her. "What is your name?" I asked her, in my levellest tone.

She stopped laughing at once, and said demurely (and oh, the cruel crooked mask on the face of R2!) "I am Elizabeth R., doctor dear, indeed I am. You must not think, doctor dear, that because I am sometimes a little bit rude to you that I do not respect you deeply, very very deeply indeed, doctor dear, very deeply indeed."

This, said with an echo of the wild laughter, and an air of mockery that shocked me, coming from a person and face still strongly reminiscent of my own R2, almost with her own voice, interrupted my next question and I was still endeavoring to collect my thoughts when she went on in the same jeering voice, "And Elizabeth is going to tell you how sorry she is to have spoken to you so, doctor dear, indeed she will, and I myself am going to make her do it."

"I should think you would," I said irritably. "Now, please, Miss R., let us continue with the questions. I should like to hear more about this annoying letter which—"

She began to laugh again, and, mindful of my nurse in the next room, I attempted to quiet her by lowering my voice slightly so that she would have to be more restrained in order to hear me. "Do you think you are able to give me any information?" I asked.

"I can tell you all about it, my good friend."

"Yes?"

"And I will, too, if only . . ." She dragged out her sentence tormentingly. "If only you will let me open my eyes," she finished, laughing again.

Letter or not, I had had almost enough of this rude creature. "You will continue to keep your eyes closed," I said sharply, "and if you can give me any information, I certainly expect you to do so. Now, after you had typed the letter—"

"I? I cannot type."

"The letter," I said shortly, "was certainly typewritten."

"By her, surely. You don't expect that I trouble myself to do *her* work?"

I was bewildered. "Her?" I said.

"Elizabeth," she said in a great shout, "your dear Miss R., Lizzie the fool, Lizzie the simple." And she screwed her face up into a dreadful parody of Miss R.'s usual vacant expression. (And forgive me, reader, if I say that in the midst of my distress I was tempted to laugh; that she should mock R2 troubled me greatly, but R1 had no such hold upon my friendship.)

"Then," I asked her, "who are *you?*"

"I am myself, doctor dear, as you will soon find out. And who, do you suppose, are *you?*"

"I am Doctor Wright," I said, somewhat stiffly.

"No," she said, shaking her head and grinning at me from under her hands, "I believe you are an imposter. I believe you are Doctor Wrong." Her voice rose again in laughter. "And you are asking questions," she went on, shouting, "which are *most* embarrassing indeed."

"If you are not quiet," I said, with all the authority I could command, "I shall awaken you." This, spoken at random—and, indeed, what I most wanted at the moment to do—turned out to be an unexpectedly useful threat; she was immediately silent, and lay back against the chair.

"May I open my eyes?" she asked meekly.

"You may not."

"I *shall* open my eyes."

"You shall not."

"Someday," she said evilly, rubbing her hands against her eyes, "I am going to get my eyes open all the time and then I will eat you and Lizzie both." She was silent, and seemed to be meditating, and then she said quietly, "Doctor Wrong. And Lizzie the fool."

"Why, tell me, do you want to harm Elizabeth?"

There was another long pause, and at last she said, with hatred in her voice, "She's *outside*, isn't she?"

This was, indeed, a dismaying turn to Miss R.'s case. The cure had seemed so simple, so much a matter of time and patience before we set our feet on the right path and brought Miss R. home to health and vigor, and now, here, barring our way, gibbering and mouthing and shouting foulness, was a demon whose evil seemed at first almost unconquerable. The mind is a curious thing, to be sure, for I found myself angry rather than frightened, much in the manner of a knight (rather elderly, surely, and tired after his long quest) who, in the course of bringing his true princess home, has no longer any fear, but only a great weariness, when confronted in sight of the castle towers by a fresh dragon to slay.

Miss R.'s treatments had now gone on for several months, and I began to see that it would be a longer matter than I had heretofore suspected. The considerable improvements in the minor aspects of her health, which she found so incredibly wonderful, were perhaps the only progress we had so far made, and we were, I confess, certainly no nearer to understanding. I know as well as any medical man that the concept of "demonic possession" has been largely given up as a diagnosis; naturally Miss R.—and her aunt, of course, a dragon of a different sort, whom I had yet to encounter face to face— were kept in ignorance of the new development in Miss R.'s case; neither of them knew more of the treatment than the superficial improvement in Miss R., and I believe that they thought the incomparable Doctor Wright was performing miracles of restoration. I felt strongly that it would be unwise to inform Miss R. of the deeper progress, or lack of it, in her case, because of the danger of alarming her and setting us back in the small improvement we had made; Miss R., being in an hypnotic trance during the greater part of her time spent with me, knew nothing of what occurred, and her aunt knew nothing because neither Miss R. nor Miss R.'s doctor told her. I had called Ryan and told him briefly my conclusions about Miss R.'s case and my proposed method of treatment, and, since he was a busy man (your jovial, hearty physician so often is, regardless of his abilities) I had not found myself troubled in that neighborhood further.

Ruefully, then, I added a new number to my notes—R3, the hateful, the enemy. Perhaps my numerical system was at fault, perhaps I was too persuaded of my belief that we could slough off the paralyzing past and bring back Miss R. as R2, perhaps the rarity of the case and the horrid aspects of it slowed down my usually acute perceptions—it was, at any rate, quite some time before I, dreaming over my comfortable fire at home, half-asleep with my book fallen to the floor and the first intimations of dream touching me—it was not until then, some time later, that I first recognized what I should have known at once, and saw through to the correct diagnosis of Miss R.'s case.

Now, for the layman, demonic possession would do as well as anything to describe Miss R. at that time, and in my heart I suspect that the pictures are close: I remember most vividly Thackeray's words, which I must have been reading before I slipped off, and which stay with me still: "All of you here must needs be grave when you think of your own past and present. . . .". And I before the fire, alone, and almost dreaming, to awaken remembering that devil's face.

But let me turn to a medical authority, whose more palatable phrases hold out hope of a cure more certain (and more permanent) than mere exorcism: "Cases of this kind are commonly known as 'double' or 'multiple personality,' according to the number of persons represented, but a more correct term is *disintegrated* personality, for each secondary personality is a part only of a normal whole self. No one secondary person-

ality preserves the whole physical life of the individual. The
synthesis of the original consciousness known as the personal
ego is broken up, so to speak, and shorn of some of its memories, perceptions, acquisitions, or modes of reaction to the environment. The conscious states that still persist, synthesized
among themselves, form a new personality capable of independent activity. This second personality may *alternate* with the
original undisintegrated personality from time to time. By a
breaking up of the original personality at different moments
along different lines of cleavage, there may be formed several
different secondary personalities which may take turns with
one another." (Morton Prince, *The Dissociation of a Personality,* 1905.)

I myself had already met Miss R. in three personalities: R1,
nervous, afflicted by driving pain, ridden by the horrors of
fear and embarrassment, modest, self-contained, and reserved
to the point of oral paralysis. R2 was, it was assumed, the
character Miss R. might have been, the happy girl who smiled
and answered truly and with serious thoughtfulness, pretty
and relaxed, without the lines of worry which so deformed
R1's face; R2 was largely free of pain, and could only sympa-
thize sweetly with R1's torments. R3 was, on the other hand,
R2 with a vengeance: where R2 was relaxed, R3 was wanton;
where R2 was unreserved, R3 was insolent; where R2 was
pleasant and pretty, R3 was coarse and noisy. Moreover, each
of the three had a recognizable appearance—R1, of course,
the character I had first met, shy and unattractive by reason of
her timidity and clumsiness; R2, amiable and charming; R3,
the rough, contorted mask. The shy, fleeting smile of R1, the
open, merry face of R2, were in R3 a sly grin or an open shout
of rude laughter; if it be suspected that I did not particularly
love our new friend R3, it can as readily be seen that I had
good reason; when my good R2 began to raise her hands to
rub her eyes, when her voice grew louder and her expressions
freer, when her eyebrows went up sardonically and her mouth
twisted, I had perforce to spend a while with a creature who
felt and showed me no respect, who attempted enthusiasti-
cally to undo any good I might have done Miss R., who de-

lighted in teasing all whom she met, and who, after all, knew no moral sense and no restrictions to her actions save only those of lack of sight; who, upon occasion, called me a damned old fool!

Now, it seemed to me that we had come closest to R3 on the question of Miss R.'s defaced letter, and perhaps that thought, aided by a chance reflection of my own, put us first directly on the track of R3; I, looking at the letter when Miss R. first showed it to me, thought irritably that I could write a better hand with my eyes shut—and had, although it was a while before I perceived it, my clue. In the course of a seemingly aimless discussion of the letter with R2, I had asked her, placing pencil and paper by her hand, to write a few words to my dictation, that I might see her handwriting, and, bringing her hands feverishly to her eyes, she first cried out "I can't, I can't, I must open my eyes," and so awoke, voluntarily, although she had never done so before. I wondered if she had perhaps not forced herself awake because of the pressure of R3 to come to the surface. Miss R., questioned again at another visit about the letter, burst into tears and refused to speak of the matter, saying only that her headache was too severe to allow of any discussion.

Steeling myself, I determined to summon R3 to an interview which I was not disposed to enjoy, but which I felt might be enlightening; I had seen almost nothing of her since her last visit, except for an occasional quick grin or gesture through R2's conversation, or now and then an echo of her mocking laughter in R2's merry voice, and, of course, the frequent gestures with her hands, accompanied by entreaties to be permitted to open her eyes. Summoning her required, I knew now, only inducing Miss R. into a deeper hypnotic slumber than that which brought R2, when she immediately began to take on the characteristic facial and vocal qualities of R3.

"So we meet again, Doctor Wrong," she said at once, and quite in the fashion of the possessing demon, "I wondered how long you could struggle on without me."

"I suspect, Miss R., that you can give me information I need."

"Not," said R3 flatly, "if you call me by that disgraceful name. I am no more Miss R. than *you* are. I am only inside her." She finished off this remark with a disgusting leer and an additional remark which was to me so distasteful that, not content to omit it from my notes, I have since made every effort to forget it, and all similar remarks made by R3. Consequently, it was a moment or so before we could get on; R3 had the disagreeable ability to confound me and render me speechless for important seconds at a time, so that I lost my train of thought and had perforce to allow her free rein during my own moments of distraction.

Now she continued, while I sat aghast, "Elizabeth, Beth, Betsy, and Bess, they all went together to find a bird's nest . . . Perhaps, you handsome Doctor Wrong, you would care to rename us? We must surely not be the first children you have brought into the world." And she burst again into her wild laughter, and—although Miss Hartley, my nurse, must surely by now be accustomed to loud noises from my office—I was half-afraid that Miss Hartley might conclude that I was being laughed at by one of my own patients, since the laughter was so clearly not hysterical. Interesting R3, or threatening her, were the only two methods I so far knew to quiet her, so I said in a low voice, "I shall awaken you, Miss R., if you do not tranquillize yourself."

She was silent at once, but murmured wickedly, "Someday you will not be able to get rid of me, Doctor Wrong; someday you will try to awaken *her*, and, when you think you have got back your disgusting Miss R., will find that you still have just me. And then," she said, her voice rising and her hands at her eyes, "and then, and then, and then!"

Fear touched me lightly, but I said, "Why, then if I find I have only you no matter who I seek, I shall have to learn to love you." I smiled wryly at the thought of loving this monster, and I suppose she detected my expression in my voice, for she said at once, "But do you suppose I could learn to love *you,* Doctor Wrong? When you wish me evil?"

"I wish no one evil, Miss R."

"Then you are a liar as well as a fool," she said. (I note down these remarks in the interests of thoroughness; I know I am not a liar and I hope I am not a fool, and I perceived that R3's object was to enrage me; I am happy to add that although I was irked at her rudeness, I endeavored, I believe with success, to keep her from realizing it.) "I know a good deal about people," she continued with complacency, "and when I have my eyes open all the time I will get along nicely. No one will ever suspect how long I have been a prisoner, I think."

I hardly dared breathe, hearing R3 rattle along so, revealing herself more with every word; this boastful chatter made it unnecessary to question her, and I would not have interrupted her for the world. "*Now*," she said, as one explaining an awkward position, "I can only get out when *she* is looking the other way, and then only for a little while before she comes back and shuts me in again, but someday very soon she is going to find that when she comes back and tries to—" She broke off suddenly, and chuckled. "Eavesdropping, Doctor Wrong?" she asked, "do you add poking and prying to your list of sins?"

"I am trying to help my friends, Miss R."

"Please *stop* calling me that," she said petulantly. "I tell you, I am *not* Miss R., and I *hate* her name; she is a crybaby and a foolish stupid thing, and I certainly am not."

"What shall I call you, then?"

"What do you call me in those notes? The ones you showed *her* once?"

I was astounded at her knowing of my notes, and that Miss R. had once seen them, but I only said, "I have no name for you, since you disclaim your natural one. I have called you R3."

She made a face at me, putting out her tongue and shrugging her shoulders. "I certainly don't choose to be called R3," she said. "You can call me Rosalita, or Charmian, or Lilith, if you like."

I smiled again at the thought of this grotesque creature naming herself like a princess in a fairy romance. "Do you also disclaim the name Elizabeth?" I inquired.

"That's *her* name."

"But," I cried, struck with an idea, "you yourself have suggested it: 'Elizabeth, Beth, Betsy, and Bess . . .'"

She laughed rudely. "Elizabeth is the simple, Beth is the doctor's darling; very well, then I choose Betsy." And she laughed again.

"Why do you laugh?"

"I was wondering about Bess," she said, laughing.

And so, my dear reader, was I.

So Betsy she was till the end of her chapter. I found that as these several different girls grew more familiar to me, and of course in the second case more dear, the names Betsy had chosen for them became easier and pleasanter to use than the cold clinical R1 and R2; R2 consented graciously and with a smile to my plea to be allowed to address her as Beth, and I think the name suited her quiet charm. I do not know if Miss R. ever perceived that I had moved quietly away from addressing her formally, or at least from calling her "my dear Miss R." to calling her Elizabeth; I suppose that she was too accustomed to constant authority in the shape of her aunt to remark being addressed as a child. Betsy, of course, was Betsy and nothing else, although she sometimes amused herself by giving herself grandiose titles or surnames, and I had no difficulty, subsequently, in identifying a note signed Elizabeth Rex as of Betsy's doing.

My immediate attempt must be, I thought, to discover the point at which the unfortunate Miss R. had subdivided, as it were, and permitted a creature like Betsy to assume a separate identity; it was my old teasing analogy of the sewer, but complicated in that I was now searching for a branch line! (I do most heartily wish that I had chosen some comparison nearer the stars; a flourishing oak tree, perhaps, but I confess that I misguidedly chose that which seemed most vivid to me, and most indicative, although ignoble, of the circumstances; I am ashamed to think that without going through and correcting all of my manuscript, and my notes, too—for this comparison found a place even there—I must abide by it.) It seemed to me that only a very severe emotional shock could have forced Miss R. to slough off the greater part of herself into subordinate personalities (until I had, with a magic touch, called them into active life) and I was fairly certain that their separate existence—although Betsy claimed a life of her own, in thoughts at any rate, ever since Miss R. had been born—must date from the most patent emotional shock in Miss R.'s life, the death of her mother. To show what kind of a problem I was manipulating, let me from my notes present the reader with the varying descriptions of this event which I received, first from R1, or Elizabeth, then from R2, the cooperative and lovely Beth, and then, lastly, from our villain Betsy.

(On May 12, to Elizabeth, in office consultation): Wright: Do you think you can tell me anything about your mother, my dear?

Elizabeth: I guess so.

W. When did she die?

E. I guess over four years ago. On a Wednesday.

W. Were you at home?

E. (confused) I was upstairs.

W. Did you live then with your aunt?

E. With Aunt Morgen?

W. Do you have any other aunts?

E. No.

W. Then, when your mother died, were you living with your aunt?

E. Yes, with Aunt Morgen.

W. Do you think you can tell me anything more about your mother's death? (She seemed most unwilling, and I thought on the edge of weeping; since I knew I could secure all the information I needed from the other selves, I did not intend to persist in a cruel cross-examination, but I did want as much information as possible for purposes of comparison.)

E. That's all I know. I mean, Aunt Morgen came and told me my mother died.

W. Came and told you? You mean, you were not with your mother when she died?

E. No, I was upstairs.

W. Not with your mother?

E. Upstairs.

W. Was your mother downstairs, then?

E. Aunt Morgen was with her. I don't know.

W. Try to stay calm, if you please. This was all very long ago, and I think talking about it will be helpful to you: I know it is a painful subject, but try to believe that I would not ask you unless I felt it to be necessary.

E. No. I mean, I only don't know.

W. Had your mother been ill?

E. I thought she was all right.

W. Then her death was quite sudden, to your mind?

E. It was—(thinking deeply)—a heart attack.

W. But you were not there?

E. I was upstairs.

W. You did not see her?

E. No, I was upstairs.

W. What were you doing?

E. I don't remember. Asleep, I guess. Reading.

W. Were you in your own room?

E. I don't remember. I was upstairs.

W. I beg you to compose yourself, Miss R. This agitation is unnecessary and unbecoming.

E. I have a headache (touching her neck).

And that was, of course, the end of my information from Elizabeth; I knew by now that her headaches, all-enveloping, would obliterate almost all awareness of myself and my questions. So I pursued my line of questioning, most pleasantly, by summoning Beth. I longed, at this time, to chat with Beth informally, and at length, and I longed to permit her to open her eyes, so that we might seem friends rather than doctor and patient, but the ever-present fear of Betsy prevented; since blindness was now the only thing I knew of which held Betsy in check, I dared not follow my inclinations and admit Beth as a free personality. I was sad, frequently, to think that Beth's whole existence had heretofore been passed only in my office, and that none but I knew this amiable girl; my conviction that Miss R. must once have been very like Beth was so far un-confirmed, and yet I deeply wanted to see Beth take her place in the world and in her family, the place to which my most un-scientific heart told me she was entitled. At any rate, it was always a great pleasure to me to call Beth, and hear her affectionate greeting. Here are my notes on this conversation, which followed immediately upon the conversation with Elizabeth which I have just described.

(On May 12, Beth, or R2, in office consultation): Wright (after preliminary trance-inducing introduction of name and place identification) My dear, I want to talk about your mother.

B. (smiling wistfully) She was a lovely lady.

W. Much like yourself?

B. Yes. Very lovely and very happy and very sweet to every-one.

W. Do you remember her death?

B. (reluctantly) Not very well. She died that day.

W. Where were you when she died?

B. I was thinking of her.

W. But where?

B. Inside. Hidden.

W. As you usually are?

B. Except when I am with you.

W. I hope we can change that someday, my dear. But you must help me.

B. I will do anything you ask me to.

W. Splendid. I am most anxious, right now, to learn all I can about your mother's death.

B. She was very kind to everyone, even Aunt Morgen.

W. You lived with your aunt at the time?

B. Oh, yes, we have lived with *her* for years, ever since my dear father died.

W. And your father died when?

B. When I was two years old, or about that. I don't remember him very well.

W. Were you with your mother when she died?

B. I? I was never allowed to be with her. I am always kept hidden.

W. Compose yourself, Beth dear. We can talk of something else if this disturbs you.

B. No, I am eager to help in any way I can; I don't want you to think badly of me.

W. I assure you, I never shall. Can you tell me, then, precisely what you did after your mother's death?

B. (perplexed) We had lunch. And Aunt Morgen said not to worry.

W. Not to worry? You mean, not to grieve?

B. Not to worry. We had lunch and Aunt Morgen said not to worry, Aunt Morgen said not to cry over spilled milk, Aunt Morgen cried. It was disgusting.

W. (amused) You will not allow your aunt her grief?

B. She cried over spilled milk.

W. (laughing outright) Beth, this is cynicism.

B. Indeed not; I do not think evil of anyone.

A man who has just spoken, however inconclusively, with Beth, does not turn hastily to a conversation with Betsy. Nevertheless, it was obvious that the information which Elizabeth and Beth found themselves unable to give must be mined from Betsy, and so, resolutely, I denied the appeal of Beth's pretty face and dismissed her for Betsy; I made an effort to keep my countenance when Beth's turned head disclosed that grinning face, even though she could not, of course, see me, and I forced my voice to remain even and controlled.

(May 12, Betsy, or R3, in office consultation): W. Good afternoon, Betsy. I hope I find you in excellent health.

By. (jeering) The others won't help, so you come and ask *me*.

W. I hoped you might tell me—

By. I know. I was listening. (contemptuously) What do you think *they* can tell you?

W. —about your mother.

By. *My* mother? Do you think I claim that poor dead thing as *my* mother? Perhaps (impudently) I have a mother of my own, question-asker.

W. (Indeed if you had, you demon, I thought, she's a fiend in damnation): Miss R.'s mother, then.

By. As you are her father? (raucous laughter)

W. Miss R.'s mother, who died some years ago. Elizabeth's mother.

By. I know whose mother you mean, old man. The one she—(here she shut her lips, and grinned mysteriously, and put her finger to her mouth in a childlike gesture of secrecy)— Talking about Lizzie when her back is turned, my dear! For shame!

W. Betsy, I would like you to trust me. Believe me, I am only a person who wants to do whatever I can to ensure that you and Elizabeth and Beth will live together peaceably and happily; would you not like to be one person again?

By. I was never one person with her, I have always been her prisoner, and you wouldn't help me if you could. You may want to help Beth, and maybe even Lizzie, but you have no place for me in your pretty little world.

W. Indeed, I am truly sorry to see anyone so bitter as to refuse help when it is so badly needed.

By. I have told you hundreds of times that the best way to help me is to let me open my eyes. (gestures of wringing hands, and bringing them up to her eyes.)—May I?—(wheedlingly)— May I open them, dear Doctor Wright? And I will tell you everything you want to know, about Lizzie and about Lizzie's mother and about old Auntie and I will even put in a good word for you with Beth if I may only have my eyes open— (This was said in a tone of such mockery that I was gravely concerned; I had suddenly the notion that Betsy was teasing me, and might perhaps open her eyes this minute if she chose, and I was genuinely frightened at the thought.)

W. I insist that you keep your eyes closed. Do you realize, young lady, that if I find that you are of no use to me in my investigations, I will surely send you away and never let you come again? (I would have liked to, certainly, and perhaps even then I still could have.)

By. (apprehensive) You will not send me away.

W. I may; it was I who brought you here in the first place.

By. I can come by myself.

W. (not choosing to press *this* point) We shall see. (carelessly) Perhaps you are fond of sweets? (I had thought of this earlier; it occurred to me that a creature so childish might be fairly treated on childish terms; I had as alternatives a doll, and some tawdry jewelry.) Shall I put a candy in your hand?

By. (eagerly) Do you have candy right here?

W. (placing in her outstretched hand a piece of candy which she consumed greedily.) I am glad you begin to find me more friendly. No one would give you candy who did not wish you well.

By. (with satisfaction) If you poisoned me, then Lizzie and Beth would die.

W. I have no intention of poisoning you. I should like to have us friends, you and I.

By. I will be friends with you, old well-wisher. But I want more candy, and I want to open my eyes.

W. I assure you, you will never open your eyes with my permission. But can we not talk together as friends, Betsy?

By. (craftily) You have not given me any more candy yet.

W. (craftier still) When you tell me about your mother.

By. (unexpectedly gentle) Elizabeth's mother? She was always nice. She danced around the kitchen one day when she had a new dress and she said "Nonsense" to Morgen and she curled her hair. I liked to watch her.

W. Where were you?

By. A prisoner, always a prisoner, inside with Beth, only no one knew I was there.

W. Were you ever free? Outside, I mean?

By. (nodding, dreamy) Sometimes, when Lizzie is sleeping or when she turns her head away for a minute, I can get out, but only for a small time, and then she puts me back. (recollecting herself suddenly) But I am not going to tell you, you are not friendly to me.

W. Ridiculous; you know now that we are friends. Were you inside when Elizabeth's mother died?

By. Surely, and I made her scream even louder, and beat on the door.

W. Why did she beat on the door?

By. Why, to get out, Doctor Wrong.

W. To get out of what?

By. To get out of her room, Doctor Wrong.

W. What in heaven's name was Elizabeth doing shut in her room while her mother was dying?

By. Now, see, Doctor Wrong, I did not say that her mother was dying, although she surely was, and yet it was not in heaven's name—(laughs wildly)—and as for what Lizzie was doing in her room, why, she was beating on the door.

W. Will you explain it to me?

By. Now certainly not, Doctor Wrong; we all went together to seek a bird's nest; do you remember the man who was wondrous wise and jumped into a bramble bush and scratched out both his eyes . . . may I open my eyes *now?*

W. No.

By. —put her in a pumpkin shell, and there she kept her very well. And so Lizzie's mother died, and it was a good thing, too. She wouldn't have cared for our Lizzie now.

W. Did Elizabeth change after her mother died?

By. (tormenting) I only said that to tease you, eye-closer. I can tell you wonderful stories about your dear. Ask Lizzie about the box of letters in her closet. Ask Beth about Aunt Morgen. (laughing wildly again) Ask Aunt Morgen about Lizzie's mother.

W. That will do, please. I am going to send you away now.

By. (suddenly sober) Please, may I stay a minute longer? I have decided to tell you why Aunt Morgen locked Lizzie in her room.

W. Very well. But no more nonsense.

By. First, you promised me more candy.

W. One more, only. We should not care to make Elizabeth sick.

By. (carelessly) She is always sick, anyway. I never thought of a stomachache, though.

W. Do you make her head ache?

By. Why would I tell you that? (impudently) If I told you everything I know, then you would be as wise as I am.

W. Then tell me why Elizabeth was locked in her room.

By. (emphatically) Because she frightened her mother and Aunt Morgen said they all went together to find a bird's nest.

W. I beg your pardon?

By. May I open my eyes *now*?

W. How did she frighten her mother?

By. She put her in a pumpkin shell. Silly silly silly silly. . . .

I dismissed her, more distressed than I can say by the odd, hinted stories she brought me, although far less inclined to credit them than to see Betsy herself as a wicked and mischievous creature, bent on making trouble, and with what fearful designs in that black heart I could not begin to imagine. When Elizabeth awakened, seeing me disturbed, she asked with some anxiety whether she had been talking foolishly while asleep, and I bade her leave me, reassuring her with the not-entire falsehood that I was not well. The next morning—a Tuesday—when I reached my office, there was on my desk a message, put there by Miss Hartley, who had taken it by phone from Miss R.'s aunt, to the effect that Miss R. had a touch of the influenza and so would not be able to keep her appointments for at least the rest of the week, and very possibly the week following. I noted on my appointment book my intention of dropping in upon Miss R. and her aunt within the next day or so, ostensibly to make a polite inquiry after Miss R.'s health, actually to determine if her recovery might not be hastened by a brief treatment from myself; I was of course aware that in such a case the attending physician would be Doctor Ryan, and had no doubt of securing a half hour or so alone with my patient.

I do not, as I believe I have before indicated, see many patients these days, and so found myself relieved by Miss R.'s illness of my greatest concern; I feel myself greatly favored by fortune in that, in the prime of life, I am, although a widower, luckily enough circumstanced to be able to avoid the pushing and scrambling which accompanies the work of many medical men, in their efforts to make a living in a field where the emphasis is upon conformity rather than upon genius (how often have I sighed over the cynicism of the old saw that a good doctor buries his mistakes!) and which is overcrowded at the mediocre level, and unfortunately not crowded at all at the top. Thackeray tells me that any stupid hand can draw a hunchback, and write Pope underneath; calumny, I know, succeeds to misunderstanding in the hearts of the best-intentioned. No one who desired my services was deprived of them, although many who needed my services were discouraged from visiting me; had I been more a crusader, I suspect, I might have had my waiting room filled from morning till night, but it has never been my way to seek out quarrels, and push an issue to a disagreement; I have been content to sit back and, knowing full well my own worth, made no effort to force it upon others. This, I submit meekly, is not modesty, a virtue with which I am not abnormally endowed (and *you*, sir?), but earnest common sense.

Thus, although Miss R. was much upon my mind during the next day or so, so was Thackeray, and the old gentleman and I spent many an amiable hour together with the office door closed and Miss Hartley outside, no doubt supposing that I was busied upon some abstruse problem of research or else— Miss Hartley is a rare humorist—napping.

On Wednesday morning I telephoned Miss R.'s residence and spoke, as I was told, to her aunt, a Miss Jones. Our conversation was brief and matter-of-fact; I identified myself and inquired after Miss R.'s health, Miss Jones told me that Miss R. felt most unwell, was running a high temperature and had been, her aunt said, delirious upon waking in the middle of the night. I was concerned, and inquired after Ryan's treatment, fearing that he regarded this illness more lightly than he should, but Miss Jones reassured me, telling me that Ryan appeared at Miss R.'s bedside twice a day, etc., and I was forced to ring off, after expressing my hopes for a swift return of Miss R.'s health. It seemed most unlikely that a personal visit from myself would be of any value at the moment, nor, indeed, could I reasonably contemplate hypnosis, with its possible unsettling effect upon Miss R. in her present condition. As a result, then, I spared a moment to wonder wryly what conceivable form Miss R.'s delirium might take which could be more frightening than what I had already met here in my office, and to hope that my next word of her might be more encouraging; I then resigned myself to hearing no further news of her for a few days and returned, with complacency, to Thackeray.

It was, then, not until Thursday evening that the blow fell. I had spent a quiet evening at home and retired and was, indeed, asleep, when the telephone at my bedside rang and, having for the last few years become unaccustomed to middle-of-the-night emergency calls, I was at first startled and then frightened and angry when I heard Miss Jones' voice, controlled but showing agitation nevertheless, asking me most urgently to hurry to her house. "My niece," she said, in that strained voice which so often accompanies terror under iron control, "insists upon seeing you at once; she has been calling your name for over an hour."

"Have you not called Doctor Ryan?" I asked, determined to keep to my warm bed.

"She won't let him in," Miss Jones said; she seemed, in her anxiety, to be unable to stop talking and I could not hush her. "She has locked the door against us," Miss Jones continued, her voice rising hysterically.

I sighed, and told her without enthusiasm that I should be with her directly. Even so, she persisted—as frightened relations so often do—in keeping me by urging me to hurry! "For a long time," she said, "we couldn't imagine what doctor she wanted; she kept calling for Doctor Wrong."

I hung up the telephone while she still talked on, and dressed with more speed than I have ever done in my life; childbirth, surgery, accidents—all these can bear to wait for the ten seconds it takes for the doctor to dash cold water on his sleepy eyes, but now I delayed for no such indulgence; there was, I knew to my sorrow, only one person in the world who called me Doctor Wrong.

And she was waiting for me behind the locked door of Miss R.'s bedroom; I could hear her shouting as Miss Jones opened the house door for me, and, hesitating only to mutter my name at Miss Jones, I brushed past her and, still in my coat and hat, took the stairs two at a time—an exertion, indeed, at my age, and one I could ill afford at the moment—and so came to the door from behind which came Betsy's voice shouting a song which surprised me only in that I could not imagine how she came to learn the words during Miss R.'s limited experience.

"Betsy," I said, tapping on the door, "Betsy, open this door at once; it is Doctor Wright."

I was aware of my own hard breathing as I stood with my head against the door, listening to the voice inside; Betsy had broken off her song when she heard my voice and appeared now to be talking softly to herself. "Is it really the old fool?" she asked—meaning me, of course—and, "I think it is Ryan again, come to tease me."

Miss Jones was coming up the stairs behind me, and I wanted badly to be into Miss R.'s room with the door closed before there was any question of Miss Jones' joining us; "Betsy," I said, "let me in immediately, I tell you."

"Who is it?"

"It is Doctor Wright," I said impatiently, "open the door."

"It is not Doctor Wright at all; it is Doctor Ryan."

"I," I said in a fury, "am Doctor Victor Wright, and I command you to open this door."

"Commands?" Her voice lingered mockingly. "To *me*, Doctor Wrong?"

"Betsy," I said as emphatically as I could; Miss Jones was rounding the landing.

"Then tell me who you are," said Betsy.

"I am Doctor Wright."

"Indeed you are not," said Betsy, laughing.

I took a deep breath and thought briefly and lovingly of punishments for Miss Betsy; "I am Doctor Wrong," I said, and very softly, too.

"Who?"

"Doctor Wrong," I said.

"Who?" I could hear her laughing.

"Doctor Wrong."

"Oh, of course," she said, and I heard the key in the lock. "If you had told me who you were sooner, my dear doctor, I would have let you in at once." And the wicked girl opened the door and stood aside as I slipped quickly in, and then she shut the door behind me, full in her aunt's face. "Poor dear," she said loudly, "did Aunt Morgen attack you?"

"Miss R.," I said, "this is intolerable. I will not be treated so."

"And I," she said, "will not be treated at all, and I am surprised that you finally came to visit me professionally instead of as my dear friend." She turned a languishing glance upon me, and for the first time I met Betsy face to face, with her eyes open, the pair of us meeting as equals without the protective barriers of my office and hypnosis and sightlessness, and I perceived, looking at Betsy, that she was as fully and acutely aware of this as I was.

"Well?" she said, amused.

I took a deep breath, endeavoring to resume my control of myself, and said as quietly as I could manage, "I see that you have your eyes open."

She nodded, and hugged herself, and laughed, and grinned, and widened her eyes to show me, and turned herself around gaily. "I told you, I told you, I told you," she chanted, and then, coming close to me and looking slyly into my face, "and what are you going to do about it, old eye-closer?"

I surmised that for all her posturing and bravado she was still honestly in awe of me and upon that surmise—indeed, the only hope left us—I decided to base my own actions. Smiling back at her placidly, I seated myself upon the edge of the bed and took out my pipe. "I understood that you were ill," I said conversationally.

"*She* was; I am never ill."

"Then," I said ironically, "a good doctor like myself ought rightly to allow you to remain until the course of Miss R.'s infection has run itself out."

She laughed. "I believe I *have* done her good," she said complacently. "If she hadn't been weak and sick, I couldn't have gotten out, and if I hadn't gotten out, she would still be weak and sick." She spread her hands as one who demonstrates an utterly reasonable point. "So you see I *am* good," she said. She seated herself on the chair next the bed and looked at me soberly. "Doctor Wright," she said—and I have never seen Betsy so demure—"don't you think that now I *am* out, I should be allowed to stay?"

She must have mistaken my silence for a hesitation as to whether or not I should agree with her, for she went on persuasively, "You can see that I am healthier and happier than she is, and I have been very patient for a long time, and it's only *fair* to give me a chance. Besides," she went on as I started to speak, "all that I used to say about wanting to do you harm and wanting to hurt her was only because I was so tired of being a prisoner and I just wanted to get out and be happy and not be a prisoner any more, and—"

"Betsy," I said gently, "how can I let you stay? Think of Elizabeth, think of Beth."

"Why should *I* think of them just because *you* care more for them than you do for me, and you expect me to give up just because *you* decide you'd rather have *them?*"

I repressed a smile at her impulsive self-interest, and told myself again that she was in actuality little more than a child, and so I said tolerantly, "Well, Betsy, suppose I make a bargain with you? Suppose I agree to let you stay tonight?"

"Let me have a week, then," she said. "A week, and no one to bother me."

"But Miss R. is ill."

"She will be well," said Betsy grimly, and then looked at me, all innocence. "At least," Betsy said, "she will not be delirious any more."

"Of course," I said, realizing. "It was you."

"I had a lovely time," Betsy said. "And poor Aunt Morgen outside the door, wringing her hands and trembling."

I could not point out to Betsy the callousness of this, any more than I could explain to her childish mind the impossibility of letting her take over, as it were, the whole personality of Miss R.; all I could do, as one does with a difficult child, was to pretend to fall in with her plans, reserving privately the right to determine with my own—and, I must say, my superior—judgment, what was best for all of us. Consequently, I continued blandly, "So, my dear Betsy, are we agreed, then? If I consent to your staying out for a day or so, will you then cooperate with me in helping to heal Miss R.?"

"I will," she said earnestly, and I do believe she thought she meant it. "I will do all I can, if I can only be free, sometimes, and be happy for a little while."

"That does not sound unreasonable," I conceded. "Now will you go back into bed and go quietly to sleep?"

"I never sleep," she told me. "I lie there inside all the time."

Again I must repress my amusement; how many children have we heard, who declare absolutely that they do not sleep, that they never sleep, that they would not know how to sleep if they tried? However, I only said, "Will you let Elizabeth come back, very briefly, then, so that I may put her under hypnosis for a minute and tell her to feel better?"

She considered, chin on hands. "Even if you do not sleep," I added solemnly, "Elizabeth must rest, and I propose a brief suggestion or two from myself to effect that. There is nothing in any case for you to do tonight unless you decide to keep your unfortunate aunt wringing her hands outside your door again, and so, if you want any freedom at all, you would be most wise to help Miss R. regain *her* health."

"She's no use to *me* sick," said Betsy agreeably. "Even if *I* feel well Aunt Morgen wouldn't let *her* go anywhere."

"That's true," I said, thanking heaven for the dragon downstairs. "But you must also promise," I added, "that while you are free you do not in any way attempt to harm Miss R. By stuffing her with sweets, for instance, or damaging her in the eyes of her friends."

"Or making her walk in front of a train," said Betsy, grinning. "You must think I'm crazy," she said, and giggled.

I stood up from the bed, and attempted to smooth the tumbled sheets. "Now hop into bed like a good girl," I said, with a heavy and most reluctant attempt at heartiness. I patted her shoulder as she climbed into the bed, thinking how extraordinarily different Betsy was from Elizabeth or Beth; I felt like an uncle putting a bad child to bed, and even Miss R.'s grown-up person did not detract from the strong avuncular feeling. I pulled the blankets up under her chin, and then sat on the bed beside her. "Now show me how you let Miss R. come back," I said, and then, as I spoke, I saw her eyes turn on me dully, and knew that without my perceiving it Betsy had withdrawn herself swiftly and completely and Miss R. lay there before me, wide-eyed and startled, as any young girl might be, who wakes up from what must have seemed a heavy sleep to find a man, albeit her doctor, sitting familiarly upon the edge of her bed and apparently continuing a conversation with her.

"Doctor Wright!" she said, recognizing me, and she attempted to sit up, but I put her gently back.

"It's all right," I told her soothingly. "You have been ill, and your aunt has sent for me." She lay back, still uneasy, and I spoke to her gently, telling her that she had called out for me in her sleep, and that her aunt had felt that I might be able to help her, so there I was, and I was planning to "put her to sleep" for only a minute or so. I could see that she had been very ill; her face was substantially thinner in even the few days since I had seen her, and she was pale and so weak that she could not protest hypnosis; I subdued her easily into a light trance, and then, speaking hastily, and dropping my voice for fear Miss Jones might be listening outside, I said, "Beth—Beth, is it you?"

She stirred, and smiled, and said, "My dear friend, I have been longing to hear your voice." My poor Beth, too, was wasted and pale, and it saddened me to see her sweet face worn by illness and hear her soft voice so tired; "Dear Beth," I said, taking her hand, "I am sorry you have been so unwell, but we will soon have you better."

"I am better now," she said, "with *you* here."

"But, Beth, you must do something for me, something extremely important; do you think you can? It will help me, and help you to be well much sooner."

"I can do whatever you tell me to."

I hesitated only a minute, debating how most forcefully to drive home my point; then I said urgently, "This is what you must do; you must insist, constantly and as strongly as you know how, that you are recovered from your illness; you must watch constantly for signs of weakness and absent-mindedness; keep insisting upon your own strength and control. Try to keep your aunt near by as much as possible. And, most important, resist absolutely any actions not usual to you. Be vigilant. If you feel yourself compelled to misbehave before your friends, or to consume quantities of sweet things, or to throw yourself before a train, or to do any of a hundred things which would ordinarily not occur to you, fight against the impulse. Now, can you promise me all this?"

"I promise," she said, whispering.

"I will help you all I can, and stay as close to you as possible. It is more important than I can tell you now, but someday I will explain it all to you."

"If you want me to, I will do it," she said.

"Dear Beth," and I pressed her hand.

She opened her eyes, grinning. "I bet you never dreamed I could do Beth so well," Betsy said.

I know not how I stumbled down the stairs, past Miss Jones halfway; "Is she all right, Doctor?" I believe Miss Jones asked me, and I, shaking my head blindly, made my way somehow to the door, and abandoned that house.

A general who retreats while his army is strong, and able to fight, is a coward, but who can condemn a warrior who, shorn of weapons, seeing his allies desert him, confronted by a field upon which his adversary reigns triumphant, withdraws from battle? I sat up late that night composing a letter to Miss Jones, resigning her niece's care; I told her I was old and ill, I explained to her that my strength was inadequate, I described to her my many pressures of business and affairs, I recommended returning to Ryan, and suggested (with what pangs for my lovely Beth) that she seriously consider some good private institution, and I closed, her humble servant, having covered four sides and said everything, except the truth, which I knew to be that I was badly frightened and unwilling to jeopardize my own health in the service of a girl who had misled me; I had placed my faith on Beth and been deceived, and although I could hardly condemn her for being no more than a weak pawn, my trust in her was gone. I wrote late, as I say, and very well (indeed, I have saved the letter, and it is before me now), but I might have slept that night, and saved my inadequate words.

In the morning, as I turned wearily from my writing desk,

Miss Jones telephoned me again. In the levellest tones, as one who endeavors not to judge prematurely and unfairly, she told me that her niece had gone. Suitcase secretly packed, her clothes hastily assumed in the dead of night, our enemy had deceived us; Betsy had carried off Miss R. and Beth, we knew not when or where.

3

BETSY

Everything was going to be very very very good, so long as she remembered carefully about putting on both shoes every time, and not running into the street, and never telling them, of course, about where she was going; she recalled the ability to whistle, and thought, I must never be afraid.

She knew that the bus left at twelve; she had planned this more carefully than they ever suspected. She had been extremely clever about packing her suitcase softly and with tiny steps from the closet to the bed, and because she had known that she was going, by then, she had chosen only the most correct clothes for wearing outdoors and on a bus; she had taken a great deal of money from Aunt Morgen's pocketbook, she had tricked the doctor roundly. Even when they discovered she had gone, it was going to take them quite a while to learn all about the suitcase and the money and the bus; she had covered her tracks exceedingly well. Whistling, she came to the corner and thought, they will never expect that I know how to get on a taxi by myself, and it will take me to the bus station in time, too. "Take me to the bus station, please," she said to the taxi driver; these were the first free words she had ever spoken, but the taxi driver only nodded and took her to the bus station. She gave him a dollar bill from her pocketbook, he gave her back change, and she said "Thank you," and "Good night," when she closed the door of the taxi. No one turned, no one shouted, no one stopped to point at her and burst into laughter; everything was going to be very very very good.

She had eleven single dollar bills in her pocketbook, and the rest, some hundred-odd dollars she had taken from Aunt Morgen's wallet, was carefully hidden in the pocket of her suitcase, since under no circumstances must she be thought careless or a fool, and the loss of all her money, besides indicating that she was not entirely able, might put her into the uncomfortable position of having to ask strangers for help. She had determined with precision that as soon as she got off the bus again she would go to a hotel, where of course in a room of her own she would be able to open her suitcase in private and take out whatever money she wanted.

Since she had both money and time, she was able to have a cup of coffee in the bus station while she was waiting, and she bought herself, also, a magazine; she did not care to read, generally, but she was attracted by the bright cover and had observed that nearly all the people standing in the station carried magazines or books, and she must on no account be thought strange or different. She had a book in her suitcase, a large dictionary for use in case she needed help in talking or writing or spelling; in any case, since she intended eventually to dispose of all her possessions, the book, which was large and solidly printed, might be a source of money sometime if she needed it, but she must remember to cross out Lizzie's name on the first page. At present, it was perfectly safe with her money in the suitcase and was hardly worth removing just to seem to be reading on the bus. She finished her coffee and set the cup back into the saucer just as everyone else did, and got down from the stool and picked up her pocketbook and suitcase and went to the ticket window. Ahead of her a woman was telling the clerk, "One way to New York, please," and, since the clerk neither looked up nor laughed, this must be the usual manner of getting a ticket; she felt a deep grateful satisfaction for the clerk and for the woman ahead and for the man who sold coffee and to the taxi driver and for all this wholly strange world; "One way to New York, please," she said, careful to get the right inflection, and the clerk neither looked up nor smiled, but passed her her change wearily. "How soon does the bus go?" she asked the clerk boldly, and he glanced at the clock and told her, without surprise, "Twelve minutes, side door."

Wondering what to do for twelve minutes, since it would certainly be remarked upon if she had another cup of coffee so soon after the first, she noticed a rack of picture postcards, and the idea of a farewell message came to her; they would naturally perceive that she had left them, but she could not forego the pleasure of telling them that they had driven her away. She chose two postcards, regretting that there were no pictures of the museum; she addressed the one with a picture of the monument to Aunt Morgen, writing with the pen which Lizzie always carried in the pocketbook. "You will never see me again," she wrote. "I am going to parts unknown. I hope you are sorry." And then, since the postcard seemed so unfeeling, and Aunt Morgen had, after all, never done her any active harm, she added, "Love, from E. R."

The other card she addressed, having saved this particular satisfaction for the last, to Doctor Wright, and for a minute she thought, pen in hand, of how most clearly and vividly in this small space reserved for messages, to say what Doctor Wright needed to be told; the recollection of the imminent departure of the bus stirred her at last, and finally she wrote quickly, "Dear Doctor Wrong, never try to find me. I will never come back. I am going somewhere where people love me, and not like you. Yours very sincerely, Betsy." This message did not particularly please her, but there was no time to try another because the man was calling, "Bus to New York, side door, leaving in three minutes, bus to New York, side door, leaving in three minutes, bus to New York, side door. . . ."

She hurried out, following the woman who had been ahead of her in the ticket line, and climbed into the bus, marveling for a moment at its size and deep comfort, compared with the smaller busses Lizzie used to ride on her way to work at the museum. After hesitating for a minute inside the door she sat down next to the woman who had been ahead of her in the line, and then got up again to put her suitcase into the rack overhead, as she observed other people doing, because of course she must not seem to be different in any way, and must not have her suitcase on the floor next to her if everyone else had their suitcases in the rack over their heads. Once settled, her magazine and pocketbook in her lap, she leaned back and sighed, and turned her head slightly to see that the woman in the seat next to her was staring at her (had she done something to be stared at? Too slow with her suitcase? Too quick, leaning back?) and so she said hastily, "How long a trip do we have?"

"Where are you going?" asked the woman, raising her eyebrows.

"To New York, same as you."

The woman frowned, glanced forward at the driver, and then said, "How did you know I was going to New York?"

"I heard you buy a ticket, so I bought a ticket the same way."

"Oh?" said the woman, raising her eyebrows again and looking sideways.

It is not going to be safe to rely on anyone, Betsy thought with quick sad clarity, not anyone at all. This woman was old, as old as Aunt Morgen, looking tired and as though she did not much relish this night trip on a bus instead of a sleep at home in bed; it was not fair that a woman as old as Aunt Morgen and looking so tired should be untrustworthy as well. Perhaps even more than wishing she was young again and full of life, the woman wished to be trusted by Betsy, because she turned now and made a big smile for Betsy alone, and said, "So you're going to New York?" and nodded, and turned her whole face and body at Betsy as though promising a home, and safety. Does she think that *I* am going to think that she is young again? Betsy wondered, and said, "I guess so. I mean, I have a ticket for New York, but I might decide to go somewhere else. Is New York exciting?"

"Not very," the woman said. She glanced again at the driver, and then leaned closer to Betsy. "No place is very exciting unless you have dear ones there," she said, and nodded again. "For me, New York is nothing—nothing. *My* dear ones are beyond."

Betsy looked past her at the dark window of the bus and thought suddenly that it was not, after all, impossible that they would not come after her; could that be Aunt Morgen's face peering in blindly through the glass, or the doctor gesturing imperiously from the station doorway? "How soon do we start?" she asked the woman, and the woman put a hand in a black glove over Betsy's hand, and said, "One longs to join them, dear, yearning for dear ones is sometimes almost a pain, a pain *here*," and she took her hand off Betsy's long enough to touch herself lingeringly on the breast, and then she put her hand down on Betsy's again.

But, Betsy thought, even if they knew now about the suitcase and the money and the bus (*could* that be Aunt Morgen, running, calling out, waving her handkerchief frantically?) they would never look for her talking to a dismal woman in black gloves, never look under the woman's hand to see if Betsy's hand lay there, and she sat back again, and turned her head courteously to the woman; they were two ladies engaged in conversation, and the bus stirred, and groaned. The driver nodded reassuringly at the station, the doors of the bus closed, and then the bus moved hugely out of the station and into the street (the doctor, was it? Stepping from a taxi, shaking his umbrella?) and then gathered speed toward the edge of town. "I guess we've started," Betsy said happily.

"—very fortunate," the woman said. "I, you see, have no dear ones awaiting me in New York. A child like yourself can never understand—"

Goodbye, goodbye, Betsy thought, turning to see the town behind them. Goodbye.

"Beyond, if only I might reach them."

"Why can't you reach them?" Betsy turned back and looked curiously at the woman who still had her hand over Betsy's and was now using the other hand to wipe at her eyes with a handkerchief. "Where are they?"

"In Chicago. I am unfortunately absolutely without means of traveling farther than New York. A child like yourself, unsuspicious, happy, free—a child like yourself, with an ample allowance—"

"I haven't got an allowance," Betsy said, and giggled. "All I have is what I got from Aunt Morgen."

"Perhaps a small loan—"

"Thank you anyway, but I have enough," Betsy said. "It's in my suitcase."

The woman glanced up, briefly, and then pressed Betsy's hand. "Such a sweet child," she said. "What *is* your name, dear?"

"Betsy."

"Is that all?"

Suddenly, perhaps because Betsy had been listening and looking through the window at the moving lights, or perhaps even just because she had allowed herself to become excited and interested—Lizzie got out, and she looked coldly at the woman while Betsy, caught completely off guard, struggled and tried to catch control again, and Lizzie said, "I beg your pardon?" and then looked wonderingly around the bus.

"I only said 'What is your name?'" the woman said, drawing back.

"Elizabeth Richmond, madam. How do you do?"

"How do you do?" said the woman weakly, and then Betsy caught onto a deep breath and put Lizzie under again, and said as politely as she could, "I don't want to talk any more now, thank you. You've been very nice, but I would rather not talk any more."

Without, she hoped, being particularly rude, she got up and went to an empty seat at the back of the bus; she could hardly try to take down her suitcase with the bus moving so quickly, but it was more important to be where she need not talk to anyone, and she could watch her suitcase easily from here. The woman with whom she had been sitting turned once, and looked at her, and then, shaking her head a little, glanced up at the suitcase and then opened her book to read. That's good, Betsy thought; perhaps she didn't even notice Lizzie speaking up like that; perhaps she has a Lizzie of her own.

Although Betsy did not sleep, and did not think she ever had, it was of course necessary for Elizabeth to sleep; ever since Betsy had been a prisoner she had watched while Elizabeth slept, lying far back in her own hidden corner of the mind, inert and almost helpless, looking as though up through a dizzying fog at the world of Elizabeth's dreams, seeing the dim figures of Elizabeth's world when Elizabeth's eyes were open, and the screaming phantoms of Elizabeth's nightmares when Elizabeth's eyes were shut; she had lain there crying out, soundless and numb, helpless to move Elizabeth's hands or feet, frantic for motion, for sight, for speech, paralyzed and wrapped in agonizing silence; now, riding the surface of Elizabeth's mind, she indulgently permitted Elizabeth to dream, and luxuriated in the picture of Elizabeth down there, dumb and helpless and waiting. Beyond Elizabeth, in the far kingdom of the mind, Beth lay, moving drowsily, unaware, not watchful, lost in soundless shadows. Betsy could feel that they were beneath, ready to rouse, as she had been, to any sharp sight or sound calling them awake. Now, Elizabeth slept, and frowned a little, and turned uncomfortably in the soft seat of the bus, and swayed with the movement of the bus, and Betsy lay back against the soft cushion of Elizabeth's dreams, planning what she was going to do, now that she was free.

She knew that she was going to get off the bus in New York, and follow everyone else out of the bus station into the street (it would be a street, she supposed, much like that she had left behind; she must not let her fears of strangeness carry her into imaginary difficulties; she must be prepared to assume a certain steadiness upon the part of the world outside) and then take a taxi, as she had done to get to the bus station—only now, she supposed, it would be daylight, and consequently easier to find a taxi, and she could look out the windows as they traveled. She would then go to a hotel. Aunt Morgen had stayed once at a hotel named Drewe; this, since she knew from Aunt Morgen's staying there that it must be a proper place and suitable for a lady traveling alone (Aunt Morgen had surely been traveling alone?) would be the best place for her to go at first. Later, when she had had time to unpack her suitcase and perhaps look around a little and get to know the city, she would move to another hotel whose name Aunt Morgen would not know; she could not remember whether Doctor Wrong had ever mentioned being familiar with the names of any hotels in New York, but thought she might safely assume that he would not be acquainted with the names of hotels suitable for ladies traveling alone. I have been very strictly brought up, she thought with satisfaction, and I shall be very well-behaved. Particularly she recalled that she had told both Aunt Morgen and Doctor Wrong that they would not be able to find her, so very likely they would not think of looking in New York, because in New York they might find her. A thought struck her, and she giggled—Elizabeth turning in her sleep—perhaps, she thought, she should have sent postcards to Lizzie and Beth, telling them goodbye; I'll do that first chance I get, she promised herself, I'll write them each a nice card from the hotel, it's no more than they deserve. Elizabeth stirred again, and groaned, and Betsy was still, wanting Elizabeth to stay asleep.

All during the dark hours of the night the bus moved on, going smoothly and rocking Elizabeth gently; because it was important not to seem wakeful when everyone else was sleeping Betsy closed her eyes, and a kind of wonder came to her, at herself going alone through the night. She was for the first time in the indifferent hands of strangers, entrusting her person to the tenderness of the bus driver, her name to the woman napping in the seat far ahead; she was going to spend the rest of her life in a room belonging to someone else and she would eat at a stranger's table and walk streets she did not recognize under a sun she had never seen, waking, before. Soon no one would even know her face; Doctor Wrong would forget and Aunt Morgen would be looking for Elizabeth; from this moment on no eyes which looked upon her would ever have seen her before; she was a stranger in a world of strangers and they were strangers she had left behind; "Who am I?" Betsy whispered in wonder, and not even Elizabeth heard, "where am I going?"

It was, then, urgently important to be some person, to have always been some person; in all the world she was entering there was not anyone who was not some particular person; it was vital to be a person. "I am Betsy Richmond," she said over and over quietly to herself, "I was even born in New York. And my mother's name is Elizabeth Richmond, Elizabeth Jones before she was married. My mother was born in Owenstown, but I was born in New York. My mother's sister is named Morgen, but I never knew her very well." Invisible in the darkness of the bus, Betsy grinned. "My name is Betsy Richmond," she whispered, "and I am going alone to New York because I am easily old enough to travel alone. I am going to New York on a bus by myself and when I get to New York I am going to a hotel in a taxi. My name is Betsy Richmond, and I was born in New York. My mother loves me more than anything. My mother's name is Elizabeth Richmond, and my name is Betsy and my mother always called me Betsy and I was named after my mother. Betsy Richmond," she whispered softly into the unhearing movement of the bus, "Betsy Richmond."

"*My* mother," she went on, half-remembering, and Elizabeth moaned, and pressed her hands together, and dreamed. "My mother was angry with her Betsy and now I am alone, I am on a bus going to New York; I am old enough to travel alone and my name is Betsy Richmond, Elizabeth Jones before I was married. 'Betsy is my darling,' my mother used to say, and I used to say 'Elizabeth is my darling,' and I used to say, 'Elizabeth likes Robin best.' "

Betsy sat up straight in the bus, so suddenly that Elizabeth half-awakened and opened her eyes and said "Doctor?" "No, no," Betsy said, and then, shivering, looked around to see if she had made any loud noise, if she had forgotten to be careful while everyone else was sleeping. It's Robin, she thought, Robin nearly woke up Lizzie. She waited a minute, trying to see through the darkness of the bus; the driver ahead seemed calm enough, and then someone far down on one side moved, and sighed deeply, and Betsy sat back in relief; it's all right, she thought, other people move and make sounds; no one cares. She sat back and looked out the window; I don't even know where Robin is, anymore, she thought, and he wouldn't remember me any more than anyone else, even if he saw me Robin would think I was someone he didn't know at all, and if my mother knew about him he'd be sorry. My mother loves me best, anyway, Betsy told herself forlornly, my mother was only teasing about not loving me best, my mother pulled my hair and laughed and said "Elizabeth loves Robin best," and my mother loves me better than anyone. My name is Betsy Richmond and my mother's name is Elizabeth Richmond and she calls me Betsy. Robin did everything bad.

She wanted to get up and move around, but dared not; it was important for Elizabeth to sleep, and even if she did go up—say—to the driver and ask him how fast they were going, or when they would reach New York, or whether his name was Robin, people would notice her and look at her, because for all she knew it might be extremely unusual for people to wonder how fast the bus was going. Thinking of Robin always made her very nervous, however, and it was important not to be nervous or afraid, and she twisted her hands together and rubbed her eyes and bit at her lip; what must I do, she wondered, if I see Robin somewhere in New York?

The bus went widely around a curve, and Betsy fell against the side of the seat and giggled; it's fun, she thought. Then, suddenly very happy because she was running away, after all, and no one could find her—so how would she find Robin, then?—she sat back and folded her hands and spoke to herself very sternly.

If I'm going to keep it all straight and make a real person by myself, she told herself silently, Robin has to be in it like anyone else; he can't get out of it as easily as that. And besides, everyone who remembers at all has bad things to remember along with good things; it would seem very funny to people if all I had for a life I remembered was good things. There have to be some bad things or it looks funny. So keep Robin in, because he was bad and nasty. We went on a picnic, Robin and my mother and me. No, she thought then, shaking her head, if it's going to be in, it's all got to be in, right from the beginning, the way things ought to be remembered, so start the remembering right from the beginning of that day, right from the top, and remember it all. No one ever remembers just a bad thing, they remember all around it, all that happened before it and after it, and of course, she told herself consolingly, one bad thing is probably enough, and when they ask you what do you remember that's bad and nasty you can say Robin, and that will satisfy them. So, she went on silently, I woke up in the morning that day and the sun was shining and the blanket on my bed was blue. There was a green dress hanging on the bottom of my bed and I thought it would look funny with the blue blanket but it didn't. I heard my mother downstairs and she was saying "A wonderful day for a picnic with my Betsy, a wonderful wonderful day," and I knew she was saying it to me and saying it on the way upstairs over and over so I would wake up hearing her say it. And then she came in and she was smiling and the sun was shining brightly on her face, and I can't remember how she looked that morning because of the sun shining on her face. "A wonderful day for my Betsy," she said, "a wonderful wonderful day for a picnic, let's go to the bay." And she came and tickled me and I rolled out of bed and she hit me with the pillow and I was laughing. Then she said "Peanut butter" and ran out of the room, and I said "Jelly," calling it after her and I put on the green dress and went downstairs and I had oranges and toast for breakfast that morning because it was hot. My mother made peanut butter sandwiches and jelly sandwiches and all the time I was eating my orange she would look at me and say "Peanut butter" and I would look back at her and say "Jelly," and it was funny because she wanted peanut butter and I wanted jelly and it was funny that two people who loved each other and had the same name liked two different things like that. She made hard-boiled eggs and packed everything in a basket with cookies and a thermos bottle full of lemonade and then my mother said "Let's take your poor old Robin along with us, Betsy, my girl. Because poor old Robin is lonesome and he is Elizabeth's darling," and I said "Jelly," and she made a face at me and said "Peanut butter, but let's take him anyway."

I pretended to throw a hard-boiled egg at my mother but she went anyway and telephoned Robin and told him to come right away and we took our bathing suits. Robin and my mother and Betsy went on the streetcar out to the bay and my mother and Betsy put on their bathing suits and Robin put on his bathing suit and the water was warm and whenever Betsy splashed at my mother Robin splashed at Betsy and he said "Betsy is a mean mean girl" and the sun was bright and there was no one anywhere around. Robin and my mother and Betsy ate the hard-boiled eggs and the peanut butter sandwiches and when Betsy said "Jelly" my mother said "Betsy, must you tease all the time?" and everyone lay down on the beach in the sun. Then my mother said, "Betsy, my nuisance, go down along the beach and collect seventy-three shells all the prettiest you can find, and we will be sirens and make them into a crown for our Robin." Betsy went down the beach and gathered shells, and she was all alone, not even strangers near her, and the water on one side and the beach on the other side and the rocks beyond, and she was singing, "I love coffee, I love tea, I love Betsy and Betsy loves me," and matching shells because she was the sea-king's daughter and she was gathering the eyes of drowned sailors to ransom her love from the sea-king's prison in the rocks. There was an empty popcorn box, and it was a coral chest where she put her jewels, and the two rocks were her throne, and when she sang the waves came running up to her feet, and she was shipwrecked, and living alone on an island, and the empty popcorn box was washed up on the shore, and inside it she found corn to plant, and a hammer to build a house. She made plates and pots out of sand, and baked them in the sun, and overhead she had a roof of seaweed and it kept out the sun. The rocks were her signal tower, to light a fire for passing ships. Pirates came by, and captured her, and the rocks were the cabin of the pirate ship where they kept the gold, and they sank a merchant ship and made all the shells walk the plank, and the popcorn box was full of emeralds and pearls. Then Betsy stood up suddenly, feeling cold, and the shells fell out of her lap and the rocks were rocks again and the sand was only scuffed and piled instead of plates and growing corn and there were no drowned sailors in the bay. "I stayed away too long," Betsy thought, and she gathered up her shells in the popcorn box and walked fast, because she was cold, and she heard Robin saying, "Leave the damn kid with Morgen next time."

"No," said Betsy, loudly enough so that people in the bus heard her, and someone turned around to look; I was having a nightmare, she thought violently, having a nightmare, is all.

She waited, tense, and then people turned and moved and fell asleep again, and no one knew that Betsy was even awake, or had been awake at all.

"My name is Betsy Richmond," she began again at last, whispering, "and my mother's name is Elizabeth Richmond, Elizabeth Jones before she was married. . . ."

When the bus stopped at last and people stirred and opened their eyes and a man down the aisle stood up and began to put on his coat, Betsy was relieved at having no longer to watch the same inside of the bus, and the windows which, whatever they framed, made it look all the same; she was among the first people standing, and she made her way hastily down the aisle, edging past the man putting on his coat, to where her suitcase was, just as the woman in the black gloves stood up and lifted Betsy's suitcase down. "Good morning," the woman said, smiling at Betsy. "Did you sleep? I'll take the bag, dear."

"I want my suitcase," Betsy said. It was not usual, she knew, to struggle over a suitcase in a bus, and she must not be angry, so she took hold of the woman's arm and said again, "I want my suitcase, please."

"I'll carry it for you," the woman said, smiling brightly at the other people in the bus. "Dear," she added, bringing her smile around again to Betsy.

This was wrong and very unfortunate. "I want my suitcase," Betsy said once more, not knowing what else to say, and not sure just how far she might trust herself to show anger; here, in a situation like this, was where her unpreparedness showed most clearly—how angry, really, might a person be when her suitcase was taken forcibly away from her? How reprehensible was this false smiling woman, with her unreal sprightliness and her tawdry dull shoddy air; might Betsy strike her? Push her back? Call for help?

She turned, wanting advice, and met the eye of the bus driver; "I want my suitcase," Betsy said to him down the length of the bus, and, because most of the people had left by now, he came out of his seat and toward Betsy.

"Something wrong, lady?" he asked the woman who still had a clinging grasp on Betsy's suitcase, and who gave him her free black-gloved hand on his arm, with a sigh of relief; "I wish this child would behave," she said, with a gesture at Betsy that endeavored to exclude Betsy from the circle of maturity in which the woman and the bus driver were naturally included. "Alone in the big city," the woman said vividly.

The wickednesses of the city were not lost upon the bus driver; he nodded and regarded Betsy with sadness. "If people want to *help* you," he began, "seems like you ought to treat them nicer."

Any needless waste of emotion in Betsy's position would be an almost criminal extravagance; "Old suitcase-stealer," she said to the woman, "Just because I told you all my money was in the suitcase."

"Well, surely . . ." said the woman, lifting her head high. "I wanted to *help* the child," she said to the bus driver. "Her money . . ." and she indicated that of all counterfeit gratification in which she dealt, money was the least regarded and the most unreliable; "alone in a strange city," she said, "someone offers to help you, and right away you start accusing them of stealing." She took away her black gloves, and gave Betsy and the bus driver each a long and unhappy look of compassion. "I can always tell your kind of person," she said flatly to Betsy.

"Lady," said the bus driver sadly, "if the kid don't want your help, you can't make her. Maybe," he added without humor, "maybe she just *likes* to carry her own money."

"Naturally," the woman said, and turned her back on them both; she took up her own suitcase and pocketbook and went out of the bus, walking with the proud step of one who does not steal. "You want to watch out about getting into some kind of real trouble," the bus driver said to Betsy. "Can't trust anybody, almost."

"I know it," Betsy said. "I plan to be careful."

"You got any people here or anything?" the bus driver asked, looking for the first time at Betsy instead of at her suitcase. "I mean, you got anywhere to go?"

"Certainly," said Betsy, perceiving clearly for the first time where she had come. "I'm going to meet my mother."

The Drewe Hotel was a sign on an awning, a gold script on

caps and vest pockets and matchbook folders; Betsy had never before walked on a carpet where her feet made no sound, and even in the museum she had not seen so high a polish on brass fittings. She was impressed by the thoughtfulness of the management on her account; someone had arranged where the bed was to go and had counted the hangers in the closet, and no disguise of satin or watercolor or walnut veneer could conceal the fact that someone had contrived a closed room where Betsy was to perform all the most private acts of her life for a space of time depending upon herself, in whatever order she chose, at her own expense, carefully and securely hidden away. When the door was safely closed and locked (Aunt Morgen and Doctor Wrong would surely not think to look for her in a room with blue satin bedspreads, but she had promised the bus driver to take good care of her suitcase, so locking the door seemed a faithful precaution) she went at once to the window and leaned out. Her room was high, and not far away, between buildings, she could see the river; leaning against the windowsill, it seemed to her that she could feel a gentle touch, as of the river moving against its banks and jarring the land in little waves, so that even the Drewe Hotel was caressed, distantly; somewhere she heard the indefinable stir of music.

A thought of the world swept over her, of people living around her, singing, dancing, laughing; it seemed unexpectedly and joyfully that in all this great world of the city there were a thousand places where she might go and live in deep happiness, among friends who were waiting for her here in the stirring crowds of the city (oh, the dancing in the small rooms, the voices singing together, the long talks at night under the cool trees, the swaggering arm in arm, the weddings and the music and the spring!); perhaps there were some, searching face after face with eager looks, wondering when Betsy would be there. A little touch of laughter caught her, like the touch of the waves of the river, and she tightened her fingers delightedly upon the windowsill; how happy we all are, she thought, and how lucky that I came at last!

Far below her, upon a narrow ledge between one of the buildings and the river, a man came, edging his way; she could not see his face or his objective, but she watched contentedly, knowing that he would accomplish with competence whatever he had started for. When he stumbled, he caught himself and sent what was surely a grin backwards over his shoulder, as one who says "Nearly lost me *that* time," and then, idly, lifted his head as though to make sure that Betsy was watching. While she held her breath with pleasure, he took one hand from his grip on the ledge and waved, although she knew it was not to her, and, grinning and wavering precariously, shouted something to someone, and made his way on across the ledge and disappeared. She looked on still at the moving water of the river, wondering at the man who went so easily, thinking of him now safely across the ledge, laughing and going on already to some new occupation, moving among his friends now and on his way perhaps to some good place where he was welcome; he may someday be a friend of *mine,* she thought; I may be welcome there too.

Now that she knew she was here to find her mother, the city had begun to take on a more coherent shape for her, because somewhere in the center was the solitary figure which was her mother, and radiating out from that figure in all directions were signals and clues which she might find and which would lead her surely to the center of the maze. Anything, she thought, looking with anticipation at the windows across the way, anything might be a clue.

Although upon reflection she perceived that her mother must always have expected that Betsy would come someday, it was impossible for her mother to foresee exactly when Betsy would be able to escape, so she could probably expect very little in the way of assistance from her mother, until her mother learned definitely (perhaps from the man on the ledge?) that Betsy had come at last, and had begun her search. They might just possibly stumble upon one another by chance, but that seemed unreasonable, considering the numbers of people in the city. Betsy decided wisely that what she must do was recall as well as possible all that she had ever heard her mother say about New York, because all that time, long years ago, her mother had been leaving clues for Betsy to find her someday, building against a future when she and Betsy might be free together.

First, then: Betsy and her mother had left New York when Betsy was two years old; consequently Betsy could not be expected to remember much about the city herself, although she had a suspicion that she might at any moment turn a corner and walk without foreknowledge onto a scene clearly remembered and more real than anything she had ever seen since. All that Betsy knew now about the city, beyond what she had seen from the taxi window, the Hotel Drewe, and her acquaintance on the ledge—although probably the bus driver and the woman with the black gloves were by now somewhere among the city people—was what she had heard her mother say, and that was little more than a dozen idle references in one or another conversation. Carefully, Betsy tried to evoke her mother's clues.

"—The one from that little dress shop I told you about, Morgen, you remember—Abigail's." Betsy recalled this remark most clearly, and even the faint impatient voice her mother had used always in speaking to Aunt Morgen; oddly, she could not remember the dress her mother had been talking about and could not even picture her mother and Aunt Morgen talking together about it; only the lonely sentence stayed in her mind, and that almost certainly made it a clue.

And then . . . had her mother not spoken longingly of the place she had lived alone with Betsy? ". . . And I danced with my baby, and sang, and in the mornings we watched the sun rise; it was like Paris." Should she perhaps consider searching for her mother in Paris? Wiser, she decided, to look here first; Paris was difficult to get to, and she already was in New York; besides, although Elizabeth knew some French, Betsy had never troubled to learn it, and she would feel extremely awkward, having to get Lizzie to translate the simplest things; no, she thought, not Paris. But we danced together, and sang, and we lived high up, because there had been many stairs (". . . and my Betsy went down the stairs and down the stairs and *down* the stairs, and I sat at the bottom and waited and waited and *waited . . ."*). She laughed aloud, leaning on the windowsill and thinking of her mother.

She would spend this first morning in her hotel room, partly because here in private she might relax her vigilance over Elizabeth for a while, and partly because she thought it would look odd if she went out again so soon after coming in; they would think downstairs that she had not unpacked her suitcase or even washed her face. This reminded her that it would not do at all, surely, to continue in Elizabeth's drab clothes, since if Aunt Morgen and Doctor Wrong were really looking for her, they would have a description: Elizabeth Richmond, twenty-four years old, height five foot six, weight a hundred and twenty pounds, hair brown, eyes blue, wearing a dark blue suit, white blouse, low-heeled black shoes, plain black hat, last seen carrying a tan suitcase. Thought to have been kidnapped by a young woman known as Betsy Richmond, about sixteen years old, height five foot six, weight a hundred and twenty pounds, hair brown, eyes blue, wearing a dark blue suit . . . no, new clothes were essential. Betsy thought wryly that if anything could impel Elizabeth to reassert her authority it would surely be the sudden spectacle of herself in scarlet shoes and sequined gown, so she reluctantly decided upon a compromise, perhaps only a red hat and some inexpensive jewelry.

She unpacked the suitcase, putting Elizabeth's neat underwear and extra stockings into the dresser drawer, hanging up Elizabeth's plain coat and clean blouse in the closet. She undressed and bathed, and then, coming out of the tub, met herself unexpectedly in the full length mirror in the bedroom and for a minute almost lost herself in surprise. Where, she wondered, is Elizabeth? Where in the tightness of the skin over her arms and her legs, in the narrow bones of her back and the planned structure of her ribs, in the tiny toes and fingers and the vital plan of her neck and head . . . where, in all this, was there room for anyone else? Could Lizzie be seen moving furtively behind the clarity of the eyes, edging in caution to peer out at herself; was she gone far within, waiting behind the heart or the throat, to seize with both hands and take control

with a murderous attack? Was she under the hair, had she
found refuge in a knee? Where was Lizzie?

For a moment, staring, Betsy wanted frantically to rip herself apart, and give half to Lizzie and never be troubled again,
saying take this, and take this and take *this,* and you can have
this, and now get out of my sight, get away from my body, get
away and leave me alone. Lizzie could have the useless parts,
the breasts and the thighs and the parts she took such pleasure
in letting give her pain; Lizzie could have the back so she
would always have a backache, and the stomach so she would
always be able to have cramps; give Elizabeth all the country
of the inside, and let her go away, and leave Betsy in possession of her own.

"Lizzie," Betsy said cruelly, "Lizzie, come out," and Elizabeth, looking for a moment out of her own eyes, saw herself
standing naked in a strange room before a long mirror, and,
turning to cower fearfully against the mirror, she began to cry,
and clutched at herself, and looked with horror into the room.

"Where?" she said, whispering, "who?" and searched with
her eyes, hoping perhaps to catch sight of her attacker, of the
villain who, enfolding her all unperceiving in a crowd, had
brought her here evilly to satisfy his white-slave passions;
"Hello?" she said finally, weakly, and Betsy laughed and
pushed her down, "You poor thing," Betsy said, looking again
in the mirror at the body which had so frightened Elizabeth,
"you poor silly thing."

And then, with Elizabeth's tears still on her cheeks, she
thought, "I wish I had a *real* sister."

She heard, as clearly as though it had been spoken in the room
with her, her mother's voice saying, "No, I want the child with
me. I won't give up my Betsy."

That was my mother, she thought, turning, my mother
was talking, she wants me to come with her. But she didn't say
that now, Betsy thought, when did she say it? When was I listening and heard my mother say that? "No, I want the child
with me . . ."

"Get rid of the little pest. Leave her with Morgen. What

good is she to *us?*" And *that*, Betsy thought, was Robin's voice. "I *hate* that child," he said, some time long ago, some time to Betsy's mother, "I *hate* that child." And had her mother said "But she's my Betsy; I love her"; —had her mother said that? Had she?

"Poor baby's cold," Betsy said, and went into the bed and rolled herself in blankets, and she could lie and think; Lizzie was restless as she grew warmer and Betsy sang, "Baby, baby, have you heard, Mother's going to get you a mocking bird; if that mocking bird won't sing, Mother's going to get you a diamond ring. . ." I wish I had a diamond ring, she thought, as Lizzie quieted; if I had a diamond ring I could tell them I was engaged to be married. If I was engaged to be married they couldn't take me back because my husband wouldn't let them. If I had a husband then my mother could marry him and we could all hide together and be happy. My name is Betsy Richmond. My mother's name is Elizabeth Richmond, Elizabeth Jones before I was married. Call me Lisbeth like you do my mother, because Betsy is my darling Robin. . . .

("You're a silly baby," her mother said.

"But I want Robin to call me Lisbeth too. Because whatever he calls you he's got to call me."

"Betsy," said Robin, laughing, "Betsy, Betsy Betsy.")

While Elizabeth dreamed of flight and falling, Betsy planned to get herself some new clothes, perhaps today if she could find Abigail's shop right away. Perhaps at Abigail's she could find a way to locate her mother at once; perhaps—and the thought made her laugh secretly and wriggle in the bed—perhaps she might, opening the door of the shop, find her mother there already, looking at herself in the glass, wondering over the sequined dress, the jewels; "Betsy, Betsy," her mother would say, holding out her arms, "Where have you been? I've been waiting and waiting and *waiting* for you."

Some time later, when she had wondered over her clothes and spent more time at the window (although the man on the ledge did not come back again) and dressed herself and Lizzie had slept, she thought of food, and was suddenly hungry. I didn't have any breakfast, she thought; with Aunt Morgen by now I'd be having lunch, soup or waffles or macaroni or sandwiches with lettuce and mayonnaise and milk and hot cocoa and little cupcakes and cookies and puddings and dishes of pineapple and pickles; she hesitated in the doorway of her room, looking back. Everything was safely put away and there was no sign of her having been there, so if they should, by some chance, come here looking for her, there would be nothing to show where she was or where she was going. She locked the door carefully and put the key into Elizabeth's pocketbook, which she was carrying for lack of any other. In it was Elizabeth's pencil and a lipstick which Elizabeth used to put a faint color on her lips, and the clean handkerchief which Elizabeth always made sure to carry, and a pencil and a small notebook and a little tin of aspirin; Betsy grinned as she closed the pocketbook, wondering how the key to an unknown hotel room would ever explain itself inside the pocketbook to Elizabeth's chaste white handkerchief, and she went down the hall to the elevator thinking here I am at last.

The most important thing she had learned so far—and it was something to know, after only twelve hours—was that she need not pretend, always, to be competent or at home in a strange atmosphere. Other people, she had learned, were frequently uneasy and uncertain, lost their way or their money, were nervous at being approached by strangers or wary of officials; this made it considerably easier for Betsy to manage, since she could go up to the clerk at the hotel desk and ask her way to the dining room without seeming odd or unwell, and she relied strongly upon getting through a meal upon the same principle; so long as she did not try to order anything with a French name, and observed carefully to see what other people did by way of sitting down, and moving plates, and summoning service, she thought that she would do nicely. She was not awed by the size or the whiteness of the dining room, after having seen the satin bedspreads upstairs, and all tables not Aunt Morgen's were equally strange to her. She sat down, thinking with humor that if she stepped on the waiter's foot, or dropped her pocketbook, or perhaps missed the chair altogether, sitting down, she could always slip off and leave Lizzie to cope. She unfolded her napkin and looked around, and sat back in the soft chair with satisfaction. Each thing, she thought pleasurably, is nicer than the last; everything gets better and better.

With an enormous feeling of delighted wickedness she ordered an Aunt-Morgen-ish glass of sherry, and did not notice the waiter's hesitation over whether she was as old as she looked, and entitled to be served, or as old as she acted, and must necessarily be refused; the waiter, however, was in the last analysis philosophical, and concluded that a woman was more likely to look her age than to act it, so that Betsy was served with sherry and she sipped it gracefully, quite as professionally as Aunt Morgen might. Because it was not possible, in this most charming of worlds, for anything to be either mistaken or out of sorts, when Betsy desired company she looked up at the first person passing her table and said "Hello."

"Hello," he said, surprised, and hesitating by the table.

"Sit down, please," Betsy said politely.

He opened his eyes wide, glanced beyond her at the empty table which had been his objective, and then laughed. "All right," he said.

"I feel funny sitting here alone," Betsy explained. "No one to talk to, or anything. At home there was always Aunt Morgen there and even when she didn't talk I could have someone to look at. Someone I knew, that is," she said.

"Of course," he said, sitting down. "Have you been here long?" he asked, taking up his napkin.

"I just got here this morning, and the bus driver told me to be careful, so of course I am, but I thought you looked all right to talk to." He seemed a very civil man, not so old as Doctor Wrong, but older than Robin, and not at all uncomfortable at talking like this to someone he had not met before. "You weren't outside my window a little while ago?" she asked him suddenly, "climbing across a ledge?"

He shook his head, surprised. "I'm not spry enough," he said.

"*I* could if I wanted to. Lizzie gets faint, but of course I never do."

"Who is Lizzie?"

"Lizzie Richmond. I brought her with me, and she wants to get out, but she can't." She stopped and looked at him suspiciously. "I wasn't going to tell anyone about Lizzie," she said.

"It doesn't matter," he said. "I won't tell."

"Anyway, my mother's going to get rid of Lizzie—we're not going to have *her* around all the time, after the trouble we've already had, getting rid of Robin and all."

"Are you having lunch?" He took the menu from the waiter, smiling at her, and Betsy said, "This is the first time I've ever been in a restaurant," and wriggled happily. "And I'm *extremely* hungry," she added.

"Then we had better make this a special lunch," he said. "Shall I choose for you?" He held the menu toward her, and said, "Or would you rather order something for yourself?"

Betsy took the menu and glanced at it briefly and then handed it back. "Lizzie speaks French," she said, "but of course I never bothered to take it up much, so you'd better choose. Only lots of things, please. Everything exciting." She hesitated. "Nothing," she said, "nothing like . . . macaroni, or pickles, or sandwiches, or things like that. Things Aunt Morgen makes."

"Well," he said profoundly. He regarded the menu in deep thought. "No pickles," he said, debating, "no sandwiches." Finally, with the waiter standing by, and both of them nodding reassuringly at Betsy, he ordered smoothly and quite as though he very frequently had occasion to order lunches for young ladies who wanted everything exciting, and no pickles. While she listened to the lovely words which meant foods so exciting she did not even know the order in which they would be served, and listened to music coming distantly from some upper corner of the room, and listened to the fine harmonious sound of forks touching knives, and cups touching saucers, Betsy told herself, this is what it is going to be like all the time, now.

"There," he said at last, handing the menu to the waiter. "I think you're going to like everything. Now, tell me—I don't even know your name."

"I'm Betsy. Betsy Richmond. My mother's name is Elizabeth Richmond, Elizabeth Jones before she was married. I was born in New York."

"How long ago?"

"I forget," she said vaguely. "Is that for me?" The waiter set a fruit cup before her, and she took the cherry from the top with her fingers and put it into her mouth. "My mother left me with Aunt Morgen," she went on indistinctly, "but she didn't go with Robin."

"The one you had such trouble getting rid of?"

Betsy nodded violently, swallowed, and said, "But I don't have to remember that part, I decided in the bus. One bad thing about Robin ought to be enough, don't you think?"

"I should think so," he said. "Seeing as you got rid of him, anyway."

She giggled, lifting her spoon. "*And* I got rid of Aunt Morgen, *and* I got rid of Doctor Wrong, *and* I'm going to get rid of Lizzie, and I'm the gingerbread boy, I am."

"I wonder if Aunt Morgen will be worried about you," he said carefully.

She shook her head again. "I wrote her a postcard with a picture on it and I said I wasn't coming back, and anyway they'll be looking for Lizzie, not me. Can I have some more fruit?"

"He'll be bringing you something else in a minute."

"I can pay for it—I have plenty of money." When she saw that he was smiling she thought, and then said acutely, "That was wrong, wasn't it? That was wrong to say—why?"

"I invited you to lunch, sort of," he said. "That means that I am going to pay, so you mustn't say anything about paying. You must wait, and then be very gracious about my paying."

"Gracious," she said. "You mean 'Thank you *so* much'? Like Aunt Morgen?"

"Exactly like Aunt Morgen," he said. "Where is your mother now?"

"I don't know just where it is. I'm still finding out. Like the

man down on the ledge. They're going to have to tell me because I'll just keep asking and looking and looking and asking
and asking and looking and looking and—" She stopped
abruptly, and there was a silence. When she looked up, he was
placidly finishing his fruit. "Sometimes," she said with great
caution, "I get mixed up. You'll just have to excuse it."

"Of course," he said, without surprise.

"So you see," Betsy said, looking with deep satisfaction into
a bowl of clear soup in which, far down, small strange shapes
moved, and stirred, and stared, and strode.

"Who are you?" asked Elizabeth, blankly.

"How do you do?" he said. "I'm a friend of yours."

Betsy looked up, gasping, and moved far back in her chair,
and scowled at him. "Don't you listen to her," she said. "She
tells lies."

"All right," he said, and moved his spoon in his soup.

"I don't want any soup," Betsy said sullenly.

"All right," he said. "It's good, though, I always like soup."

"Aunt Morgen likes soup," Betsy said. "All the time."

"And pickles?"

Betsy giggled, in spite of her annoyance. "Old Aunt Pickle,"
she said.

"Old Doctor Pickle," he said.

"Old Lizzie Pickle."

"Elizabeth Jones that was?"

"What?" said Betsy.

"Elizabeth Pickle before she was married," he said.

"You stop that right now," Betsy said furiously. "You just
stop talking like that. I'll tell my mother."

"I'm sorry," he said. "It was a joke."

"My mother doesn't like jokes. Not mean jokes, and when
Robin made mean jokes my mother told him to stop and when
you make mean jokes you sound like Robin."

"And you'll get rid of me?"

She laughed. "That was smart, how I got rid of Robin," she
said, and then, breathlessly, "Oh!" turning to look at a tray of
pastries being wheeled past her chair. "Can I have one?"

"First eat your lunch. Your nice soup."

"I want cake," said Betsy.

"Your mother wouldn't want you to have dessert first."

Betsy was quiet suddenly. "How do you know?" she said. "How do you know what my mother would want?"

"She *certainly* wouldn't want you to be sick. That would be silly."

"That's right," Betsy said joyfully, "Mother's Betsy can't be sick, Betsy is Mother's baby and she mustn't cry, and Aunt Morgen said stop spoiling the child."

"I think," he said slowly, "that we don't like Aunt Morgen, do we, you and I? I don't think Aunt Morgen is so much."

"Aunt Morgen says to make the child stop fawning on Robin all the time. Aunt Morgen says the child is too old to scramble around with Robin like that. Aunt Morgen says the child knows more than is good for her."

"Old Aunt Pickle," he said.

"I want cake," Betsy said, and he laughed, and gestured to the waiter with the dessert wagon. "Only one," he said, "and then you eat the rest of your lunch I ordered for you. We're not going to have you sick, remember."

"Not *me*," said Betsy, bending lovingly over the tiny rich cakes, her eyes sparkling with the reflections of whipped cream and chocolate and strawberries; "it's Lizzie who gets sick," she said; one had bananas and one had chopped nuts and one had cherries; Betsy sighed.

"And you say they'll be looking for Lizzie?"

"Maybe the little square one," Betsy said. "Just to start. I choose the little square one," she said to the waiter. "Because then later I can try another kind and if any of them are very very good I can come back and have them again, after I've tried them all. Because I live right upstairs," she said parenthetically to the waiter, "so I can keep coming back and coming back. So I choose—"

She broke off as the headwaiter came to their table. "Telephone for you, Doctor," he said.

"Doctor?" said Betsy, rising. "Doctor?" She snatched at her pocketbook, and said in anger, "You're just Doctor Wrong in another face and you tried to fool me—"

"Wait a minute, please," he said, putting out a hand to stop her, but she brushed past him, her lips trembling and her hands shaking with anger. "It was mean of you," she said, "and I'll tell my mother you pretended to be friends, and now I can't have the little square one." She started off, and then remembered. "Thank you *so* much for paying," she said, bowing her head graciously, and then, almost running, left the restaurant and went through the hotel lobby into the street. A bus, she was thinking, always take a bus to get away, and she turned to her right and hurried down the street. She could see a bus coming to the corner to stop, and she ran and got onto it and sat down with relief, next to a woman in green silk, who looked at her briefly.

When she caught her breath, she leaned forward to look out of the window past the woman and said, "I wonder where *this* bus goes."

"Downtown, of course," the woman said stiffly, as though Betsy had somehow impugned the honor of the bus, or, worse, the discrimination of the woman in green silk; "this bus goes downtown."

"Thank you," Betsy said. "I hope I can find the place I'm looking for. It's not very likely, just starting out like this, but I can try, anyway."

"Some people," said the woman, consideringly, "think it's harder to find places downtown. Myself, I always have a *good* deal more trouble uptown. Are you going far?"

"Well, of course I can't be sure," Betsy said. "I'm just looking. Lots of stairs. And pink walls," she went on, remembering, "and there's a view of the river from the window."

"That would be the west side, then," the woman said. "They've all got stairs, there." She sighed. "I live east, myself," she said, "but of course we're moving in the fall."

"West of what?"

"West of the bus, of course," the woman said. "To your right as you get off."

"Then I turn right, and just anywhere might do?"

"Just anywhere?" said the woman, with a delicate inflection, and she turned emphatically and looked out of the window.

People keep getting so mixed up, Betsy thought helplessly, and she said, "It's because I'm looking for my mother, and I don't know exactly where she lives because I haven't been there in so long."

"Really?" said the woman, looking out of the window.

Oh, dear, Betsy thought, and she put her hand timidly on the woman's arm. "Please," she said, "if you don't mind, can I just ask you?"

The woman turned, hesitating as though half-convinced Betsy might have in mind an improper question—whether she had always lived east, perhaps, or did her building have an elevator?—and then nodded briefly. "Naturally," the woman said, "I can't answer *every*thing."

"I need only a kind of direction," Betsy said. "A clue. I know where I'm going, of course, and I'm positive I'll recognize it at once, but I'm just not quite sure of which house. The window looks out over the river, and the walls are painted pink—"

"Pink?"

"And," Betsy said triumphantly, "I remember there was one good picture on the wall." (And heard, distantly, her mother's voice, "And, really, if you have just one *good* picture you don't need. . ." Need what? Flowers, was it? Beds? Betsy?)

The woman next to her was thinking gravely. "You remember the street?" she asked hopefully at last.

"Downtown, I'm sure. Because of the stairs."

"Well," the woman said. "I *do* know," she went on at last, "that some people we knew once—not friends, of course, not anyone I *knew*, not the *sort* of people—"

She gestured with a small dismissal, and Betsy said eagerly, "I know lots of people like that, yes."

"*They* had, these people, a place over on . . . let me see; it was Tenth because when we came out we went directly . . . no, no, I'm a liar. Sixteenth, I'm positive. Middle of the block."

"Middle of the block," said Betsy. "Could you see the river?"

"The reason I remember it, now you mention it," the woman said, "because of course I never went *back,* not really knowing the people and it was just a party, and all, was because they had a picture they thought a lot of. Painter, *he* was."

"Oh," said Betsy. "No, she's not a painter, my mother."

"Oh, not *professional*," said the woman. "Not *bohemian*. I'm sure I wouldn't send you any place you shouldn't go. After all," and she folded her arms and turned her face firmly to the window.

"I didn't mean that at all, I'm sorry," Betsy said. "I just meant it didn't sound like the right place."

"Well, you *did* say a picture," the woman said.

"You see, it's my mother," Betsy explained again. "She's waiting for me to come after a long time."

"You get off here," said the woman, with finality.

"Thank you," said Betsy, rising. "And thank you for telling me where to go."

"No need to mention me when you get there," said the woman. "They probably don't even remember my name."

The street was not one to be joyfully remembered; she looked eagerly at things which would, unmolested, tend to be permanent—the view down to the end, down to the narrow spot where it disappeared, presumably into the river, but the long sight of it was not prettier than the nearer view, and the sidewalk beneath her feet was not inscribed in the cement ELIZABETH LOVES BETSY and the dirty fence on her left bore no recognizable carving and even the arrow in chalk and the scrawl "go this way" indicated only a low gate with "clubhowse" uncertainly inscribed over it. Not my club, Betsy thought, my mother's not *there*, anyway, and that's at least one place ruled out. Middle of the block, she said, middle of the block, view of the river, and not a place marked ROOMS, Dressmaker, Canaries for Sale, Medium. Across the street was a white stone apartment house, crowding defensively against its neighbors advertising ROOMS, and Betsy crossed the street to get to it; it announced its number and the sizes of its apartments in bold emphatic placards, but said nothing about whether or not there were stairs, and Betsy, wondering at which point now the sudden recollection might begin, went hurriedly down the path of the canopy and up the one shallow step—perhaps only ostentation, since directly inside there was another step going down the same distance—and into the small foyer, where there was a mural of orange fish against a black sea. However live the fish may have been when the mural was painted, they were long dead now, floating miserably upon the painted surface of their water, fins dragging; perhaps at one point they might have been saved, when, gasping for breath, they first came to the surface and turned their agonized suffocating eyes upon the casual guest entering the foyer of the apartment house; a little fresh water, a kindly look, might have revived the painted fish and made the visitor welcome in the dim light. The fish had died, however, and there was a stout woman in a plaid cotton dress sitting at a table, searching eagerly for gentility; "You want a room, I guess?" the woman said, leaning forward against the table and resting herself heavily upon her magazine, and the reassuring weight of her bosom upon the table recollected her, because she sat back and said, "May I ask whom you are looking for?"

"My mother," Betsy said.

"She's *here?*" Again the woman recollected herself, and sat back. "Name, please?"

"My name is Betsy, but I'm looking for my mother. Is she here?"

"I couldn't say, dear. What apartment you want?"

"I'm not sure. But it has pink walls and a view of the river, and one good picture, because if you have one good picture you don't need . . ." Betsy stopped, but the woman could not help; she was staring absently at an advertisement in her magazine which promised to teach her engineering in six weeks. "Pink walls?" the woman said when Betsy stopped.

"And a view of the river."

The woman glanced up, then sideways, then down. "Makes you think you got a mother *here?*" she asked. "Anybody's mother's *here, I* certainly don't know it."

"But she said—"

"Pink walls," said the woman irritably, in some obscure impatience with a world where there could be pink walls, and she spent her days seeing orange fish on a black sea; "one of those decorators," she added, in ultimate condemnation.

"Then my mother's not here?" asked Betsy despondently.

"No," said the woman, "she's not. Poor kid. Lost your mommy, have you?" She turned the pages of her magazine quickly as though looking up a reference, and said, "You run along, now, you hear me?"

Betsy turned obediently and went past the dead fish again, and as she came to the step up which would correspond to the step down outside, she heard the woman saying with disgust, "Always want something you haven't got. Pink walls!"

Outside, she started off again down the street. There did not seem to be any other possible place to look, and Betsy gave up almost immediately the idea of trying from door to door, and then, when she saw someone coming down the street toward her, indistinct in the shadows of the buildings, she thought it would surely do no harm to ask, and when they took word back to her mother they could report that Betsy was really trying hard.

"Excuse me," she said, reaching out to touch the man on the arm, "but have you seen my mother? Mrs. Richmond?"

"Hello," he said.

"Robin?" said Betsy, and then, again, "Robin?" and then turned and ran, and heard him laughing behind her, as one whose hunting is leisurely, his quarry sure; then she came to lights and safety.

"Give me Doctor Wright, please. I must speak to the doctor, hurry, please."

"Who?"

"Please, I'm on a public telephone and I've got to hurry. Please, Doctor Wright. Tell him it's Beth."

"Who you want?"

"Please, the doctor. Doctor Wright."

"You got the wrong number, lady."

"Sure I got the wrong number, you silly fool. You think *I'm* crazy?"

Safely back in the hotel, she was still both frightened and angry, and yet did not dare indulge herself in either fear or anger, since both used up vital stores of control. She was angry at Beth for getting slyly to a phone and nearly ruining them all; she was afraid of the man who said he was Robin and yet let her run away. Mostly, in the hotel, she was angry and afraid of that doctor who stayed around watching for people in trouble, so he might offer to buy them lunches, and then betray them; it was not going to be safe, Betsy reminded herself bitterly, to trust anyone at all. She sat down heavily in the chair by the desk, the door of her room soundly locked and the key back in her pocketbook, and tried hard to think. Things were not going well, not at all as well as they had gone at first. She had done something wrong, obviously, and she was fairly sure that it had been her talking to the doctor at lunch (had he not promised to be a friend during the brief moment when Lizzie got out; did he not mean, therefore to be a friend to *Lizzie?*); fortunately, Robin's presence had warned her in time against the neighborhood she had visited tonight; her mother was not there. Therefore, although she had surely grieved her mother, she was not abandoned altogether; she must only be more careful with the next clue and not risk running directly into Robin's arms. ("Darling Robin," she said aloud, "call me Lisbeth.") Then, when she turned cold and suddenly trembling, she saw clearly that everything was not all right; something had happened.

She thought immediately that she had been caught, and then realized that she was alone still, with the first light of morning coming over the buildings across the street. Suddenly, wildly she ran at the door, pulling at it frantically to make sure it was locked, and almost cried with relief when she found it secure; she didn't get away, then, Betsy thought, and then wondered, Who?

It was still almost too dark to see in the room; when Betsy turned on the light next to the door, her hands still trembling so that it was difficult for her to touch the little switch, she saw first of all Lizzie's suitcase lying open in the middle of the floor. "So she found the suitcase," Betsy said aloud, and then, cold and still, said into the continuing silence of the room, "Lizzie! Where are you?" But there was no answer.

There were tears on her cheeks, Lizzie's tears again, and Betsy brushed them away irritably, thinking, the messy messy *sloppy* thing, can't she leave my stuff alone? The suitcase was half-packed, clothes thrown in wildly, and, as though Lizzie had given up despairingly in the middle of packing, other clothes were strewn around the room, torn and scattered. Lizzie's own best white blouse lay over the end of the bed, collar ripped off and buttons hanging by threads, and Betsy, looking slowly around the room, saw with fear the sheets pulled from the bed and cut with the nail scissors, the pillow slashed open, the paper from the desk tossed wildly in a scattered heap, as though swept off altogether by an arm wild with fury; the curtains were pulled down and lay on the floor, the shades pulled askew, and even one corner of the rug had been tugged aside and turned back on itself; "Don't be afraid," Betsy whispered, "Betsy is my darling, my darling." She pressed hard against the wall, feeling still the weakness of panic, and knowing that if she yielded only the smallest particle of her strength she was gone again; she could not afford anger or fear or despair; she could not waste a moment to look behind her. "I am Betsy Richmond," she whispered, "my mother's name is Elizabeth Richmond . . ."

Gradually she became quieter. The light in the room grew, coming stronger over the tops of the buildings, and she thought of the man on the ledge and was heartened. At last she stood away from the wall, sighing deeply like a child who has finished crying, and walked around the room slowly, thinking, wouldn't you think she'd have more respect for other people's things? She picked up a stocking, hacked with the scissors and tied into knots, and then laughed suddenly. Why, Betsy thought, she's learning from *me;* this is *my* kind of thing, not hers, and she's even with me now for spoiling that letter of hers. And she's got more life than she ever had before, Betsy thought, laughing still, as she took up the soft white blouse ripped apart; the picture of Elizabeth's tired hands pulling wildly at the weak seams of the blouse caught Betsy suddenly as irresistibly funny, and she fell back onto the bed and rolled in helpless laughter. Poor baby, she thought, working so hard to spoil my things, poor frantic baby. Her face and hair were full of feathers from the torn pillow, and as her laughter eased, she found that she could blow a feather into the air again and again, catching it each time as it fell; then, luckily, the sunlight touched her face, luckily because of course she still had a great deal of work to do about finding her mother, and could not afford to lie on a bed playing games with feathers. She rose, and looked at herself in the mirror with distaste. Her clothes had certainly suffered during the night; they were covered with feathers and disarranged, and for a minute she wondered that they too had not been cut and torn, before she realized that of course Lizzie had been planning to escape, and in these clothes. She wondered idly if Lizzie had attacked the room desperately because she had tried to escape and could not find the doorkey, or if she had destroyed the room first, vengefully, planning to escape afterward, and been caught by exhaustion; "Poor silly baby," Betsy said again, and, whistling, began a hunt for any piece of her comb so that she might smooth her hair. Then, suddenly, one hand on the suitcase, she turned as cold and sick and frightened as she had ever been. The big dictionary she had brought with her, so that she might check spelling and various usable words, was lying just inside the suitcase, its binding torn off, its pages pulled out and crumpled, its millions of good, practical, helpful words hopelessly destroyed.

"Lizzie," Betsy said aloud, backing off, "but Lizzie wouldn't ever have done anything to her own *book,* not to her own good book—"

Suddenly, madly, she took up the book, and rising and turning, threw it as hard as she could at the mirror. "There," she said out loud, through the crash, "that'll show you I'm *still* worse than you are, who*ever* you are!"

Sometime later, back on the bed playing her game with the feather, she was quieter again. This only meant, she reasoned, that she had less time than she had thought. She must quite simply get to her mother just as quickly as possible.

It was by then nearly noon, and she could not remember whether or how she had had dinner the evening before. She turned her back resolutely on the icy little reminders that there seemed to be a good deal of time unaccounted for, all around; why, for instance, had it been afternoon when she left the lunch table, and night when she returned after meeting Robin? She thought she had probably not had dinner, because she was now so extremely hungry, and she dwelt with gratitude upon her hunger, which was surely a healthy and a normal feeling, and not at all dangerous, except that it entailed going out of her hotel room. At last she reasoned shrewdly that if the doctor was still watching for her downstairs he had to stop sometime to eat, too, and if he stopped to eat his lunch or his dinner he would put someone else to watching her, and whoever he got to watch her would have to have dinner or lunch, too, so she would be, to all effects, invisible, if she was only having dinner or lunch, and might come and go as she pleased. Thinking of the little cakes, she moved hastily to the shattered mirror and arranged her hair and then, taking her pocketbook—thankful that because she had Aunt-Morgen-ishly hidden it on the closet shelf, it had escaped the ruin of the room—she unlocked the door of the room and locked it again, leaving the chaos inside, and dropped the libertine key into Elizabeth's chaste pocketbook and went down the hall to the elevator. When she came into the dining room she walked proudly, and even stopped for a minute inside the door to consider and choose a particular table; she sat down with perfect ease, and ordered herself a glass of sherry.

"But then why did Robin run away?" he asked.

"Because I said I'd tell my mother what we did." She looked up, dumfounded, fork in hand; "no," she whispered, staring fearfully, "no," she said, and then, just like Elizabeth, "why?" looking from him to her plate to her fork to the pastries, "why are you talking to me?" she said.

"Please," he said, half-rising, "please, it's all right, Bess, really—"

"Bess?" she said. *"Bess?"*

———

Now she knew concretely that she had almost no time; she had wasted so many minutes, looking out of windows and gloating over cakes, and they were close behind her now, the doctor in the dining room and Aunt Morgen and perhaps even the betraying bus driver, and the whole city still to search for her mother. Perhaps, she thought, stopping in her flight to stand for a minute in the half darkness apart from the hotel entrance, perhaps if I just stand here she might come. Mother, she said silently at the people going past, mother, come and find me; I'm lost and I'm tired and I'm afraid, come and find your baby, please?

"My dear child," he said, coming silently up behind her, "do come back inside; I promise you I only want—"

"It's Robin," she said, and ran again, going in and out between people, not wondering if they saw her or thought she was strange, listening only to hear if he was following her. She came to a corner and turned, and went into a lighted doorway into an endless bright store; "Too late, closing," a girl said to her, just inside, and she turned without speaking and ran out another doorway into another street and down the street and on until she saw a crowd ahead and thought, "He's in there, waiting," and turned and ran back down the street and turned at the corner and stopped.

"How can he find me?" she thought, reasonably at last. "He doesn't even know my name." She breathed deeply, standing against the wall of a building. This corner was darker and there were fewer people passing, going always toward the lights beyond; for a few minutes she watched the street light turn red and green and red and green, and then she thought no sense wasting any *more* time, no one could ever find me here, and she laughed that she still had her pocketbook, because all the time the strap had been firmly hooked over her elbow.

"Where is a bus?" she asked a man passing by, and the man stopped, and thought, and then said, "Bus to where, miss?"

"I don't care," she said.

"Well," the man said, "if you don't *care*, why take a bus? Why not walk?"

"I don't know," she said. "Where are *you* going?"

"I'm going over across town about three blocks," he said. "I'm going to get my wife a birthday present, a necklace."

"Can I come? My mother likes necklaces and things like that."

"Come along," he said. "You can help me pick it out. She likes," he went on, as Betsy walked along beside him, "she likes jewelry, but not ordinary jewelry. Not the kind you get just *any*where. Unusual stuff."

"That's the best kind," Betsy said. "Of course, almost anything is unusual if you're not used to it."

"Well, that's what I mean," the man said. "There's this little shop I know about, and of course *she* doesn't. So it's got to be a surprise."

"I'm sure she'll like it very much," Betsy said. "Coming from you, that is."

"Well, I guess she will," the man said. "She likes just about everything I pick out, because of course I always look for unusual things."

"Of course I do too," Betsy said. "Right now, I'm looking for my mother and being new here I don't know what's unusual or not, but my mother will know. She lives here somewhere."

"It's a pretty good town," the man said, consideringly. "Of course you have to live here to appreciate it."

"I'm going to live with my mother when I find her," Betsy said.

"She live in Brooklyn?"

"Probably," Betsy said doubtfully.

"How're you going to *find* her?" the man asked.

"Well," Betsy said, "you're looking for something, and I'm looking for my mother, and so if I go along with you maybe I'll find my mother."

"*My* mother now," the man said, "you could find *her* any time."

"Well, you see, I came here to meet my mother and I just haven't gotten to her yet. It just takes looking. Does your wife live in Brooklyn?"

"No," the man said, surprised. "She lives with me."

"Where do you live?"

"Uptown." He stopped, and looked at her searchingly. "You all right, kid?" he asked.

"Of course," Betsy said. "Why?"

"Thinking I lived in Brooklyn," the man said, going on. "At this time of night."

"Does your wife," Betsy asked, hurrying to catch up with him again, "know you're getting her a birthday present?"

"Sure," the man said. "Only she doesn't know where, you see."

"How about a cake?" Betsy asked. "She ought to have a cake, with 'Happy Birthday' and candles."

"Golly," the man said, stopping again. "Golly. Let's see," he said. "You figure a cake costs—what? Say, sixty cents?"

"Just about that, I guess," Betsy said.

"And then you got to have candles," the man said. "Now, let's think this over. You say candles cost maybe a dime? And the cake sixty? Because then you got to get a thing says 'Happy Birthday' and that's maybe twenty-nine cents, you find a five and ten open if you *can*. So there goes another buck. So the necklace costs—"

"*I* know," Betsy said. "*I* get the cake and all. *You* get the necklace. Then it's all right. Cake from me, necklace from you."

"Right," the man said. "Cake from you, necklace from me. You say chocolate, maybe? Mocha?"

"I like chocolate," Betsy said. "Get a nice card, too, and tell her it's from me." She stopped under a street light and gave him a handful of change from her pocketbook. "Because," she pointed out, "if you're going uptown or to Brooklyn it's no help to me anyway, because my mother's the other direction. But thank you very much anyway."

"Right," the man said. "Cake from you," he went on, worried, "necklace from me. But listen—" he called, as Betsy turned to go the other way, "who'll I say? On the card and all?"

"Tell her it's from Betsy, with my love."

"Right," the man said. And as Betsy hurried down a side-street she heard him calling, "Hey—thanks."

"Many happy returns," she called back, and went on her way. Although she had very little hope of finding her mother so soon, she was glad she had remembered the cake anyway. We always have cakes on birthdays, she thought; my mother would be disappointed if I forgot; my name is Betsy Richmond and my mother's name is . . . She stopped short and laughed aloud; things were good again at last.

"I beg your pardon," she said, stepping out among the people passing; she took hold of the arm of a woman going by alone and said "I beg your pardon" again.

"Well," said the woman good-humoredly, "if you're not a cop, you can beg my pardon and get away with it. Something you want?"

"Do you know someone named Elizabeth Richmond? Where she lives, I mean?"

"Richmond? No. Why," the woman asked, peering at Betsy, "you looking for her?"

"It's my mother. I'm to meet her, and I've forgotten where she lives."

"Whyn't you look in a phone book? Under R, for instance?"

"I didn't think of that," said Betsy blankly.

The woman laughed. "You kids," she said, and went on.

It was so easy Betsy was almost afraid. She walked down to the corner to a lighted drugstore, went inside and directly back to a rack where the phone books were piled; it was too easy, she thought dubiously, not willing to touch the pages, it was a trap; but how could she ever look at her mother and say she had taken so long because she thought it was a trap? Could people afford to be afraid if they were going to their mothers? Why would her mother want to make a trap for her Betsy who was her darling?

RICHMOND, ELIZABETH. It stood out from the page, blackly, and then, below it, RICHMOND, ELIZABETH, and below that, RICHMOND, ELIZABETH, and, again, RICHMOND, ELIZABETH. Who, Betsy thought, staring, who? My mother's name. . .

She turned hastily away from the telephone books and then told herself sternly no, no traps, and turned back again, and put her finger down on the page. Silly, she thought, lots of people have the same name. *I* have the same name. And anyway it's the *place* I want, I already *know* my mother's *name*. So find an address, and it's somewhere near Sixteenth, she said, and anyway how many people are having birthdays tonight? It's west of the bus, I know *that,* and you can see the river, and I'll just be careful not to tell anyone where I'm going because of traps.

One of the addresses said West Eighteenth, and that seemed good, and so did West Twelfth, and the others were East, and one of them was a hundred and something, which seemed fairly uptown, so that narrowed it down to two, and *now,* Betsy thought triumphantly, things are getting very very good, because now I've got the best clue of all, and I can go right there and maybe even be in time for the candles.

When she came out of the bright drugstore into the darker street she realized that it had really gotten quite late, and she did not dare look for a bus, with so little time; she got, instead, into a taxi, and told him West Eighteenth Street. Her time was growing shorter; she felt the minutes pulling at her, and when she looked out of the taxi window at the lights outside she felt them surge sickeningly against her, and had to hold tight to keep her eyes from blurring and she wanted acutely not to breathe. Just a little while more, she whispered, just a little while more, Betsy is my darling. The taxi let her off at the corner of Fifth and Eighteenth, and the driver showed her which way to start. She hurried, because it was better, walking, and the streets were almost empty. I said I'd do it and I will, she whispered, I said I'd do it and I will, *my* mother is waiting for me and the rest of you will die.

She could not remember at all whether the first address had been twelve or a hundred and twelve or twelve squared or a hundred and twenty-one; twelve seemed to be a shop and as she looked into the darkened windows, going by, she saw that it might be a dress shop and, although she could not read the name darkly on the window, she knew that it must be Abigail's and she knew she was right, at last; here I come, she whispered, I am coming and my name is Betsy . . . It must be a hundred and twelve or a hundred and twenty-one; they were almost across the street from one another and she stopped and looked at the lights of a hundred and twelve and thought, here it is, this is it.

No fish here, she thought, entering, and wondered with surprise why it should seem important not to have fish painted on the walls. "Excuse me," she said, putting her face close to the little barred window which seemed so absurdly small for her mother to get through, "I'd like to find Mrs. Richmond. Elizabeth Richmond."

"Not here."

"But I'm sure this was the address. Do your rooms have a view of the river?"

"Naturally, miss. *All* our rooms—"

"Then she might be using her other name. Try under Jones."

"Not here."

"But I'm sure—"

"Try over across the way."

Of course, she thought; it was the place with the fish after all, they probably just pretend to see the river. She crossed the street, setting her back firmly to the useless apartment house, and came into another lobby; no fish *here,* she thought with satisfaction. "I'm looking for my mother," she said, standing with her knees tight against the desk in the lobby; the lady behind the desk had a pink dress on and of course that was a very *very* good sign. "My mother," she explained.

"Name?"

"Richmond. Elizabeth Richmond. Or maybe Elizabeth Jones."

"Make up your mind, which."

"She'd be up there now, getting ready; we were going to have a party because it's her birthday."

"No noise allowed after ten P.M. No parties any time."

"Just for our birthday celebration. Just my mother and me and I'm going to buy her a necklace."

"No parties here. Try somewhere else."

"But my mother—"

"Try over across the way."

She went out proudly, because she was ashamed at having been misled into talking to strangers about her mother and giving both these people her mother's name; what would the man on the ledge think of her if he knew she was going around telling people where her mother lived? Here she was, so close to her mother, and she could have spoiled it all right then by telling the fish; "I beg your pardon," she said, and took the arm of a lady passing by, "you're not my mother, are you?"

"Well, *really*," said the lady, and then laughed. "Your error," she said. "Excuse it, please."

"Richmond," she said. "Elizabeth Richmond."

The woman turned, and scowled. "Her calls herself Lili?" she demanded. "Lili?"

"Maybe." Betsy tried to draw away, but the woman held her tight. "If that's your mother, young lady," she said, "and I'm not saying it *isn't*, you're the one to know, after all, but if *that's* your *mother*, I'd be ashamed to say so, and that's final."

"Richmond," Betsy said.

The woman nodded, keeping hold of Betsy's arm. "And that's the one," she said, nodding, "and I'd be ashamed if it wasn't that *I* had nothing to be ashamed of in all of it, and doing my share and pulling my weight and here all the time he was after *her*, see? And coming to me with a straight face, and me not even knowing, what I mean, unless you got a suspicious turn of mind you don't *think* about that kind of thing."

"Robin," Betsy said. "I already know about Robin."

"Another one, is it? But of course sooner or later they're going to find out, what I mean. What I mean, *some*thing's going to happen, you can't stay a dope forever. So when he came to me there I was and he said hello same as usual and me—what I mean, I wasn't letting on at first, see?—I said hello and then he says what's wrong and I don't answer and he says it again, like this, 'Hey, what's wrong?' and then, what I mean, I let him have it. You think I'm a dope, I said to him, you think I'm going to stand for this thing forever, you think I'm going to wait and wait and wait and wait and wait and you after *her* all the time? It isn't the money, I told him straight out, it isn't the money—"

"It was Robin," Betsy cried out, pushing against the woman, "it wasn't anybody except Robin, I *know*."

"Maybe you *do* know, too," said the woman with hatred,

holding Betsy off to look at her, "maybe you *do* know all about it, and I for one wouldn't be surprised, being well aware that I was the *last* to know, so he says what are you talking about—innocent, see?—and I said how long you think I'm going to wait and wait and wait and wait and wait for *you?* People are talking already, I said, and I guess I'm the last to know. You think I'm crazy? I asked him right out. So then don't you think he had the gall to admit it? And *tell* me? I was so mad I couldn't even *cry* and me, I cry when I'm mad, whenever I'm real mad I can't help it, you know what I mean? And so he says she's nice. What do you mean, I ask him, nice? You mean nice? What's a nice girl got to do with you? I asked him right out."

"Not Robin," Betsy said forlornly. "I'm a nice girl, aren't I?" She caught her breath and said tightly, "You wouldn't let me go around Robin again?"

"Carnal," the woman said with satisfaction. "Carnal desires, and that's what you call *nice!* And, what I mean, can you take that kind of thing forever? So I came right out with it and I told him, either her or me, I said, and you can make up your mind while I stand right here waiting, either her or me. I mean I wasn't going to make any kind of a fuss, if he wanted her, she was what he got, and if he wanted me, all he had to do was prove it. So I came right out with it, see, I never liked beating around the bush and I wasn't going to give him any satisfaction, see, and any chance to say I tried to hold him when he wanted to go, you know, if he wanted to waste his carnal desires with her he could go ahead with my blessing. Because it had gotten to that point, see, where it was either her or me."

"Where is she?" said Betsy.

"Halfway down the block. See that light, there? Likely," said the woman, whom Betsy now perceived to be Aunt Morgen, "you'll find them together."

Now, she thought, striding greatly down the street, now I am really very angry with this mother of mine, hiding away with Robin and trying to keep me from finding Robin all this time, and all I ever wanted was to be happy and it was lucky Aunt

Morgen happened to tell me, because otherwise they'd just keep on getting away with it, and pretending it was her birthday all the time. No fish here, she noticed, coming up the low step which compensated for itself by going immediately down again; lucky for *them;* "I want my mother, please," she said to the man at the desk just inside. "They'll be trying to hide."

"Your *mother?*"

"They probably haven't been here very long. They wanted to be all by themselves, and hide. But she's my mother."

The man at the desk smiled. "The rose room?" he suggested significantly.

"Yes," said Betsy, "the rose room."

"Miss Williams," said the man, leaning back in his chair to speak to the girl at the telephone switchboard. "Anyone in, in 372?"

"I'll check, Mr. Arden. That would be our rose room?"

"I believe so, Miss Williams. This young lady is inquiring."

"Number 372 is busy, Mr. Arden. There must be someone there, since they're using the phone. In our rose room, Mr. Arden."

"The rose room," said Mr. Arden tenderly. "Miss Williams, did the management send up champagne?"

"I'll check, Mr. Arden. Champagne and a rose corsage. Compliments and congratulations. This morning, Mr. Arden."

"Splendid, Miss Williams. And now this young lady is inquiring." He turned and smiled on Betsy. "A little ceremony," he explained. "Compliments of the establishment. The . . ." he hesitated. "The *personal* touch," he said, and blushed visibly.

"Can I go right there?" Betsy asked.

"Are you expected?" he asked in return, raising his eyebrows.

"Of course," Betsy said. "They're waiting for me."

"Well," said Mr. Arden, and turned one hand eloquently. "Are you *sure?*"

"Of course," said Betsy. "And I'm late now."

Mr. Arden bowed. "Miss Williams," he said, "take the young lady up to our rose room."

"Certainly, Mr. Arden. Will you come with me, please, miss?"

There were no fish painted on the walls of the elevator and that was a very *very* good sign, and the walls upstairs were pale green and not at all like sea water, even though pale green was a color for deepness and going down and losing and fading and sinking and failing; "Our rose room is very popular," Miss Williams said walking softly as they left the elevator. "The management *invariably* sends up champagne and a corsage of roses for the bride. Compliments of the hotel, of course. Such a charming custom."

"They'd be wanting to hide," Betsy said.

"Right down here. Last room on the left. Privacy, you know." Miss Williams giggled, but very softly.

"Here?"

"No, no," said Miss Williams. "Let *me* knock, if you please." She giggled again. "Always knock *twice* on the door of our rose room," she said, and giggled.

"Someone said to come in," Betsy said.

"Good evening," Miss Williams said, opening the door. "Here's a young lady you were waiting for, Mr. Harris."

"Good evening, Betsy," said Robin, grinning hideously from across the room.

"No, no," said Betsy, stumbling back against Miss Williams, "not *this* one, not Robin again?"

"I beg your pardon?" said Miss Williams, staring, "I *beg* your *pardon?*"

"I won't let you, not ever any more," Betsy said to Robin, "and neither will my mother." She turned and struggled violently past Miss Williams in the doorway, broke free, and ran. "I'm *terribly* sorry, Mr. Harris," Miss Williams said behind her, "in our rose room . . . I didn't dream . . ."

"It's perfectly all right," he said. "A mistake of some kind."

And she could hear him after her, down the hall and down the stairs, praying not to stumble, not Robin again, it wasn't fair, not after all she'd done, not after all she'd tried, not Robin again, it wasn't fair, no one could do *that* again, praying to move quickly enough, to be safely out of it and away before he could touch her, to be safely out of it; "Robin," she said, "Robin darling, call me Lisbeth, Lisbeth"; was he following? To be out of the light and invisible, to be easily around the corner and gone, to lose him long behind . . . was he below? In the doorway? Waiting grinning with his arms wide to catch her, could she go any faster? There was the end of the stairway ahead, and the door leading out, and she threw herself against the opening and it opened and there he was, as always, waiting for her always, and she said "No, no more, *please*," and went under his hand and sobbed and hurried for the door; "Thief," someone called in a loud voice, and someone else cried, "Help?" and beside her she heard him laughing as she hurried and she put her arms up to hide her face and ran and nearly stumbled on the low low step which went up and down; there were lights, and she opened her eyes a little and never dared to look behind her because she heard him coming.

"Robin," she said, "Robin, call me Lisbeth, Lisbeth, call me Lisbeth, Robin darling, call me Lisbeth." And fell, and fell, and could not be caught, and fell.

She was in the hotel room, and trying to pack into her suitcase what fragments of clothing seemed worth taking with her. She had ripped and torn at the clothes and the curtains and the bedpillows because she was angry, but now she had the pocketbook and the key, and felt only a pressing need for hurry, because—and she knew clearly where her great danger lay—Betsy might come back at any moment. It was on the desk, among the broken pens and spilled ink, that she discovered the highly important paper which she knew was to be hidden among her things and delivered to someone as yet unidentified. Although she did not understand how anything of vast importance could be written on such a tiny slip, she knew perfectly that it must not fall into Betsy's hands; she had the swift impression that it was an artificially valuable thing, like the thimble in hide-the-thimble or the handkerchief in drop-the-handkerchief, of value only so long as the game went on, and then of interest to no one. Besides, she could not read it. It resembled the hundreds of small papers which come into people's hands every day, enclosed in packages of laundry, for instance, recommending dry-cleaning of curtains for the spring, or the labels which certify that Easter eggs are pure, or the slip of paper enclosed in the theatre program pointing out that there was an inadvertent mistake on page twelve, where Miss Somebody's name had been mistakenly rendered as Miss Something Else; at any rate, she could not read it.

She had no idea who had written it, or why, or who it was supposed to be given to, or how, or when, but she put it into her pocketbook anyway, since if Betsy was not to see it that in itself was sufficient reason for her to conceal it and make every effort to see that it was properly delivered. She wasted precious time attempting to read it, and, puzzling, could only decide that it seemed to contain numbers of some kind, and words which, while clear and distinct to any passing glance, turned into meaningless markings when she brought it close enough to read. Because she was so sure of its desperate importance she decided to pin the paper into the money in her wallet; she knew she would not take out a bill to pay for candy or magazines or the taxi to the bus station without considering very carefully, and so ran no chance of losing the little paper.

There was not much she could find to put in her suitcase. It was irritating to reflect that if Betsy had been sensible and given up the key without trouble none of this would have happened and her good clothes, which, after all, cost money, need not have been ruined, but Betsy was a dangerous, scheming girl, and was, besides, a wastrel; consider, for one thing, this hotel room, which must surely have been an unnecessary expense and would have to be paid for with other people's money. She badly wanted to be paid up and out of the hotel before the hotel people found out about the damage to the room; it had been Betsy's fault, after all, and they would almost certainly expect her to pay as well for the mirror which Betsy had broken.

When she had packed the suitcase with everything she thought could be mended, or patched together, or used for something else, she snapped the suitcase shut and stood up to look around the room for anything she might have overlooked. Then, moving quickly, she slipped into her coat and took up her pocketbook and the suitcase. Then she stopped and stood perfectly still; Betsy was coming back.

There was no time now for the suitcase, and she dropped it and scrambled the key out of her pocketbook and ran for the door. Just as she touched the key to the keyhole Betsy found her and with a furious shout snatched at her hand and bit it until she dropped the key and Betsy grabbed for it as it fell. If Betsy once got a hand on the key there was no hope of escape; wildly, she got a hand in Betsy's hair and pulled, and dragged her back away from the key, and it lay there on the floor while both of them, panting, stood back and waited for one another like two cats circling. Then, with unbelievable speed, Betsy went for the key again, the tips of her fingers just touching it, and she put her foot down hard on Betsy's hand and held it there.

Nothing could pain Betsy, she knew; no kind of hurt could register on that black mind, and so she could only try to over-power Betsy physically, and force her down; with quiet slow strength she put her hand almost gently around Betsy's throat and tightened her fingers as slowly and surely as she could; she made no sound, because she needed all her breath, but Betsy screamed, and gasped, and then ripped at her hand with sharp, cutting nails, and kicked out, and screamed again, sinking; the heel of Betsy's shoe caught in the light cord and brought the lamp smashing down; the noise will bring someone, she thought. She felt Betsy's nails rake the side of her face, and then Betsy called out "Mother!" and was vanquished.

She took her hand from Betsy's throat and, sobbing for breath, rolled over on the floor and got the key in her hands. Then, moving slowly and with pain, she stood up, got the key into the door, and turned it.

"Well," said the nurse with great enthusiasm, "you *have* had quite a sleep. Feeling all chipper now?"

Many rooms have white walls and many beds have white covers, but only hospitals have white walls and white covers

and a bed table with a glass of water and a glass bent straw
and nurses who speak with quite that quality of enthusiasm;
"Where?" she said, and it hurt her achingly to talk.

"Mustn't chatter," said the nurse, holding up a playful finger.
"We've got a pretty sore throat there, haven't we? But we're not
going to think about it at all; we're going to have a nice wash-up
and then Doctor will be here and give it a look-see. And we're
not going to talk and we're not going to get excited and mostly
we're not going to think about what happened, because after all
it was pretty horrid, wasn't it? Let's just turn our head a little,
so I can go over those scratches on your cheek without hurting.
Now." The nurse stood back and beamed with wholehearted
simplicity, "Soon be just as pretty as ever," she said gaily.

"Where?"

"Where what? You do say the *silliest* things." The nurse
laughed, and held up her finger again. "We're going to be in
trouble," she said, "if Doctor comes in and finds us talking.
And won't he be pleased to see how nice we look today, after
the way we looked yesterday! And I must *say* that we were a
pretty smart girl to be carrying around that little paper, we
were indeed." She turned, and almost curtsied, her jolly air re-
placed immediately by one of extreme gravity. "Good morning, Doctor," she said.

"Good morning. Good morning, Miss Richmond. How's
the throat this morning?"

"Hurts."

"I imagine it does," said the doctor. He hesitated, and then
went on, "I don't want you to talk any more than you have to,
but I'd like you to try and give me some idea of how it happened. Do you know who tried to choke you?"

"No one."

"Miss Richmond," said the doctor, "someone has had a
hand around your throat, making those violent bruises. Do
you mean that you don't know who did it?"

"She scratched me."

"Who?"

"Doctor," said the nurse, coming forward in an ardent little
rush, "Miss Richmond's doctor is here, just outside."

"Bring him in, by all means. Miss Richmond, thanks to the memo we found in your pocketbook, we have been able to locate your aunt and your doctor and get them here quickly." He rose, and went to the door, where she could hear him speaking quietly. "Since last night," she heard him say, and another voice speaking, questioning. "—an eye on her in the hotel," the doctor said.

The nurse came over and looked down on her with vast kindliness. "You've been a lucky girl," said the nurse enigmatically.

"—self-inflicted, but it's impossible that—"

"Aunt Morgen?" she asked the nurse.

"Downstairs," said the nurse. "Came to take her girl home."

The door opened wide, and the doctor came back, with another, smaller man, who walked with small steps and seemed pale and worried. "A paper with my name and address," he was saying as he walked, seemingly in confirmation of what had just been said, and the doctor nodded; they both came and stood looking down at her from the two sides of the bed, and the nurse stepped hastily back. "I wish she could talk more," the doctor said. "She can't seem to tell us who did it."

"I know who did it," the little man said absently; he was looking down at her gravely, and then he reached out and touched the scratches on her face briefly and withdrew his hand. "Poor child," he said. "We were worried about you," he told her.

She looked up at him, perplexed. "Who in sin are you?" she said.

4

DOCTOR WRIGHT

Since I do not anticipate making the history of Elizabeth R. into my life's work—although I can conceive of lives spent on less—I do not think it necessary to enter into as much professional detail in what I now see as the second, and concluding, stage of her treatment at my hands. On the one side, I feel strongly that although the layman cannot be too well instructed in the uses and values of the several therapeutic methods employed, too detailed an examination of such a case as Miss R.'s may in some respects lessen the efficacy of similar treatment in further cases, the patient being already too well familiarized with the slow progressive steps and prepared for them, as it were; on the other side, my own feelings about the case are mixed, and I am most unwilling to complicate my account with unnecessary detail. Moreover, I strongly suspect that readers today (what, still with me, my friend? Our numbers have grown no larger since we last saw eye to eye; literature is—and I insist upon it to you, sir—a diminishing art) will not sit docilely under a description of a piece of work carefully and painstakingly done; with little patience to lavish upon their own performances, they have none for the work of others.

In any case, I shall curtail my presentation of Miss R.'s case, and go as quickly as I can to my conclusion. I believe I may have given my reader the notion that I am not an even-tempered man by nature; few are, in truth, I believe. I was hugely annoyed by Miss R.'s abduction at the hands of Betsy, and hardly less aggravated at being called upon, some three days later, to travel to New York—a spot which I particularly loathe—and by airplane, which is, to my thinking, a mode of travel only slightly less nauseating than riding camelback. I traveled with Miss Jones, the venerable aunt of Miss R., and Miss Jones' company did not materially improve my voyage. She was alternately enormously amused at my discomforts in the airplane, and reproachful over what she deemed my "letting the child escape"—which, since it was I alone who kept Betsy under so long as she did stay, seemed to me both ungrateful and ungratiating; I have, altogether, rarely undertaken a less rewarding journey.

We found our young lady substantially the worse for her holiday. No one knows, even now, the entire story of what had happened to her, and my most astute questioning, since, has not uncovered all the facts, by any means; we knew, of course, from the phone call which told us she was in hospital, that she had been taken unconscious from the floor of a hotel corridor, that she had been beaten, scratched, and half-strangled, and that she seemed to be suffering from what the New York doctors called, with unshakable assurance, partial amnesia. I myself came into her hospital room with some misgivings, having reason to doubt the cordiality of my reception by Betsy, and found upon the bed a girl whom I would unhesitatingly have denounced as an imposter, had I not, in the past, seen the facial changes produced when Elizabeth R. became Beth, and then Betsy. This girl—she impressed me as considerably younger than either Elizabeth or Beth, Betsy of course being physically ageless—seemed slighter, somehow, and almost frail; even allowing for the probable harrowing effect of her miserable days in New York, she did not impress me as a young woman of robust health. She resembled Elizabeth strongly, but her face was sharper and of a more cunning turn; I thought she had a sly look.

At any rate, she and I were strangers. She addressed me civilly enough, but was surprised that I should have come so far to see her, and concluded of her own accord that it was done in duty to her aunt, in whose name she thanked me courteously. Her medical attendant, she further informed me, was Doctor Ryan, and she supposed that if I called at his office upon my return to Owenstown he would be willing to oblige me with any future bulletins with regard to her health, should my interest in her continue so long. She spoke very lamely because of the painful condition of her throat, but we none of us, the attendant physician, the nurse, or myself, had any difficulty whatsoever in determining that Doctor Wright's services were superfluous to the present Miss R.

I confess I felt a momentary pang of sympathy for whoever had gotten a hand around her throat, but bowed in silence and retired with what grace I could muster, amused privately at the chagrin of the hospital doctor, who had summoned me in haste because a slip of paper containing my name and address was found in Miss R.'s pocketbook. I assured Miss Jones that her niece was in most capable hands; then, very willingly, I abandoned Miss R. to her aunt to bring home, and a pleasant trip I wished them both. I myself returned by train, a longer but less unsettling mode of travel, and reached my own office and my good fire with an aching head and a deep desire never to hear more of either Miss R. or her aunt. I felt, not to put too fine a point on it, that Miss Jones would probably be completely satisfied with the girl we had found in New York, that my own Miss R. was gone, probably for good, and that I had undertaken a wild goose chase for nothing more than to be mocked in a hospital room by an impudent girl, and to risk my life in an airplane with her fright of an aunt; I found in myself nothing but a kind of sublime impatience with Miss R. and all her family.

Two things I knew which I do not believe anyone else suspected: that Beth had written the note with my name and address and tucked it into Miss R.'s pocketbook, and that the bruises on Miss R.'s throat were made by the fingers of Betsy; I believe they would have thought me mad in New York had I proposed either as a clue to Miss R.'s condition. I contented myself, therefore, with my anger, and did well with it.

I was not, nevertheless, altogether dumfounded when, two days after her return, Miss R. came to my office; Miss Hartley, of course, announced her only as Miss R., and it was a genuine pleasure to me to find myself greeting Elizabeth who, timid and hesitant as always, sat down as though she thought she had an appointment, and indeed, upon questioning, it developed that she really thought she had. The poor girl knew of nothing that had passed, and assumed, in all innocence, that she was merely continuing her regular series of visits! I was touched, and perhaps a little guilty over my anger with the poor creature, and so it was with great cordiality that I affected to act as though nothing untoward had occurred since our last meeting.

"Have you completely recovered your recent illness, my dear Elizabeth?" I asked her. "You look extremely well." There were still dark bruises on her throat, which she had tried to cover with a silk scarf under her collar, and the scratches on her face had not entirely faded, but there is no doubt but what she looked better than she had the last time I had seen her—or the time before that, for that matter.

"I feel better," she said. "I have been sick a long time, I think."

"You caused your aunt much concern." With a genuine sense of well-being I opened the desk drawer and took out the notebook which I used for recording my conversations with Miss R., and smiled at her rueful face when she saw it. "We have a good deal of time to make up," I told her. "How long has it been since we last talked together?"

"About a week?" She was doubtful.

"It seems to have done you good, at any rate. Now, let us begin with our usual catechism. Headaches?"

"None, except for a slight one a day or so ago, when I woke up from a bad dream."

"I assume," I said, "that since you woke up, you had been asleep, and from that I deduce that your insomnia has not been so troublesome as before?"

"I have been sleeping soundly. Except . . ." She faltered. "Except . . . I have had very bad dreams."

"Indeed? Can you recall anything of them?"

"I was standing," she said reluctantly, "and I was looking at myself. There was a big mirror—it went as high as I could see. And even though I don't want to speak unkindly of anyone I

think it is cruel of Aunt Morgen to lock my door at night. I am
no longer a child, you know."

My eyes were on my notebook, but I heard the curious
change in her voice, and asked, without looking up, "Did you
write my name and address on a slip of paper?"

"You did see it, then?" Her voice was delighted. "I was so
frightened, and I tried to telephone you, because I knew that
you would *always* come to help me, but the man wouldn't call
you to the phone, and I was so frightened."

I looked up at her; it was surely Beth, come to me voluntarily without hypnosis, pale and tired and brutally disfigured
by her scratched face, but my own lovely girl nevertheless. "If
you hadn't written that note," I told her, "we could not have
rescued you."

"Rescued me?" she asked wonderingly.

"I will explain it in good time. Let me only say that you
were most wise to make that note. There are a great many
things I am anxious to discuss with you, but I fear that you are
not entirely well even yet, and I think you should rest." I had
not until now met Beth face to face, and—just as when I first
saw Betsy with her eyes open I recognized suddenly that she
was an independent personality, a being whole and apart from
any other, rather than a mere angry manifestation engendered
solely in my office—I saw that Beth now, looking about her
and drawing herself together, was endeavoring to *form* herself,
as it were; let my reader who is puzzled by my awkward expla-
nations close his eyes for no more than two minutes, and see if
he does not find himself suddenly not a compact human being
at all, but only a consciousness on a sea of sound and touch; it
is only with the eyes open that a corporeal form returns, and
assembles itself firmly around the hard core of sight. This was,
at any rate, my impression of Beth's growing consciousness;
she had been at first no more than a voice and a look, but as
she hardened into an individual the separation between her
and the other personalities grew visibly greater; it was impossible, for instance, to look now at Beth, as I was doing, and
believe her the same person as Elizabeth, who had been sitting

in that chair not ten minutes earlier; except that they wore the same clothes, and their faces, although subtly different, wore the same ugly scratches, they were two entirely different girls. Thus, my growing clumsiness with Beth; I can only say again, helplessly, that there is a world of difference between a wraith-like shadow and a real girl. So, I stumbled and got through my stiff sentences, and made a note which read—I swear it; I have it in my notebook still—"Elizabeth Beth brillig; o borogrove" and then Beth said primly, "Do you know that I have never seen you before, doctor?" and I thought that perhaps my own expression had been fairly fatuous, being accustomed to deal-ing with Beth sightless. I asked her if she felt well enough after all, to talk with me for a while, and she was eager to stay, add-ing that Aunt Morgen was "so cross all the time now."

I was not very much surprised at that, to be sure, and asked her what her aunt thought of her continuing to visit my office.

"She said I could come," Beth said. "When I go out she wants to know where I am going and when I am coming back, as though I were a baby still."

I wondered at this; from what I had seen of Aunt I would have expected her to keep her runaway niece chained to the bedpost, but I suppose that actually, short of a legitimate con-finement in an institution, she could hardly endeavor to keep her niece under constant supervision; she knew only the hospi-tal's diagnosis of "amnesia" and so imagined, I suppose, that her niece had forgotten that she ran away, and why, and might be assumed to be fairly safe from another attempt. I sighed, and Beth said quickly, "It is *you* who are tired, and I have stayed too long."

"No, no indeed," I said. "I am only perplexed."

"I know," she said. "You are worried about me, and won-dering over my health, and hoping I will be well." She thought. "Are you going to put me to sleep?" she asked.

I most certainly did not want to attempt hypnosis; indeed, I wanted only to send her home until I might prepare myself more adequately for returning to her case. But she had come to me faithfully, and I was still her physician. "I shall," I said steadily. "If you wish it, we shall resume our regular treatments now."

Perhaps because she was excited she was most difficult to subdue into a deep hypnotic slumber this afternoon; with her eyes closed and lying back in her chair she more nearly resembled the Beth I remembered, the girl who had once been only R2! I had never before put Beth under further hypnosis without arriving at Betsy, and perhaps that thought, too, delayed our achievement of her hypnotic trance; time after time she would open her eyes and smile at me and I, smiling back, would begin again, patiently. At last her eyes closed and she began to breathe evenly and I, hardly daring to speak above a whisper, said, "What is your name?"

Her eyes snapped open, and she scowled at me. "Monster," she said, the scratches showing red on her face, "wicked man."

"Good afternoon, Betsy. I trust you are rested from the fatigues of your journey?"

She turned her face away sullenly, and I repressed a great jubilation at seeing her so chastened; here was no wild laughter and tormenting teasing, but only a vicious creature trapped and held fast. "Betsy," I said, abandoning my ironic tone, "I am truly sorry for you. You treated me unfairly, but I am sorry, nevertheless, to see you so miserable, and I still offer to help you in any way I can."

"Let me go, then," she said, to the wall.

"Where can you go?"

"I won't tell," she said sullenly. "You haven't any right to know."

"Then, Betsy, will you tell me where you went, when you ran away? We found you in New York, you know—did you go there directly?"

She shook her head mutely.

"Why did you run away, Betsy?" I asked her, most gently.

"Because you wouldn't let me be free and happy. And when I was in New York I was happy all the time, and I had lunch in a restaurant and I went on a bus and everyone I met was nice, not like you or her or Aunt Morgen."

I confess I could have found it in my heart to feel sorry for the young sinner; a giddy day or so, a few hours of freedom, a taste of luxury—they would appeal to the best of us. But, I told myself sternly, the best of us would not thereby jeopardize the lives of Beth and Elizabeth, and so I went on, "And in the hospital?"

"I wasn't there," she said, and it was a cry of agony, "I wasn't even there!"

"You mean you were inside?"

She shook her head. "I was gone," she said. "I didn't even know about it, and I *always* know *every*thing, what Lizzie does and what Beth does and what they say and think and what they're dreaming and now I know about the hospital just because I heard *her* talking to Morgen, and I wasn't even *there*—"

"Her?"

"Her," Betsy said with loathing.

"Then," I said, with an attempt, at geniality, "it was not you who denied me in the hospital."

Betsy grinned. "I heard about it," she said. "*She* said that you—"

"The subject is not worth discussion," I said. "We have more important things to worry about, and primary among these is the question we were working on before Elizabeth fell ill; I mean, of course, the death of your—of Elizabeth's mother."

"I won't talk to you," she said, sullen again. "You don't like me."

"I don't," I agreed readily. "You have been most unfair to me. But I believe that I should like you a good deal more if you answered my questions sensibly."

"I won't talk to you," she said, and made the same answer to everything I said, and finally would not speak at all.

I found in her sullenness the conviction that she knew she was beaten, and, much heartened by this taming of the villain of our piece, I gave up my questions, and wondered if I might untangle my hypnotic snarl by awakening her, but I found this almost as difficult as I had found hypnosis in the first place. Again and again I found Betsy's hating eyes fixed on mine, and

I began to suspect that matters among these several personalities were coming to a head, as it were, and that instead of slipping from one to another easily through hypnosis, they were each of them enough aware of individuality to resist being pushed under, and were clinging tenaciously to the surface, each in hope of finally establishing dominance. It seemed reasonable to assume that power was closely coordinated with conscious control, and the more time any personality spent governing the others, the stronger that personality would be, bleeding the others of their precious consciousness. I already knew that here knowledge was surely power, and the personality most basic in Miss R. was the one to whom the mind was most open; Elizabeth had lost, and was losing, a large portion of her conscious life, with no conception of what was going on when she was under, and my poor Beth was very little better off; Betsy had, so far, with her ability to comprehend both Elizabeth and Beth, seemed easily the most basic of the ones I had met, and yet how unwilling I was to admit it! Now, however, Betsy's dark hints of a "she," to whose mental workings Betsy did not have constant and easy access gave me hopes that perhaps Miss R. might be coming to herself again, although I trusted that the girl I had met in the hospital was not to be the entire final form of the personality; I could have wished her a little of Beth's sweetness!

I finally put Betsy aside, then, and awakened, as I thought, my friend Beth; she opened her eyes, looked around, sighed and sat up at once. "Again?" she said, as though to herself, and then her eyes fell on me. For a long minute she looked at me, and then she said deliberately, "I thought I asked you not to bother me any more. If you will not leave me alone I will tell my aunt."

It may be imagined that I was not overly complimented by this address; I resisted a strong impulse to rise and show her the door, and said only, "My name is Victor Wright. I am a doctor and you have been, miss, my patient for upwards of twenty months."

"I? Impossible."

"I thank you," I said stiffly. "It is not quite so impossible as you think; there are, in fact, those in this town who could, if they would, point to me as a man of science and integrity. However, madam, it is not my credentials which are in question, but your own. Can you tell me who you are?"

She flashed a look of dislike upon me. "If I have been your patient for as long as you say," she told me arrogantly, "then you must have found out my name by now." And she gave a short laugh which reminded me disagreeably of her aunt.

"Your name," I said flatly, "is Elizabeth R., although in any future conversation between us I am going to surprise you by calling you Bess."

"Bess?" she said, more nettled than surprised. "But why?"

"Because I choose to," I said, just like Betsy. I believe that if she had not reminded me of her aunt (a picture which will always remind me in turn, most vividly, of my experiences in the airplane) I should have not been so brusque; I ought to have spoken to her kindly and patiently, and brought her slowly to an acceptance of myself, but even a man of science cannot always be impartial, and sensible, and invulnerable, and she had antagonized me hopelessly.

She was not stupid; she perceived this at once, and perhaps had some inkling of future favors to be gained from me, for she changed her tone and said more civilly, "I am sorry to be rude. I have not been myself since my mother's death; I have been very nervous, and I may say things I never really mean to. I was very much affected by my mother's death." She seemed to consider this a most handsome apology, and flounced and simpered at me to show that she bore me no ill-will for having insulted me twice before.

I thought her tawdry, and artificial, and mincing, and I did not at all care for her obvious attempts to sound refined; how, I wondered, could Elizabeth and Beth speak like quietly-educated girls, and this one speak so lispingly, and then thought that the mind behind this one was surely faulty, although strong, and must be securely incorporated with Elizabeth and Beth to manufacture a final endurable personality. As soon as I felt that I might answer her with composure, I said, "I am not surprised, of course, that you felt grief at your mother's death; it would be unnatural if you had not. But surely, in this length of time . . ."

I paused, and she lifted her handkerchief to her eyes.

"After all," I continued, when it appeared that she was too much "affected" to speak, "your aunt was also devoted to your mother, and she has succeeded in overcoming her loss."

"Aunt Morgen has no fine feelings at all." This coincided very nearly with my own view of Aunt Morgen, but I said nothing; after a minute she went on, "Besides, Aunt Morgen is old and fat and foolish, and I am young and" (she simpered) "attractive and rich; surely it is a shame that sorrow should—"

"Blight?" I suggested ironically.

She gave me another look of dislike, and continued, "Many people have told me that I look very much like my mother when she was younger, except that my hair has a better color than hers did, and my ankles are narrower." She regarded her ankles with pleasure, and I could not resist saying, "Then let us hope that those scratches do not leave scars on your face."

She looked up at me and for a minute she was as badly frightened as anyone I have ever seen. Then she said, with a false smile, "They won't, thank you for asking. I checked with Doctor Ryan."

"Did you tell him how you got them?" I asked.

"I fell," she said quickly, still desperately afraid. "I don't know why you keep asking about them, it isn't polite and it doesn't matter anyway."

"And Betsy?"

She stood up, trembling, and said ferociously, "There isn't any such thing as Betsy, and you know it, you want to frighten me again and I won't *have* it!" She stopped, caught her breath, and then went on more quietly. "I told you that I have not been myself since my mother's death. I sometimes . . . imagine things. I am a very nervous person by nature."

"I see," I said. "And how long did you say it had been, since your mother died?"

She lifted the handkerchief again. "Three weeks," she said.

"I see," I said. "Most distressing. But your aunt has completely gotten over it?"

"To tell you the truth," she said, sitting down again and obviously relieved that we had gotten away from the scratches on her face, "Aunt Morgen and I don't get on very well. I expect to be moving out on her soon."

I did not envy Aunt the graceless society of this young lady, and would have liked to send her home Miss R. in the form of Elizabeth, as a gesture of common humanity, but I could not really see my way clear to proposing soberly to Miss R. that I put her into an hypnotic trance, so I only said, "I trust your agitation will have abated somewhat, Miss Bess R., by our next appointment."

"Our?" she said in absolute astonishment. "My dear man, you do not suppose that I am coming here again?"

"Indeed?"

She laughed, with a return to her former arrogance. "There are so many people who speak so well of you," she said, "that you hardly need to beg for patients to come to your office. I told you I had seen Doctor Ryan; *he* is *my* doctor, and I am telling you plainly, once and for all, that I do not want or intend to be any patient of yours. There is nothing personal in it, and I have told you already that I am sorry for being rude before, but just because I apologized to you, you needn't expect to send me a bill and get paid for this short conversation. I may be rich, but I am not going to be taken in by every . . ."

I showed her the door at last.

Without enthusiasm, I added R4 to my notes, and hoped she was the last; each of Miss R.'s varying selves, I thought, proved more disagreeable than the last—always, of course, excepting Beth, who, although weak and almost helpless, was at least possessed of a kind of winsomeness, and engaging in her very helplessness. I found myself, lying awake that night in bed— one finds, I think, that even with a clear conscience there comes an age when sleep forsakes the weary mind; I am not elderly, but I frequently, now, court sleep in vain—that I was telling over and over, as though they were figures in a charade, my four girls: Elizabeth the numb, the stupid, the inarticulate, but somehow enduring, since she had remained behind to carry on when the rest of them went under; Beth, the sweet and susceptible; Betsy, the wanton and wild; and Bess, the arrogant and cheap. I perceived that no one of these could possibly be permitted to assume the role of the true, complete (by very definition none of *them* could be complete!) Miss R., and, equally, none of them could be judged "imposters"; Miss R. would be at last a combination in some manner of all four, although I must admit that the contemplation of a personality combining Elizabeth's stupidity with Beth's weakness, Betsy's viciousness with Bess's arrogance, left me with an urge to throw the blankets over my face and hide myself!

I saw myself, if the analogy be not too extreme, much like a Frankenstein with all the materials for a monster ready at hand, and when I slept, it was with dreams of myself patching and tacking together, trying most hideously to chip away the evil from Betsy and leave what little was good, while the other three stood by mockingly, waiting their turns.

As I sat the next morning at my desk, putting my notes in order, I heard Miss Hartley's surprised voice in the outer office, and then the door to my private office slammed open, and Betsy ripped in, raging like a fury, shaking and white; "What is this, you old fool," she shouted, without even closing the door, "what is this I hear, that you have chosen this proud cold beastly bitch* to manage all of us now? Do you think I'm going to let you get away with anything like that? Do you suppose—"

"Close the door, please," I said quietly, "and moderate your language. Even if you are not a lady, you are addressing a gentleman."

She laughed, uncaring for the harm she did her own cause by angering me, and I swear that I thought for a moment she

---

*These are Betsy's words, not mine; I hesitate to copy them, but accuracy compels. V.W.

might strike me; she came up to the desk and leaned over (and I most heartily grateful to be securely behind such a solid piece of furniture) and shouted into my very face, "Madman! What are you doing to all of us?"

"My dear Betsy," I said imploringly, "do compose yourself, I beg of you; I cannot possibly discuss the matter with you so long as you are in this overwrought state."

She quieted somewhat, and stood with her hands shaking and her eyes, flashing, pressed close against the other side of the desk. Still more than half afraid that she might suddenly spring at me, I held myself tense, back against the wall, and with an effort kept my voice quiet and steady as I asked her to sit down. "For," I added, "we cannot talk quietly, you and I, until we sit together like human beings, and do not hold one another at bay like animals."

Apparently seeing that I was not afraid of her, she gave a re-signed shrug and threw herself into her usual chair, where she sat with her face turned from me and her hands still clenched into fists. I took the first real breath I had drawn since she entered my office, and passed warily around her to close the door. "Now, my dear," I said, returning to my own chair behind the desk, "tell me what has upset you so."

"Well," said Betsy, as one diagramming an enormous injustice, "Lizzie and Beth and I are all your old friends, and even though you don't like *me*, it's not fair to pick a stranger to take charge of us."

"I am not going to put anyone in charge, as you call it. This Bess is merely another self, just like yourself and Beth and Elizabeth."

"She's not like *me*," Betsy said. "She's awful."

I smiled at the pot calling the kettle black, and continued, "My intention is not to choose among you, but to coax you all back together into a whole person again. Why should you suppose that I am discriminating against the rest of you in favor of Bess?"

"She says so," Betsy said sullenly.

I was growing excited; somewhere in here it was going to be possible to define the precise area of consciousness of each of these characters, and, when I could break down the barriers of silence between them, my cure was more than half accomplished; "How?" I asked, and then, when Betsy looked up in surprise, I said more evenly, "How do you and Bess communicate?"

"So there *are* things the old man doesn't know?" said Betsy with sudden amusement. "Well," she said, lying back in her chair, "why should I tell *you?* Suppose I just don't tell you anything so long as she's around? How do you like *that?*" She got to her feet, and looked down at me from across the desk. "You can't be friends with her *and* me," she said flatly, and turned toward the door.

"Betsy," I said urgently, but when she turned her face to me again it was politely disdainful and my heart sank—I confess it—to see that I had for the moment lost Betsy, with our quarrel still unsolved, and was entertaining Bess. "Why don't you leave me alone?" Bess asked, surveying me without anger, but surely without cordiality.

"I regret," I told her coldly, "that you were brought here without my desiring it. My patient—"

"Your patients do not concern me," she said. "I was a little excited a few minutes ago, and I hope you are going to forget what I said. About people being put in charge of other people."

"You are aware of everything that has been said in this room since you entered?"

"Of course." She was surprised. "I am sometimes very nervous, and say wild things. My mother's death—"

"I know," I said hastily. "Will you come back and sit down? I badly need your assistance."

She hesitated. "If you need any assistance," she said, "I will stay for a minute, but since I am not consulting you as a patient—"

"No bill will be sent *you* for my time," I told her, with absolute conviction, and, reassured, she came back and sat down again. As soon as she was seated, "Tell me, then," I said, "why you deny the actuality of any other personality in yourself?"

She wet her lips, and glanced nervously about her, as though afraid of retaliation from Betsy, perhaps, for what she was about to say. Finally she said haltingly, "I was so sick when my mother died, and I am only beginning to get well again. If I get to thinking that there is some other person making me do things, they will all believe that I'm *really* crazy, and maybe lock me up somewhere, and Aunt Morgen will take all the money."

"I see," I said. "And if I tell you that I do not believe that you are 'crazy,' as you call it, and that together we may overcome this illness of yours, will you then agree to help me?"

"If there really is someone else," she said slowly, "then I was stronger than she was, when we were in New York, because I drove her down. So why should I go to the expense of hiring you to drive her away, if I can do it myself?"

I felt as though I were going mad along with her. "Miss R.," I said, "out of the kindness of my heart and friendship for Doctor Ryan I undertook your case. Since I first began, with nothing but the purest scientific integrity, nothing but your own good health my objective, no cause to serve and no glory to gain beyond the sight of Miss Elizabeth R. well and happy and prepared to assume a normal place in the world—since I began, I say, I have met with nothing but insolence and obstruction from you and from your sisters; only Beth has in any way tried to help me and she is too weak to remain consistently loyal. If I had my way—" and I am afraid that, in my turn, I raised my voice—"if I had my way, Miss, you would be soundly whipped and taught to mind your manners. As it is, you leave me no choice but to give up your case; as of this moment, Miss R., my association with you is ended."

"Oh, Doctor Wright," she said in tears, and it was Beth, "what have I done to anger you so?"

I was a man bedeviled. Wordlessly I rose and stamped out of my office, leaving the field to my enemies, whose wild triumphant laughter echoed behind me.

I do not suppose that even my least cynical reader will expect that my association with Miss R. ended here, on such a strong note of my own; I was prepared without further question to give up Miss R.'s case, upon what I thought full and sufficient provocation, but I could not persuade Miss R.'s case to relinquish me; I might as well have shouted my tirade to an empty office as to Beth, who was as little able to understand me as if I had been babbling Greek, and my heroics went for nothing. Elizabeth presented herself at my office promptly the next day, sat in the chair across the desk, and told me she had a headache.

Betsy about this time became addicted to a kind of spiteful practical joke, practiced largely against Bess, her particular enemy (it was amusing, incidentally, to see how Betsy's loathing of Elizabeth and Beth had modified itself when Bess appeared on the scene) but sometimes Betsy was not above entertaining herself with dull Elizabeth or guileless Beth; one afternoon Miss R. was extremely late, and I had almost decided to await her no longer, when Beth telephoned; she could not get out of the house, because her aunt had gone out after locking the back door, and someone (and I knew who, although Beth, of course, did not) had pushed a heavy desk before the front door, so that Beth could not get out; she was too weak to move the desk and too self-conscious to be seen climbing from a window, and so home she stayed, until her aunt returned to unlock the back door and help her move the desk. When I scolded Betsy for this prank she explained innocently that she had intended it for Bess, who had planned to go shopping that afternoon, and had thought that if Bess could not move the desk she would remain at home and so permit the other personalities to pay their usual visit to my office.

Again, Betsy was not above a kind of petty dishonesty; several times Elizabeth exhausted her small supply of strength walking to my office because Betsy had stolen all her money and hidden it. Poor Elizabeth would rather walk to my office than not come at all; I think it was one of the few spots where the unfortunate creature was allowed any freedom, with the more powerful personalities lording it over her at home.

Bess was most particularly sensitive about her money, and strongly disliked spending it upon anything but herself; she grudged every penny her aunt spent for household items, but lavished large sums upon clothes and jewelry of her own. One of Betsy's favorite tricks, and one which never failed of driving Bess to a frenzy, was to assume control of the personality and then, as Miss R., distribute Bess' possessions generously among everyone she saw; she gave an expensive coat to the old woman who cleaned house for Miss R. and her aunt, and sums of money to beggars on the street (I think, myself, that Betsy was more able to take control of the personality when someone approached who needed money; Bess was very apt to become nervous and excitable when she thought she might be asked to give away her precious pennies, and easier of access to Betsy; this, however, may be pure malicious reasoning on my part); each time, wickedly, bringing Bess back in time to hear the fulsome thanks of the recipient of Betsy's charity. Bess spent long hours shopping, and many times (since, we discovered, she had still only the most partial access to Betsy's actions), believed she had been shopping when the rest of them were with me at my office; we were something of a clandestine crew, with Betsy on guard. For several months after my last scene with Bess, Betsy took it upon herself to protect the rest of us, and, gleefully, stood watch while I talked with Elizabeth or Beth; at the first sign of Bess' coming Betsy would hastily shepherd Miss R. out of the office and into the street and when Bess arrived she would find herself standing gazing into a shop window safely outside. Betsy's favorite spot, by the way, was the window of a shop across the street from my office, which sold sporting goods, and Betsy reported with mirth that Bess was not able to understand the peculiar fascination the window of the sporting-goods shop held for her; she knew only that several times she had strayed unconsciously toward it, and had found herself gazing raptly at a display of tennis rackets, fishing rods, and golf clubs.

Careful questioning uncovered the reassuring fact that, although Betsy felt perfectly free to play her tricks on her fellows, and to tell me about them, she was enough in awe of her aunt to stay relatively circumspect when there was a chance of her aunt's discovering her. The girls all seemed to behave fairly well around Aunt Morgen, and I am sure that Aunt—

although she could hardly have avoided perceiving that her niece was odd—had no notion of the real state of the case.

During all this time Betsy's attitude toward me was changing materially. We could never trust one another entirely, but she knew, of course, of my treatment at Bess' hands, and felt that in any balance of power I would stand on the side of the angels, which, to Betsy's mind, meant no one but Betsy. I was greatly appreciative of the assistance Betsy was giving me, in numberless ways, to enable me to mine information from Elizabeth and Beth; I still knew that the final personality of Miss R. could only be one which was fully cognizant of Miss R.'s life and experiences, full and entire, and my present hope was to strengthen Beth, by whatever means, and bring her slowly to a complete open realization of the whole personality. Beth already knew of the existence of herself and Elizabeth; I now told both of them about Betsy and Bess, taking a great deal of time, and explaining as slowly and patiently as I could. The minds of Betsy and Bess were still closed to them, of course, just as Bess could still shut Betsy out for spaces of time, exerting maximum control, and Betsy could do the same for Bess. I found that as the four of them became more distinct they drew farther away from one another, also, so that what once might have been mere cracks of cleavage were now gulfs between them.

I grew quite accustomed to my little group of girls and we were frequently very merry; Elizabeth and Beth were astonished at Betsy's knowledge of their actions, and I think she even developed a kind of fondness for them; she never really liked Beth considerably, but she became really quite protective toward Elizabeth, and several times helped Elizabeth, unasked, when Elizabeth was in trouble; being tireless, and given to fits of enthusiasm, she twice did all of Elizabeth's personal laundry, scrubbing and ironing with great fervor and little efficiency; once, when Bess put on a blouse which Betsy had freshly ironed, Betsy irritably poured a bottle of ink on her head; her fondness for Elizabeth did not, of course, exempt Elizabeth from being the victim of various practical jokes

which occurred to Betsy, but whenever Elizabeth became innocently entangled in some snare Betsy had set, we were sure
of a contrite apology from Betsy, and a wide-eyed declaration
that the trap had, of course, been set for Bess.

I have among my notes numberless instances of various possessions spilled, torn, or hidden by the indefatigable Betsy, of
the long walks she would take in order to leave Beth or Elizabeth stranded far away in an unfamiliar spot, with no way of
getting home except to walk upon legs already wearied by Betsy's brisk pace; she sent Bess screaming hysterically through
the house one night, a result of finding her bed full of spiders;
she brought me affectionate little gifts stolen from Bess' desk,
and a red candy box full of Betsy's own letters which she said
she had taken from Elizabeth. When I showed this last to Elizabeth she was utterly taken aback, but confessed that she
had received the letters before she had ever begun treatments
with me, while she was still employed at the museum. Oddly
enough, the discovery that these letters had been composed by
Betsy only increased the fondness which they felt for one another. Betsy, unless she was sulking, rarely afflicted Elizabeth
now with aches and pains, reserving all her malevolence
for Bess, and when Betsy discovered that I disapproved of her
pranks against Bess, even though I felt little sympathy for
her victim, she stopped reporting these details to me, so that
for this period of several weeks I heard little or nothing of
Bess, since Betsy would not tell me about her, and Beth and
Elizabeth could not.

This period—which I may perhaps be pardoned for calling
Miss R.'s golden age—came to an abrupt period one afternoon when, expecting my friends, I was both shocked and surprised when Miss Hartley, announcing Miss R., ushered in
Bess. I had almost forgotten the sharp face and the snapping
eyes, the unpleasant voice and manner, and it was not a joy to
me to see them again; I had hoped to be far better prepared before I tried to deal with Bess. She flounced to the chair, and sat
herself down, and gave me a condescending smile, and said at
last that she supposed I was surprised to see her and—I admitting this without comment—that she hoped I bore her no mal-

ice. I told her that I did not, which was not true, and she explained to me that her mother's recent death had left her very nervous. I told her dryly that I was sorry to see her still grieving and she gave me a suspicious glance and then, settling herself more firmly in her chair, went on, "That's one reason I'm here, you see. I don't seem to be recovering as quickly as I should, and I am a little worried about my health."

"Let me see," I asked her. "How long ago was it? Your mother's death?"

"Three weeks," she said.

"Still three weeks?" I asked. "Surely, a good time ago, you told me—"

"I guess I know when my own mother died," she said flatly.

"Of course," I said. "And the nature of this nervousness of yours?"

"You mean, why do I think I'm nervous? I've *always* been nervous; I was a very nervous child."

"I meant, what particular causes do you have, to worry about your health? Headaches, for instance, or insomnia?"

"I . . ." She hesitated, and then said rapidly, "I'm just frightened, all the time. Someone is trying to kill me."

"Really?" I asked, thinking of three people who would have enjoyed killing Bess if they could, "why do you imagine such a thing?"

"Because they are. They want my money."

"I see." I thought. "Why?" I asked.

"Because she hates me, and the day before yesterday I was coming down the stairs and she caught my foot and I almost fell, and then today when I was cutting tomatoes for sandwiches for lunch she turned the knife right around in my hand and c-cut me." I thought she was about to cry; she held out her left hand, inadequately bandaged in a handkerchief. I came round the desk and took away the handkerchief and examined the cut; it was neither deep nor serious, but must have bled freely and to Betsy's satisfaction. "It could hardly have proved fatal," I told her. "Betsy would not—"

"Betsy?" she cried out. "Who says it was Betsy? There isn't any such thing."

"Then who do *you* think is trying to harm you—your aunt?"

She could not pretend to believe that, and she dropped her eyes and slowly rewound the handkerchief around her hand. "I'm left-handed," she said. "This is very awkward for me."

This was of some interest to me; Elizabeth and Beth and Betsy were all right-handed. I said to her gently, "I think a great deal of your fear would be dissipated if you could bring yourself to face the reality of Betsy. You could at least give up thinking, then, that your life is in danger; Betsy could not harm you without harming herself."

"There isn't any Betsy."

"Very well. Did you put spiders in your own bed?"

She stared at me. "Who told you that?"

"Betsy did," I said blandly.

She dropped her shoulders and looked away resignedly, and I felt for her. She was taking a bold stand on Betsy, and perhaps by steadfastly refusing to admit the existence of any other personality to Miss R., she might have succeeded eventually in eliminating Elizabeth and Beth, but Betsy was made of stronger stuff and poor Bess was fairly cornered; she had either to bow to the fact of Betsy's existence, and admit that she was not the only Miss R., or explain to herself why it had come about that—say—she had gotten into a bed full of spiders, or cut her own hand, or pushed herself downstairs.

"Look," she said earnestly at last, leaning forward as though she wanted to avoid being overheard, "*I* get the money, no one can take it away; Aunt Morgen even admits that the money is mine. And I'm not going to let any Betsy or anyone come along and pretend she's me and try to take it all away."

"But surely the money is not that important; consider—"

"Of course the money is important," she said, interrupting me sharply. "You idealists always think you can invent something better, but I notice that when it comes to paying the rent—"

"Young lady," I said, interrupting in my turn, "I do not care to be called names by a person who has only the vaguest idea of what her words entail. I am not interested in whose money it is, or what Aunt Morgen says; I am only interested in—"

"I know you *say* that," she said coolly, "but what you'd better know is, if you've made some arrangement with Aunt Morgen, say, about this Betsy of yours, and you're trying to fix up something to run me out so's I have to give up the money— well, what I want to say is that whatever Aunt Morgen or this Betsy or anyone has promised you, the money is *mine,* and I'll make you a better offer than any of them, and *I'm* the one can back it up."

"Good heavens," I said, hearing her through because I lacked words to speak to her, "Good heavens, my dear Miss R.! What a deplorable . . . I mean to say, how outrageous!" And I believe I was almost struck dumb; I gasped, and floundered, and have no doubt I turned purple in the face; she apparently accepted my shock as genuine, because she had the grace to hesitate before she continued, "Well, if I'm wrong, I'll be the first to say I'm sorry, doctor. But I do think you ought to get it clear that I'm the only one really able to offer you anything. Because after all, if you were taken in by someone who *said* they'd pay you, I'm just doing you a favor by making sure you know they won't. Because the money—"

I believe that only my knowledge of the fear behind her words saved me from an apoplexy; in spite of my speechless fury, I noted that under her brazen assurance, her lip was trembling, and beyond her arrogant gestures her right hand moved constantly over to touch the bandage on her left hand, to tug at it and fold it back, to move and turn and clench itself, as though it held. . . . My anger gone, scarcely attending to her unending financial monologue, I carelessly slid a pad of paper across the polished surface of the desk, and sent my pencil after it. When the pencil touched her arm her fingers seized it, and then— poor Bess continuing all this time about the obligations of wealth, and the luxuries she had had to forego because of her aunt's extravagances—Bess' right hand, without her knowledge, took to scribbling on the pad, while I drew a deep sigh and sat back in my chair, smiling and nodding like a great idol who has just seen a whole calf roasted at his altar. (I am not an irreligious man, but I suspect myself occasionally; here the analogy is irresistible, and I think it is because this present satisfaction was utterly worldly, almost akin to spite, and I do not, certainly, find human pettiness an aspect of the Almighty; thus, perhaps, the pagan conception.) At any rate, I eyed the scribbling pencil with far more attention (although disguised, surely) than I gave to Miss R. and her large, if diaphanous, plans for endowing hospitals and setting up charitable institutions for the poor.

"Certainly," I said occasionally, and nodded, and sometimes I said, "By all means," or "Not at all." I have no notion of what I may have agreed to, but I do not think she was listening in any case, any more than she was attending to the earnest labors of her own hand with a pencil. At length, seeing the top page of the pad entirely filled with writing, I reached forth again casually—although I believe I might have snatched the page, without noticeably withdrawing Bess from her monetary devotions—and took off the top page, her hand holding back while I did so, as though waiting to start another.

"Do you not think I have a case, my dear doctor?" Bess asked me just then, and I looked up, and shook my head with great deliberation, and told her I hardly knew what to think, and she sighed, and said it was very hard for a young woman alone, and so went on, and I bent my gaze ardently to the page of paper.

"doctor wrong," it read, "aunt m lawyers stop money poor bess ask her ask her where is mother what aunt m says ask her ask her she is not saying true ask her i am here and i am here and she is not no money poor bess laughing betsy"

And thus ended my page, but the pencil wrote on and on. I put my hand down firmly and flat on the page I held, and lifted my head, and said, into a pause where Bess stopped to draw breath, "My dear Miss R., what did you do to your mother?"

There was a dead silence, and then she said, whimpering, "You're angry again, Doctor Wright; what have I done?"

"Nothing, nothing," I said, as to a fretful child, "nothing, Beth."

"You don't always call me the way you used to. I think you don't like me any more, and I think that now you'd rather talk to Bess, and I never thought you'd like *her* better than you do your own Beth, but I guess that if you'd rather—"

"Oh, Beth," I said, and sighed. "I only want Bess to tell me about your mother's death."

"If I'm in your way," Beth said, "you just don't need to call me again. You can spend all your time with Bess; *I'll* never know. I thought you *liked* me, though."

"Oh," I said in weary desperation, "I'd rather have Betsy."

"Fine," she said, grinning. "I *never* thought, my dearest doctor, my dearest dearest Doctor Wrong, that I would hear you calling upon Betsy as you would call upon—"

"Stop," I said, "no blasphemy; is it not enough that I am driven and tormented by all of you; must I be blamed, too?"

She giggled maliciously. "You were clever to give me the pencil," she said. "I couldn't get out until you drove *her* away." She added more seriously. "Aunt Morgen made her come see you today."

"I rather imagined that there had been some crisis; Bess would not have risked a consultation fee without grave provocation."

"Well," said Betsy, consideringly, "first of all, she was scared. She cut her hand, you know," and the imp glanced at me demurely. "But it was really Aunt Morgen deciding to write to the lawyers that made her come—*I* told you, with the pencil."

"I don't really understand it, however; it has to do with her precious money, I assume?"

"Indeed it does; Aunt Morgen wants to tell the lawyers that *she* can't have the money because . . ." Betsy hesitated, with a long, innocent face ". . . because she has been so *very* nervous since her mother died," said Betsy. Then she asked me bluntly, "Are you going to let her pay you money for telling the lawyers and everyone she's all right?"

"Certainly I am not going to become involved in any such foolishness. I don't want any money, or at least not *hers,* and I have no intention of discussing her with lawyers or anyone

else, and I am furthermore prepared to abandon the subject of
this infernal financial lunacy forever; I am neither an accoun-
tant nor a bank clerk, and I am heartily tired of dealing with a
ledger when I am concerned with a flesh-and-blood—"

"Fiddle-dee-dee," said Betsy, "fiddle-dee-dee. The mouse
has married the bumblebee."

"*And*," I said roundly, "I fully intend to discover what hand
you, Miss Betsy, had in all this mischief."

"Me?" said Betsy. "Fiddle-dee-dee."

"Did you, for instance," I wondered aloud, "hint to your aunt
of some irrational behavior over expenditures . . . did you, perhaps, *demonstrate* some such silliness?"

"Fiddle-dee-dee," said Betsy, eyes cast heavenward in
innocence.

"I should not be surprised if you had—say—torn up, or
burned, some large bill in your aunt's presence—"

"You mean," Betsy asked, "like lighting a cigarette with a
ten-dollar bill? Fiddle-dee-dee."

"I see," I said.

"I *did*," Betsy continued with great candor, "put a little notion into Beth's head about how you were always talking to
her these days. I thought maybe when you heard how bad it
made Beth feel you'd be a little nicer to us all."

"That was unkind," I said.

"Tell Beth," said Betsy, grinning, and turned to me Beth's
tearful face.

"I don't want to talk to you any more," Beth said.

"Beth," I told her with irritation, "I tell you that I have not
seen Bess for weeks until this afternoon when she walked into
my office. I did not invite her here, and I assure you that I view
her with the most sincere dislike. There is no reason in the
world for you or anyone else to be upset; I am a doctor and in
order to make any progress upon this case—"

"If you don't like her," said Beth sullenly, "then why do you
talk to her all the time instead of me?"

"Oh, Betsy, Betsy," I cried, in despair.

"She's just jealous," Betsy said. "She'll get over it. Fiddle-
dee-dee," she added, with a giggle.

"If I could only persuade you to behave," I said wearily.

"Do you know," said Betsy, falling suddenly back into her familiar sullenness, "do you know that if you had left me alone I could be free now? I would be with . . ." She stopped abruptly, and when I looked up questioningly she was turned away.

"Tell me about it, Betsy," I said.

"No. Besides, if I told you about Robin you'd be angry with me and hate me worse than you do now, even, because that was a *bad* thing. And I wouldn't tell you about the rest of it because then you'd find out about Robin."

"And suppose I promise not to be angry?"

She laughed. "Fiddle-dee-dee," she said. "Said the mouse, 'Dear bee, will you marry me, will you marry me, sweet bumble-bee?' Can you sing, Doctor Wrong?"

"Poorly," I said. "Betsy, I am persuaded that in all of this, even including your nonsense, there is a pattern of sorts to be discovered, and I am determined that it shall not remain hidden. At every crucial point of Miss R.'s life one or another of you steps forward to confuse and bewilder me; you tell me meaningless trifles when I require absolute facts, you babble nonsense at me when I come close to home, you mock me."

"Fiddle-dee-dee. I treat you very nicely, I think."

"And," I continued, "I have observed that whenever I am speaking to you or to Bess, and my searching becomes too sharp for comfort, you withdraw and send Beth with her tenderness and her tears, and evade my questions. I think that you and Bess between you can tell me my story, and I fully intend that you shall. Therefore—"

"Beth won't come, anyway," Betsy interrupted, giggling. "Beth's mad and I'm glad and I know what will please her; a bottle of wine, to make her shine, and Doctor Wrong to—"

"Betsy," I said, "in heaven's name!"

"Now who's blaspheming?" she said pertly.

"I want you to take a note to your aunt," I said in sudden decision. "I'll tell you what I shall write, since I expect you would read it in any case. I shall ask Miss Jones to call here at my office, at any time convenient to her, to discuss the progress of her niece's case."

Although I had serious misgivings about entrusting such an errand to Betsy, I felt that I had no choice; I disliked addressing Miss Jones through the common post, and could not endeavor to communicate through Elizabeth, who would most probably not be allowed to remain conscious long enough to carry a message, or through Beth, who was in the same state of subjection, and angry at me besides, or through Bess, who would surely find the message of ominous import to her security. I might have telephoned Miss Jones, indeed, but, to own it frankly, I was very reluctant to converse with the lady on any grounds but my own, safe in my own office with my own books and my good stout desk before me. I dreaded her mockery, and it was a delicate subject I brought her.

All of these doubts passed swiftly through my mind as I wrote a quick note to Miss Jones, asking only that she call on me to discuss the health of her niece, while Betsy sang to herself in her chair; I then thought to fortify the safe delivery of my message by remarking, as I handed the folded note across the desk, "I expect that you will keep this from Bess."

"I will," she said, and added slowly, "if I can." And then, in a rush of words that seemed born of a terror not until now acknowledged, "I think she is getting stronger all the time."

I glanced up at her frightened face, and said easily, "I believe we shall have her down yet. Don't be afraid of her."

"Mother's Betsy mustn't cry," she said, and turned and left me quickly.

Well, then, I sent my note, and had my answer, and my exasperation for my pains; a letter reached me two days later, and a staggering surprise it was—although my reader must do me credit, and suppose that I was not, after the first moment, altogether taken in—to read: "My dear Doctor Wright: I don't think you seriously meant what you said in your letter, and if you did, you should be horsewhipped. I am a poor lone woman but you are a bad old man. Sincerely yours, Morgen Jones." This odd document, laboriously composed, had an air unmistakable, and even though it caused me some honest amusement, I was acutely aware of my own folly in supposing that Betsy's seeming friendliness was to be trusted for a moment; I

had been taken in by her cheerfulness and seeming cooperative spirit. When I thought, finally, of what nonsense might
even now lie in Miss Jones' hands, purporting to be from me,
I was inclined to berate myself for a madman. I do believe,
however, that this superlative insolence of Betsy's put the final
stamp upon my conviction that matters must be brought to a
head as soon as possible; I perceived that my present policy of
tactful patience had been shortsighted, in allowing Betsy to
wander almost freely, and Bess to establish herself almost
firmly; knowledge is power, I told myself, and determined to
seek my knowledge from Miss Jones, and, armed with my
knowledge, lead an unscrupulous flank attack upon her niece.

I was, moreover, deeply concerned at the blatant tricks Betsy
seemed willing to employ in order to avoid a meeting between
her aunt and myself; I wondered that Betsy so much feared her
aunt. That these obstructions came from Betsy I had no reason
to doubt, and any question in my mind concerning the author
of the letter I received was banished when I discovered, on the
afternoon of the same day, that although Elizabeth came in re-
signed misery to my office, and turned shortly to Beth, from
whom I had ten minutes of reproaches and tears, I was not
able, that afternoon, to bring Betsy by any ingenuity. I asked
her politely to come, I called her, I scolded and entreated, and
the best I could do was Bess, who fell immediately to lamenting
her aunt's criminal activities with regard to the bank account.

I had never found Bess so trying as on that afternoon; I attempted again and again to drive her away, and she only stayed
on like an unwelcome guest, greeting my questions with blank
stares or foolish answers, and relating every subject brought
forward to her tiresome money. Again and again I tried to
bring her to an understanding of the true state of her affairs,
again and again I tried to explain to her that she was no more
than one-quarter of an individual, that there were three others
who shared her life and her person, and must be granted a
share in the consciousness of Miss R., but each time I reached
a point of final definition, where it seemed that surely this time
she must comprehend, she turned aside from me and went
back to her unending talk of money; it veritably seemed that

she would willingly sacrifice three-quarters of her conscious life, if she might only be allowed to hold onto four-quarters of her money. I had put a pencil close by her hand, but sulky Betsy refused to write, and at last I said in disgust, "Miss R., this cannot continue. I am unable to go on today; we shall take up this conversation at another time, after I have spoken to your aunt."

"What are you going to speak to my aunt about?" Bess demanded with suspicion.

"I must give her a report on your present condition," I said thoughtlessly.

"What will you tell her?" Bess spoke imperatively, and I thought with anxiety; she leaned forward and asked again, "What will you tell her?"

"Merely my own opinions with regard to your mental health," I said; now, indeed, her hand was writing, and I thought more of that than of Bess; this time she caught my glance and looked also down at her hand; "I have done this before," she whispered, gazing in horror at her writing hand, "my hand is moving by itself." She seemed horrified and filled with loathing for her own hand, and yet fascinated, for she made no attempt to lift her hand from the page, but leaned forward to see what was written. A ghostly kind of conversation then commenced, with Bess, speaking in a kind of muted sick voice, communicating with her own right hand. The hand had written: fool fool fool do not let him go he does not love you

Bess: (speaking) Who? Who does not love me?

Hand: (it was clearly Betsy, and so I shall call it) robin does not love you or coffee or tea or girls love me

Bess: What do you want? Why are you writing? (to me) I can't even feel it; it goes right on moving and I can't make it stop.

Doctor Wright: (to Betsy) Indeed, there has been wickedness done.

Betsy: fiddle-dee-dee.

Bess: This is how my hand cut me with the knife, then.

Betsy: cut your head off next time ha ha dear bumblebess

Doctor Wright: Betsy, I think I shall forgive you for your impertinence to me, but will you fare so easily with your aunt?

Betsy: aunties mad and im glad

Bess: *Her* aunt? Does she mean Aunt Morgen?

Betsy: Go marry the mouse you filthy bess

Doctor Wright: (at something of a loss) Here is an honor I had not expected. Bess, this is Betsy; I thought you two had already met.

Bess: This is some kind of a joke, I suppose. Or else you are trying to frighten me, Doctor, and I promise you that I am not going to think better of you for these cruel tricks. You seem to think that all you have to do is say "Betsy" and I'll come running to you for help; I wish I could make you understand that this is not at all the way to deal with me. I am willing to be reasonable and helpful, but I won't have you thinking I'm a fool.

Betsy: foul dirty thing

Bess: I hope, Doctor, that you won't think *I* am as vulgar as this writing; I assure you that—

Doctor Wright: I have known Betsy for a long time.

Betsy: old man knows well i am not tame bess will know someday bess darling go away leave go away live somewhere else never come back find someone richer

Bess: I thought that sooner or later we would come around to talking of money. Just because I will be very rich, everyone thinks they can play tricks on me to get money.

Betsy: poor bess no more money do not let him go

Bess: Who?

Betsy: old doctor money-taker tell aunt m

Doctor Wright: Betsy, I will not endure any more mischief from you, remember.

Betsy: better hide nestegg went together to find

Bess: (lifting her hand violently from the page, and speaking to me) This is more than I can stand, my own fingers holding a pencil and speaking to me so rudely and then you play tricks and try to take away my money and Aunt Morgen is angry, and all I want is to be left alone and not bothered and I would be so happy!

Doctor Wright: I am not able, seemingly, to persuade you of my good intentions; there is nothing more I can do.

Bess: (writing again) My hand won't stay still—Doctor, can you make it stop?

Betsy: all went together to find a nestegg elizabeth beth betsy and bess

Doctor Wright: Betsy, if you will not come yourself, will you send Elizabeth?

Betsy: fiddle-dee-dee

"I think I have overstayed my time, Doctor Wright," Elizabeth said, rising and pulling on her glove. "My aunt will wonder why I am late."

"Will she worry?" I asked, rising.

"No, no," said Elizabeth, "she knows where I am, of course. But she doesn't like waiting dinner."

"Goodbye, then, until day after tomorrow," I said.

She stopped in the doorway and looked at me over her shoulder. "Fiddle-dee-dee," she said, and closed the door behind her.

I have in my notes the record of the preceding conversation between Betsy and Bess; I naturally preserved Betsy's scrawl, and noted down Bess' remarks in my book. This odd performance was repeated only once, to my knowledge, and at Bess' insistence, on the occasion of Miss R.'s next visit to my office. Betsy had again refused to put in an appearance, and had showed no sign of her presence; I had spoken briefly to Elizabeth and even more briefly to Beth, who was still downcast, and who had broken off in the middle of a sentence to turn abruptly into Bess, who was seemingly so anxious to talk to me that she could not observe even fundamental good manners, but must interrupt her sister to catch my attention. She had been thinking, she informed me earnestly, and had concluded that it was unjust to suspect me of trickery. (She had been very nervous since her mother died three weeks before.) She had, however, been vastly entertained by my cleverness in causing her hand to write of itself, and hoped that I would show it to her again. Could I, did I think? Would I be so kind?

Betsy's writing seemed to have a kind of horrid fascination for her, the kind of delight so many of us experience when told of our babblings when asleep, or the half-wary excitement of having one's fortune told; I suppose there is a kind of stimulation in a stranger's catching one off guard, as it were; I have felt it myself. At any rate, Miss Bess was charmed with the conversation of her own right hand, and eager to test it again. From the nervousness which possessed her I think that she half-hoped, too, to catch Betsy and Doctor Wright in some kind of a conspiracy against her, so that she might triumphantly reveal a plot against herself and her fortune and emerge victorious from our insidious conniving; in this last, I fear, she was sadly disappointed.

We sat ourselves down, then, Bess with the pencil in her right hand (grasped now, I noted, in the clumsy fashion of one who habitually uses her left, and not at all in the easy manner in which Betsy wrote) and a larger pad of paper provided for the purpose; I with my notebook on the shelf below my desk, quite out of Bess' view, since I did not put it past her to suspect me of a kind of written ventriloquism. Then, after waiting for some few minutes, and Bess watching her hand avidly, and I wondering to myself at her eagerness, and Betsy perhaps off chasing butterflies, for all the writing that was being done, finally Bess leaned a little forward and spoke tensely to her hand.

"Now," she said, "you wouldn't do it at home because you were afraid. And *I* wasn't afraid, so I came here and I'm sitting here waiting, and if you're anything at all, show yourself, or I'll laugh myself sick thinking how silly you are."

It seemed to me that this was no way to summon Betsy, who was not, in my experience, intimidated by strong words, so I said quietly, "Perhaps if you spoke more civilly, and called her by name, she might come."

"She isn't worth it," Bess said with contempt. "All I want is to prove she doesn't exist, and I don't need to worry anymore. It's nothing—" she turned the hand holding the pencil over in a gesture of mockery, "nothing but my imagination. And now are *you* convinced, Doctor?"

"Betsy," I said, half-humorously, "now *you* must defend *me*."

Immediately her hand turned, and wrote on the page, and I felt an unworthy satisfaction in the thought that Betsy had resisted all challenges until I asked her support. All the hand wrote at first, however, was "Doctor, doctor"

Bess: (ironically) She seems to prefer *you*, Doctor Wright; perhaps *you* would rather hold the pencil?

Betsy: doctor open my eyes

Bess: Betsy darling—if you will not be offended at my speaking familiarly to you?

Betsy: hateful

Bess: Now, that is rude, and I am being so polite. I don't even believe that you exist, and yet I am far too polite to say so; I am even calling you Betsy to please you and your dear doctor.

Betsy: bumblebess

Bess: I don't think that's very polite, either, and I think you and Doctor Wright should know that it's much better to be polite to *me*.

Betsy: polite to a pig

Bess: That's much better; at least you show that you can understand what I'm saying. Now listen to this: I am so displeased at your manners that I am quite seriously planning to get rid of you for good, You *and* (to me) your doctor.

Doctor Wright: (without anger) You have tried before, I think.

Bess: But this time little Betsy knows I will manage. Poor Betsy is going to be badly hurt if she troubles me again.

Betsy: cut your head off

Bess: But you can't, can you? You tried again with the knife and I was too quick for you, wasn't I? I was watching for you, wasn't I?

Betsy: sleep

Bess: No, indeed; you aren't strong enough now. I think you are hardly able to keep writing from weakness.

Betsy: fiddle-dee-dee

Bess: I think I hurt you, when I caught you in the hotel, and I think you've been afraid of me ever since because I was stron-

ger and I brought you back from your little escapade; Betsy
darling, shall I tell Doctor Wright where you were going and
what you were looking for?

Betsy: (suddenly stilled; then) no one knows

Bess: *I* know, darling; you've forgotten that pleasant doctor
who treated you to lunch—shall I tell you what he told me?

Betsy: no

Bess: (mocking) You must have told him all sorts of things,
Betsy darling.

Betsy: if you tell i will tell too

Bess: And you know how they are all going to laugh at you,
when I tell them, Doctor Wright and Aunt Morgen and that
nice doctor in New York, that you went wandering and whining all over the city looking for your—

Betsy: now i will tell what you and aunt morgen did and
when she came in the door you went to her and said is this true
what aunt morgen said and when she looked at you and smiled
a little because she was drunk you took your hands—

At this point Bess raised her left hand and dashed the pencil
from her right hand, in a gesture of such violence that I was
shocked, and half-rose to expostulate.

"This is frightful," she said, her voice still shaking with
anger. "That I should have to sit here and read the ravings of a
maniac . . ."

"Then you concede that it is Betsy?" I asked her dryly.

"Indeed not. It is . . ." She thought deeply. "Hypnotism,"
she said at last.

"Remarkable," I said. "You make me out an amazing per-
former."

She reached down slowly and picked up the pencil and put it
again into her right hand. Then she said slowly and with
venom, "Goodbye, Betsy darling. Say goodbye like a nice girl
and I won't hurt you any more."

The pencil wrote, laboriously, "doctor open eyes"

"Betsy," I said sharply, "you may open your eyes."

She took a deep breath and said with relief, "I feel sometimes like I would like to start eating at *her* from the inside
and eat away at her until she was nothing but a shell and then

I would crack her in half and throw her away. And then I would take the little pieces and—"

"She is not an attractive girl," I conceded with a sigh. "What were you going to write, when she struck you?"

"Nothing." Betsy spoke more quietly than usual, and when I looked at her I could see that she was suffering from this unending battle; more than either Elizabeth or Beth she was dejected, and weaker. She saw my glance, and perhaps read a kind of sympathy into it, for she said, "It's harder now for me to come out, almost as hard as it was at first with Lizzie."

I wondered if Betsy was not perhaps ready to give up, and I said, "Elizabeth and Beth cannot fight her."

Betsy grinned wanly. "I used to want you on my side," she said. "I always told you she would be worse than I was."

"Actually," I said frankly, "she is infinitely worse."

"I used to know everything," Betsy said wistfully. "All that Lizzie did and thought and said and dreamed and everything. Now I come out sometimes when *she* lets go for a minute, and it's harder every time, and harder to stay out, with *her* pushing at me. Funny," she went on, "if I went back under now, after all I've tried."

"You are none of you going to be 'under,' as you call it. When Elizabeth R. is herself again, you will all be part of her."

"Like raisins in a pudding," Betsy said.

"You might just tell me," I suggested, "why you are trying to keep me from your aunt."

"I'm not sure," Betsy said, and I think she was telling the truth. "I think it's because I know something's going to happen and I'm afraid of Aunt Morgen."

"What could be going to happen?" I asked cautiously, but Betsy only stretched and made a face at me.

"Fiddle-dee-dee," she said. "Let *her* walk home; I'm too lazy."

Bess, sitting in the chair, apparently perceived that she was putting on her gloves, for she rose to go. "I think," she said, as though nothing at all had happened since she bade goodbye to Betsy, "that I shall not care, Doctor, to try your game again. I am satisfied that it is no more than hypnotism, or a trick like spiritualism."

Nothing could be more calculated to infuriate me, but I said with restraint, "I am no more anxious to continue than you are, Miss R."

"Good afternoon, then," she said.

It was clear to me from her voice and actions that she knew nothing of Betsy's brief visit, and I was greatly relieved to think that, even now, Betsy could still come without Bess' knowledge. I bade her goodbye with some cheerfulness, and took up the telephone to call Miss Jones. I knew that her niece could not reach home, walking, for a good twenty minutes, and I felt that it was no longer possible for me to attempt dealing with my four Miss R.'s without Miss Jones' active and knowledgeable help. If it meant some sacrifice of dignity on my part, that was, I told myself sternly, a minor hazard of my profession, and I kept my voice extremely businesslike, asking Miss Jones only for the privilege of an appointment with her, in order to "discuss the illness of her niece," and adding that, if possible, I should like our conversation to be unattended by Miss R., and, in fact, kept secret from her, since I had medical details to communicate which were best kept, at present, from Miss R.'s hearing. Miss Jones, as icy and formal as I myself, readily agreed to grant me an audience on the following evening, but preferred not to come to my office; would I consent to attend her at home, since her niece would be hearing a concert with friends.

I should point out, I think, that Miss R. was at this time so much quieter than she had been at various previous times— Bess and Betsy having apparently established a kind of equilibrium in their warfare, and both believing that any overt hostile act might endanger the perpetrator more than the victim— that it was felt by Miss Jones, and approved by me when consulted by Elizabeth, that Miss R. might with safety be allowed into public under supervision. As I have pointed out before, no one, without using actual restraint, had much control over her actions generally, and she came and went largely as she pleased when alone. To public functions such as concerts, where she would certainly be seen by people who had known her since childhood, and her slightest abnormality remarked, she went only when accompanied by her aunt, or by trusted old friends. She did not leave her home often, except for visits to my office, and when she went out alone it was always by day, and for never longer than an hour or so; I was confident that, operating under the dangerously poised balance of power between Betsy and Bess, so delicate that neither dared jolt the other unduly, she had heretofore kept her actions under strict control, but I made a point of discovering from Betsy where Miss R.'s journeying had taken her. There was, I thought, no longer any need to fear Betsy's eloping again, with the powerful opposition she must meet from Bess in any such attempt, and when it began to be apparent that Betsy was going to need all her strength to cope with Bess, and so must give up her unkind practical jokes upon Elizabeth and Beth, there was not even any danger of her repeating her favorite prank—taking them too far away to get home, and abandoning them. She spent much time walking, and even more time, when Bess was dominant, in going from one bank to another, where she stood outside and examined the architecture of the institution, presumably trying to decide upon the one least vulnerable to bandits; she sometimes went alone to soda shops—this usually Betsy's doing—where she indulged herself in quantities of chemically sweet concoctions; once she went to the museum and entered as a visitor, going from exhibit to exhibit, and showing the greatest interest, quite as though she had never come near the place before. She never visited any place of amusement, such as a theatre—which I believe she knew instinctively might overexcite her and shake her stability—but spent her time, largely, in mere wandering. She once rode a bus as far as the bay, and spent an afternoon looking out over the water, and, of course, mainly, there were Bess' famous shopping trips, where she went earnestly from store to store, fingering cloth and sniffing perfume, and lavishing upon herself numerous small rich indulgences.

It was thus relatively easy for Miss Jones to guarantee that her niece would be absent during our interview, and my cold tone and insistence upon my entire preoccupation with business had, I think, the effect of persuading her that she was entirely secure in both honor and reputation (oh, that I knew what Betsy had written her in my name!) in permitting me to visit her alone in the evening. Indeed, I felt as I set down the telephone that my disagreeable task was half done.

Betsy, unchastened still, made one more attempt to prevent my seeing her aunt, although I do not believe that she was aware that our appointment had already been settled. I had half-expected to see Betsy on the afternoon following my conversation with her aunt, but I reached my office late, after having been unavoidably detained by a most disagreeable session at the dentist's, and found upon my desk a note, written in a childish, unformed hand. This note was from poor Beth, and it said, "Dearest dearest Doctor, I did think you liked me in spite of everything and I didn't ever think you would really want me gone, but if you want to there isn't anything poor Beth can do. I guess there's no one in the world who likes me any more now that you have given me up. I guess I will just be lonely and sad all the time. Your own Beth."

I was grieved, and a little perplexed, at this epistle, and at a loss how to reassure the poor child until, happening to glance into the wastebasket to see if my pen had accidently fallen within, I took out several sheets of my office paper. The top one was a note of my own, left on my desk when I went out, and meant to tell Betsy that I would be a few minutes late that afternoon, because of an unavoidable appointment elsewhere. Below this, on the same sheet was scrawled, in the stylish handwriting which Bess affected, "Dear Doctor, just dropped by to say hello. Sorry I missed you. Elizabeth R."

On another sheet, and written with my pen instead of the pencil which the others had used, I found Betsy's characteristic blind scrawl: "i wont go i will stay you cant make me remember i can tell" and, again, "i will write what i please you cant hurt me i will tell him about what you did"

And, on still another sheet, in what seemed an attempt at

imitating my own handwriting—an attempt, I must confess, which would delude no one but the sillier Miss R.'s—but the same attempt, I reflected wryly, that Miss Jones might have read—was written the following composition:

"Miss R., although I have been patient with you for a long time, and put up with a good deal of your nonsense, I will not stand for your bad habits any longer. This is therefore my final and only notice that I am giving up your case, permanently and for ever. Do not come to my office again, if you please. Notify your aunt. Yrs. very truly, Victor J. Wright."

Even allowing for the execrable literary style of this masterpiece, I found it one of Betsy's more entertaining pranks, and amused myself in endeavoring to plot out what had taken place: I imagined that Bess had for some (probably financial) reason come to my office, and found my note. She had, reasonably enough considering that it was Miss Hartley's day off and the office was therefore empty, jotted down a note telling me she had called, and, of course, once Betsy got the pen between her teeth (oh dear; I am trying to learn to do without metaphors, and would have said I was getting on nicely, but see what comes up here to plague me!) she was off into a conversation with Bess, taunting and tormenting, and driving Bess closer toward that dark area where Bess felt herself in danger and was easily overcome, until, once dominant, Betsy could hold her precarious position for a while. Then, with what malicious gigglings I could only imagine, I thought that Betsy had with loving care composed the pseudo-letter from me in which I so blithely gave up Miss R.'s case. Betsy would then retreat, bring Beth forward, and lie back in delight while Beth remained long enough to read the unkind letter (which by a positive effort of silliness she might believe was actually from me) and write her plaintive answer.

I later learned that my recapitulation was largely correct, although Betsy had, in the refinement of her wickedness, first allowed Elizabeth out to read the letter of dismissal, before she summoned Beth, thus, if I may be permitted to phrase it so, killing two birds with one stone; Elizabeth had been too shocked and hurt to do anything but retreat silently, and Betsy, returning, had with great delight gathered up and thrown away all but Beth's final sad cry, and left *that* one for me.

It is a kind of practical joke of which I must warn the reader to beware, involving as it does the swift and almost certainly bewildering shift in identity of the joker—although if, as in this case, successful, an alarmingly thorough kind of prank! I should call it, as a matter of fact, a completely *practical* practical joke, not for the general order of person, but most effective if one just happens to have four warring personalities, and one pencil.

Having been so roundly dismissed, I dined pleasantly, and then, donning a dull necktie and a forbidding medical scowl, and forgetting my overshoes, I made for Miss Jones'. My steps were labored, for I went rehearsing the sounding phrases with which I intended to bring Miss Jones to an understanding of the precarious situation of her niece; withdrawn as I tried to hold myself, I could not help an involuntary feeling that we were all "choosing sides," as the children call it, and Miss Jones was too powerful a figure in our game to remain long unsolicited.

I dare not, in my capacity as writer, essay an attempt at describing either Miss Jones or the house in which she lived with her niece. My feelings with regard to Miss Jones are, I fear, too strongly tinged with prejudice to enable me to picture her with absolute accuracy, and, as for her house, I thought it an abomination. Let me only say, then, that I regard Miss Jones as a singularly unattractive woman, heavy-set and overbearing, with a loud laugh and a gaudy taste in clothes, as much unlike the prettier aspects of her niece as could be conceived, although it must be admitted that Betsy bore a strong family resemblance to her aunt. The house where they lived, in a neighborhood generally regarded as the most exclusive in our town, had, I thought, been put together by some family eccentric whose taste found its most perfect expression in the bleak, pudding-colored style so popular not too long ago among our grandparents, when taste and financial security were felt to be most surely expressed by a kind of ruthless ornamentation. I do not mean to say merely that Miss Jones' home was ugly; to my mind it was hideous. It had been freely embellished outside with many of the small details which so depress a lover of the classic in architecture; it was heavy with wooden lace and startling turrets, and gave the impression (and here I confess I am malicious) of having been assembled by the same unartistic hand as Miss Jones.

Miss Jones was, I should think, an accurate heir of the designer of the house, for she had assumed its aesthetic education in much the same state of mind as must have fired the dream which first envisaged those turrets, and Miss Jones had at her disposal fashions more repelling than were dreamed of a hundred years ago. (And, before Madam approaches me with a fire in her eye and a swatch of turkey-red in her fingers, let me hasten to admit that I, a peace-loving man, spend my leisure hours in a room executed by a woman's taste: my late wife, whose silken dreams were luckily limited by her means; I am still however, in undisputed possession of my worn leathery old chair, sir—are you?) Where the original Mrs. Jones had hung brocade at the narrow windows of her new house, the present Miss Jones had substituted a calico kind of thing, with great hideous "modern" designs; she had tried to compensate for the turrets outside by an equally fungoid growth within, a kind of embellishment which I have heard her describe as "art"; in the front hall, where one of my pedestrian generation would fully have expected to find, say, a marble urn, or a hatrack, or even a mirror (and I am persuaded, myself, that Mrs. Jones kept there some sort of inlaid table which held some sort of beaded and painted card tray)—in the front hall Miss Jones had settled a lifesize (I *presume* that it was lifesize) figure of black wood, unclad, and exhibiting much the same random unbeautiful physique as Miss Jones (and I have caught myself forcibly withdrawing my mind from the irresistible sense that it may very well have been a representation of Miss Jones; in that case it would have been only just barely lifesize, but I have no grounds whatsoever for this supposition which, as I say, I have steadfastly refused to entertain; for one thing, the statue had no hair and Miss Jones had). Beyond the hall, the stairway, once certainly handsome and sweeping, was now utterly vulgarized by a series of paintings on the wall supporting it, which I am not willing to suppose the work of Miss Jones' own hand. I used to shudder when I remembered those paintings, and think of the many Misses Jones who must have come as brides, blushing and smiling beneath their veils, decked in the pearls which I am positive good Mr. Jones hung about the necks of his daughters on their wedding days, down that staircase to pause and toss a bridal bouquet, and then I would try to picture a contemporary bride, perhaps our own Betsy, grinning like a jackanapes, turning under those unmaidenly paintings to hurl her flowers into the hall, where they would be caught, surely, by the black outstretched hand of the wooden figure below.

Oh, well. I have taken a roundabout way to get me to Miss Jones' house, but I have outgrown the minor vices of my youth, and am unwilling to find them painted on people's walls today. Enough; I have brought myself with laggard steps (and without my overshoes!) from my own fireside and into Miss Jones' front hall, and am regarding the black wooden figure with misgivings while Miss Jones gallantly takes my hat and coat and throws them, with an incomparable air, roughly over the end of the balustrade; and I, all unmanned, must needs follow her into her living room, a spot uninhabitable for human creatures. I wondered irreverently at the comparative mildness of Miss R.'s mental illness, looking at the great mounds and masses of bright colors, the overlarge furniture (overlarge for me, overlarge for Miss R., but of course suited nicely to Miss Jones), the great splashing decorations, of which the "modern" design upon the curtains was not the least, the bizarre ornaments. I sat myself down timidly upon a chair covered over with orange peacocks and found at my elbow a shivering creation composed entirely of wire and bright metals; as I breathed this airy creature moved and fluttered, swung half around and back, and continued pendulum, while I hesitated to breathe again, for fear I should send it lofting altogether out of sight and lose Miss Jones a precious object. I had hoped briefly that there might be some spot in it for a man to lay his pipe, but no: the ashtray was a hand, reaching out avariciously as though to snatch away my pipe—and indeed, my pouch and matches, too—in its porcelain grasp, and I thought, again in wonder, of how everything in this house seemed to have an air of seizing at a person, and I put my pipe away. It is a fine pipe, and I should hate to have it taken from me, but I had then perforce to accept a cigarette from Miss Jones and allow her to light it for me. During all this time—since she was of course not utterly insensate—she had kept up a kind of conversation, wanting to know how I did, and how I liked the weather, and did I find my chair to my taste, and would I take brandy?

When, thoroughly wound about with spider webs, I consented to a glass of brandy, she poured me a generous share in a goblet which, it pleased me to fancy, the grandfather of the patriarchal Jones had brought home in his piratical loot, and I set it upon the table next me, where it provoked my airy acquaintance into a frenzy of oscillation. Miss Jones, then, composed herself with her own brandy and the bottle with it, onto a sofa of radiant pink and green, which did not become her; "Well?" she said squarely, "what do you have to say for yourself?"

"Madam," I said (and I had upon her very step concluded upon addressing her as "Madam"; I feared that too free an address might defeat my end, and mark me as much interested in "Miss Jones" as "Miss R.'s aunt"; "Madam," therefore, I began), "I cannot imagine that you have gone for this long time in entire ignorance of your niece's deteriorating mental health." (Thinking, you see, that by an implied reproach over lack of interest I might compel her to listen to me respectfully, since surely no one could accuse *me* of lack of interest, or of ignorance on the subject!) She signified slightly that she conceded the first point—if I may so call it—to me, and I continued as delicately as I could manage in my formal, prepared speech: "I have been most anxious to discuss these matters with you, since it is now apparent to me that Miss R. is approaching a climax in her illness, and one of which we must take immediate advantage. I propose, if you will allow me, to lay before you the full history" (the devil; I had absolutely de-

cided to use some such phrase as "ensure that you have been
fully informed," in order to drive home the point about her
lack of interest, and even hint that her niece may not have been
entirely truthful with her always; but it was done now, and I
continued fairly smoothly) "of the various manifestations of
Miss R.'s illness during this period when she has been my patient, and to see if you will agree with me in my outline for
further treatment" (should we have at Bess, all together, I was
asking her, but hardly liked to phrase it so) "and to ask, naturally, for your assistance in bringing about a complete and
final cure."

There, I thought; she cannot complain of a lack of polish in
me; surely she has not for a long time sat patiently under such
a well-turned speech, or one, I must admit in honesty (and you
thought, reader, that I did not know it?) so entirely meaningless.

There was a short silence, during which Miss Jones, apparently in meditation, sipped of her brandy, and touched her
necklace, and regarded the floor, and nodded slowly, and then
she raised her eyes candidly to me, and began with a grave inclination, "My dear doctor, in the past few years with my
niece, I have frequently thought of—and even suggested—her
taking professional advice. Believe me, I should not have recommended what is for me such an extreme step (and you will
forgive me, I know, for this attitude, understandable in a
layman) if I had not felt that a person better qualified would
better understand and assist my niece than one who, like myself, has had little or no experience with the mentally ill. Except," Miss Jones continued reflectively, "with her goddamned
mother. But certainly I believe that your superior judgment
must be consulted first, and I shall of course be prepared to
follow through on any course of action suggested by yourself."

Score one for Miss Jones, I thought, a veritable tiger among
women; I myself would have shaded the ironic inflection upon
"layman," but it is of course a matter of taste; we all have our
preferences and I would be the last to deny my own; now I said
smilingly, "Then you will not prevent me from describing to you
what gives me a good deal of understandable satisfaction—my
own conduct of Miss R.'s case so far?"

"Indeed not," she said. "More brandy?"

I permitted her to refill my glass, and most generously, too, and then launched—having come already prepared with my notebooks—into a detailed account of Miss R.'s case, omitting only those factors which might prove distressing to Miss R.'s own aunt—an occasional off-color reference in Betsy's activities, and of course the greater part of her animadversions upon myself, and various slighting remarks upon her aunt and, naturally, all reflections upon the unfortunate dead woman who had been mother to the one, and sister to the other. As I spoke—and I spoke well, having so thoroughly rehearsed myself, and having my notes besides—Miss Jones listened attentively, with every appearance of great fascination; she interrupted me once with a question about Betsy's early appearance—whether it was possible that Betsy had been able to express herself briefly and violently before my first awareness of her; she recounted to me the incidents of an evening spent by herself and her niece at a friend's house, which had directly influenced her in seeking medical assistance. I listened to her with patience, since of course all facts are vital, but during her interruption I was strongly afraid of losing the thread of my own narrative, and its perfect balance, and had at last to cut her off in order that I might continue. Again, she asked and insisted on a more detailed and simpler description of the dissociated personality, as described by Doctor Prince, and again I must break off and give it her. We were wasting time, I thought, since I knew the subject perfectly and she need not know any more than she did, and always present in my mind was the approaching return of Miss R., so I said at last, "Then, Miss Jones, you agree with me that an attempt must be made to force these various personalities into assimilation?"

"Your superior judgment . . ." she murmured. "More brandy?"

I had by his time taken so much of Miss Jones' keen potations: her flattery, her brandy, her stimulating intelligence, that I was perhaps a little heady; at any rate, I permitted her to fill my glass again, and I continued, "My dear," and then stopped, with my face no doubt as scarlet as I felt it to be, "I *beg* your pardon," and I stumbled. "I am afraid that I was assuming, most unintentionally, the tone and manner which I employ for your niece. I *do* beg your pardon."

The amiable woman laughed outright. "It is not an address which I hear often," she said. "By all means feel free to honor me as your dear."

I laughed in turn, and felt most comfortable; we were beginning to understand one another better, I felt, and was moved to say in a kind of sadness, "Our generation, madam, yours and mine, was a kinder one as regards the small graceful ways of life . . ."

"I never found it so," she said. "Indeed, when I think back on my own youth—"

"But to Miss R.," I said. "I look forward to seeing *her,* at any rate, gay, and happy, and free of worries and pain; it is within *our* power, my dear Miss Jones, to set her free."

"Work together, and bring a new being into the world?" asked Miss Jones, without inflection.

"Ah . . . precisely," I said. "In a manner of speaking."

"I would be pleased," said the girl's aunt, "if she could just get around the house without falling over the furniture. First I couldn't talk to her because she used to sit there with her mouth open and her hands hanging down like paws, and then she goes wild, laughing and yelling and all cheerful and fine, and then she runs away and when I bring her back . . ." She shivered dramatically. "Look," she said finally (and I sitting speechless) "try to understand my position, if you can." She smiled at me winningly. "You know that I have no knowledge about these things, and I am afraid very little sympathy; I have always been very sound, I think, and have the ordinary person's feeling that being cr—mentally ill is a disgrace." She held up her hand as I was about to interrupt. "No," she said. "I realize perfectly how foolish I sound. But kindly do not forget that all the time Elizabeth was growing up, and having the devil's own time with adolescence and getting into all this mess without anyone even noticing—and you can thank *me* for that, I guess; *I'm* the one who cared for her, really; anyway, during all this time, I was not only trying to keep a decent home here for the child, and something she could be proud of, but I was also taking care of a brutal, unprincipled, drunken, vice-ridden beast. Her mother."

Miss Jones stopped abruptly, overcome by emotion, and for a moment I only sat helpless, avoiding looking at her as she sat with her hand over her eyes; at last she sighed deeply, and lifted her head. "Sorry," she said. "I guess confessions like this are the usual thing for you, doctor, but it hurts me to have to speak so of my own sister. Brandy, I think."

For a few minutes we sat in silence, sipping our brandy and I, for one, brooding upon the mournful revelation of the character of Miss R.'s parent; at last poor Miss Jones sighed again, and then laughed a little. "Well," she said, "I've told you our secret, and I think I feel better. I suppose I've spent so long trying to forget what my sister was like, and trying to believe it couldn't touch Elizabeth . . ." She let her voice trail off, and I could only nod sympathetically.

Finally I shook myself together, and set down my glass with a sigh of my own. "I appreciate your distress," I said. "Why did you lock Elizabeth in her room while her mother was dying?"

"Well, goddam," she said. "You *have* been getting it out of the girl." She laughed, as though I had made some huge joke, and then finally she began, not, perhaps, so solemnly as before, "All right, then, but I warn you it was better the other way. I didn't want Elizabeth around when I saw her mother that morning, because I was honestly scared of the effect her mother's dangerous state—dangerous, I mean, because she was dying; not her moral state *that* time—might have on a girl of Elizabeth's delicacy. She had been through a severe nervous strain during early adolescence, and I thought . . ." She looked up and saw my smile, and shrugged. "Well," she said defensively, "she *did* have a hell of a time when she was about fifteen."

"I am sure you did your best for her," I said obscurely.

"I'm sure I did better than that," she said. "And I find I am beginning to like you, doctor, so I have decided that I will be doing my best still if I tell you the truth, which I suppose is what you want."

"If you can bring yourself to it," I said, and she grinned, reminding me of Betsy again.

"Well," she said, looking deep into her glass, "maybe you'd better know what kind of a person my sister was." She looked up at me curiously. "You know the kind of person who walks all over other people without really meaning to, and then goes back to pick them up and apologize and steps on their heads again? She was like that, a really pretty girl, and delicate and fragile—not like me." She stopped for a minute, until I thought that she had forgotten the train of her narrative. Then, when she went on, her tone was colder, almost dispassionate. "She just seemed to do everything the wrong way. When she wanted a new dress, it always turned out to be just the only dress that would have looked nice on someone else, if *she* hadn't gotten it first. She contaminated everything, even when she didn't know she was doing it. Whenever she decided to go to a dance or a party or a picnic, it always turned out that her going would mean inconvenience or trouble for someone else—maybe someone had to stay home because there wasn't room for everyone on the hay wagon, or the only fellow left to take her was just getting ready to ask someone else . . . I remember once," she added with an odd smile, "there just weren't enough sandwiches to go round. Anyway, no matter what she did, even when she picked out a man to marry, she always managed to do it at the worst possible time, in the worst possible style. I didn't really hate her, you see," she said, raising her eyes to mine. "No one could."

"Was she older than you?"

"Yes." She was surprised. "But only a year or so." Silently she rose and poured more brandy into my glass, and filled her own. "When—when her husband died, she left the place where they had been living in New York and came back here to live with me, and she brought Elizabeth with her. Elizabeth was only two then, named after her mother, naturally. Who would ever think of naming a baby Morgen?" Again she was silent, thinking, and then after a minute she went on. "It was the only time in her life she couldn't get her own way, with Ernest's money. Even Ernest," she continued slowly, "wasn't completely taken in by her, and he figured just the way everyone else always did—when you have trouble with Morgen's pretty sister, get Morgen to take care of it for you. Anyway, if *you* had a lot of money and wanted to be reasonably sure your baby daughter would get some of it when she grew up and needed it, Elizabeth Jones would be the last person you'd think of giving it to. I think," she said, "that he tried to tell me *then* how much he had always cared for me, but the lawyers made him take it out."

"Then your niece is actually an heiress?"

"In about two months, when she's twenty-five. And," said her aunt darkly, "when she gets it she won't find a penny of it wasted unless you count what was spent on educating her a waste of money. In *spite* of what she says."

Miss Jones scowled fearsomely, and I said in haste, "Miss R. has mentioned her inheritance to me. I believe, however, that when she is herself again you will find her more just with regard to your management."

"If Ernest ever thought I wanted the money," Miss Jones said plaintively, "he would have given it directly to me."

"It certainly is a pity," I agreed, "that the question of this money has entered into Miss R.'s case; we were quite confused enough without it, and it can certainly have no bearing upon her cure, except insofar as a feeling of personal security can help to tranquilize her mind."

"She had the gall to tell me that she was going to spend whatever she liked anyway, and buy all the clothes and things she wanted no matter who paid. As if I hadn't always let her do what she pleased, for no thanks either, and given up all the dresses and picnics all the time, because Morgen was so good-humored and didn't care whether she stayed home or not; at least," said Miss Jones with satisfaction, "I outlived her."

"But how did she die?" I asked at last, softly.

"Badly. As I knew she would—whining and saying it wasn't her fault and she was sorry and if she didn't die everything was going to be different." Miss Jones looked up at me grinning, although I think she had largely forgotten who she was talking to, and even, indeed, if she was addressing anyone at all; "She was mud clear up to the neck," Miss Jones said. "I told her I was sorry she was dying, too, and I cried for her. It was the best I could do. And of course I insisted upon Elizabeth's grieving for her too."

"Quite natural."

"Certainly. I don't know what people would have thought. Anyway, Elizabeth *was* sick again for a while, the way she was before, what everyone kept saying was growing pains. A kind of nervous fever, *I* called it, and it was good enough for my mother."

Not caring to unravel this dubious piece of medical effrontery, I said, "I suppose the actual death of her mother was most trying for your niece."

"Most trying," she agreed solemnly. "As a matter of fact, I cannot remember a time when my niece behaved better."

"It happened . . . when? In the morning, I believe you said?"

"About eleven, I think. I remember I was having a hell of a time with Elizabeth about where her mother *was* that morning; there was some foolishness about a party, or something—as a matter of fact, it may have been my sister's birthday, although I'm not sure—they had so *many* little things together—anyway, *I* couldn't give the girl any new story about where her mother had been all morning and all night and all the day before. I knew she was out somewhere, that's all, but it's a *hell* of a thing to have to explain to her own daughter, when she's seen enough of it already to begin to wonder a lot. And then the door opens very softly, like she hoped to get in before we noticed, and she was standing there . . ."

"Smiling," I said softly.

"Smiling, kind of fearful, and wondering, hoping she'd gotten away with it one more time. She had to hold onto the door to keep from falling. And I'd just been saying to Elizabeth . . ." She stopped, and shook her head, and took up her glass.

"And?"

"Well," said Miss Jones, "Elizabeth was very upset, natu-

rally, when we realized that there was something wrong—
really *wrong,* that is, this time—and I took her right upstairs
and told her to lie down and I'd take care of things, and naturally I called Harold Ryan and he came over. *He* can tell you
more about it than I can, naturally. When Elizabeth was told,
it was, naturally, a great shock to her. Another nervous fever,
as a matter of fact."

"Unfortunate," I said prudently. "And terribly hard on you."

"I enjoyed every minute of it," said Miss Jones. "I felt kind
of sorry for Elizabeth, of course, losing her mother so suddenly, but we were both better off afterward. You can't bring
up a child in an environment like that, not that I condemn my
sister for her way of life, but she should have given the child to
me outright. *He* wanted me to have her. It was like my own
child."

I was suddenly seriously alarmed for fear she might begin to
cry, and was hardly reassured when she chose, instead, to refill
my glass and her own, moving with a steadiness which I found,
even then, impressive. When she had settled down again and
taken up her glass she looked at me dreamily for a moment
and then, fetching a deep breath, smiled and said. "Let's not
talk about it any more. It makes Morgen very unhappy. So tell
me about *your* wife."

"*My* wife, madam?"

She smiled still. "Yes," she said, "tell me about your wife."

"She is dead, madam."

"I know." She looked up at me with surprise. "But what did
she use to be like?"

"She was a fine woman," I said, and then, because I thought
that I had perhaps shown a shade more curtness than was my
wont when discussing my unfortunate wife, I went on more
gently, "she was a woman of intelligence, of spirit, and of
kindness. A truly great helpmeet, and a sincere loss to those
she left behind."

"Ah," Miss Jones said happily. "And who did she leave behind?"

"Myself," I said. "She was a great loss to me."

"Ah," said Miss Jones. "Irremediable, I suppose?"

"Precisely, madam."

"I wonder sometimes what it would be like to suffer from the loss of a loved one. Does one tend to become reconciled?"

"Indeed, madam, I cannot tell. For my own part . . . in any case, your sister, madam. Surely. A woman among thousands . . ."

"And who gave you the idea she was among thousands?" Miss Jones laughed rudely. "I knew some of them," she said, "the thousands she was among." She laughed again. "I wouldn't be caught dead with any of them," she said.

She lost herself again in her obscure musings, and I, sitting back in my chair, touched briefly by the aerial creature at my elbow, pipeless and overfull of bad brandy, endeavored to clarify my mind and decide whether I might with politeness take my departure. It did not seem that Miss Jones had any further information she was prepared to give me, but from what I already knew I was able, I thought, to define my next attack upon Miss R. Carefully, my eye fixed almost unseeing upon a painting which may have been black polka dots on a red background, or a red field filled with black holes—and my eyes, without my mind's attention, focusing in and out, from holes to polka dots and back again—I set up my little mental figures: Elizabeth, relaxing into stupor, situated between a foul-living mother and a foul-tongued aunt; Bess, grieving for a mother only three weeks dead; Betsy, not grieving for a mother she had never believed she had; could I bring these three, together, face to face with their mother, let them see her clear, if I dared?

I know myself, surely, and not at any time with more accuracy than at that moment; I am a man easily weakened, and by nothing more surely than the temptation to yield. I could not afford the picture of Miss R.'s stalwart knight, the road behind him strewn with dragonish corpses, bringing his princess safely home and then, full within the citadel, turning her over once more to the wicked enchanter who had first put her into jeopardy; if I had time, I thought, it might almost be safer to bring Bess cautiously along the narrow path of days and years into the present. But there was not time—

"And then, by the great god, I *told* her so," remarked Miss

Jones, turning violently at me, and seeming to think that she had been speaking aloud all this time, "and I will not hear any voice that says I did wrong."

"My dear madam, I—"

"I have *never* admitted to doing wrong, not in my whole rotten misbegotten sodden flodden ambergodden life, not wrong, not evil, not trespass against, no, nor adultery neither."

"Surely you do not accuse me of—"

"And now I will be heard." And with a great shout Miss Jones arose, towering in that great room, and lifting a voice almost great enough to shatter her fragile ornaments, some of them so dangerously close to my person, "and when I choose to be heard, the lowest legions of hell may turn in vain to silence me and when I choose to speak not all the winds of earth can drown my voice for I speak truly and well and raise not your hand to me, sirrah, for I might strike you down as a reptile or a craven bellyful wanderer upon my green earth if you so much as whimper; I charge you, sirrah, look not on me."

"Indeed, madam. . . ." I was dismayed, and hoped, somehow, for some auspicious catastrophe; one of her feet to smash through the floor, perhaps, or a flailing arm to crash down a wall; "Indeed . . ."

"Now listen, rascal, and be alarmed, for I shall not be tampered with nor restrained; when I speak, you will tremble and be afraid."

Good heavens, I thought, trembling in verity; might I with any optimism anticipate an apoplexy? After the quantities of brandy she had taken, if she continued thus . . .

"And now I tell you that having let your devils loose upon me you look to see me fall, and your horrid revenge accomplished, and filthy and crawling you hope to spit and gulp at my blood and snarl over my flesh and scratch and claw at one another to catch your teeth in my bones and I will not have it, for I alone and in myself will defy you and your legions, and defy me if you will! For I challenge you and I dare you here on this spot and I challenge you—do you dare to touch me? Will you defile me in the manner of *my* death? Am I to be done by children and by changelings, by yappings and by mutterings, by blood-drinkers and by bone-suckers, am I to die underfoot? Indeed, am *I* your little creature, to suffer whimpering under your hands and submit with tears to your hardness and take joy in my lowness? Surely when you question *me* you mistake; surely there are those who bow lovingly to your words and your sharp looks and your little touchings and will talk and talk and talk and I charge you here, sir, look well before you come to me! For I have done it, and I say I have, and I tell you here in my own voice that I have—"

"Goodnight, Miss Jones," I said, offended at last—as who would not be, since she had in so many words announced that she despised my questions?—and making ready to leave her.

"You are not half a man, clown, and not worth my presence!"

"Madam," I told her civilly enough, "if you were half a woman you would have had your sister's husband." I thought this a final shot, and would have fled hard upon it, but she shouted after me, "I had her child—will you deny it? I stole my sister's child—"

"Morgen *dear*." It was a voice cool, and dispassionate, and I turned, thinking to find a stranger (and in confession I will say here that I, too, had touched too heavily upon the Jones brandy, for I could not at once determine who stood in the doorway, fresh from outdoors, and icy).

"Doctor Wright will have a very bad opinion of our family," she said, coming forward into the silence which was, after that peroration, overwhelming.

"Not at all," I said, caught off balance.

"I hope you weren't listening to Aunt Morgen, doctor. She is worried about me, and I think she has been losing sleep, listening at my door all night."

"Go away," said Miss Jones flatly.

"Doctor Wright came to see me, you know; he is my physician. I think he would be relieved if you went to bed."

"Of course," I said, with almost unseemly haste. "But I greatly fear that I also—"

"I shall stay, until I have told what I have to tell, and I defy the legions of . . ." But it was weaker.

"Now, please, both of you." She turned, holding out her hands prettily to her aunt and to me. "I know how worried you both are over my health, and I would be the first to admit that I haven't been entirely certain of *myself*, but now you must both stop fretting yourselves; you are two dear people, and I love you both very much, and it makes me very happy to know that I can promise you both that there isn't going to be any more trouble. I'm all well now."

"My God, she looks like her mother," Miss Jones said to me. "All these years I've been trying to make her see what her mother was like, and now she *looks* like her."

"My mother was your sister," her niece said reprovingly, "and you're not going to talk like that any more, with her only three weeks dead. Morgen, will you leave us, please?"

"Now you see her," Miss Jones said to me. "Help me."

"Not I," I said, honest to the last; I would not have given her the aid of my hand for worlds; I was seeing defeat as possible for the first time, and knew it; I had no strength to spare for another dragon. "Indeed, madam," I said, "we must leave her."

"I defy—"

"Not *me,* Morgen."

"Betsy," I said wildly, "Betsy."

"Please." Her voice was quiet, and contained; I should not, even without the brandy, have recognized it; I am a man deeply afraid of failure, and yet I would not even have recognized her voice. "This is going to be the end of it," she said. "I tried to be nice about it, and yet here is Aunt Morgen shouting at me and calling me names, when I would have treated her kindly and never said a word against her, and here are *you,* doctor, and I thought better of you, I admit, but now you're after me again. I am going to tell you both, finally and flatly, that I do not need anything from either of you. I," and her voice grew very cold, "am going to get along very much better without you two."

I looked at Morgen; speech—although she had denied it me, when in full possession of the room and the air in it—seemed now to be *my* prerogative, and I knew that if I spoke, defeat for me was certain, for I was genuinely and honestly and sincerely angry; I had been insulted in my profession, my manhood, and my associates, and was in no temper to submit quietly to this impertinent girl; I can, however, neither justify nor explain myself by admitting that I knew in advance that submission at the moment was my wiser course; all the cures for all the Miss R.'s in the world would not, I think, have at that moment moderated my rage. "My dear young lady," I said then, in a voice full as measured as her own, "I assure you that this kind of childish insolence will gain you nothing save further misery; you will not speak again in my presence unless it be an apology; consider that it is only through my misguided sufferance that you continue to exist at all. This temporary power, this brief and insecure dominance, will not endure; take thought now of the months of preparation which brought you into being, kept you safe when you could not defend yourself, preserved you without harm until this moment; do you think that you may with impunity bring your pert words to bear against a power like that? If I relinquish you—and I am going to; I tell you now, Miss Bess, you have made your last charge against me—how long do you think you will survive, alone, without a guide or a friend or an ally? You are at best, young lady, only a slight, only a poor and partial creature, and for all your fine words, you will not stay long; I am leaving you in the entire conviction that without my aid you will only for a while be suffered to trouble your friends with your arrogance; I promise you, here and now, that you as a person will, with the knowledge of you I have, cease, absolutely and finally and without possibility of petition, cease, I tell you, unalterably cease to exist!"

Surely—I can see it now—a very substantial and well-rounded diatribe for a doctor dedicated to quiet and stealth; I confess to a little adjusting at this distance—surely no one, possessed of such an opportunity for such a fine speech, could resist altering a period here and there—but in truth I was very angry, angrier than I believe I have ever been before, and rendered reckless besides. I stormed out of the house—had I ever left it in peace?—and the black figure in the hall caught my coat sleeve as I passed.

I thought to myself as I came into the cool evening air that I

would be repentant soon enough, and I believe the first coherent thought I knew reached me as I came off the Jones walk
onto the street; I heard clearly the name of my wicked enchanter, to enrich whom I had slain so many dragons—it was
Victor Wright. Thus comforted, I could spare a pang for poor
Bess, blundering through another girl's life inadequately
equipped; had I the temper, I thought, I might have stayed by
her, coaxing her back into Betsy, and been impervious to her
clawed words; she, on her side, had no such recourse, and
could only, by calling my name, bring an even more unsympa-
thetic, if less brandied, Doctor Wright.

Understand, then, reader—if you have stayed with me,
cheek unreddened, all this while—I, too, repudiate all of this;
it was a shameful scene for a quiet man whose pipe had been
forcibly taken from him; I am now, thinking of it, still embarrassed at the picture of myself standing, eyes blazing and pos-
ture threatening, against these two women, one of whom I
loathed and the other of whom I often dominated; I cannot
believe that I so stood, and declared myself, and laid myself
low; I hope—I appeal it to you—that you cannot so see me,
driven by anger into outrage and repudiation.

We are all measured, good or evil, by the wrong we do to
others; I had made a monster and turned it loose upon the
world and—since recognition is, after all, the cruelest pain—
had seen it clearly and with understanding; Elizabeth R. was
gone; I had corrupted her beyond redemption and in the cool
eyes which now belonged entirely to Bess I read my own vanity
and my own arrogance. I reveal myself, then, at last: I am a
villain, for I created wantonly, and a blackguard, for I destroyed without compassion; I have no excuse.

5

AUNT MORGEN

Breakfast, never at all an auspicious meal for Morgen Jones, was never less ingratiating than the morning after her talk with Doctor Wright, only half-remembered in this cold spring sunlight, but disagreeably vivid in many aspects; Morgen recalled, for instance, that the doctor had left in a rage, nearly toppling the Nigerian ancestor figure in the hall, that someone had been making a good deal of noise, and that her niece had been insolent again. Her intended breakfast this morning had included warm sweet buns and butter, somehow reminiscent in spiced richness of the impractical meals she might have if she were—say—living alone on a tropical island, tasting fruit hot from the sun, or lying upon cushions in a tented harem, accepting lazily of comfits from a sandaled eunuch; the doctor had been poor company last night, she thought, and set aside her cinnamon buns, unwarmed. In her most optimistic recollections she could not believe that the interview had gone well; even before the doctor had become so unaccountably angry there had been a flavor of disagreeable insistence about the evening. Morgen had spoken at length about her sister Elizabeth, when, actually, Elizabeth was easily the least interesting subject to be taken up; at the thought of the untraveled countries of their conversation Morgen sighed, and looked at the clock to see if she might safely have three more aspirin. The sight of her niece entering the kitchen was not calculated to brighten Morgen's breakfast, and she watched with a cold and resentful eye as her niece poured a cup of coffee at the stove and then sat down at the table. She avoided her aunt's eye and did not speak, and at last Morgen—knowing that surely, as the day bore on, she would get to further aspirin and an eventual return of her good humor—said darkly into her coffee, "Thought of putting out four cups. One," she explained with care, "for each of you."

Her niece looked at her speculatively. "He likes to hear himself talk," she said. "I didn't think *you'd* get taken in by it, though."

"Then do me a favor," Morgen begged. "I promise to keep it a secret, but I've got too bad a headache for arithmetic this morning. Just tell me how many of you there really are."

"Me. Your niece Elizabeth."

"Well, now, *there's* something *doesn't* take me in." Morgen said, setting down her cup to nod, and then regret it. "Something I *know,*" she went on, holding her head still, "is, you're not *Elizabeth,* anyway."

"Don't be silly, Aunt Morgen. Just because I used to—"

"You used to be well-behaved and a lady; no matter what other damn fool things you did, you knew how to behave. And now, you sweet baby, you act like your mother."

"I refuse to discuss my mother with you. I am still too deep in grief—"

"Oh, shut up," said Morgen. "I can get awful sick of hearing you blabber about your grief. Anyway, the doc says you're only a splinter named Bess."

"Well," said Bess, stung, "he called *you* Madam and you're—"

"Common civility is as much beyond your infantile comprehension," Morgen said grandly, "as . . . as . . . oh, hell. Anyway," she went on, amused, "maybe I *am* a Madam, for all you know. I've got a house full of nice girls." And she laughed in spite of her headache.

"I don't know how you can *talk* like this," Bess said viciously, "with your sister just dead, in a house of mourning, and me an orphan."

"Look," Morgen said, "I'm going to go right on talking however I please, and it's *my* house and there's no mourning in it, for your mother or anyone else, and I would like to take this unparalleled opportunity of letting you know that, orphan or not, I have been for the past six years feeding you and dressing you and doing everything but wiping your nose and all of a sudden you turn around and try to tell me I don't know what year it is and you're an orphan. Orphan!"

"I tell you this," said her niece, pointing a butter knife at her aunt, "it may be a good story about feeding and dressing me and spending my money for me, but pretty soon you and a lawyer are going to have a little talk about what's been happening to that money since my father died. Because I'm going to get a lawyer to make you give it all back."

Morgen snorted. "You're going to get a spanking, better," she said. "And stop fidgeting with the silverware, because it's mine."

"Nothing is yours," said Bess, "and if I don't see an accounting of my—"

"You know," said Morgen, leaning back with some pleasure, "if you don't watch yourself with all that wild talk one of these days Auntie is going to get *really* mad and let you have it. And if you don't stop scrabbling that butter knife around right now my headache is liable to get worse and then I will take that thing out of your hand and slice off your fingers one by one."

She giggled. "You scare her with that kind of talk," she said. "She hates people talking about hurting her."

"Hello," said Morgen agreeably. "You're supposed to be another one, aren't you?"

"Betsy," she said. "I'm the one you like best."

"Well, keep mighty quiet, then. Auntie feels like hell."

"Too bad," Betsy said. "I don't *ever* feel bad; I don't even know what it's like to feel bad."

"Dandy," said Morgan heartily. "I wish it was you instead of me."

"Poor Morgen."

"That damned doctor," Morgen said. "Why couldn't he stay where he belongs?"

There was a silence, and then Betsy said fearfully, "You mean Doctor *Wrong?* Was he *here?*"

"Last night. We had a long heart-to-heart-to-heart-to-heart little talk. Oh, lord," said Morgen, putting her hand over her eyes.

Betsy was quiet for so long this time that Morgen uncovered her eyes to see if Betsy was still there. "What's the matter, kiddo?" Morgen asked. "You don't like him either?"

"He doesn't want anyone to enjoy themselves," Betsy said. She leaned forward across the table and said persuasively, "Look, Morgen, first thing you know he'll be lecturing and ranting at *you*, too. Don't you talk to him any more."

"Couldn't if I wanted to," Morgen said, remembering. "He's not coming back any more. He doesn't like any of us much."

"Who cares?" said Betsy. "Good riddance to bad rubbish."

"I wish he'd gone before he came," Morgen said. "I *do* feel sad." She closed her eyes and rested her head against the back of her chair.

"*I* know," Betsy said brightly, "I'll send you someone feels worse than you do." Her eyes fell, and lifted timidly and the smile died on her face, and she looked up apprehensively at her aunt. "Hello," she said. "Aunt Morgen."

Aunt Morgen opened her eyes, and closed them again. "No," she said. "Go away, child. Auntie loves you but she's already got troubles enough. Just go away."

"I'm sorry," Elizabeth said falteringly.

"God almighty holy God almighty go away," Morgen said. "You make a big horrible muddy dirty black cloud come down over the whole goddam world when you give me that long face; go away go away go away go away go—"

"All *right*," said Betsy, coming back laughing. "Now don't you like your nice Betsy?"

"You just stay around for a while," Morgan said earnestly, "and don't leave me with that clam again."

"Be nice or I'll send Beth," Betsy said. "She's the one who calls you 'Auntie darling' and says you're all she has in the world and do you still love her?"

Morgen groaned.

"Tell you about that doctor," Betsy said conversationally,

"what *he* wanted to do was set Bess up as me, and let her go on pretending to *be* me all the time, so's they could share up all that money."

"I'm going to give that money to a home for stray cats," said Morgen. "So help me."

"Well, *I* don't want it," Betsy said.

"*That* one," said Morgen, as one to whom a vast injury has been done, "that puny white-faced slimy bitch, she doesn't think Auntie ought to take a glass of brandy after meals. Account for every penny!" She glared at her niece. "Me!" she said.

"*I* wouldn't do that," Betsy said. "I don't want the money at all."

"Look," Morgen said with great reasonableness, "I'm a simple character. All I want is to be comfortable, and sleep and eat and drink and talk the way I always have, the way I *like* to eat and drink and sleep and talk. For a long time I got along fine. I had this niece, and she wasn't much good to anyone, but I liked her fine, and I thought she liked me, and we used to talk to each other and she listened to me when I got sounding off and maybe I wasn't always careful to be so delicate with her, but I always thought things were going along all right. I just thought that if I liked her and she liked me and we got along together it didn't matter if maybe some people thought she was lacking a little, so long as I kept an eye out for signs that she was going like her mother. Because one thing I *did* know," said Morgen with a sigh, "was that *there* she needed watching. But I wasn't bright enough to see how things were going till it was too late, so now I've got *you*. I'm not complaining, and I brought it on myself, and anyway you're a little brighter than she—you—used to be, but I spent a long time with her. The way I see it, no matter what the doc says or you say or old moneybags says, you're all of you still my niece, and I'm responsible for you. But I'm not used to being teased and defied and coaxed and whined at, and I like people to keep their voices down when I have a headache, and I don't like having people's problems dumped in my lap, and one thing I've got to

say for the old Elizabeth I had for so many years—she never
had any problems *I* knew about, except how to sit down in a
chair without falling off the seat."

"Well," said Betsy, with something of embarrassment, "of
course, a lot of that was me. I guess she would have gotten
along a little bit better if it hadn't been for me."

"Don't tell *me* about it," Morgen said. "You kids can fight
your own battles. I don't care if there are twenty of you, what
you all boil down to is still my niece Elizabeth, and you can
play all the games you want with yourself, so long as you lay
off me."

"Perhaps," she said sweetly, "if I were dead?"

Aunt Morgen raised her eyes briefly, and then dropped them
again. "If you were dead," she said, "I could maybe get a little
quiet to drink my coffee. In case you care."

"I don't," she said. "And don't *you* think for a moment that
I was joking about that lawyer. Because if I don't get an
accounting—"

"Why was I ever born?" Morgen asked rhetorically, and got
up and left the table. "I am going back to bed," she said over
her shoulder. "Soak your head in the coffee pot."

Left alone, Bess poured herself out a fresh cup of coffee, and
sat down again at the table. After a minute she got up again to
search for a pad of paper and a pencil in a corner of the kitchen
counter, and then sat down again and tried to figure, starting
with the estimated amount of her father's fortune and, trying
to remember all she could about interest and capital, and puzzling over what it might cost Morgen to run this house, and
feed and clothe both of them, and how much Morgen had
probably used of her own money, and how much from her
niece's inheritance. The terms of her inheritance were not at
all clear to Bess, and she had been unsuccessful in any attempt
to learn more from her aunt; she knew only that what sounded
like a vast sum of money was waiting for her, and that Aunt
Morgen had probably helped herself freely by pretending to
buy clothes and food for her niece; Bess had been vainly hoping to make Aunt Morgen give her a lot of money in advance,
but Aunt Morgen was quite unreasonably stubborn about al-

lowing her niece access to liquid funds since they had come back together from New York, and the best Bess had been able to manage was the ability to buy whatever she pleased from the stores in town on her aunt's accounts. Lately, however, since various small silly things had been happening—like the time Aunt Morgen had walked in and found Bess taking money from Morgen's pocketbook, although Bess had surely no intention of stealing, and had, in fact, no actual consciousness of being anywhere near Morgen's room—anyway, lately, Morgen had closed all the accounts and hidden her household cash, and now Bess couldn't buy the smallest thing unless she got permission first, and couldn't even have carfare unless she begged it from Morgen. It was no way to treat a nineteen-year-old girl who was going to have all the money she wanted someday. Bess sat back and looked at her page scribbled with figures. They *looked* like money, all with dollar signs in front, and decimal points; a good lawyer would know what to make of them. Suddenly, with curiosity, Bess switched the pencil to her right hand and held it over the pad.

"Come on, silly," she whispered. "A penny for your thoughts."

The pencil stayed unmoving in her relaxed hand, and Bess, looking at it, fell to wondering about rings, when she had her money. She did not care for diamonds, she thought, and most rings she had seen in the jewelry stores had such small stones it was hard to see them, much less know whether they were real or not; something like a ruby was more to her taste, but a big one. She fell back then before Betsy, who thoughtfully took up the pencil and drew heavy black lines through all of Bess' figures, tasted her coffee, and then dosed it richly with sugar and cream. For a few minutes Betsy amused herself with the pencil and paper, drawing circle heads with eyes and noses and mouths, which she labeled "Doctor Wrong" and "Aunt Morgen" and "Bess." After a few minutes Betsy wearied of the pencil and paper, yawned, and disappeared before Elizabeth, who touched the back of her neck daintily, looked with nausea on the coffee, and got up to take the cup and saucer to the sink, where she rinsed it out thoroughly, and then moved back to the table to gather up the coffeepot and Aunt Morgen's breakfast dishes. When she had washed and dried the dishes, and while she was on her way to the refrigerator for a glass of milk, Bess reestablished herself and took herself into the hall where she listened carefully for a minute to hear if Aunt Morgen was stirring, then put on her coat and hat and left the house softly.

When Morgen came downstairs again, early in the afternoon, it was with the deep sense of well-being which comes with the general over-all effect of many aspirin judiciously administered, and the consequent rosy and painless impression of walking in a cloud; her headache was gone, as was her humiliating consciousness of the night before, and so, as a matter of fact, was her ordinary conviction that her feet were touching the floor as she walked. Her hand, as she opened the refrigerator door, was independent and intelligent, and the smile upon her face was beatific. I shall have a little something to eat, Morgen was thinking; soft-boiled eggs? I am an invalid, barely convalescent, and something buttery and soft . . .

The refrigerator was full of mud. Morgen stood for a minute staring at it, not at all comprehending the ugly slimy mess where she had expected to find white and shining shelves, with eggs and butter and cheeses neatly arranged; the inside of the door was smeared and the ice trays were oozing, and somewhere within, where the cold meats were kept, a worm stirred, almost frozen and yet still moving, turning blindly toward the light. Morgen stepped back, her stomach turning, and then without closing the door fled. She could not dress, could not wash; when she looked at her hands she thought there were worms on her fingers, working their way in and out and between and over, wet and cold, and she put her hands under her pillow and closed her eyes and held her mouth tight shut to keep the worms out, and screamed silently in her bed. I am all alone and I am an old woman and I will die without love, she thought, with her face hidden in the pillow, and at last slept again.

When she awakened she was well, without the intercession of aspirin, and she rose firmly, straightened her clothes and her hair, looked at her hands carefully, and told herself she was an old fool, and ten times an old fool. She went downstairs into her spotless kitchen, where the refrigerator stood clean and immaculate, regarding her askance, and the breakfast dishes were neatly back on the shelves, and the coffeepot scrubbed and put away. After a minute Morgen (I am an old fool, she thought) touched the handle of the refrigerator and pressed it and swung open the door, and inside the white eggs and clean yellow butter box shone on her, although she knew without question that she did not care for food. A drink, she thought, not daring to put her hand or even a finger to the ice trays; a glass of brandy to insure that I am well now, and she took down the brandy bottle from the shelf and poured steadily into a glass. Your health, she thought, raising her glass to herself.

Morgen Jones, of the Owenstown Joneses, was not by any means to be described as a fool. Her life was circumspect, rigid, and extremely private, because she found very little in the world outside to tempt her into mingling with its people. A woman well-educated when a good education was still thought of among her mother's friends as somehow the best possible occupation for an unmarried girl—better, surely than going out as a governess, or taking up the painting of china—she had been bred to reason and comprehend and read whatever she pleased, and in the very particular workings of her mind now, there was much humor, some tolerance, a great deal of unexpressed affection, and no space whatever for the appreciation of the remarkable. Morgen had been, for a very long time, the most remarkable object in her own landscape, and anything stranger than herself was, to her mind, either an obvious sham, or non-existent.

She was, therefore, unprepared to accept in her niece any more startling manifestation than an entirely ladylike "nervous breakdown," and in all that she had seen of Elizabeth, and in all that she had been told by Doctor Wright, she found nothing to worry her. She had watched, and nodded, and her mind had been actively dismembering, analyzing, separating, and scrutinizing, grinding up all information into a palatable mixture of nervous illness in her niece and fanciful phraseology in the doctor; she was confident, finally, of her stern ability to bring a sensible matter-of-fact eye to bear upon the situation, and in short order reduce the niece and the doctor to separate embarrassed creatures, wholly well, and slinking away to bury their romances realistically in everyday life. If Morgen's practical eye could be said to perceive a cure where she did not acknowledge a disease, it might be phrased as "Don't appear to notice," or "They're only doing it to get attention," or even—in extreme cases—"Humor them."

She had not materially altered herself in more years than she chose to remember. Her manner of dress, of speech, of doing her hair, of spending her time, had not changed since it first became apparent to a far younger Morgen that in all her life to come no one was, in all probability, going to care in the slightest how she looked, or what she did, and the minor wrench of leaving humanity behind was more than compensated for by her complacent freedom from a thousand small irritations. At first she had found it necessary to remind herself often of the clamors and demands other people made upon one another, the attentions expected, the answers awaited, the gifts and visits and good wishes to be returned, the affections to be reciprocated, but with the securing of her niece she found at last that there was nothing other people had which she needed to regard, any more, with a longing eye. Elizabeth immediately assumed the position of most importance in the little group of mortal folk with whom Morgen still held converse of one kind or another, and it was assumed by all of them that Elizabeth felt as much deep affection for her aunt as Morgen felt for her niece.

Although Morgen had not changed in so many years that she had fallen to regarding the world outside her windows as in a state of constant fevered activity, she was fond of her own whims—changes in the decorations of the house, for instance, which, although in a world of styles and ages, never strayed from the basic pattern of the architecture: one of extreme and loving ugliness—and did not take kindly to having them disputed. One of Morgen's notions had set up the Nigerian ancestor figure in her front hall, and she disliked having her niece's doctor jostle it when he left in anger. She was deeply pleased with the sound of her own voice, and did not care to be interrupted; she had been prepared to frown upon Doctor Wright because she felt that in some obscure fashion he was responsible for the change in her life which came with the change in her niece. She discovered herself, in all honesty, to be further annoyed with Doctor Wright because he seemed to regard her without proper attention to her uniqueness—surely ungallant in a man so prepared to find realms in her niece—and had, finally, showed himself as almost entirely devoid of meekness and sweetness of temper, qualities which Morgen admired to excess in people with whom she came into intimate contact.

When she learned that Doctor Wright and her niece were conspiring between themselves over the romantic idea that Morgen had a niece Elizabeth, a niece Beth, a niece Betsy, and a niece Bess, she was first of all startled, and then enchanted with the novelty of a chameleon personality, reflecting that this was a highly-colored version of an idea she had sometimes used to deck herself. She thought with humorous self-deprecation of the times she had seen in herself a Jekyll-and-brandy personality, of the wise Morgen at midday who at evening turned into a cynical Morgen and at morning became a snarler over breakfast, and when she had identified this in herself, she was prepared to countenance it in Elizabeth. When she found herself angry at Elizabeth, she thought, she need only remind herself of the morning Morgen to speak more gently, and when Elizabeth whined or spoke rudely or smirked, it must be recalled that the girl had spent many years with the many Morgens and so, perhaps, deserved a turn of her own. Then, having reasoned to this point, pleased with her own perception and more pleased than not with her niece's unexpected variety of imagination, Morgen came downstairs with the drag end of a bad hangover and found her refrigerator full of mud.

Swift-change artists she could countenance, mad doctors and fiendish scientists she might accept, burbling nieces with notions of stolen inheritances she could regard with composure, but she could not and would not endure any tampering with her refrigerator, which was where she kept the greater part of her food. Moreover, her mind was where she lived the greater part of her life, and the cleaning of the refrigerator before she came back a second time was a deliberate attempt to clog up the workings of her mind. Although she would sooner have given up thinking than eating, she resented being pushed into depriving herself of either; she had no difficulty whatsoever in reassuring herself that she was sane, hangover-Morgen or not, and she was thus the victim of a wicked trick, performed in a cruel and vicious manner which would automatically set a distinction between the reasonable, regular alterings of a sensible person—Morgen—and the unreasonable, erratic alterings of a non-sensible person—Elizabeth.

Morgen's first sensible thought—to slap Elizabeth's head right off her shoulders—was quickly abandoned in favor of saying nothing and waiting; Morgen was a splendid person at getting even with people, and if she accused her niece of filling the refrigerator with mud and Elizabeth denied it, revenge would be far less satisfactory, and would probably have to be taken in a more subtle form than if the subject were never mentioned or dealt with until an opportunity turned up. Musing thus, drinking her brandy, Morgen sat at ease in her own living room, among her own possessions, which she felt for the first time she was called upon, vitally, to defend.

When a key turned in the door and she heard her niece's step in the hall, Morgen was quiet for a minute, listening; her niece closed the door gently, and set her pocketbook down on the hall table. Then, from the sounds, she opened the door of the hall closet to hang up her coat and hat; such neatness and order established that either Elizabeth, who was neat from bewilderment, or Bess, who was neat because of a profound respect for her own property, had come in; the quietness and ease with which the actions were performed argued with certainty that it was not Elizabeth.

"Bess?" said Morgen, raising her voice.

"Yes?"

"Will you come in here for a minute, please?"

Bess came to the living room doorway, narrowing her eyes

to see in the darkened room. "What's the matter with *you?*" she asked, without rudeness, but without solicitude.

"A slight malaise," said Morgen comfortably, "the weakness of the living and the sight of death, the abandonment of worldly care in the face of holiness; I decided that you were going to make dinner tonight."

"Go to a restaurant," said her niece. "I've already had dinner."

"Who with?"

"None of your business."

"Someone must have paid," said Morgen. She sat up. "Have you been into my pocketbook again?"

"Certainly not," said Bess, and then, after a minute, added reluctantly, "I found an old penny bank, if you must know."

Morgen began to laugh, and swung around to turn on the lamp on the table next to her. "You poor baby," she said. "You can have dinner anywhere you like. Tell me next time and I'll give you a couple of dollars."

"You don't know how I'm going to get even with you someday," Bess said. She spoke slowly, and she looked at her aunt with hatred. "You don't know all the things I've been thinking of to do to you. When I have all my money, and I don't have to live with you anymore, I'm going to spend half my time doing nasty things to you."

"All right." Morgen was unconcerned. "Seems to *me,* though, my pretty wealthy darling, that you've started out fairly well, on that refrigerator."

"What refrigerator?" said Bess innocently.

"Know what I ought to do with you?" Morgen said, lying back to look up at her, "I ought to take you and rub your nose in it, and maybe I will. Or maybe I'll just turn you over my knee and spank the hell out of you."

"You wouldn't dare," said Bess, backing away.

"Indeed I would," said Morgen, genuinely surprised; she had in all her life found few things she did not dare to do, although there had been a number of things, which, fortunately, had not occurred to her. "I'll do just as I please, as a matter of fact," said Morgen, "with you or anyone else."

"I don't care what you do to anyone else," Bess said. "But when I get a lawyer—"

Aunt Morgen laughed again, with such honest and uncontrollable hilarity that tears came into her eyes and she had to sip at her brandy to keep from choking. "You'll have a sweet time with a lawyer," she said helplessly, "when you can't even find out what year it is. *My* problem, sir," she went on in a mincing voice parodying Bess, "is that I'm going to come into all this money when I'm twenty-five years old, and I'm going to *be* twenty-five in a few months, but I *think* I'm still *nineteen*, and *no* one can tell me any *different* . . . Oh, lord." And Aunt Morgen sighed weakly, while Bess sat tense and angry and looked at her. "Anyway," Morgen said at last, more firmly, "you let me know when you get your lawyer, kiddo, and I'll pay his bill for you."

"I wish my mother was alive to see how you treat me," Bess said, and her aunt looked up angrily.

"Maybe you've forgotten how your *mother* treated you," she said. "When you talk like that you make me mad enough to—"

She sighed; Bess had turned abruptly into Elizabeth, who was sitting watching her aunt with numb fear.

"Who *you* staring at?" Morgen demanded, annoyed at herself for having, as always, said more than she intended to.

"Nothing. I mean, I guess I don't feel very well."

"Well, go to bed, for God's sake," Morgen said, turning impatiently away.

"May I make myself something to eat?"

"I thought you had dinner."

Elizabeth shook her head miserably. "If you'll let me, I'll have a sandwich or something."

"Go ahead," said Morgen. "Make me something, too."

Elizabeth got up with eagerness. "I'll make you something nice," she said. "I think I'd feel better if I ate something."

Wearily Morgen took up the magazine she had been reading last night when the doctor came. "Don't knock yourself out," she said, and then, with some remorse, "If you need any help, yell."

"I'll be all right." Elizabeth went busily away, and Morgen

hesitated, and then refused herself more brandy. For a few minutes she half-listened, wondering if Elizabeth would be able to
manage, and then she shrugged and told herself that Elizabeth
had been capable of feeding herself for a long time now, and
she gave only a fragment of her attention to the faint sounds
from the kitchen, alert for a fall or a scream. After a while,
when she heard returning footsteps, she set her magazine aside
with pleasure, and turned to the doorway to watch her niece
entering with a tray. "What you got?" Morgen inquired.

Betsy giggled, tilting the tray dangerously. "That *Elizabeth*,"
she said. "You could starve to death before she got around the
kitchen; I finally had to come and do it myself. Cheese sandwiches and milk."

"Mustard?" said Morgen.

"She did most of it, though, really," Betsy said. "It isn't fair
to say she didn't. I poured the milk, anyway."

She set the tray down on the coffee table which Morgen
cleared for her, and drew up a chair on the other side. "You
know," Morgen said, taking a napkin, "this is the first food
I've had since . . . oh, Jesus." She sat, staring for a minute, and
then began frantically brushing the bite of sandwich from her
mouth, choking and making frightful sounds of disgust.

"What is it?" Betsy half-rose, backing away. "Robin?"

Morgen threw the sandwich across the room and emptied
her mouth into the paper napkin. "Bitch," she said, "bitch, nasty
bitch."

Betsy looked at her own sandwich. "What?" she said.

"Mud," said Morgen, "sandwich full of mud." She twisted
her face and looked away. "I'm sick," she said.

"Mine's all right," Betsy said. "Eat it." She held her sandwich
out but Morgen pushed her hand away. "I'm sick," she said,
"go away."

"What's wrong, Morgen dear? Has something upset you?"

"Get out of here," Morgen said wildly, "get out of here before I throw something at you, you dirty filthy bitch."

"Really," said Bess, "I should think you'd make an effort to
behave yourself; throwing food around and making horrible
noises; it sounds perfectly—"

"Will you get out of here?" Morgen demanded, rising and lifting her hand, "you lying monster—"

Elizabeth began to cry. "You're always picking on me," she said. "I didn't do anything."

Morgen caught her breath and was silent; perhaps she was saying "morning-Morgen, morning-Morgen" over and over to herself, because after a few minutes she spoke gently. "Sorry," she said. "I was upset. I don't mean to frighten you, kiddo. Come on, I'm going to see you safely in bed before I do another thing." She rose, and Elizabeth followed her almost cheerfully. "I'll be glad to go to bed," Elizabeth said, coming after her aunt to the stairs, "I'm tired and I haven't been sleeping well again. Maybe I could take a hot bath."

"Good idea." Morgen was remorseful, and brought a quality of unfamiliar enthusiasm to the prospect of a hot bath. "Just what you need to make you sleep, a hot bath and I'll give you a little blue pill."

"All right." Elizabeth went toward the door of her room, and Morgen, saying "I'll start your water," went into the bathroom. She started the water in the tub and then, because she was truly sorry to have made Elizabeth cry, she got a jar of pine bath salts from her own dressing table; it had not yet been opened and Morgen had been promising it to herself as a particular luxury tonight, bath salts being a fanciness for which she ordinarily did not have time; now, however, it was no more than what was due to Elizabeth, and she poured a generous helping of pine bath salts into the tub. When Elizabeth came into the bathroom the air was already warm and rich with an odor only faintly reminiscent of outdoors and trees and growing things; Elizabeth bent over the tub to turn the water off and smiled gratefully.

"Wonderful," she said. "Just what I needed." She hesitated, standing beside the tub in her robe and slippers, and from the timid smile she turned on her aunt it seemed that she was almost going to speak with tenderness; at last, with an effort, she said, "Won't you . . . Aunt Morgen, won't you stay in here and talk to me while I bathe?"

Morgen, perceiving without effort Elizabeth's attempt at affection, and moved by it, said, touching her niece on the shoulder, "Sure, kiddo. I used to give you a bath all the time, you know."

She sat uncomfortably on the bathroom stool and caught Elizabeth's robe from the floor and held it. "Warm enough?" she asked as Elizabeth got into the tub, and Elizabeth nodded and said "Fine, thanks."

"You feeling any better?"

"I think so, Morgen," and she stopped, soap in hand. "Did the doctor tell you about . . . about the others?" she asked.

"How do you know the doctor was here?" Morgen said.

Elizabeth stared. "I guess I heard you say so."

"He made me mad. But yes, he told me."

"Did he say I was going to be . . . well?"

"Depends on what you mean by well," Morgen said cautiously.

"Like I was before."

"Well," said Morgen, "you weren't so well then." She was wondering, now, what to say; she had a clear idea that in a spot like this the most reasonable, the most sensible, the most reassuring statements were invariably the most dangerous, and she very much did not want to frighten Elizabeth again; it came to her with an acute, almost physical pain, that the reason Elizabeth spoke so much more fluently and freely tonight might be that it was the first time in many months she had found tenderness in her aunt. "I want you *really* well," she said awkwardly, and then found Elizabeth looking at her with eyes full of tears. "What'd I say *now?*" Morgen demanded.

"It's because. . ." Elizabeth faltered, and patted the water with her hand. "He said, the doctor, that when I was cured it would be that all of us, Betsy and Beth and all, were all back together. He said I was one of them. Not myself, just one more of them. He said he was going to put us all back together into one person."

"So?" Should Elizabeth be speaking of this, concerning herself over it? Even haltingly, clumsily as she spoke, should she be allowed to continue? "Why not wait and see what happens?" Morgen suggested, inspired.

"Look." Elizabeth turned and looked at her. "I'm just one of them, one *part*. I think and I feel and I talk and I walk and I look at things and I hear things and I eat and I take baths—"

"All right," Morgen said. "Conceded that you do it all, what's wrong with it? I do too."

"But I do it all with *my* mind." Elizabeth spoke very slowly, feeling her way. "What he's going to have when he's through is a new Elizabeth Richmond, with *her* mind. *She* will think and eat and hear and walk and take baths. Not me. I'll maybe be a part of her, but *I* won't know it—*she* will."

"I don't get it," said Morgen.

"Well," said Elizabeth, "when *she* does all the thinking and knowing, won't *I* be . . . dead?"

"Oh, now, look," said Morgen, and then sat helplessly, facing the definition of annihilation. Finally she shook herself, and said with great briskness, "Now, look, kiddo, *I* don't know anything about these things, and neither do *you*. You just figure that everything's going to turn out for the best, that's all."

"I guess so." Laboriously, Elizabeth rose and stepped out of the tub and took the towel Morgen handed her. She turned the handle which let the water out of the tub, and began to dry herself. When she finally had her robe and slippers on again she spoke. "Anyway," she said, "when you've got her you won't have someone sick all the time."

"I won't think about it, and neither will you," Morgen said, but she was speaking to Bess.

"What are you doing in here?" Bess demanded. "Watching me every minute?"

"I came in," Morgen said, "to draw your bath for you."

"Well, do it," Bess said. "I don't mind."

"Look," Morgen said, "what makes you think I wouldn't drown you?"

"You couldn't get the money *that* way," Bess said. She turned around and bent down to start the water in the tub, and said, "Mind if I use your bath salts?"

"Not at all," Morgen said. "Help yourself." She watched, speechless, while Bess put bath salts in the tub, and got in herself, handing Morgen her robe to hold. Bess scrubbed herself diligently and thoroughly, chattering all the time. "This *is* nice of you, Morgen," she said. "There isn't really any reason why we can't be friends, you and me, you know, even if I *do* get the money. Maybe I sometimes say things I don't mean, but so do you, you know, and if I'm willing to make allowances for *you,* I guess you ought to do the same for me. Besides, I'm going to be wealthy, and the way I see it I'll have a position of great responsibility—the responsibility of wealth, you know—and I can't afford to hold grudges and hate people, even you. A person in my position has to keep the same distance from everyone—no enemies, and no friends, because of course if they pretend to be friends it's really only the money they're after. Because—"

"Indeed yes," said Morgen earnestly. "And no one in your position can *ever* be *too* careful."

"Of course not," Bess agreed. "Morgen, I've been thinking that I'd like to get you something, pay you back, sort of, for taking care of me all these years. A nice pair of gloves, maybe, or some handkerchiefs. What would you like?"

"Well," said Morgen thoughtfully, "I *have* been needing a new nail file. But whatever *you* say."

Bess rose and stepped out of the tub. She waited for a minute until Morgen reached over and found her a dry towel, and then she began to dry herself. "Something to remember me by," she said. "Because of course we won't be seeing much of each other when I get my money. I'll be too busy with charitable pursuits and shopping, and things."

Morgen rose, taking a deep breath. "I've decided that I *will* drown you, after all," she said. "Better than a new pair of gloves, even."

As she had expected, Bess fled when Morgen approached, and Beth, untying the cord of the bathrobe which Bess had just tied, said happily, "Did you come to see me have my bath? How *nice,* Aunt Morgen dear."

"Just came to start the water for you," Morgen said straight-faced. "I thought you'd sleep better for a hot bath."

"You darling." Morgen successfully dodged as Beth tried to kiss her, and leaned past Beth to turn on the hot water tap. "Do not," Morgen said, "forget your bath salts."

"These for me? Morgen, how *lovely*."

"Not at all," Morgen said, going back to her stool. She watched in a kind of stupor as Beth filled the tub, got in, and deliberately soaped and scrubbed the same neck and feet and legs and arms and ears that Elizabeth and Bess had been scrubbing for the past forty minutes. "Bath feels good," Beth said, flicking a bubble with her finger. "I'm glad I thought of it."

"It's very relaxing at bedtime, a hot bath," Morgen said.

"It's nice to have you sit here while I take my bath, the way you used to."

"Oh," said Morgen, "I've watched you take a lot of baths."

"I don't get much chance to talk to you anymore," Beth said, turning her wide, innocent eyes to her aunt. "I wish I *did*, Aunt Morgen. I wish we were more intimate, because I *do* think just the world of you, and *I* wish we could be . . . well . . . *pals*."

"Pals," said Aunt Morgen.

"I could take *such* good care of you, if you'd only let me. We could have real fun together."

"Yes," said Aunt Morgen. "Well, we must try to see a lot more of each other from now on."

Beth turned to her, eyes tearful among the soap bubbles. "You *don't* really like me," she said. "No one *ever* does. I don't have a single friend in all this whole wide world, because no one loves me, not even my own *aunt*."

"I gave you my bath salts," Aunt Morgen pointed out.

Beth sniffled, and then wiped the soap off her face with the back of her hand and stood up in the tub. "Don't want any bath," she said. "I'm just too *miserable* to take a bath."

"You weren't very dirty anyway," Aunt Morgen said heartlessly.

By the time the water had gone out of the tub and Beth was dressed in her robe again she had recovered her usual silly self, and she was just saying, "But Auntie, we've got to get you some *clothes,"* when she vanished and Betsy, clean and scrubbed, turned and bowed ironically to her aunt.

"Well," said Betsy, "everyone wash behind their ears?"

Morgen began, at last, to laugh. "Betsy, my girl," she said, "come on downstairs and have a spot of brandy with Auntie."

"Can't," said Betsy. "Got to have my bath."

"Heaven save me," said Morgen, "I will go mad if I watch you scrub your feet again. Couldn't you give up your bath just this one night?"

"No, oh, no," said Betsy, "what would the rest of them think?"

"I thought," Morgen said with curiosity, pausing on her way to the bathroom door, "I thought Bess always knew all that the rest of you were doing?"

Betsy shook her head, her look of ironic amusement fading before a kind of puzzlement. "She used to, most of the time," Betsy said. "The last few days, though, she hasn't been any better than the rest of us. That's why she's so scared, too," and Betsy capered on the wet floor.

"Betsy," Morgen said slowly, "what did you have to do with all that mud?"

"Mud?" said Betsy, "what mud?" She looked complacently down at her naked body. "No mud on *me,*" she said.

"Yeah," said Morgen. "I'll be downstairs, kiddo. Get nice and clean."

As she went down the stairs toward the living room the bathroom door behind her opened and Betsy shouted, "Say, Morg—you mind if I use the rest of your bath salts? There's only a little left."

Morgen awakened the next morning out of sorts and worn with a weakness which she finally identified as hunger; for a minute she lay in bed, thinking that she had not eaten anything at all the day before, that someone had once told her that brandy contained all the necessary minerals and vitamins to sustain life for an indefinite length of time, that she might, had she been born somehow differently, been at this moment awakening into the boudoir of Madame de Pompadour, a jeweled page kneeling beside her bed proffering chocolate. She rose, fancying herself among turquoise satin hangings, and asked herself, whistling, whether milady would wear the ruby tiara or the pearl stomacher. Dressed at last, in the corduroy housecoat she always wore in the mornings, her hair combed and her feet in splendidly comfortable old sheepskin slippers, she went, still whistling, down the hall to the bathroom, amused at the thought that her niece might be still in the tub, and washed her face and hands and took up her toothbrush, which she held under the running water to wash the mud out of it. Then she dropped it, and moved back and held her hands, trembling, against the lock of the door and wanted to cry and heard herself whimpering, "I'm an old woman."

"No more, no more, no more," she said at last, and unlocked the door, leaving her toothbrush where it lay in the basin, and went stamping downstairs to the kitchen. She looked carefully into the coffeepot and rinsed it out thoroughly before starting the coffee, and during the time the coffee was cooking she stayed in the kitchen all the time, and did not touch anything without looking at it twice. When the coffee was done she poured herself a cupful, after washing the cup, and drew out a chair at the table and looked carefully at the seat of the chair and at the floor under the table before she sat down. Then, in a clean chair with a clean cup of coffee, she leaned her head down to let the hot clean fragrance come freshly to her, and tried to think.

First of all, it didn't matter, not at all, whether it was Elizabeth or Bess or Beth or Betsy fouling her, dirtying everything she touched; it wasn't important, because the whole pack of them were leaving. For the first time Morgen isolated and looked clearly at what she now knew she intended to do; she had, in the back of her mind, a confused and terrible picture of what she called an "institution," which had until this minute revolted her because of a medieval uneasiness about chains and barred windows and dark wormy food; now that the

Richmond fortune had been brought into such prominence, it seemed an equivocal thing for an aunt to send her only niece off to be bound in chains in darkness, and continue to live alone with that niece's money. For the moment there was no mud anywhere in sight, however, and Aunt Morgen endeavored to see the question impartially. There are places, she thought, I've certainly heard of places like country clubs, where they live in luxury and get the best of care and food, and places like that cost plenty, too, so she'd be getting her share of the money after all. I'd probably have to cut down here considerably, as a matter of fact, to keep her in a place like that, and no one could say . . . We could both go, Morgen thought wryly; one more mouthful of mud and I'd be ready; maybe I could leave her here and go myself, and get the best of care and food. She laughed, thinking of what people would say then: of course, Morgen got the money and all, and there she is, off in that loony-bin, living on the fat of the land, and her poor crazy niece half-starving at home. . . .

No, Morgen thought suddenly and firmly. She's infected me; I can't even think about what's best to do for her without beginning to wonder what people will say about the money; this is not intelligent of me. No one *needs* it, she thought, no one *cares,* only Bess, and then the minute she mentioned the money we all stopped being able to think about good things like eating and drinking and being well, and just started squabbling; I'll give her a big bag of silver dollars, Morgen thought; she can take it in her suitcase when she goes. I'll tell her she's got it all. No, *no,* Morgen thought, I will decide this without ever once thinking again about that money. Now. In order to take any steps at all in even locating the proper place—one near enough for visiting, where Morgen might, personally, inspect at regular intervals the quality of the food, the cleanliness of the floors, the servility of the attendants, one where the lawns were green and the tennis courts well rolled, where Bess could stroll and Betsy could romp; where, to put it most distinctly, Morgen might visit without feeling uncomfortably under restraint—in order to find such a place, it was distressingly necessary to apply to Doctor Wright; Harold Ryan would know, too, of course, but to Doctor Wright Morgen's decision would seem fair, without justification or explanation, might even seem humorously overdue. Harold Ryan would have to have too much talking done at him, and it was important, Morgen thought, to get moving at once on a thing like this; if 'twere done, she thought, surprising herself, 'twere well it were done quickly.

She laughed, tasting her coffee, and began aloud, declaiming "—that struts and frets his little hour upon the stage; it is a tale—"

"Good morning, Morgen," said Bess, from the kitchen doorway. "You praying or something?"

"Good morning," Morgen said, thinking, I know now that she is going soon; done quickly.

"Did you make coffee? Fine." Bess poured herself a cup of coffee and came to sit down at the table. "Before I forget," she said, looking delicately at her spread fingers, "I want you to pay for some things I ordered sent home. They'll probably be coming today."

"What?"

"Some clothes. A few things for my room. Nothing that really need concern *you*."

"They don't concern me at all," Morgen said, "because I won't pay for them."

Bess smiled. "Morgen, *dear*," she said, "*I* am paying for them. You just give the man the money."

"I won't *do* it," Morgen said flatly, and then rage caught her again and she slammed her hand down onto the table and opened her mouth to shout, and then was quiet at Bess' smile. "If I get sore," Morgen said, "you'll run away. And if I can't get sore, what *can* I do?"

"Try to behave like a lady, dear," said Bess. "Try to behave like *me*."

"Tell you what I'll do," Morgen said, controlling herself and thinking: how soon she will be gone, "We'll compromise. Some of the things you ordered—" (the ones you can take with you, she was thinking) "—you can keep, and the others we'll send back. That way, each of us is giving in to the other, and we can both be satisfied."

Bess thought. "All right," she said at last, "but *I* do the deciding."

"We'll make a list of everything," Morgen said. She left the table and went to her desk in the living room to get a pencil and paper; when she came back Elizabeth was heating herself some milk at the stove and Morgen's coffee was suspiciously thick and dark; without tasting it Morgen made a mouth of disgust and set the cup in the sink. "How'd *you* get here?" she asked Elizabeth.

"Good morning, Aunt Morgen," Elizabeth said. "I had a wonderful sleep last night."

"Fine," Morgen said, "fine." She hesitated, not knowing how to say it, and then began carefully, "Elizabeth, I hope you'll try to understand when you know what I'm doing. If I didn't think that it was the only possible way—"

Elizabeth poured her hot milk into a cup and sat down at the table, and said, looking wistfully at her milk, "I wish just once they'd let me stay long enough to eat something *I* like."

"Why not try?" Morgen asked with interest. "I mean—when they push at you, push back."

"I guess so," Elizabeth said vaguely; "I wish you wouldn't keep *meddling*," she said. "I'm perfectly all right."

"I'm waiting for you to tell me what you ordered," Morgen said. "We'll have to send back anything too expensive, because we simply can't afford it."

"Don't be silly," Bess said. "I can afford anything I want."

"Yeah," Morgen said.

"Well, a little radio," Bess said. "It's coming from that big store. I had lunch there," she said, "and there's a fountain in the restaurant, and goldfish."

"Arnold's," said Morgen, writing. "Radio. I thought you had a radio?"

"This was smaller than mine," Bess said. "And I ordered a coat, dark green with a fur collar, leopard, and a little hat to match."

"Green's not a good color on you, anyway," Morgen said.

"And some stockings and underwear and gloves . . . I don't know. I went around picking out things and the girl was going to put them all in a package together and send them."

"And I'll keep them all in a package together and send them back," Morgen said.

"And some costume jewelry. I even ordered a necklace for *you*, Morgen. Little shells."

"Great," Morgen said. "So I could hear the sound of the sea?"

"I beg your pardon?"

"Never mind. Is that everything?"

"Yes," said Bess, looking away.

Morgen put the pencil down and sat back, looking at the list. "Not too bad," she said. "You don't need the radio and you can't have the coat. I don't want the jewelry, and you have more underwear and stockings and gloves now than you can wear. We'll send it all back."

"If you expect any favors from me," Bess said, "you'd better be careful now."

"What favors?" Morgen laughed rudely.

"I was going to let you go on living here," Bess said. "Last night, when you promised to treat me better, I half-decided to give you an allowance."

"Generous of you," Morgen said. "That's more than I'd do for *you*."

Bess took up Morgen's pencil and pointed it dangerously across the table. "Someday," she said, "you are going to come crying to me, and then—"

"All right," Morgen said agreeably. "When I come crying to you for a dark green coat with a leopard collar and a little hat to match, you may take great pleasure in denying it me. As," she said, "I am doing to you."

"Morgen," Bess said, "if you won't let me get what I want today, then tomorrow I'll go again and order the same things sent all over again, and if I can't get them from the same store I'll get them somewhere else, because I plan to have what is due me, and I'm just going to go on and on buying whatever I please with my money."

"So long as it keeps you happy," Morgen said, watching Bess' hand and the pencil and paper. While Bess was talking her hand had added, not neatly but clearly, "wristwatch," "cigarette case," "pocketbook" to the list of items Bess had bought, and Morgen began to laugh. Bess looked down and saw her hand writing, and scowled.

"Stop," she said in a whisper, and tried to unclench her fingers from the pencil; while Morgen, sitting back, watched without expression, Bess tried with her left hand to twist the fingers of her right hand away from the pencil, tried to lift her arm from the table, whispering, "Stop, stop, I won't *let* you."

"hahaha," Bess' right hand wrote, the letters scrawling across the page as Bess tried to drag her hand away.

"Morgen," Bess said in appeal.

"*I* won't help you," Morgen said, and grinned. "After you changed your mind about my allowance?"

Bess abandoned her struggle with her hand to look long and angrily at Morgen. "I suppose you think this is going to work out fine for you," she said, and her hand wrote freely; Morgen looked away from Bess' hand, sickened at seeing the thing released and capering off in pursuit of its own mad ends; "I can't make it stop," Bess said, looking at her hand.

Morgen rose and came around the table to lean over Bess' shoulder and read what Bess' hand was writing. "It's beastly," Bess said.

"It's loathsome," Morgen said. The hand had written: "poor cinderella bess poor cinderbess no pumpkin coat no ball"

"It never writes anything but nonsense," Bess said.

"cinderbess sitting in ashes and mud up to neck."

"Mud up to the neck," Morgen said. "That's funny." She smiled down at the back of Bess' head. "*I* say that," she said.

"cruel sisters," said the hand, and made a kind of final heavy line, as though a telling point had been made.

"Someone," said Bess, very carelessly, "keeps a suitcase all packed in my room. I don't know who it belongs to, but it looks like someone is planning to sneak away some night. Again," she finished.

"no morgen no morgen no morgen poor betsy ask bess mud."

"This is silly," Bess said, trying again to lift her hand.

Morgen laughed. "You girls keep telling on each other," she said, "first thing you know, no one's going to have any secrets left."

"poor lizzie," the hand wrote, "poor lizzie poor morgen poor betsy not paris never now"

"Are you Betsy?" Morgen asked, leaning forward.

"betsy over ocean betsy over sea"

"Betsy broke a teacup, and blamed it all on me," Bess said. She tried to lift her hand again, "I cant *stand* those things," she said.

"What things?" Morgen was puzzled.

"Nursery rhymes," Bess said. "She does it—" She stopped abruptly.

"hahaha," Bess' hand wrote.

"I remember your mother teasing you with that rhyme," Morgen said, looking from Bess to Bess' hand and back again. "When you were a baby."

"Kindly do not recall my grief," Bess said grandly.

"Rubbish," Morgen said, and then, "She's gone." The pencil lay idly in Bess' hand. "Well," Morgen said at last, "I've got to make a phone call. And I don't want you listening."

"I? Aunt *Morgen!*"

Morgen closed the kitchen door with a slam, leaving Beth in tears at the table, and went into the hall to the phone. When she took up the receiver it slipped and turned in her hands and she let it drop and sat for a minute, choking back nausea and whispering to herself. Then, valiantly, she found her handkerchief and used it to hold the phone, almost amused at herself for dialing the doctor's number without having to look it up. When his nurse answered, Morgen said, keeping her voice low, "Doctor Wright, please. This is Morgen Jones."

And, after a minute, the doctor's sharp voice said, "Good morning, Miss Jones. Doctor Wright here."

"I'm sorry to disturb you, doctor, but I badly need your help."

There was a silence, and then he said, "I am extremely sorry,

Miss Jones, but I could not be of any possible assistance to you. Perhaps Doctor Ryan?"

"No," she said. "I have . . ." she thought, searching for a noncommittal phrase, aware with certainty of Bess pressing her head against the kitchen door to listen. "I have decided," Morgen said, "to follow your example." An idea came to her. "Birnam wood has come to Dunsinane," she said.

"I beg your pardon? Is this Miss Jones?"

"Don't be an idiot," she said. "I'm trying to tell you something."

"I assure you that if you are in this manner endeavoring to revive my interest in your niece—"

"Look," said Morgen dangerously, "I am most goddamn certainly in this manner endeavoring to whatever you call it. The fact that I can forget my own dignity long enough to listen to you chattering ought to convince you that you're just as much tangled up in this as any of us, and I want you over here *fast*."

"You do not mean to be impolite, I am convinced," the doctor said coldly. "And if you stop to think for a minute you must certainly agree that my objections to seeing your niece again are legitimate; I can be of no conceivable help to either her or you."

"To *me*, you can," Morgen said. "As a matter of fact, now I think of it, I don't believe you *can* get things into a muddle like this and then quit on me. So I think if you don't get over here as fast as you can travel I'll call Harold Ryan and get you unfrocked."

"Disbarred from practice," said Doctor Wright with some amusement. "I can hardly come if you threaten me."

"I take it back," Morgen said. "It's almost impossible for me to talk clearly."

"There has been trouble?"

"Yes. I am—" She glanced back over her shoulder at the kitchen door "—very much disturbed."

"I can appreciate that," said the doctor. "I can be there within an hour."

"Right," said Morgen.

"I hope you realize," the doctor said, "what violence I am doing to my own pride in resuming the care of your niece, Miss Jones. Only my conscience—"

"If you're worried about violence," said Morgen evilly, "you'd better keep quiet to me about your conscience." And she hung up, pleased to think that she had had the last word, but that he would be coming anyway.

The kitchen door was shut tight, and Morgen turned her back on it and went into the living room, where she sat tiredly on the couch and wondered what was best to do. She had a fear of putting into motion, through Doctor Wright, legal forces overwhelming and uncombatable; it was one thing to take your niece, nervous and failing in health, to a highly recommended physician, but another thing entirely to turn her over to a faceless, mechanical operation of papers and committments and, perhaps, publicity; I'll tell everyone she's gone off to have an illegitimate child, Morgen told herself consolingly; it's better than admitting I had her locked up. She looked up, then, and said, "What do you want now? Or are you just following me?"

"There's a man here," Elizabeth said. "He has a package to be paid for."

"And she sent you to tell me, did she? Well." Morgen got up heavily and went into the front hall, where a delivery man stood with a package which might have held a radio or a green coat with a fur collar or even a cigarette case. "The order," Morgen told him moderately, "has been cancelled. I'm sorry."

"Sure." He took up his package and put his hand on the door. "You don't want it now?" he said, looking back over his shoulder.

"We don't want it now," Morgen said firmly.

"You're the boss." He opened the door and was turning to shut it behind him when Bess pushed Morgen aside and called out, "Wait—wait a minute!"

"Yeah?" said the delivery man, pausing.

"We *do* want it; bring it back."

"Okay," said the delivery man, turning.

"We *don't* want it," Morgen said. "Take it away."

The delivery man hesitated, holding the package without affection. "Look," he began reproachfully. He gave a little shove with the package, as though to toss it out through the door. "*I* don't want the package," he said to Bess, "*she* don't want it," and he gestured with his head at Morgen, "*you* say wait, wait, you *do* want it. All right. There's thirty-seven dollars and eighty-five cents on this package. Tell me now, I either go out the door with the package or I leave the package here and I go out the door with thirty-seven dollars and eighty-five cents. Well?" He stopped, holding the package out ingratiatingly.

Morgen cocked her head at Bess. "Well?"

Bess stood undecided, her face flushed and angry. She was unused to easy communication, and she did not think quickly. She looked from the man to Morgen, both watching her with interest, and then turned abruptly into Beth, who was first aware of Morgen's regard, and then perceived the delivery man and the package.

"Ooh," said Beth, "is it something for me? Morgen, did you get me a present?"

"No," Morgen said. "The man is going to take it away."

After a minute the delivery man shifted the package, sighed, and opened the door again, waiting for a minute on the threshold as though expecting to be called back again. "You never get *me* anything," Beth said. Two large tears started down her cheeks. "Everyone gets presents but me, and I guess no one likes me, because no one *ever* gives *me* presents."

The door closed gently. Through the glass of the door Morgen could see the delivery man going down the steps to his truck. He stopped once, and looked back at the house for a minute, and then shrugged and tossed the package into the truck.

"Someday I'll get even with you, Morgen."

"Oh, stop *talking* like that." Morgen stamped back into the living room and felt that Bess was following her without sound; Morgen turned, with a faint cold chill going up her back and said, over-heartily, "Come on, Bess, be reasonable; I *told* you the stuff was going back."

"You said I could keep half of it."

"You said you had given me the whole list."

"Who'd tell the truth to *you?*" Bess said scornfully. "You never heard of the truth in your life—you tell lies and you make up lies and you try to hurt people with lies, and you won't let anyone come around you unless they tell you lies. You're a bad bad bad—"

"Now look," Morgen said. The quick apprehension she had felt at Bess' approach stayed with her; she was a little bit unsure, and she raised her voice. "Now look," she said, standing with defiance in the middle of her own living-room carpet, chosen and put down under her supervision, surrounded by walls whose color she had dictated, and windows whose view met with her approval, standing firm and not to be shaken by any alien fear, "now look," she said, "this is all I am going to take from you." She swept her arm largely around, as one who calls forces to her support, and said in a less emphatic tone than she intended, "You've driven me out of patience, the way your mother did before you. You blame me the way she did, and call me names, and when I look at you all I can see is her whining face. And do not—" she said, gesturing, "try to give me any phony tears or stories about your grief; I know what you thought of your mother."

Bess wavered, on the edge of tears, or perhaps on the edge of Elizabeth; she brought up her handkerchief and looked from side to side, but Morgen said, "If you send Elizabeth and run away, now, you'd better not come back. Because if you ever *do* come back, I'm going to be waiting right here for you, like a cat on a mousehole, and the minute I see you looking out at me, I'm going to be after you; so, if you want to go, go, but remember I tell you not to come back once you're gone."

"I'm not going," Bess said, taking down the handkerchief. "I," she said, smiling at Morgen, "am not *ever* going. You can just plan, Morgen, on having me from now on, thinking of anything I can do to make you miserable, lying awake nights hating you, and wishing you were dead. You won't," she finished, with loving slowness, "you won't *ever* be rid of *me*."

"You sound like your *mother*," Morgen said. "You sound

exactly precisely not to be mistakenly like your goddamn whining mother and if I were you I would stop it right there because, believe me, Miss Elizabeth Beth Betsy Bess, your mother is the last person I want to hear talking right now—you hear? I spent one rotten lifetime with her and I was just as glad to see the last of her as I'm going to be to see the last of you." Shouting, Morgen turned and swept wildly up and down the room, but never came close to her niece. "We're going to put you in a place," Morgen said, speaking quietly again, her voice shaking, "into an institution, a madhouse, a head-whorehouse, where you can take yourself apart and put yourself together again like a goddamn jigsaw puzzle and all the pretty doctors will stand around and clap their hands when you subdivide like a building lot and all the nice nurses will pat your head when you split four ways from Sunday and then they'll all giggle and drag you off and lock you up and *I'll* be rid of you and the *world* will be rid of you, and your precious doctor will be rid of you and the world will be a better place with you going to pieces in private. And, now I think of it, just to make you happy I'll take your piles and piles of money and I'll buy up a couple of acres of swampland and I'll dig it up and go and pour it on your late lamented mother's grave, so the world will know what I think of what she did to you and me. And if they ever let you out again—which they won't, I tell you—and you come all whining and old to me and begging for me to take care of you—which I can tell you *I* won't—and your mouthing doctor to come and put the pieces back together—which I will just bet *he* won't—we can shove the mud off your mother's last resting place and dig up enough of it to put you in, and your poor old Auntie will buy a marble bench to come and sit on and snicker over the two of you dead. And to think," Morgen said at last, and wearily, "that I thought your father was the finest man who ever lived."

She sat down on the couch, tired and miserable and afraid. I can't back out now, she was thinking, and she moved defensively as Bess took a step forward.

"I don't believe you," Bess said flatly. "You won't in all your life be as good or as nice as one-*quarter* of my mother. It's true," she insisted defiantly, as Morgen raised her head in fury, "and *you* know it too. And everyone else knows it, and I'd even rather go to . . . go to a place like you said, than stay here with you. Even Betsy," she cried wildly, crossing her arms and holding her shoulders, as though keeping herself compact, and solid, "*she* wants to run away again, doesn't she? Away from you? *She* hates it here, doesn't she? She wants to get away and find her mother again, doesn't she? What do you suppose she wants from *you*—love?"

"What mother?" Morgen said softly, looking up. "Whose mother?"

"*Betsy's* mother, in New York. That's what she was looking for, and she's going back as soon as she can, and when she finds her mother *she* won't ever come back here because her mother wouldn't let her near you."

"*Her* mother?" Aunt Morgen's voice was enormous. "*Her* mother? That foul thing that married her father? She wants *that?*"

"Give me a pencil, and ask her."

"Bring Betsy here." Aunt Morgen was commanding, imperial. "Bring that girl to me at once."

"But you said—"

"Bring me Betsy."

"Well?" Betsy smiled provokingly.

Morgen leaned back and breathed heavily. With Betsy, at least, she need not be so on guard; Betsy represented no danger and brought no hatred. "Why did you go to New York?" Morgen asked quietly.

"None of your business," said Betsy.

"Betsy, I want to know."

"None of your business."

"Were you listening while I talked to Bess?"

"Couldn't. Tried, but couldn't, I heard you yelling, though." Betsy giggled. "Even *that* far down I couldn't miss your yelling."

"Tell me this, then, Betsy, honestly. Are you going to try and run away again?"

Betsy tossed her head. "In came the doctor, in came the nurse, in came the lady with the big fat purse."

"Betsy, I command you—"

"Try and make me."

"Doctor Wright is coming," said Morgen, who found herself wanting almost irresistibly to laugh. "He'll keep you in line, young lady."

"I won't stay," Betsy said. "How's he going to make me?"

Elizabeth, coming to the surface, found herself chanting, ". . . Maw told Paw; Johnnie got a licking, hee haw haw." She turned red, looking at her aunt. "I'm sorry," she said.

Aunt Morgen suddenly found it safe to laugh. "You silly baby," she said, laughing and full of relief.

"You're not mad at me?"

"Not at you, I'm not. How do you feel?"

"Fine," said Elizabeth, pleased. "I really do feel fine. Except," she added, after a minute and with reluctance, "I guess I do have a headache."

"Well, take something for it," Morgen said. "There's going to be a lot of noise around here for a while."

"Have I done something?"

"Nope." Morgen sighed, and looked at the clock. "Your doctor's on his way."

"To see you, Aunt? I never thought—"

"Kiddo." Aunt Morgen sighed again, and then said, "Another ten minutes, and I'd pass for a patient. They could give us a room together, maybe."

"I don't understand," said Elizabeth, falteringly.

"I didn't know when I was well off, is all," Morgen said. "I had to send you to a doctor, we were doing all right till then."

"I won't go any more if you don't want me to. I only went to please you, anyway. I always . . ." Elizabeth came forward timidly and touched her aunt on the arm. "I always tried to do what you wanted me to."

"Why, kiddo?" Morgen looked at her clearly for a minute. "*I* never did anything *you* wanted me to; why would you want to be nice to me?"

Elizabeth smiled shyly. "Just because my black hen laid eggs for gentlemen; I always thought you lashed him and you slashed him and you laid him through the mire—"

"Will you please shut *up?*" Morgen said. "I don't really think I can stand—"

"I'm sorry." Elizabeth's eyes filled with tears. "I only wanted to—"

"Oh, lord." Morgen patted her on the head. "I wasn't talking to you, kiddo, I was talking to—"

"Me, dear?"

"Yes, *you,* goddamn it. Oh, *lord.*" Stamping, Morgen made for the kitchen and came back with the brandy bottle. "Eleven o'clock in the morning or not eleven o'clock in the morning, Morgen is going to have a big full intoxicating glass of brandy and I defy the pack of you to stop me."

"Sot," said Elizabeth, but when Morgen swung on her she was standing, unaware, smiling fearfully through her tears.

"Oh god oh god," said Morgen, sitting down on the couch. "Elizabeth, do Auntie a favor, will you?"

"Yes?" said Elizabeth, coming forward eagerly.

"Just don't *talk* to me anymore, not for a while, not till the doc gets here, will you?"

"Jumped into a bramble bush and scratched out both his eyes. Of course not," said Elizabeth. "I mean, if you *want* me to be quiet, I'll keep perfectly—"

"Thanks," said Morgen.

"There was an old woman lived under the hill," said Elizabeth. "If she's not moved away—"

"Brandy, brandy," said Morgen. "Food for the mad."

"—got a licking, hee haw haw."

"Elizabeth, sister Elizabeth," Morgen said, "is that the doctor coming?"

Elizabeth went to the window and looked out carefully, as she had been taught, between the curtains. "I think so," she said doubtfully. "I've never seen him with a hat on before."

"He can keep his hat on if he wants," Morgen said. She rose and Elizabeth turned from the window and came over to her and put her hands firmly on Morgen's shoulders and pushed her down again onto the couch. "What the devil?" said Morgen, struggling, stunned because for a few minutes she had forgotten to be afraid. "What the devil are you *doing?*"

Bess laughed, one knee on Morgen's chest. "You're *old*," she said, in pleased surprise. "I'm stronger than you."

"Get out of my way, you misbegotten jellyfish," Morgen said fiercely, "I'll step on you."

"I don't think so," Bess said, and laughed again. "Poor Morgen," she said. "He'll ring the doorbell and ring the doorbell and *ring* the doorbell, and he'll decide that it's another of Betsy's tricks and he'll go away again. And then when he's gone I'll let you get up again. Maybe."

Morgen was helplessly caught, as much by the indignity as by the weight of her niece pressing her down; she looked up into the flushed, wicked face of her niece, and closed her eyes in distaste, trying to gather her strength, to move, without even breath to shout.

"Now you know how *I* feel," Bess said, "when you're talking to Betsy."

"Betsy," Morgen said. "Betsy."

Betsy gasped, and moved aside, scraping her shoes against Morgen's legs, digging in her elbows trying to scramble off; "You're lucky she was frightened," Betsy said. "I almost couldn't get out."

"*She* was frightened!" said Morgen fervently.

Betsy looked around at her nervously, and shivered. "I can't stay," she said. "I almost couldn't get here at all. Everything's mixed up." The doorbell rang, and Morgen, who had put her arm affectionately around Betsy's shoulders, found that she was embracing Bess, and drew back violently. "Don't think I'll forget this," Morgen said quietly to Bess, standing off. "Laying hands on *me*." She started carefully around Bess, out of reach, to get to the door, but Bess moved quickly, and darted past her, screaming, "I'll kill her, I won't let her do it anymore—I'll *make* her stop it," and Morgen could not catch her before she ran down the hall and threw open the front door and then fell back before Doctor Wright.

"Good morning," said Doctor Wright civilly, and then, to Morgen, "Good morning, Miss Jones."

"Good morning, Doctor Wright," said Morgen, blowing slightly, "nice of you to drop in."

"No trouble at all, I assure you. Although I ordinarily see patients only in my office, in this case, naturally I was willing to make an—Bess? Is something wrong?"

"Where did you put her?" Bess demanded, staring from one to the other of them.

"Odd," said the doctor. "Where *would* I put her? Since I assume you mean your aunt?"

"I thought she was coming again," said Bess, breathless, and staring wide-eyed.

"The chances are remote. Since I assume you mean your mother," said the doctor. "May I put my own coat on the bannister rail, Miss Jones?"

"By all means," said Morgen. "My niece and I were just talking of you."

"Complimentary, I hope." The doctor beamed genially at both of them. "Now, then," he said. "Bess upset?"

"Overexertion," said Morgen evilly. "Shadow-boxing."

"Pity," said the doctor. "Come in and sit down, Miss Bess. If you will forgive," he said over his shoulder, "my presumption in making free with your house."

"Certainly," said Morgen. "Not at all."

"Now, then," Doctor Wright said, and gestured Bess to go ahead of him, but she pushed him aside and turned wildly to the door. "I *can't* talk to you," she said, "don't you see that she's got to be stopped? She'll ruin us all . . . it's her birthday," she told the doctor tearfully. "No one remembered."

"It was, too," said Morgen. "I had a present for her and afterwards I took it out and threw it in the trash."

"My mother's coming home," said Bess, and turned unexpectedly, saying it, into Betsy, who made a face at Morgen. "I got back after all," she said, pleased.

"Good morning, Betsy," said Doctor Wright.

"You here at last? Good morning, wondrous-wise."

"Betsy," said the doctor urgently, "tell us what Bess was trying to do—do you know?"

"She wanted," said Betsy hesitantly, "to . . . to walk a crooked mile and find a crooked sixpence."

They were still standing, the three of them, in Morgen Jones' front hall; behind the doctor the Nigerian ancestor figure grinned and waited and held out its hand, and Betsy sat down on the low bench near the door and looked up at Morgen. "I can't tell you," she said finally.

"Why not, Betsy?" asked the doctor, but Morgen came forward and said angrily, "I don't see why you won't, Betsy, my girl—*she* told on *you*."

"Told what?" Betsy, sitting on the bench between them, shrank back and seemed to cower. "Told what?" she asked, but her fear seemed to be of Morgen. "I was just going to go away," she said. "I wasn't going to do anything bad, I was just lonesome. *You'd* go away if you weren't happy."

Morgen smiled sadly. "I would if I could," she said. "But you can't go anywhere, Betsy, because there's one thing you don't know. When Bess went running to the door, ready to hurt someone, she was . . . looking for *your* mother."

Betsy shook her head wisely. "Not *my* mother," she said with confidence. "*My* mother is safe."

"No longer." The doctor stepped aside as Aunt Morgen kneeled beside Betsy. "Your mother is gone, Betsy. Elizabeth Jones, my sister, the prettiest girl in town, Elizabeth Richmond. She's gone."

"Elizabeth Richmond? There were four of them in the telephone book."

"I was with her when she died," Morgen said helplessly.

"Not *my* mother," Betsy said.

"She stood right there in the doorway," Morgen said insistently, "you remember it as well as I do, smiling and kind of frightened, because she knew she'd done something terrible, with your birthday celebration waiting here for her, and no one even knowing where she was for two days—not worse than she'd done before, in a dozen different ways, but this time you were waiting and waiting and waiting for her, and I kept telling you kiddo, be patient, she'll come; don't you remember—I said we'd pretend it was *my* birthday, instead? And you sat there and looked out the window and waited and waited and then we heard her coming?"

"I remember," Betsy said, moving uneasily. "It was *her* mother who came."

"No," said Morgen, "it wasn't. We heard her key and the front door slammed open and you went running down the hall and there she was standing there smiling and frightened, and that was when I knew you were angry, because she could see your face, and I couldn't, and she was frightened—and she said—"

"She said," said Betsy levelly, "she said, 'Hello, am I late for the birthday party?'"

"No, she didn't," Morgen said. "She said, 'Hello, Betsy my darling, am I late for the—'"

"She *didn't*," said Betsy, rising and catching at the doctor's hand, "she didn't because *my* mother loved her Betsy and I was her darling and when *she* was there I was inside laughing because I wasn't *her* darling, she didn't *say* Betsy darling . . ." She turned in frantic urgency to the doctor, and he shook his head, watching Morgen.

"You were her darling, you were her baby darling," said Morgen tonelessly. "It was all I ever liked in her. She used to sing to you and dance with you and you wouldn't let anyone else near you. Even when she was out somewhere, you wouldn't let me sing to you."

"Who shook her and shook her and shook her?" Betsy demanded, pulling at the doctor's hand, "who ran at her and hurt her?"

"Bess." Aunt Morgen made a gesture of helplessness and spoke to the doctor. "I took her up and locked her in her room," she said. "And please don't think that I believe for a minute that my niece . . ." she took a breath ". . . killed my sister," she said. "My sister was a strong woman, and the shaking she got from her daughter was nothing, really. When I talked to Harold Ryan afterward he said it was bound to happen anyway, it was no one's fault, not to worry, and not to trouble the child with guilt she couldn't understand. He said it wasn't anyone's fault."

She might have gone on talking endlessly, saying these things which of all things had not been spoken of in years, but the doctor touched her on the shoulder, and she followed his glance down to Betsy, who was sitting crying broken-heartedly, as a baby cried. "She believes you now," said the doctor.

And when Betsy raised her eyes, tear-stained, she was Bess, looking at Morgen with eyes wide and blank and clear. "You told her," Bess said to Morgen, "you told her, and you blamed *me*."

"It was you," Morgen said.

"No, it wasn't," Bess said. "Because I waited and I looked out the window, and I knew she was coming soon, and you told me, 'She's off with some man; you think she ever cares for *you* when there's a man hanging around?' And you said she never loved me, only because of the money, because she couldn't ever get the money unless she stayed with me, and you said if it wasn't for the money she'd go and never come back. You said not even when my father was alive—"

"Don't you talk about your father, you foul bitch," said Morgen.

"Poor Morgen," said Bess to Doctor Wright, "she wanted my father and she wanted me and all she's going to get is the money; I wish *I* had the money," she said wistfully.

Morgen stood up suddenly and walked across the hall; she stood with her back towards both of them, looking up into the black wooden face, her hand almost resting in the out-stretched wooden hand, and said quietly, "I cannot believe, somehow, that I have managed all this very well, Doctor Wright. I have never tried to make any secret of the way I felt about my sister, or the way I felt about her husband. I always loved my niece, too, and all those times when I used to wish that we were alone together, Elizabeth and I, I pictured our life, I am afraid, as pleasant and peaceful. Not the way it is now. I thought that once my sister was gone, all her badness would go with her; I was afraid of what was happening to my niece because she loved her mother. I suppose," she said, without turning, "you've heard about this fellow Robin, Doctor Wright. That was entirely her mother's fault, keeping a child around the two of them all the time, letting her see and hear things she shouldn't, until she got herself in real trouble."

"Robin," said Bess, and laughed.

"Well," said Morgen, turning to smile tiredly at her niece, "I suppose you're right. That kind of thing looks worse to someone outside it, like me. But," she went on, raising her voice a little, "it was *me* Robin called to come and get you that night, and it was *me* took care of you when your mother died, and ever since, and before you were old enough to know the difference, it was *me*, plenty of times, who dressed you and put you to bed and saw you got fed. And it's me," she said, "who's going to help Doctor Wright lock you up forever. That's what I want to do," she said to the doctor.

The doctor came over and touched Morgen's arm reassuringly. "I don't think," he said, "that you need feel *quite* so desolate. Bess, after all, does not represent your niece in a state of health, and what she says is motivated largely by malice; surely your own heart will acquit—"

"Morgen!" Bess said, and Morgen and the doctor turned, startled at what had seemed almost a cry for help. Bess was standing, looking at them fearfully; her hands were clasped in front of her, and as they watched, her right hand got free.

"Hold Betsy!" the doctor shouted, and Morgen, thinking, now *I* have lost my mind, ran to Bess and caught her right arm and held it, pulling and straining against its strength. The doctor had thrown his arms around Bess, holding her still and away from Morgen, who clung desperately onto Bess' right arm; how could she be so strong, Morgen wondered, how is it I can hardly hold her? "We're going to rip her in half," Morgen said, gasping, and the doctor answered grimly, "I wish we could."

Then the strength pulling against Morgen slackened, and she looked up to see that Betsy lay, relaxed and grinning, in the doctor's arms; "Don't *pull* so, Morgen," Betsy said with amusement, "you'll have us all on the floor." She stayed so quiet for a minute that involuntarily they loosened their hold on her and then suddenly, without warning, she was scratching at her eyes and Morgen sobbed and strained to get her hands down; "I don't want to hurt you, Morgen," Betsy said, "so let go."

"No," said Morgen doggedly.

"*Please,* Morgen." Betsy's voice rose entreatingly. "I never did anything to *you,* Morgen, and I don't think I'll get any more chances . . . Morgen, *please* let go."

"No," said Morgen. She looked beyond Betsy to the doctor, who had his arms tight around Betsy, imprisoning her other arm, and he shook his head violently.

"Morgen," Betsy said quietly, "I'll get rid of her for you. She'll be gone, and never come back. Because I don't think I'm coming back any more, either."

"Goodbye," said Morgen, setting her teeth.

"Morgen," said Betsy despairingly, and fled.

Morgen looked up again, thinking that they were again holding Bess, but it was Elizabeth, white-faced and helpless, lying back against the doctor; it seemed suddenly laughable to be clinging madly to Elizabeth's limp arm, and Morgen stood back, letting the arm drop to Elizabeth's side. The doctor relaxed his hold and stood free, but cautiously close.

"Elizabeth," said Morgen weakly, "how do you feel?"

"Fine." Elizabeth looked uncertainly from Morgen to the doctor and back to Morgen again. "I'm sorry," she said.

"My dear child," said the doctor, breathing hard, "you have little to be sorry for."

Morgen put her hands behind her because they were shaking, and Elizabeth said, "They all went together to find a bird's nest. Aunt Morgen," she went on seriously, "you were always very kind to me."

"Thank you," said Morgen, past surprise.

"And Doctor Wrong," said Elizabeth, "thank *you,* too."

Her face seemed to waver; she half-grinned, and swayed. "The money," she said. "No one likes me."

"Not Bess," said the doctor, "I pray that it may not be Bess; Morgen, can you influence her?"

"Elizabeth," said Morgen, "Elizabeth, come back."

"I'm back," Elizabeth said. "I never went away, auntie dear, I never never did." She looked at the doctor and said clearly and without faltering, "I did it. I'm the real one, Doctor Wrong, I am the one who gets the money and who never did anything, and I jumped into a bramble bush and I am going to close my eyes now and you will never see me again."

"God *almighty*," said Morgen. She turned and moved to the other side of the hall and leaned her head despairingly against the shoulder of the black wooden figure, who had seen and heard everything. I was wrong, she thought, I did harm; I coveted.

"You will never see me again any more," said her niece.

Quickly, Morgen came back to put her arm around her niece and hold her tight. "Baby darling," she said, "Morgen's here."

Between them they carried her into Morgen's living room and set her on the couch. She opened her eyes once and smiled at them together, and then slept.

"What do we do now?" Morgen asked, whispering, and the doctor laughed.

"When she awakens," he said dryly, "we can ask her. Meanwhile, we, you and I, can wait."

"We'll make coffee," Morgen said. "Maybe she'll want some when she wakes up." Turning to follow the doctor out of the room, she stumbled and was made aware of her old robe and battered slippers; it was probable, she thought, that the doctor had not noticed, but when she came into the hall she said to him with some awkwardness, "I'll dress, if you'll excuse me."

"Morgen?" said the doctor; he was standing looking with dislike into the face of the black Nigerian figure.

"Yes?"

"I want you to get rid of this fellow," the doctor said. Then he turned and smiled. "I beg your pardon," he said. "I should put that more tactfully; I am not myself. But he offends me, this creature; he does nothing but watch and listen and wait hopefully to snatch at people."

"All right," said Morgen lifelessly.

"A good many of our sins may go with him," the doctor said, and he reached out brazenly, and patted her on the shoulder.

6

THE NAMING OF
AN HEIRESS

Three months later, when the warm weather had really come to stay, and rain and cold and dismal dark days seemed set aside forever, Doctor Wright's patient, who had been his patient for a little more than two years, Aunt Morgen's niece, who had been her niece for a little more than twenty-five years, found unexpectedly that she wanted to run down the sidewalk, instead of pursuing the sedate crisp walk she had heretofore found so fitting. She wanted to pick flowers and feel grass under her feet, and she stopped not half a block from Doctor Wright's office and turned slowly and wonderingly around in a full circle, approving even the geraniums staunchly blooming in the doctor's windowbox; it was the first time she had looked at anything with her own true eyes; I am—and it was her first privately phrased thought—all alone; it was clear and sparkling as cold water, and she said it again to herself: I am all alone.

She had come up and down this street many times, and the geraniums were not strangers to her. Gropingly, holding firmly to Doctor Wright's hand, keeping her eyes upon Aunt Morgen, wandering and bewildered and faltering, she had been brought slowly to remembrance; much of what she recalled now was sharply distinct, present in her mind as it would have been if it had really happened to her; she could remember the outlines of emotions, and the looks of places, and the gestures of yearning, and the patterns of movements. She could lift her head, still, and hear sweetly the far faint sound of music (I was in a hotel, she would notify herself, that was when I was in a hotel) and see far away the diminishing figure of the doctor (of course; I was in a bus, and thought I saw him) and sometimes, superimposed over other pictures, tennis rackets and boxing gloves and saddle soap (in the window of the sporting goods store, naturally; I looked often into that window); she could remember in perfect detail the room at the hospital, and the Nigerian ancestor figure that Doctor Wright had made Aunt Morgen put away in the attic, and she could, moreover, answer freely all their questions: "Who put the mud in the refrigerator?" Aunt Morgen asked her, and she answered, with simple truth, "I did."

The act of recollection, at first halting and uncertain, had soon become compulsive; now, when she looked at the doorway to the doctor's office, she saw reflected against it the countless entrances she had made; Aunt Morgen's eyes were layers of doubt and surprise and love and anger, Aunt Morgen's voice echoed in infinite turned phrases, from as far back as time stretched; the doctor's office was crowded and shifting, kaleidescopic with her own visits there, and during the past week or so, when she sat down in the doctor's office she wondered always if she was sitting down this time or just remembering sitting down the last time, if she had come at all, or if she had perhaps made only one compressed actual visit, to be expanded infinitely in her memories of it. She was clouded with memory, bemused with the need for discovering reason and coherence in a patternless time; she was lost in an endless reflecting world, where only Aunt Morgen and Doctor Wright followed her, as she pursued them. When she turned to Aunt Morgen, crying her name, Aunt Morgen might answer from fifteen years ago, her voice clear but her arms never reaching far enough to provide a refuge; when she clung to Doctor Wright his hands might hold her steady, but his voice came to her from some pinnacle of mockery, rounding a splendid period of nonsense.

She was awakened from her enchantment at a quarter to four on an afternoon in July, brought back from a weary contemplation of the composition of her own mind. Her first clear thought was that she was all alone; it had been preceded by a rebellious, not-clear feeling that she had succeeded in remembering absolutely all her mind would hold; the second thought she ever phrased clearly she phrased almost aloud: I haven't any name, she told herself, here I am, all alone and without any name.

Everything was astonishingly bright and rich; all about her were the commonplaces of the present, the one-at-a-time actions which had no echoes in the past, the thoughts which were new, and the streets not habitually followed. She perceived this with genuine pleasure, and walked past the doctor's office. The sidewalk on the untraveled section beyond the doctor's office was a little more carefully put down: one block of cement met the next block of cement without more than the slightest line to trouble the eye with uneasiness; although she knew that she had come along here before she realized without question that it was not necessary, any more, to make an effort to remember the precise time and occasion; I am through with remembering, she thought. Turning the corner onto a busier street she went more slowly, and stopped at last because she had come to a shop where she might have her hair cut. She had not before felt any intention of cutting her hair, but, once conceived, the idea would not die, and she went into the shop, and smiled at the pretty young woman dressed in blue, who came forward through the fragrant dimness to speak to her.

"I would like to have my hair cut, please."

"Surely," said the young woman, as though people had their hair cut every day, and they both laughed, because everything was working out so nicely, and so agreeably.

She sat in a chair with a blue bib around her, and the cold scissors against her neck made her shiver suddenly; "I've never cut my hair in my life," she said, and the young woman murmured, "In this heat . . . so refreshing." She watched herself from out of the mirror, watching the young woman in blue move the flashing scissors, and cut off the hair she had worn when she was a small baby and her mother touched it gently with a soft brush, the hair which had curled around her face when she came down the stairs and down the stairs and *down* the stairs, and cut off the hair which had been growing when she gathered seashells on the beach and the hair which had been long and gath-

ered back with a ribbon when Aunt Morgen said not to cry over
spilled milk and which had been braided and folded over itself
but still growing when Doctor Wright asked her if she was
afraid, and growing still and not well combed when she met the
strange man at lunch in the hotel, and brushed by the nurses in
the hospital and pulled and tangled and washed and wound
around her head for all the twenty-five years of her life, and the
pleasant young woman in blue pushed it aside on the floor with
her foot, and held up a mirror behind and said, "Well, how do
we like ourselves *now?*"

"So that's what I'm going to look like," she said.

"You'll find it makes a difference, getting rid of that weight
of hair." The young woman shook her head approvingly. "You
are a different girl," she said.

She was entertained, walking back down the street, to find
that now she had to think constantly of holding her head high,
because she had no weight of hair to pull back against her, and
she felt an inch or so taller without any hair, the top of her
head closer to the stars. Best of all, when she turned and
started up the steps to the doctor's office, she knew that now,
of all times, she was coming in actuality, since in all her pictures and reflections of herself coming to the doctor, and sitting with him inside, there was no time when she had come
with her hair short and her head high.

Doctor Wright was cross. He rose briefly when she entered,
nodded at her, and sat, unsmiling and wordless, at his desk. He
noticed that her hair was cut, she knew, because he was accustomed to noticing everything about her, and when at last she
said, "Well, good afternoon, Doctor Wright," he glanced up, his
eyes touching the top of her head, and then looked down again.

"It is five and twenty after four," he said at last. "I am able
to recollect, much as you may doubt it, that youth feels little
sense of time, with all the future at its beck and call; regretta-
bly, we who have had the pressure of years forced upon us—"

"I had to have my hair cut," she said.

"*Had* to have your hair cut? Did you gain your aunt's permission? Because, to my knowledge, you had not mine."

"It's such a lovely day."

"Hardly relevant," he said dryly. "Such a lovely day for disposing of one's hair? A sacrifice, might be, to ensure a temperate summer? Or perhaps, a shorn lamb, you hope to appease a wintry blast?" He sighed, and set straight the inkwell on his desk. "I am annoyed with you," he said. "We will not spend a great deal of time today; I am annoyed, it is late, I preferred your hair the way I was used to it. What is the state of your health—aside—" his glance touched her head, briefly, again— "aside from the probability of your catching cold?"

"Excellent. And if you insist, I shall wear a hat until the rigors of the July climate have abated."

"You are mocking me, young woman. You are shorn and bold."

She laughed, and he looked at her in surprise. "I'm happy," she said, and then stopped and listened to the echo of her words, surprised in turn as she became aware of their meaning. "I am," she confirmed.

"I have no objection," he said. "You may even laugh if you like. Has there been any difficulty with your aunt? Any quarrels? Embarrassment?"

"No." She was uncertain. "She seems quieter, though."

"Her experiences, recently, may have been somewhat unsettling for one of your aunt's . . . ah . . . placid temperament. You treated her unkindly, I think."

"The mud?" She frowned, puzzling out a way to explain. "I don't think that was *against* Aunt Morgen, exactly. I can remember doing it, and it seems to me that it wasn't to hurt her or anything, but just because something *had* to happen, there had to be some kind of explosion, and it had to come from outside, because there wasn't any force in me."

"Perhaps." The doctor, who much preferred doing the talking himself, cut her short and went on, "A decisive gesture was necessary, certainly, to bring matters to a climax, and the struggle between personalities had reached a point where their very counter-tensions made them static. The balance between them had to be shaken, weight had to be thrown on one side or another: Aunt Morgen had to be brought into the fray, to shatter the violent equilibrium in which they were locked.

A . . ." he paused, and looked up at her speculatively. "A death struggle," he said, and then nodded, amused. "The two cats of Kilkenny," he said. "Instead of two cats, there weren't any."

Could I have behaved like that? she wondered, was that *really* what I did? With my own hands, wearing my own face, walking on my own feet, using my own head (and she could still feel the mud on her fingers, hear herself laughing), did I really *think* of things like that? She looked down at her clothes, and remembered with an odd kind of tenderness that her own hands had torn this blouse when she was angry in New York, and ironed this skirt in a deep rush of love toward herself; she had scratched her own face. She looked at her hands with their round nails and their soft fingers, and lifted her right hand and put it gently around her throat, tightening the fingers with slow care; the doctor spoke quickly, sharply, and she shook her head (its hair cut short), and laughed. "I'm just playing," she explained. "I can *remember,* but I can't think *why.*"

He was lighting his pipe, not looking at her. "Do *you* think they are gone?" he asked; he had not, in all this time, asked her pointblank before.

"Yes," she said. "Gone," and she thought, searching down and half closing her eyes and feeling, as one moving in the dark with hands outstretched to touch a solid object; "Melting together," she said, "like snowmen."

He nodded, his pipe going satisfactorily. "I suppose we could say that you had absorbed them," he said.

"Eaten them all," she amended, and sighed again happily.

"We are not out of the woods *yet,* by any means. You are confident, you cut your hair, you are easy with me, you call yourself 'happy.' But may I point out that you have just eaten your four sisters?"

"You can't catch me, I'm the gingerbread man," she said impudently. "Doctor Wrong."

He frowned at her. "We are not, as I say, out of the woods yet. At the moment you may choose to amuse yourself at the expense of your doctor, but—since you at the same time assure me of your great good health—we may plan to commence, at your next visit, a severe and thorough series of treatments and hypnotic explorations; we shall scrutinize with extreme and tiresome exactitude every aspect of your illness, until we have determined the *why* which you say you do not know; we will not rest until—"

"A punishment?" she asked. "Just because I laughed?"

"Have a care, my dear young lady. You have interrupted me again, and you speak pertly. I am attempting to describe a great concern for your future welfare. We shall study your past in order to discover—"

"My future? But suppose *I*—"

"There," he said. "You have interrupted me once again. Three times in ten minutes. I think it is easily time you went back to your aunt. I hope that by the time we meet this evening you will have somewhat recovered your usual good manners."

"I may be worse," she said, still possessed of an irresistible tendency to giggle. "I've run away from a little old woman and a little old man."

"I beg your pardon?"

"I'm the gingerbread man," she said.

He shook his head, and rose to show her to the door. "It is gratifying, I must confess, to see you cheerful," he said. "Although I am not fond of good humor at my own expense. Until this evening, then."

"When we're with Aunt Morgen I can interrupt you all I want to."

"On the contrary," he said. "When we're with Aunt Morgen, it is Aunt who interrupts. A splendid woman," he said, "but overly fond of talk."

She came out of the doctor's office laughing, feeling her head cool and aware for the first time of this day as separate from all other days; she walked lingeringly toward the corner where she would catch her bus, thinking, I am all alone and I have no name; I have cut my hair, I'm the gingerbread man, and wanting to prolong this little time of perfect freedom, although she thought that she would never lose it completely now; without more concrete thought than, it's Thursday, closing's not till seven, she crossed the street to wait for a bus that would take her to the museum.

She could remember, of course, that she had gone to the
museum every day, and she could remember whole paragraphs and pages of letters and lists she had written; she knew
perfectly the look of the desk where she had worked, and she
knew, too, that she had gone, afterwards, to the museum one
afternoon, but had not gone above the first floor; had wan-
dered without purpose or interest through the most available
rooms. If she had known that day what she was looking for,
she could have remembered it now, but all that that grey afternoon brought back was an intense loneliness, untouched
by the people who walked through the rooms with her; she
had sat on a bench and watched others go by, stepping firmly
through a world to them almost secure. I wonder why I went
that day, she thought, leaning forward in the bus to see where
she was; she remembered all the other buses, and all the running away. She was simultaneously awake and asleep; she was
talking with a lady in green silk; she was holding tight to her
suitcase.

The bus stopped directly in front of the museum, and she
came down from the high bus step and turned to look at the
austere white stone of the building. It looks well, she thought,
it hasn't changed since I left; how pleasant, she thought, to
come calling on the scenes of one's past, and find the past of
all the ages there too; how can I tell that the girl who used to
come here and call herself me was not just a remnant of a
stone age culture—no, a glacial deposit?

Just outside the museum entrance was the white stone statue
of General Zaccheus Owen, in whose questionable honor the
museum had been erected; General Owen sat as he always had,
not having even recrossed his legs in all this time (although, of
course, he *could* have crossed and recrossed them any number
of times, so long as he finished with them the same way he
began), and he still rested his head on his hand and his elbows
on a white stone table, and he studied still in his white stone
book, weary and bored and hopeless, although he might very
well have turned over a page or two in all this time. He was
not a proper general, she thought, to sit reading while the battle surely raged; he had been thought to represent the conquest

of brute force by intellect, and his sword, unwieldy with its great ribbons of white stone, lay idle at his feet.

"Good afternoon, general," she said at last. "If you belonged to Aunt Morgen, Doctor Wright would put you in the attic." There was no one around at the moment—or else, naturally, she would not have spoken aloud—but the general apparently did not dare risk turning over another page; he bent his eyes down doggedly, and perhaps only glanced at her for one swift second. "I probably won't be seeing you again, general," she said, "so goodbye."

The general did not speak as she went on inside, suddenly aware that she had not come to see the general, but to visit a particular painting on the second floor. The painting had never attracted her before with any personal communication, and she did not know why she wanted to see it now, but, coming through the museum entrance, she suddenly wanted to go and look at it, and she remembered where it was and how to turn to reach it, how to go up the main wide staircase with her hand on the wide stone balustrade, and she remembered, with a kind of sadness, that she had never before come to look at this picture, although she had passed by it many times. Here at last, she thought, is a choice entirely my own.

When she stood before the picture she thought only, at first: I would like to have that; then she looked at it more carefully, wondering why she had longed for it so, and telling herself at the same time that for a long time to come she must study every thought carefully, and test its reality, and examine it for flaws and for traces of weakness or sentiment, for invitations to turn back. The picture was bright and lovely against a background of black silk, a thing of small jeweled greens and blues and scarlets and yellows; an Indian prince sat in contemplative happiness against a clean colored pattern of eight-petaled flowers, with his feet close together on a tiny mosaic floor and his small hand open before him. He was touched with gold, on the belt of his robe, at the corners of his eyes, and beyond him lay a green meadow ending in a row of even little trees topped by precise little mountains, and at his feet lay a basket of oranges. She stood and looked at him, deeply satisfied with the

clarity of the tiny jewels glowing against the black silk, and
when she turned away her eyes, blinded by the colored flowers, there was a reflected light in the white stone ceiling of the
museum, and a glitter along the floor.

She knew the hidden stairway that led to the third floor of
the museum, and went up its iron steps without hesitation, although she had not been up here for a very long time. It, too,
had not changed, and she turned with assurance down the
hallway and to the door of the big office room where she had
at one time come every day, and, entering, looked at once to
the last desk on the left, where she suddenly half-expected to
find her work set out as she had left it, her letters demolished
by crude messages, her back still aching. The office was empty,
because it was late, and the desks were neat and bare; she did
not want at first to leave the shelter of the doorway and then
perceived that it was because she badly wanted to turn to her
right and hang her hat and coat on the rack ready there for
them. Not ever again, she thought, and moved resolutely forward toward her own desk.

"Were you looking for someone?" She turned, and smiled.
There was a girl standing in the doorway, looking severe because of course visitors were not allowed on the third floor,
and yet tentative, because her jurisdiction extended only so far
as the third floor went, and visitors to the museum were a special order of trespasser, and a girl who might freely order
strangers away from the third floor must herself leave the museum by the iron stairway which, hidden, went all the way
down through the museum to the employees' entrance in the
back basement; she was carrying a flower in her hand, far too
small for the buttonhole of General Owen and overblown for
the garden of the jeweled prince. She held the flower with care,
because it was made of metal and had been carved and fash-
ioned and created with the hands and so was very likely worth
money; the stem had been sharply broken off and as the girl
stood, staring but patient, she caressed the hard petals, running the tip of one finger around them.

"I'm sorry to walk in like this. I used to work here, and I
just wanted to look around again."

"Yes?" said the girl, undecided. (There *was* another way to get off the third floor, then?)

"*That* was my desk, the last one on the left."

"That's Emmy's desk," said the girl defensively, holding the flower close to her.

"Really?" There was nothing more to say; she had seen her desk, and the flower was broken off, and Emmy had gone home for the day; there was nothing new to be found up here. She nodded her head at the desk, remembering, and said, "Once there was a big hole in that wall. It went right down through the whole building."

"A hole?" said the girl. "In the wall?"

Aunt Morgen was in the doorway, peering out, tapping her fingers, biting her lip, frowning. "God almighty," Aunt Morgen said, "am I going to spend all my *life*—what in sweet heaven's name have you done to your head?"

"I've been to the doctor's. I cut my hair."

"I called the doctor. You left there an hour ago. He said you were—" Aunt Morgen broke off, and made a small ceremony of closing the door behind her niece. "Have you and the doc been squabbling?" she asked, once the door was safely closed behind her, and dropping her voice a little, as though the very air might carry her irreverent words to the doctor's ear; "he said you were light-headed."

"And so I am. Look at me."

"It doesn't suit you," Aunt Morgen said, after a minute. "You'll have to let it grow again."

"I can't; I'm the gingerbread man."

"What?"

"I've run away from a little old woman and a little old man."

"I sometimes think," Aunt Morgen said amiably, following her into the kitchen, "that a nice home for old ladies is what I really need. The kind of a place where they play croquet. And wear brooches made out of the hair of all their dead friends."

"And Doctor Wright would come every Sunday evening to call on you," said her niece, settling happily into her place at the kitchen table.

"For our weekly hymn sing," said Aunt Morgen. "I made cabbage and sour cream, merely because you *used* to like it, although I must say that with your majesty's tastes shifting the way they do, I hardly dare—"

"You suppose they'll let you cook in the old ladies' home? You're one of the best cooks in the world."

The table looked pretty and warm in the soft light of the kitchen corner. Aunt Morgen was using new dishes, yellow on a brown cloth, and when she touched the round edge of her yellow cup she wondered that she had not noticed it sooner; Aunt Morgen had changed a number of small things, relinquishing, it seemed, the harsh defiant colors, the sharp, out-flung angles, the obtrusive patterns; "Morgen," she said, "you're getting mellow."

"Hm?"

"Your new dishes. And the tablecloth. The front hall."

Sitting, Morgen said, "—lives to thy service," and passed the rolls to her niece. "I didn't know you noticed," she said, and sighed, looking without enthusiasm at her butter plate. "I don't suppose you want to talk about it," she went on finally. "I've been waiting until you said something, or the doc, and I figured I'd spent so long never catching up with what was going on that I could afford to hang on a while longer. But." She put her fork down with sudden determination, and looked sternly at her niece. "All these jokes about old ladies' homes," she said. "I keep feeling as though the house was empty now, everyone gone for the summer, place closed up, windows boarded, everyone off in the country. Like I was left all alone, sitting here wondering where in hell everyone's got to. Did you know I went and bought you that green coat you wanted and it's been hanging in your closet for three weeks?"

"I didn't even see it," said her niece blankly.

"That's what I mean," Aunt Morgen said. "I thought you really *wanted* that coat. I've been waiting for you to mention it. And now you've gone and cut your hair," she finished helplessly, and pushed her plate away.

"You thought I really wanted that awful coat?"

"You either really wanted the coat, or else you were trying to buy it to show me who was boss or to make me miserable or

maybe just to make up to yourself for all the things you figured I should have done for you and gotten you and never did.
So I talked myself into thinking you really wanted a new coat."

"I suppose it's too late to take it back to the store."

There was a silence, and then Aunt Morgen said, "Yes, it's
too late to take it back. You'll have to wear it and maybe pretend you like it. Pretend," she went on carefully, "that it was a
gift from a doting old relative in the old ladies' home and you
have to wear it to avoid giving offense. Because," she said,
"with a thing like that it is very easy indeed to give offense;
you have really no idea how touchy old ladies get about their
gifts." Shutting her lips tight, Morgen held her breath for a
minute, and then got up without speaking and took her plate
over to the sink. "I'll leave the dishes," she said in a voice almost normal. "We're a little late; the doc should be here any
minute."

"I'll help you with the dishes when we get back."

"Thank you," said Aunt Morgen. "Thank you very much."
Silently she cleared the dishes from the table and put them in
the sink. Then, impulsively, she turned and came back to the
table and sat down next to her niece. "Look," she said, and
stopped, and put her elbows down on the table, and lighted a
cigarette, and fussed with the ashtray, and rubbed her nose
foolishly with the back of her hand. "I'm *damned* if I know
how to say it," she said. "I keep trying and trying—maybe the
doc can get a straight answer from you; maybe *he* can get to
you. Me, all I keep doing is wondering and worrying and praying it's all going to come out all right, and maybe I'm wrecking
everything speaking out like this—*I* know I'm clumsy and silly
and I've got no head for all this fancy figuring you do with the
doc, but here all of a sudden, here I never had any trouble in
all my *life* making myself understood and my wants known,
and here all of a sudden I can't even *talk* to you after all these
years. All I want to know is this." She stopped, and carefully
set her cigarette down in the ashtray so she could fold her
hands and turn attentively to her niece. "Where do I fit in?"
she asked.

Seeing her niece regarding her with curiosity, but without

comprehension, Morgen faltered, and gestured, a pathetic little turn of her hand. "You don't understand," she said. "I suppose I *am* really talking? I'm not just moving my mouth and waving my arms and not making any noise? You *do* hear me? Because it is beginning to look to me like you don't care in the least whether I talk or not, or whether the doc sees you or not, or whether we go out or stay in or whether we eat or don't eat or whether I live or don't live or whether I'm happy or not; I keep feeling that when I work to make something special for your dinner that you used to like once and then forget to tell you what it is you don't even know what you're eating."

"Dinner was very nice, Aunt Morgen."

"I *know* it was very nice, I made it and it was very very very damned nice and if I hadn't told you what it was you could honest to God have sat there all through dinner moving your fork and putting it in your mouth and maybe if it's my lucky day just happening to notice that for the past month we've been using new dishes. I keep telling myself it isn't *possible,* not after all this time." Morgen put out her cigarette with care, and said, "I don't want to sound like the kind of person who says I've got a right to your affection just because I've spent a lot of time taking care of you as though you were my own child. I'd have to be pretty damn silly to think that people had *rights* to other people's love; in my life I've earned more love and got less than anyone I know. But I could have sworn," she said, making her tone light, and smiling a little, "I could have sworn *you* wouldn't let me go off alone to an old ladies' home."

She was watching Aunt Morgen carefully, looking at the big earnest ugly face and the false little smile and the mouth still a little open, and she thought, people shouldn't ever look closely at one another, they're not like pictures. There was not any sure way to know, from the eyes of her aunt or the mouth of her aunt or the hair or the eyebrows or the lines in the face of her aunt, whether the expression stated by her aunt's face was a faithful delineation of fear or anxiety or expectancy; it might be a kind of ecstasy, or it might be wholly false, and not at all the expression corresponding to Aunt Morgen's thoughts. There was too much there to be defined clearly; the jeweled prince was beautiful, General Owen was tired, but Aunt Morgen's face was a portrait too heavily shaded, with too much detail. And that is because, she thought, in a picture all the unnecessary misleading parts of the face have been eliminated, all the extra lines are gone and the painter has only left in the useful things; painting Aunt Morgen's face and calling it *Agony,* she thought, one would probably have to eliminate the greater part of the nose, which detracted sensibly from the composition of the whole, and surely avoid the sense of bestial, inarticulate pain introduced by the eyebrows, which were overheavy; a general thinning of the design . . .

"I think I'm being patient," Aunt Morgen said, and her voice was cold.

"Aunt Morgen," she said slowly, "you know what I was thinking, today in the museum?"

"No," Aunt Morgen said, "*what* were you thinking, today in the museum?"

"I was thinking what it must feel like to be a prisoner going to die; you stand there looking at the sun and the sky and the grass and the trees, and because it's the last time you're going to see them they're wonderful, full of colors you never noticed before, and bright and beautiful and terribly hard to leave behind. And then, suppose you're reprieved, and you get up the next morning and you're not dead; could you look again at the sun and the trees and the sky and think they're the same old sun and sky and trees, nothing special at all, just the same old things you've seen every day? Not changed at all, just because you don't have to give them up?"

"Well?" said Aunt Morgen when she stopped.

"That's what I was thinking today in the museum."

"Were you now?" said Aunt Morgen, rising heavily. "Well, if you don't mind," she said, taking up the coffee cups, "I'll save it. Think about it some other time, when I'm not so worried about my own affairs. My own *tawdry* affairs," she said, and slammed the new cups into the sink with a crash.

"She has still a great deal to learn," said the doctor soothingly, and quite as though he and Aunt Morgen were walking all alone; "she has a long path to retrace. We must not make too many demands upon her."

"Goddamn unfeeling heartless icicle," said Aunt Morgen roundly. "I mean *you*," she said over her shoulder to her niece.

"I have the constant impression," the doctor went on, "that she is . . . how shall I say it? . . . as a vessel emptied, if she can forgive me such a graceless comparison. Although she seems to be, my dear Morgen, in undisputed possession of the citadel, too many of its defenses are down, too much has been lost in victory." He stopped, and for a minute they walked on, unperceiving, and then realized, and turned to him as he gestured at them eloquently with his rolled umbrella. "Such a pleasant evening for a walk," he said, "you must not stomp along, Morgen. Let us put it this way, then. Much of what was *emotion* has been lost; the facts are there, the memory clear, but the feeling for these things is suspended. Take, for instance, some person toward whom she has displayed, in these troubled times, mixed reactions." He thought, started to speak, stopped, and thought again. "Doctor Ryan," he said at last, with satisfaction. "At different times, she has felt differently toward Doctor Ryan; under one influence she very likely hated him violently, and under another influence she may even have valued him enormously. Now, suppose her to remember perfectly the circumstances under which she at one time admired, and at another time detested, Doctor Ryan; the circumstances recalled, which emotion, presuming them equally strong, which emotion might be expected to remain with her?"

"Who *cares* about Ryan?" Morgen demanded. "For twenty-odd years I've been—"

"If you please," said the doctor, holding up his umbrella, but falling into step again with Aunt Morgen, "allow me to continue. You will recall that there was—I believe I may say this with entire safety from contradiction, even from *you*, Morgen—no area so far explored in which there was not dissension. Almost, if I may be permitted the term, open warfare. Absolute diametric opposition," said the doctor, walking rhythmically, "on every point. Thus," he continued, holding up his umbrella again at Aunt Morgen, who had raised her arm to gesture, "emotion has been, so to speak, cancelled out. No resolution has taken place, no compromise has been reached, no workable truce declared in that warfare. And *our* responsibility, Morgen," he went on, raising his voice slightly, "*our* responsibility is, clearly, to people this vacant landscape— fill this empty vessel, I think I said before—and, with our own deep emotional reserves, enable the child to rebuild. We have a sobering duty. She will owe to us her opinions, her discrimina- tions, her reflections; we are able, as few others have ever been, to re-create, entire, a human being, in the most proper and reasonable mold, to select what is finest and most elevating from our own experience and bestow!"

Morgen said disagreeably, "You can be her mommy, and I'll be her daddy, and what I am going to bestow on her is a good swift—"

"We always quarrel," the doctor said ruefully. "We strongly resemble an old married pair, I think. The wicked enchanter marries the dragon, after all, and they live happily ever after."

Aunt Morgen laughed. "You and your empty vessels," she said, suddenly good-humored again. "Hollering down a rain barrel, *I* call it. Well, come on," she said to her niece, catch- ing her niece's hand and holding it, "we'll start all over again like friends. You like the hair?" she asked the doctor across her niece.

"Unwomanly," said the doctor, "but not unbecoming, I think."

"I suppose I'll get used to it," said Morgen. She turned, tak- ing precedence going up the narrow walk to the front door, and said, stopping and turning, "Now, remember, for heaven's sake, *don't* ask Vergil to sing."

"Morgen!" said Mrs. Arrow with delight, as she opened the front door for them, "and it's Doctor Wright, too, isn't it? So dark, with no moon, but of course I *did* know you were com- ing, didn't I? So how could it be anyone else? And how are *you,* my dear?"

"A lovely night, lovely," said Mr. Arrow, with his back to

the door, and standing with both arms out ready to receive the coats his wife took away from their guests and handed to him; he held his arms wide and even their three light coats seemed heavy for him, with Doctor Wright's hat and umbrella neatly on top; he seemed wondering, suddenly, where to put all of this, and he turned vaguely around and around until Mrs. Arrow led him to the closet, and took everything away from him, lifting carefully from the bottom, and then Mr. Arrow stood the doctor's umbrella in the umbrella stand and hung the doctor's hat on a peg and then carefully put the coats one by one onto hangers.

While Mr. and Mrs. Arrow were giving the coats back and forth, and making small anxious gestures at one another, in extreme concern lest the tail of Doctor Wright's coat should touch the floor or Aunt Morgen's scarf mingle commonly among the Arrow mufflers, Aunt Morgen, as senior guest, who had known Ruth and Vergil Arrow since they were all children together and had been free with their house for long years, led the way into the Arrows' living room, followed by her niece and the doctor. "Well," said Aunt Morgen, touched with a faint embarrassment because these people were her friends and Doctor Wright had not been here before, "here we are." She sat down without looking, as one who knows absolutely that in a room belonging to the Arrows the furniture does not permit itself to be moved from one place to another; "sit here, kiddo, beside me," she said, and bit her lip. "In case you should feel called upon to repeat your remarks on Vergil's singing," she said, and grinned at her niece.

"Perhaps she would be more comfortable over here," said the doctor; he was poised uncertainly between the sofa, which showed by a deep indentation in one corner that it was dedicated to an Arrow, and a chair whose trim lines bespoke, at first glance, a background not in keeping with the rest of the furniture, until a second, and more critical, observation showed its unmistakable ripeness, the line too long, the curve too full, which had surely brought it favor in Mrs. Arrow's eye; "would you sit by me?" the doctor asked.

"Leave her here," said Aunt Morgen. "She's all right."

"Near me, if you please," said the doctor.

They looked at one another, in a kind of quick wonder, and then Mrs. Arrow came between them, gay, and almost clapping her hands. "I'm so *glad* you came at *last*," she said. "Morgen, it's been *years!* And the doctor, too, of course." She turned, admiring everyone. "And I do believe *you've* cut your hair," she said.

"This afternoon."

"So nice. And it *looks* nice, too; Vergil?"

"Very pretty indeed. Sit down, doctor, sit down."

Pressed, the doctor made his decision and reconciled himself to the ill-made chair. He adjusted his well-proportioned limbs with difficulty to the inaccurate composition of the chair, wriggled uncontrollably once and then, never utterly inarticulate, turned politely to Mrs. Arrow. "A charming home," he said. "So conveniently located."

Mrs. Arrow, who was about to regret their long walk coming, was caught unprepared, and could only say, "So nice that you came. And Morgen, too."

"Kiddo," Morgen said, turning to look over her shoulder, "won't you light somewhere? Makes me nervous, you wandering like that."

"It's such a lovely night; I'm looking out at the garden."

Mr. and Mrs. Arrow, who had confidently supposed that all their windows were securely blockaded with the backs of chairs, and small tables holding potted ferns, rose immediately and approached from opposite sides of the room, Mr. Arrow intending to move a chair a little sideways to clear a passage to a window, Mrs. Arrow offering to loop back the curtain; "The roses are not as rich as usual this year," Mrs. Arrow said apologetically, and Mr. Arrow pointed out that the lilac had not done as expected, "but the hedge," he said, "the hedge is coming marvelously well. That back privet," he said, turning, to Morgen, "would amaze you; you wouldn't believe it."

"Edmund is there," Mrs. Arrow said softly, "in the back, under the roses."

"Could I go out for a while? It looks so quiet."

"That's kind of you." Mrs. Arrow was touched. "Come along, dear; I'll take you through the back." She nodded reassuringly at Morgen. "It's perfectly all right," she said, "we've got that high fence," and then, turning red, said, "I mean, no one can get *in* or anything," and went hastily out of the room.

"Put on a sweater, kiddo," Morgen said.

"Veil that naked head," said the doctor.

"It's a nice night for the garden," said Mr. Arrow. "Often spend a few minutes out there myself. Bench, and all." He sat down again, on the end of the couch near Doctor Wright, and turned to say, with masculine concern, "You given any thought, Doctor, to this new idea about street lighting? Waste of money, *I* call it; when you consider—"

Mrs. Arrow hurried back into the room and over to Morgen. "*Perfectly* happy," she said. "Quite warm enough, sheltered, quiet, and I thought she was so sweet about Edmund. He was genuinely fond of her, you know."

"We let her do pretty much as she pleases," Morgen said solemnly.

"You know, she *looks* better," Mrs. Arrow said confidentially. "Tell you the truth, Morgen, last time *I* saw her—that must have been nearly a year ago, wasn't it? that day I met you two in the restaurant, and she was laughing so?—well, anyway, I thought *then* she seemed poorly, not at *all* herself. Has she been . . ." Mrs. Arrow paused delicately, and lifted her eyebrows at Doctor Wright inquiringly.

"A nervous fever," said Aunt Morgen smoothly.

Mrs. Arrow turned and looked openly at Doctor Wright. "I would have thought," she said, "that Doctor Ryan . . . of course, he's a *younger* man."

"We have the greatest confidence in Doctor Wright," said Morgen, raising her voice slightly to be heard with clarity across the room. "*Complete* confidence."

"Not unlike," said Doctor Wright to Mr. Arrow, "the familiar practice of impaling a living man on a maypole. Disagreeable only to the victim, if, indeed, he himself is not transported with ecstasy. I would not suppose, however, that in the present day . . ."

"Not," said Mr. Arrow valiantly, "with the town manager system the way it's set up most places."

Mrs. Arrow put her hand over Morgen's. "I just want to say that I think you've been pretty brave, Morgen, just pretty brave. There aren't many people," she finished, and nodded emphatically. "I wonder," said Morgen, half-rising. "I'll just take a look at her through the kitchen window."

"Of course." Mrs. Arrow smiled sympathetically. "I *know* she's all right, though; you mustn't worry so."

"I just want to know if she's still there," Morgen said.

Mrs. Arrow smiled at Morgen's back, shook her head with a tender little sigh, and turned to the gentlemen; "A glass of sherry?" she asked brightly.

"Ah?" said Mr. Arrow dimly.

"Sherry, Doctor Wright?"

"Thank you, thank you. On the other hand, although I am at best only very slightly informed in these matters, I would suppose that the mandrake, which shrieks, you will recall, only when uprooted—"

"You all right, kiddo?" Aunt Morgen said, looking down from the kitchen window.

"Yes, thank you, Aunt Morgen."

"What you doing?"

"Sitting on the bench. The roses are lovely."

"You warm enough?"

"Yes, thank you."

"All right. Call me if you need anything."

"—And I think Morgen will bear me out in my theory that witchcraft is little more than the judicious administration of the bizarre."

"Yes, indeed," said Morgen, seating herself. "She's fine," she told the doctor.

"Certainly. This is overprotection, Morgen; our lamb will not leave the fold, particularly since the fence is so high. Morgen's interest in what is called 'modern' art—"

"Modern rubbish, *I* call it," said Mr. Arrow, stung to vehemence. "I don't know about your interest in music, sir, but I always say that a ten-year-old *boy* could do better."

"You're talking to the man who wanted to burn all my paintings, Vergil," said Morgen. "Until I offered to throw him in after them."

"I have very little desire," said the doctor dryly, "to stand in as a human sacrifice to ensure the fertility of Morgen's artistic self-expression." He gave a pleased little wriggle in his uncomfortable chair.

"*I* wouldn't have minded," Morgen said.

"Each life, I think," said the doctor, "asks the devouring of other lives for its own continuance; the radical aspect of ritual sacrifice, the performance of a group, its great step ahead, was in organization; *sharing* the victim was so eminently practical."

"And such a social occasion," Morgen murmured. "I can just see you, Victor."

"And you wouldn't be the first, either," said Mr. Arrow, coming squarely to grips with the conversation. "You take Kipling, and all the great musicians. *They* didn't have anyone to help them."

"Kipling?" said Doctor Wright injudiciously.

"Mandalay, I was thinking of. Maybe, if you haven't ever heard it, I could—"

"Lovely," said Morgen, looking at the doctor with evil intensity. "Victor would love to hear you sing."

"I should be delighted," said the doctor. "I was speaking of the custom of human sacrifice; I have been led to understand that although it is, as a practice, deplored generally today, the initiate into the secret society—"

"What exactly *was* wrong with her?" Mrs. Arrow, coming up to Morgen with a tray, spoke too loudly, and there was silence in the room. Mrs. Arrow looked around, discomfited, and then said boldly, "Well, we've known her ever since she was *so* high, and I think we've shown enough interest to be told."

"*Very* old family friends," Mr. Arrow confirmed.

"A nervous fever," Morgen said.

The doctor spoke slowly, in a measured voice, seeming to estimate the suitability of each of his phrases for the ears of

Mr. and Mrs. Arrow: "The human creature at odds with its environment," he said, "must change either its own protective coloration, or the shape of the world in which it lives. Equipped with no magic device beyond a not overly sharp intelligence," and the doctor hesitated, perhaps lost in wonder at his own precarious eminence, "intelligence," he went on firmly, "the human creature finds it tempting to endeavor to control its surroundings through manipulated symbols of sorcery, arbitrarily chosen, and frequently ineffectual. Suppose a gazelle, discovering itself to be colored blue when all other gazelles—"

"A nervous fever, you said?" Mrs. Arrow whispered to Morgen, and Morgen nodded.

"My cousin—" Mr. Arrow began in a low voice, but Doctor Wright frowned him down.

"—will take refuge, first, in disbelief, in a convincing refusal to perceive colors, a state of confused bewilderment—"

"Like that fellow you mentioned, the one on the maypole," said Mr. Arrow, hoping to atone for his previous interruption by a show of intelligent comprehension.

"In any case," said Morgen, overwhelmingly, "I think our pet gazelle had better come indoors." She rose. "I'll get her."

Doctor Wright turned alertly to Mr. Arrow, but this time Mr. Arrow was ready. "Since you were kind enough to ask me," Mr. Arrow said, "I'll just get out my music."

Later, walking home companionably through the warm summer night, she put one hand through Morgen's arm and one hand through the doctor's arm and walked in step between them. "And all that faradiddle," Morgen was saying.

"Not faradiddle at all." The doctor was hurt. "I thought I did it very nicely."

"Hah," said Morgen. "And the way you play bridge."

"Bridge is a game for the undivided intellect," said the doctor. "Like your own." He bowed to Morgen, as well as he could, walking through the night with her niece between them.

"You know what I was thinking, out in the garden?"

"What?" said Aunt Morgen, and "Yes?" said the doctor.

"I was looking at the flowers, thinking of their names, as though I were naming them, and had to see that each one had a name, and it was the right name. It's harder than it sounds."

"Like what?" said Morgen.

"And the stars—I named some of the stars, too."

"And yourself?" said the doctor.

She nodded, smiling.

"This child is without a name," the doctor said across her to Morgen. "Did you know?"

Morgen thought, and then laughed. "I guess she is," she said, "but I hadn't noticed." She laughed again, and pressed her niece's arm. "If you're taking on a new name, how about Morgen this time?"

"Victoria?" suggested the doctor.

"Morgen Victoria," Morgen amended generously.

"Victoria Morgen," said the doctor.

She laughed, too, holding both their arms. "I'm happy," she said, just as she had that afternoon. "I know who I am," she said, and walked on with them, arm in arm, and laughing.

ALSO AVAILABLE

DARK TALES
Foreword by Ottessa Moshfegh

THE HAUNTING OF HILL HOUSE
Penguin Classics Deluxe Edition
Introduction by Laura Miller

LIFE AMONG THE SAVAGES

RAISING DEMONS

THE BIRD'S NEST
Foreword by Kevin Wilson

THE SUNDIAL
Foreword by Victor LaValle

HANGSAMAN
Foreword by Francine Prose

THE ROAD THROUGH THE WALL
Foreword by Ruth Franklin

COME ALONG WITH ME
*Classic Short Stories and
an Unfinished Novel*
Foreword by Laura Miller

**WE HAVE ALWAYS LIVED IN
THE CASTLE**
Penguin Classics Deluxe Edition
Introduction by Jonathan Lethem
Illustrated by Thomas Ott

 PENGUIN CLASSICS   PENGUIN BOOKS

Ready to find your next great classic? Let us help. Visit prh.com/penguinclassics

P.O. 0005388990 20230922